Bandages

Other Books by S. L. Kassidy

Please Baby

Scarred Series
Scarred for Life - Book 1
New Cuts, Old Wounds – Book 2

Bandages

By

S. L. Kassidy

Desert Palm Press

Bandages
(Scarred Series – Book 3)

by S.L. Kassidy

© 2016 S.L. Kassidy

ISBN-13: 9781942976097

Desert Palm Press
1961 Main Street, Suite 220
Watsonville, California 95076
www.desertpalmpress.com

Editor: CK King (https://www.facebook.com/RavensEyeEditing)
Cover Design: Jamani Hawkins-El (http://www.maddrandom.com)

Printed in the United States of America
First Edition March 2016

DEDICATION

This book is dedicated to my family, who supported my writing long before I thought it was worth anything, and to my friends, who helped me believe in myself and allowed themselves to be conscripted into betareading stories, whether they wanted to or not. Thank you all.

Table of Contents

Stitches

"OKAY, SO I SHOULD be back for them by six," Adam Wolfe said to Nicole. Even though he spoke to her, his dark brown eyes were focused on his children, Luke and Thomas. They were in Nicole's living room with their aunt, Danny, who was hyping them up about the day they were going to have.

"We could easily bring them to your house." Nicole's gaze drifted toward her girlfriend and the little boys.

The sight brought a bright smile to Nicole's face. *They look so small and adorable, standing next to Danny the giant.* She liked to give her lover as much time as possible with the boys. Danny loved her nephews, but didn't spend as much time with them as she liked because their mother didn't trust or like Danny. There was a story there, but Nicole didn't ask. Danny seemed to only know she was hated for being a lesbian. They both suspected there was more.

"No, I'll still be out, so I'll just come get them." Adam's anxiety cutting into his voice.

Nicole decided not to argue with him. He wouldn't yield and she didn't want to make things uncomfortable. Adam didn't want to risk Danny running into his wife, Sharon, especially with the boys around. Nicole wasn't sure what Adam thought would happen between the two. Danny ignored most insults, and all Sharon did was snipe. She didn't even do that to Danny's face. It wasn't like they'd have a fistfight if they occupied the same space at the same time.

"Fine," Nicole conceded with a small shrug. "Well, we should get going then."

"Let me say goodbye to my little guys," Adam said. "Hey, guys!"

Luke and Thomas didn't bother to turn around. They were now enamored with Haydn, Nicole and Danny's white shepherd puppy. Adam grabbed them up into a single hug. They squealed and Haydn let out a surprised bark, circling around Adam's feet as if trying to figure out where to attack.

"Haydn, come," Danny ordered, standing a couple of feet away. Haydn made another noise and continued circling until Danny repeated the command.

"Those obedience classes seem to be paying off," Nicole said, as she stepped over to her girlfriend. While Adam bid his sons farewell, Nicole decided to check on her lover. "Are you sure you're up to this?"

Danny ran her hand through her short, onyx locks. "I watch the boys enough to take them to your grandparents for a simple cookout, right?"

"Yes, you do, but that's not what I meant, baby. Technically, you're still healing. Are you up to hanging out with my family?" Nicole asked for possibly the hundredth time. She had been asking since the beginning of the week when her grandparents invited them to an end of summer barbeque. The spontaneous cookout was thanks to the nice, warm weather lasting to the end of September.

"Chem, I'm fine. Stop worrying," Danny replied with a smile. A car had hit her some months earlier. Her ribs had healed over a month ago, but the cast on her right leg had only been off for a few weeks.

Rolling her eyes, Nicole shook her head. "You know I can't," she replied with a bright smile.

A warm smile spread across Danny's face again. "I know. I appreciate the concern."

They turned their attention back to the males in their home as the goodbyes were finished between the anxious father and eager sons. Luke and Thomas quickly returned to cooing over the puppy. Adam gazed at his sons, almost as if he was scared they'd forget him. Danny didn't bother with her older brother, but Nicole at least walked him to the door.

"It'll be fine. We're just going to my grandparents' house. There'll be other children for them to play with and everything," she assured him for quite possibly the tenth time. He clearly didn't spend a lot of time away from his children. She found his separation anxiety to be sweet, even though it obviously irked Danny.

"Okay. Call me if anything happens," Adam said, his eyes wide and slightly wet.

"We will, but it'll be fine. It's just a small, family barbeque. Nothing more than that."

Adam nodded and she finally ushered him out of the door. Nicole breathed a sigh of relief as she shut the door. Okay, so his anxiety was sweet, but also exhausting. She turned her attention to Danny and her nephews.

"Are you guys ready to go?" Nicole asked with cheer in her voice and a grin on her face.

"Yeah!" the boys cheered and the happy noise made Haydn yelp.

"All right, let's get moving. Everybody have everything they need?" Nicole inquired.

Danny grabbed her guitar, which was resting by the couch, and took Luke by the hand. Nicole attached Haydn's leash to his collar and took Thomas' hand. The group exited the house and the boys were buckled up in the backseat. Danny held onto the pup in the front seat, while Nicole got behind the wheel.

"Okay, are we sure we have everything?" Nicole asked again just to be sure. She knew small children needed every chance possible to remember anything they might need.

"Yeah!" Luke answered for the boys. He hugged his backpack. His little brother had one, too, but Thomas had just dumped his bag on the floor.

"Then let's go have fun and eat hotdogs," Nicole cheered. The boys shouted their approval, which made Haydn yelp and Danny smile.

***

Nicole's family was in the backyard of her grandparents' house. The barbeque was already in full swing with everyone there, including Nicole's parents. Nicole looked around and Dane could've sworn her girlfriend looked embarrassed. For just a second, Nicole's cheeks were almost as red as her hair.

"Hey, everybody." Nicole waved to her family.

"Nikki, we were scared you weren't going to show up," Raymond said, as he moved away from the card game he was playing. The other players included Nicole's aunts, Kimber and Katrina, and Kimber's son, Philip. Raymond grabbed her into a hug.

Nicole smiled and returned her father's embrace. "We had to wait for Luke and Thomas. Danny thought they'd have fun here."

Dane noticed Thomas grip Nicole's hand a little tighter as if to remind her he was there. For some reason, this made her chuckle a little. Luke and Thomas weren't boys that would let anyone forget them. Nicole smiled down at Thomas, giving him the acknowledgement he wanted.

Raymond turned his attention to the towheaded boys. He was familiar with them after meeting them at Dane's birthday party a couple of months ago. He offered the boys his hand, which they both shook like little men.

Nicole thought they were cute mimicking the adult behaviors they saw. Of course, the fact they were dressed in khaki shorts and white polo shirts tickled her as well. Dane didn't get the appeal, but if it made her lover happy, it was good enough for her to just accept.

"Good to see you two again. Have a good time, okay?" Raymond smiled down at the boys and they seemed to almost puff out their chests because of the attention.

"We will!" Luke proclaimed, while Thomas grinned and nodded. Haydn yelped again. Dane was certain she and Nicole were raising a little glory hound.

"You brought your dog, too? Is he ready to be out around people or another dog?" Raymond asked, nodding toward Katrina's dog in the yard.

"We'll find out," Nicole replied with a smile.

Raymond nodded. "Be careful," he cautioned them and patted Dane on the shoulder as a greeting. She smiled at him before turning her attention elsewhere.

Dane thought Katrina's dog was bigger than she remembered, but that was expected. She hadn't seen the creature in months. She remembered the dog was friendly and Haydn was affable. In fact, Haydn had yet to meet a person or dog he didn't like.

Dane decided to see sooner rather than later by letting Haydn off of his leash. He charged off to investigate his new environment. The large backyard set off a rather average house. Luke and Thomas took off after him and Dane followed. Katrina's kids, Eddie and Sabrina, came over almost immediately with their dog. Haydn eased back, settling next to Dane.

"Hey, Danny! Who are they?" Eddie asked with a bluntness that Dane knew would get him in trouble in a few years. But, his cherubic dimples and slightly wavy, dark-chocolate locks would get him right back out of trouble...well, with most girls and adults anyway.

"These are my nephews and my dog. Luke, Thomas, meet Nicole's cousins, Eddie and Sabrina." Dane introduced the duos. She hoped they'd get along, even though her nephews were younger than Nicole's cousins.

"You don't look anything like Danny." Sabrina seemed amazed.

It was quite true, they didn't appear related in the slightest. Luke and Thomas were blonds with creamy complexions, while Dane had a caramel skin tone and black hair with blond highlights. Luke had brown eyes like his father, and Thomas had blue like his mother; Dane had grey eyes. They shared almost nothing in common with Dane, except maybe chubby cheeks.

"You don't look like Nick," Luke countered. He and his brother had taken to calling Nicole by the nickname Dane used. Nicole's family did the same with Danny.

"I'm not Nikki." Sabrina shrugged.

"We're not Dane," Thomas countered.

Luke just moved on. "Dane's puppy's name is Haydn. It's a weird name. What's your dog's name?"

"Beanie." Eddie grinned. "Beanie can do tricks."

As Beanie went through his tricks, Haydn checked him out. Beanie was older than the shepherd pup, but he wasn't too much bigger. Beanie was a mixed breed Katrina had rescued as a puppy. Dane could understand why Eddie and Sabrina loved the sweet dog.

"Beanie's cool," Thomas declared as Haydn nudged Beanie with his nose.

Dane only laughed. She suspected they'd go home, demanding a dog of their own, again. They had done so when they first met Haydn. She also suspected they'd spend a lot of time trying to teach Haydn tricks. With luck, Haydn might actually learn something.

Dane stuck close to her boys, but acknowledged everyone at the cookout with a wave. Nicole's family waved back and let Dane go about her business. The only one who gave Dane more than a nod was Jarred, Kimber's husband. He was working the large grill and pointed toward the food that he had already finished cooking. She shook her head to decline the offer, for now.

"Does Haydn know any tricks?" Eddie asked, once Beanie had gone through all of his little doggie tricks.

"Only if you count whining and jumping on things he shouldn't." Dane smiled, as she reached down and petted the rambunctious pup. Haydn yipped and licked her fingers.

"Sabrina does those tricks, too." Eddie laughed.

Sabrina didn't seem to get the joke, which was for the best. They moved on from dog tricks to chasing the dogs. Dane moved around with them, but couldn't run with them. Even without just being healed from her car accident injuries, she wouldn't have been able to keep up with them because of her lame leg. Still, they called for her participation, so she did what she could.

***

Nicole settled down next to her grandmother, Alicia, who was at the small picnic table that was slowly being covered in food. Nicole's mother, Kate, was there too. Nicole happily kissed both of their cheeks as greetings.

"Hi, sweet pea. I was worried when your mom beat you here." Alicia snickered.

Nicole laughed. While she was hardly the first person to arrive at a family function, her mother was always the last one. But, her mother didn't have two small kids and their worried father to get out the door.

"Luke and Thomas came late and their dad wouldn't leave once he showed up. So, that's why we're the last to show."

Alicia nodded. "The little angels are related to Danny?"

"I know Mommy already told you those are Danny's nephews. They're her eldest brother's sons. They love her," Nicole replied in a delighted tone. She liked talking about Danny and her relationship with her nephews. She wanted everyone to know how good Danny was with children.

Alicia glanced over at the group. "She looks really good with them. How often do they go places with you?"

"Not often, because Danny doesn't go places often. They come over to the house every weekend now. She always makes sure she has stuff to do with them. They play video games, or go to the park, or just walk the dog. They're very nice boys."

Her grandmother made an odd noise, but it sounded pleasant, so Nicole didn't take offense. "I'm sure they are. So, Danny's good with kids and I see there's a ring on your finger..." Her eyes drifted down to Nicole's hand. The gold band with a small row of diamonds that probably bankrupted her lover sat pretty on her left hand, letting the world know she was taken.

The words ring and finger seemed to be a gathering call for the other women, except for Danny. Nicole's aunts and teenage cousin Jody practically flew over to the table to see the simple ring. Jody went as far as to grab Nicole's hand for a closer inspection.

"I expected better from Danny," Jody declared, while Kate glared at

6

the piece of jewelry.

"It's not an engagement ring, just so we're clear. It's a promise ring. So, you can all get pictures of my wedding out of your heads," Nicole informed all of them. Her mother was the only one that did not look disappointed.

"Sweet pea, your grandma is an old woman." Alicia sighed dramatically and made sure to look extremely pitiful, putting a hand to her forehead. "You want to give me great grandchildren, don't you?" She sniffled.

Nicole gave her grandmother a playful swat. "Not just yet, no."

"She needs to find the right guy first," Kate chimed in.

Kimber rolled her eyes. "Kate, don't start. Danny's a wonderful person and so in love with Nikki that she probably can't see straight, which I guess suits her since she's gay. She's put up with your attitude toward her and she's still here, smiling all the way through. She only wants the best for Nikki, and she's willing to go through hell for it, apparently. I'd think you of all people would recognize that."

Katrina chimed in. "Seriously, how often did Raymond's family try to run you off?"

Kate glared at her younger sisters, which was enough to silence them on the subject. Nicole was aware that her father's family were not fans of her mother, but she didn't know the real details. Her aunts sometimes let things slip, so she knew her mother was resented for what the Cardell family viewed as her transforming Raymond from a carefree, fun-loving guy into a serious lawyer. Nicole thought that was crazy and couldn't help noting the irony in her mother's feelings toward Danny.

"Nikki, you hold onto Danny if she's the person you love. You marry her when you feel the time is right. You have babies with her when you feel the time's right," Alicia said.

"Mom," Kate huffed, but she didn't dare to glower at her mother.

"What? I told you the same thing when you complained about Raymond's family trying to chase you off. I told Kimber the same thing when your father was trying to run Jarred out of here because he wasn't Christian."

Katrina chuckled. "I was the only one that didn't require this little pep talk?"

"Just remember it when Eddie, Sabrina, and Wayne start dating," Alicia said. Katrina laughed again as she nodded.

"Where is Wayne, anyway?" Nicole asked, hoping to get off the subject of her ring.

"He's been asleep for about an hour now," Katrina replied. "This is his usual nap time, so that's good. I don't have to worry about him staying up extra late tonight, as long as I don't let him take another nap after he wakes from this one."

"So, you're not engaged?" Jody asked with bright eyes and a smile practically beaming at Nicole.

Nicole smiled back. "Nope, not engaged. Engaged to be engaged maybe." With luck, that'd be the end of the matter for now.

***

"What's going on over there?" Dane asked Philip, Eduardo, and Benito, nodding toward the picnic table across the yard. She sat by them at the now abandoned card game. Raymond had gone over to help Jarred clear the grill.

Eduardo, Katrina's husband, chuckled. "I guess you're the guy in your relationship if you missed the female version of the Bat signal."

Dane only arched an eyebrow. *What the hell? I feel like I should be insulted.*

"Somebody said the word ring, so we're guessing you bought Nikki a ring," Benito, Nicole's grandfather, said.

Philip's head snapped to the side as he stared at her with wide eyes. "Whoa, you're engaged to Nikki?"

Dane shook her head. "No. Not an engagement ring. It was a promise ring."

"That explains why they haven't come over here to talk to you," Benito said with a shrug. Then he looked her right in the eye, almost like a warning. "They will be bugging you about marrying her."

She nodded. "I will one day. I just need to mature some more. Gotta get to a better place."

"You'll know when your ready," he assured her with a warm smile. She nodded, believing he was totally right. "And don't let anyone try to talk you into doing it before you're ready. Nikki's a special girl and she deserves the best."

"Yes, sir," Dane completely agreed. She definitely wouldn't ask Nicole until she felt totally worthy of her and also completely comfortable with herself. She still had a journey ahead of her, but she'd get there. She knew that because of Nicole.

"Hey, Danny, you brought your guitar, right?" Philip suddenly asked with hope in his eyes. There was another nod and he grinned. "Cool, I've got mine, too. We can jam and you can see how my lessons are going."

"Okay, but just to warn you, once those boys see me with that guitar, they're gonna want in on the action." She pointed over at her nephews.

Philip just shrugged before going off to get his guitar. Dane groaned as she climbed to her feet to fetch her own instrument. She barely had her hand on her guitar case before her nephews were in her face.

"Are you playing? We'll play, too." Luke pointed to himself and his brother.

"Yeah, I'll play the drums." Thomas threw his hands up.

"And I'll be the lead singer and play the guitar," Luke said.

Dane smiled. "Okay, but I gotta play the guitar too, and so does my friend Philip."

Luke nodded in agreement and Philip found himself the member of a band by the time he returned. He was a good sport, even though he didn't know he was part of a game Dane often played with her nephews.

"One, two, three, four." Thomas banged together the drumsticks he traveled with. Dane was sure he'd end up an actual drummer as he got older. Thomas played his pretend drums, while Philip played his real guitar, and Dane followed his lead.

Luke squinted as he watched the pair playing the guitars and his little brow was so furrowed Dane wondered if his forehead would drop off. For a moment, Dane thought Luke would object because he didn't know the song. Instead, he didn't try to sing, but played his air guitar with them. Dane laughed a little, glad Luke was so cool about things.

***

"What are they doing?" Kimber asked, nodding toward the band.

Nicole smiled as she noticed the scene. "Oh, that's their band. The boys love music as much as Danny, so she plays this little pretend game with them like they're a band. They seem to love it."

"Indeed they do, if the little one carrying his own drumsticks means anything. I'm glad Philip's getting the chance to play with Danny. I don't know who this guy is that gives him lessons, but every time Philip comes home, he has some crazy story about Danny in high school," Kimber said.

"Danny actually went to high school?" Kate sneered.

"Be nice," Katrina scolded her older sister.

"Is his guitar tutor an old high school buddy?" Kimber asked Nicole.

Nicole shook her head. "He's someone she knew while she was in high school, but he didn't go to school with her."

Danny had gone to an alternative high school and was a loner even there. She didn't know or interact with many of her classmates. During her teen years, all of her "friends" were older musicians who respected her musical ability and vice versa. The musician she referred Philip to knew not to tell him about any of her wilder exploits as a teen, but was free and clear to tell whatever embarrassing tale came to mind.

"So, what type of stories does Philip come home with?" Kate asked, undoubtedly hunting for ammo to use against Danny to prove her point that Danny wasn't worthwhile.

"Oh, just like she knocked herself out stage diving once. She somehow managed to completely miss the crowd," Kimber told them, earning a laugh from the ladies, except Nicole.

Nicole couldn't laugh. She knew the audience would probably have been quite sizable for one of Danny's performances. Likely, she had been so high she couldn't hit a single person in a crowd. Sighing, her eyes went to her lover, and she decided she didn't want to hear any more unintentionally sad stories involving her lover.

"You should see Danny and Luke freestyle. He's adorable," Nicole said.

Katrina clasped her hands together and grinned. "Oh, God. Can you get him to do it, please?"

"He's a huge ham. All you have to do is ask. There's not a shy bone in that kid's body," Nicole said with a fond smile. *It's probably a Wolfe family trait.*

Sure enough, right after the band finished playing, Nicole called Luke over for him to do a freestyle rap. His face lit up, and he called Dane over to do it with him. Nicole noticed her grandmother, aunts, and cousin all gave Luke an odd look as he referred to Danny as Dane and didn't attach aunt or any variation of the title. He barely got started before Haydn charged over, yapping at Danny.

"Oops. Time to feed the pup," Danny realized and then she checked her watch. "Time for you little guys to eat, too." She ruffled the top of Luke's golden head.

Haydn got his first taste of people food that day, sharing some hotdogs and burgers with Beanie. Nicole made a plate of food for

Thomas while Danny took care of Luke. They sat to eat with the boys and Haydn curled up at their feet when he was done. The boys, however, were off as soon as they finished and pulled Danny with them. Nicole tried to ignore the looks as she cleared their plates.

"You really need to have some babies," Alicia said with a sparkle in her brown eyes.

"Danny's really good with them, so you'd both make good parents," Kimber concurred. There were nods and even Kate couldn't disagree.

Nicole shook her head. "We're not going to have kids anytime soon, so just stop, Grandma." She could see herself having a child with Danny, definitely, and she hoped it was in the future. But, it was something for years down the line.

Alicia smiled and shook her head. "I can't do it. I really think you'd enjoy having a family. I'll let it go for now, though."

"Why do Danny's nephews call her Dane?" Katrina asked.

"That's how she was introduced to them by her brother. It's complicated," Nicole answered. *The entire Wolfe family is complicated.* "The important thing is that they like her and she likes them, not what they call her. It's good they want to be around her."

A teasing glint flickered through Kimber's eyes. "Sure you don't want kids now?"

"How's school going?" her grandmother asked to save her eldest grandchild.

Nicole's mother couldn't take it anymore and got up from the table. Nicole followed her mother with her eyes, momentarily, but she didn't say anything to Kate. Her mother disliked her partner and the fact that she was going to school for a chemistry degree, but she wouldn't change either of those things. So, her mother was just going to have to stay upset or get over it. Nicole was done kowtowing to her parents as she had done her whole life.

"School's fine. I just started two new classes. I've got twelve credits already," Nicole answered her grandmother's question. "Jody, how's school for you?"

Jody sighed dramatically, pressing the back of her hand to her forehead. "It's harder than you told me it would be, Nikki." The adults chuckled, knowing Jody wasn't serious.

Jody was a freshman at a local university. She wasn't sure what she would major in, but they all knew it'd end up being something with computers. Jody was into computers like Nicole was into chemistry. The thing that Jody had on her side was that her mother was more laid back than Nicole's mother. Jody would not be pressured to follow in Kimber's footsteps.

***

Dane found herself inside, watching football with the guys. She didn't know much about football, but Benito had taken it upon himself to educate her on his favorite sport. Philip was his assistant in that regard, as he also enjoyed football and wanted Dane to like it, too. Football was the sport of choice for all family gatherings, so Dane figured she needed to learn it if she wanted to be accepted.

"So, who're we rooting for again?" Dane chuckled to let them know she was joking. She earned a playful swat from Benito.

Benito wagged a stern finger at her. "Just pay attention."

Dane laughed, but obeyed. She had plenty of serious questions that were handled by every guy there, including Eddie when he wandered by every now and then. Part way through the second quarter, Thomas staggered in and fell asleep on her lap. Not too long after that, Nicole came in. She took a picture of the scene with her phone before she said anything.

"Danny, it's time to go, so we're not late," Nicole said.

Dane frowned and checked her watch to see her lover was right. Her frown deepened. She was having a good time and she wished they could stay a little longer. Her desire must have been written all over her face, because green eyes softened.

"We'll come back soon, sweetheart," Nicole promised.

Dane sighed, but didn't argue. She rose to her feet, careful of Thomas. She had to give the boy to Nicole, because there was no way Nicole would allow her to carry him. Goodbyes were said as they collected Luke and Haydn. Eddie and Sabrina were near tears that their playmates were leaving.

"Luke and Thomas will come back soon, okay?" Nicole assured her cousins.

That didn't work and Katrina had to go save her niece from her children. With Katrina's help, Nicole and Dane were able to escape, even though it was hard to get Luke to leave. By the time they pulled up to the house, Adam was already there, pacing by his car, and it wasn't even six yet.

"You're early." Dane scowled as they unloaded from the car.

Adam looked sheepish, but that didn't move her. She hated when he loomed, as if she couldn't be trusted with the boys. Of course she wasn't alone with them, so it was like he didn't trust her or Nicole.

Ever the diplomat, Nicole chimed in as she gently pulled the still sleeping Thomas from the car. "You missed your boys, didn't you?"

He smiled. "I did." He turned his attention to Luke. "Hey, buddy, ready to go home?"

"No, I wanna go back and play with Eddie, Sabrina, and Beanie again!" Luke actually stomped his foot.

Dane blinked. *Who is this kid?* She was used to her nephews being well behaved and fun loving. She never saw them throw a real tantrum, and she wasn't in the mood to see it either. She rubbed the top of Luke's head to calm him down.

Nicole smiled softly. "He was having a lot of fun with my little cousins and their dog." She handed Thomas over to Adam.

Adam nodded while Dane stayed back. She was tempted to say something nasty to her brother for showing up early, but she didn't want to curse him out in front of her nephews. So, instead, she gave Luke a hug farewell and ruffled his hair.

"See you next weekend, guitar hero," Dane said to the little boy. Luke was clearly unhappy, but he nodded and tried to give her a smile.

Adam said his own goodbyes before taking his sons to his car. He and Luke waved as he pulled off. They were gone before Nicole and Dane got to the front porch.

***

"You okay?" Nicole asked Danny. They were cuddled up on the couch watching a movie. Danny was uncharacteristically quiet during the very cheesy horror movie.

Danny thought about it for a moment. "Yeah, I'm fine. I was just thinking about how much fun today was. Hanging out with the boys and with your family is so *normal*. I love it."

Nicole smiled. "I'm glad you like being around my family. They like you a lot."

A small smile settled on Danny's face and she nodded a little. "I can tell, and I like them. Your grandfather's great. I've never really had a grandfather, so having him like me is really cool. I just really enjoyed today."

Nicole wrapped her arms around her lover and pulled her closer.

"That's great. So, we'll go to Sunday dinners more often, okay?"

"Okay. No problem. It'll be a new thing for me."

Nicole sighed. She hated that so many things she took for granted—loving family, grandparents, and family dinners—were novelties for her girlfriend. She wanted Danny to experience as many normal things as possible.

"Hey, did your grandma and aunts think your ring was an engagement ring?" Danny took Nicole's hand and played with her ring finger for a second.

Nicole glanced down at Danny's hand. "They did. You saw them mob me?"

"Yeah, and the men folk had to explain to me what was going on." Danny chuckled.

"I explained it's not an engagement ring, but they want us married with kids, like now." Nicole grinned.

Danny laughed. "Kids? I only just got qualified to take care of a dog and that's only because you're here."

Nicole rested her head on Danny's shoulder. "Do you want kids?"

"Never thought about it. Do you?"

"I do. I want at least two. But, I'm not in a rush and we can talk about it seriously later on, when you've had time to think about it. I already told you, I want to get married before I have kids."

Danny nodded. "Sounds good. Right now, I just want to hang out with you, Haydn, and the boys every now and then."

A smile settled onto Nicole's face. She felt the same for the moment. She also wanted to help her girlfriend experience a few more normal things in life before anything else. Danny needed some of life's simple pleasures and Nicole consciously decided right then and there to make that happen as soon as possible.

Heavy Metal Poisoning

"WHO'S A GOOD BOY? Huh? Who's Dane's good boy?" Dane asked Haydn, as she leaned down to detach his leash from around his collar. He licked the end of her nose and nuzzled her cheek. She grinned and rubbed him down.

Haydn was four months old. She and Nicole had owned him for two months. He was their proud, happy bundle of energy and a bright spark in their lives. He wiggled against her, as she petted him lovingly.

Dane continued to grin. "Let's go brush your coat. You'll like that, won't you? I know you will. Then we'll start dinner, so our girl Nick will have dinner when she comes in."

Haydn yapped in what Dane took as agreement. She was so happy to finally have her cast off, from when she was hit by a car a few months ago, and be able to do simple things with Haydn. She'd had her cast off for a couple of weeks and before being able to do things with Haydn, the new freedom had allowed her to do a number of things with Nicole. Of course, being intimate with Nicole was the best thing, but taking care of Haydn ranked high on her list of things to do. She had always wanted a dog, and Nicole had fulfilled that desire by getting her precious white shepherd pup as a birthday gift. He turned out to be a gift for both of them. Haydn brought the couple closer and that only made Dane love the little guy more.

"Guess we can get you a treat too, since you were such a good boy," Dane cooed.

She hung the leash by the door and Haydn barked again. She couldn't help leaning down, petting his head. He rubbed his head against her hand and barked in approval. As they moved toward the kitchen the phone rang. Dane glanced at the caller ID on the living room phone and rolled her eyes.

"It's Christine again, Haydn. Think I should take her call this time or just wait until Chem notices she's called like eighty times and asks me if I want to get the number blocked or something?"

Haydn responded with another yap, which Dane decided meant she shouldn't answer the phone. She brushed the pup's fur and gave him a treat before leaving him with a toy to chew on. She and Nicole had found out the hard way that he was in a chewing phase and had rushed out to get him plenty of toys before he ruined the coffee table and his own mouth from biting hard wood.

She showered and went to start dinner with the puppy keeping her company in the kitchen, as he rolled around with his toy. Everything was almost done by the time Nicole entered the house. Dane poked her head out of the kitchen while Haydn charged the door.

"Hey, honey," Nicole called out. Seconds later, a cuddly ball of white fur was at her feet. She bent down to pet and hug the pup. "Hey, Haydn! Have you been behaving for Danny? Have you?" she prattled, scratching his ears.

"He's been a very good boy today. Took him to the park and actually let him off the leash. He was good. He came when I called and stayed away from any unfriendly dogs. We met a few new people and dogs, and he got to play around with his new friends. We had a good time." Dane stepped completely out of the kitchen.

Nicole placed her briefcase securely on top of the end table that was near the stairs. Another lesson they had learned the hard way was that Haydn thought Nicole's briefcase was a plaything whenever it was within his reach. He knew better than to try that with Dane's guitar, though.

Nicole and Dane walked to each other and embraced. As they wrapped themselves in each other's lips and arms, Haydn bounced around their feet. They pulled away, and Nicole turned her attention to the phone. The blinking light undoubtedly caught her attention.

"Baby, how often has your mom called here?" The light meant they had voicemail, and she had gone through this enough to know why Dane hadn't answered the phone. Nicole picked up the phone and went through the call log. Shaking her head, she sucked her teeth. "Dozens. I should've known."

"Uh..." Dane tried to think of some response to all of those calls. Nothing came to mind.

"Sweetheart, if you're not going to talk to her, at least do something about the voicemail. Someone else might call and need to leave a message." Nicole gave her a teasing smile.

Dane nodded, scratching the top of her head. "You're right. Should I listen to them, or should I just erase them?"

"That's up to you, love." Nicole smiled and ran her hand through Dane's hair because she knew Dane was about to do it.

Dane pouted. "Not fair," she pretended to whine.

"That's life." Nicole placed a small kiss to Dane's moue. "Besides, you know what I'd say, but I'm done interfering in this part of your life. I'll only step in when you ask me to."

Dane snorted. "I'm asking you right now."

"When you ask me and it's something you truly cannot do without me."

"Damn you and your fancy lawyer tricks." Dane huffed and pushed the button to play the messages.

The first message played. "Uh...hello, this is Christine...I'm calling for Dane. I was just wondering how you're doing. That's all."

The second message was nearly the same. "Hello, it's Christine again. I'm calling for Dane. Perhaps you would call me back."

Dane groaned and massaged her temples, as the messages droned on and on. "Why the hell can't she take the hint? I don't wanna talk to her!"

By the tenth one, Dane rested her forehead against Nicole's and prayed for the messages to end. After the fifteenth, she just erased the rest. Sighing, she turned her attention to Nicole.

"Any advice on what I should do about her?"

"My first piece of advice would be talk to her if you don't want her calling so much. If you don't say anything, she'll just keep calling with the hope that eventually you'll respond. I'm sure if you even yelled at her a little, it'd give her pause," Nicole answered.

Dane scrunched her face up. "But, there's no way to just get rid of her?"

Nicole offered a small smile and her emerald eyes sparkled with sympathy. "I doubt it. But, my guess would be to start with seeing what she wants. If you at least give her that, she might back off if she sees that you don't want it. But, of course, I also think you should talk to her for your own peace of mind."

Dane sighed and nodded. "I know, I know. I just can't talk to her. Every time the phone rings and I see it's her, my brain comes up with a million things to do to keep me from answering. The only time I talk to her is when you pick up and then hand me the phone because you don't check caller ID."

A light laugh escaped Nicole. "Well, excuse me for assuming my parents might be calling me at home or your nephews might want to talk to you."

"You could still check the caller ID. You know she's always calling. Anyway, you really think I should talk to her? I mean, over the phone is so impersonal and I always hang up, like I can't stand the sound of her voice. I dunno..." Dane's hand glided through her short hair, as her face scrunched again.

Nicole nodded and placed a gentle kiss to Danny's cheek, which helped settle her. "I think you're right. The phone is impersonal and I've seen how frustrated you get when you're on the phone with her."

"Maybe I should send her an email."

Nicole burst out laughing. "You don't even have an email address, and that's even more impersonal than the phone. Do you want me to help you?"

"Uh...haven't I been saying that all along? So, where are we gonna hide the body?" Dane chuckled as she rubbed her palms together.

"I wouldn't give that sort of help with your mother. Now, your father on the other hand..." Nicole tittered.

Dane laughed. "Okay, fine. So, what're you going to do?"

"Well, first, I'm going to take a shower, and then I'm going to eat dinner. Finally, I'm going to cuddle on the couch with you and little Haydn while watching some pup-friendly movies."

Dane laughed again and stepped away. She swatted Nicole on the butt, earning a yelp and a smile from the attorney. "Go do all of that, you smartass."

"I will, and then I'll worry about Christine." Nicole walked away, making sure to sway her hips as she did so.

"Tease!" Dane called after her. She could hear Nicole giggling all the way to their bedroom.

***

"This is your idea of helping?" Dane asked, as she and Nicole walked down the street. Haydn was on his leash, taking in the sights and smells of a totally new area.

"What? You said the phone was impersonal. I thought a face-to-face would be best for both of you. This way, you can see if she's sincere or if she's just trying to torment you further. Seeing you might also help her get to her point sooner."

"Her point? Her point's to keep harassing me now that I don't need her at all anymore because I've got you." Dane rolled her eyes.

Nicole didn't argue. The galvanizing force behind Christine Wolfe's sudden interest in her youngest daughter was because she no longer had any excuses to keep tabs on Dane. Once upon a time, Christine was the only person who could get Dane out of trouble—usually a medical emergency. But, after an incident where Dane had shown up on Nicole's front lawn looking like death warmed over, that changed.

Dane was now covered under Nicole's health insurance—something Nicole still didn't want to discuss at length—so Dane had no need for help in that area. Besides, Nicole would not only pay for medical problems, but stick around to make sure that Dane healed. Christine couldn't make that claim.

Not being needed had turned Christine into a needy pest as far as Dane was concerned. While Dane was recovering from being hit by a car, and Nicole acted as her overprotective nurse, Christine tried to speak with Dane more often than Dane wanted. Well, wanted *now*, anyway. Christine was too late in trying to be there.

Nicole did plenty of things that Christine couldn't lay claim to. It was just that, up until Nicole, Christine had been the only game in town when Dane was in serious trouble, like when Dane was beaten and hospitalized a few years ago. If Nicole had been around then, Dane might've even healed properly, because someone would've been watching out for her. Now, Dane had no need for anyone beyond Nicole and it seemed to bother her mother.

"Look, it's just lunch. We'll eat and when we're done we'll take Haydn to the park. Maybe our young man might make some new friends. What do you say to that?" Nicole gave her a bright smile.

Dane frowned. "Why do you know exactly how to bribe me?"

With a shrug, Nicole gave her another smile. "I dunno. You sleep next to a person for a few months and you just pick up things about them." She took Dane's free hand and gave it a squeeze.

Dane laughed and shook her head. She was now out of excuses and saw her mother waiting for them at the outside café Nicole had picked. *At least we can have Haydn with us. It's one silver lining.*

"Hello, Dane, Nicole. I'm glad you invited me out." Christine forced out a smile, but her voice shook slightly. She rubbed her hands together before motioning to the empty chairs, silently inviting them to sit.

"It was our pleasure," Nicole replied, which was a lie and they all knew it. Still, the couple sat after Dane pulled Nicole's chair out for her. They were silent for a moment, before Christine glanced down at Haydn.

"Luke and Thomas were telling me that you have a dog now. He's adorable," Christine said with a small smile.

Nicole glanced over and Dane knew her lover expected her to just open up since Haydn was the perfect topic to discuss. Dane loved talking about their pup. Her eyes drifted down to Haydn, but Dane didn't sing his praises like she usually would.

"I gave him to Danny as a birthday present."

"Really? He must be a lot of work," Christine said.

"He is, but Danny and I enjoy taking care of him. Danny's especially enjoying it, and she's very good at handling him. She's always wanted a dog."

"Oh." Christine couldn't hide the surprise in her face. The surprise could've been from the idea that Dane actually took care of something or that Dane might've always wanted a dog. Dane took it as the former since she couldn't understand why her mother would think the latter.

"Yeah, believe it or not, I can actually take care of myself, my girl, and a dog. Who knew?" Dane huffed and rolled her eyes. "This is bullshit," she added in a grumble, folding her arms across her chest.

"Baby," Nicole reprimanded Dane softly and patted her thigh to keep her calm.

"What? We've been sitting here for three seconds and she's already acting like I'm a fuck-up." Dane motioned to Christine with one hand.

"You assumed that. Come on, you said you'd try," Nicole whispered before leaning over and kissing Dane's cheek.

Dane sighed. "Fine." She turned her attention back to her mother. "So, here we are."

"Indeed..." Christine sighed. Her eyes went to the table and it seemed like she searched her brain for something to discuss.

They were all saved for a moment, as a waiter came over to give them menus and take their drink orders. Of course, all too soon, he was gone again and they were left with awkward silence.

Christine was the one who broke it. "Adam tells me you've been spending more time with his boys. They seem to like you."

"Yeah, I know it's hard to believe." Dane snorted and glanced away for a second. After all, Luke and Thomas were the only people in her family who seemed to like her.

"Danny." Nicole gave her another pat on the thigh.

Dane growled and threw up her hands. "You know, I can't do this! I just can't." She hopped out of her seat and marched off. "Come on,

20

Haydn. Let's go to the park and chase some squirrels." The pup gave a yap of approval.

Nicole sighed and gave Christine a shrug before chasing after her fleeing lover. "Danny, wait for me!"

Dane slowed down just enough for Nicole to catch up to her. "Sorry for that," she said as soon as Nicole was by her side.

"It's all right. I know this was difficult for you to begin with." Nicole took Dane's free hand.

"Was a good try with the face-to-face thing. You just forgot that I, unlike most human beings, don't mind making a scene. I think this would've worked out if only I didn't give a shit about hearing what she had to say." *Maybe I'll never be emotionally ready to talk to her.*

"Is that it? You don't have an interest in what she had to say?" Nicole asked, as they rounded the block. They were taking the long way to the car, it seemed.

Dane ran her hand through her hair and then scratched her head. "Not sure. I mean, I do, but I don't. I feel like if I can avoid talking to her, then I will. I don't know what to do about that. I just feel like being spiteful to her. I dunno." She shrugged.

Nicole squeezed her hand. "It's okay, honey. Take it as slowly as you feel you need to."

"Yeah?" Dane gave her a sidelong glance.

"Hey, I told you, I'll support your decisions when it comes to your family. So, I'll do whatever you tell me to do in regards to them. Well, I might step in with your nephews, because you tend to get immature around them." She offered Dane a teasing smile.

Danny laughed. "They get me in trouble!"

Nicole arched an eyebrow and chuckled. "How? How is it they get you in trouble? I don't think it's them shoving chips and cookies down your throat until everybody has a stomachache."

Dane smiled and linked their arms together. "One time! Besides, I'm an aunt. I get to be irresponsible. I'd never do that if we had a kid. I'd be really strict." *Whoa. Did I just say that? Be cool, Dane. We're not even near ready for that. Hell, I'm not ready for that. I can't even talk to my own mother, so definitely not in the right space to be one.*

Nicole laughed again. "Just like you are with Haydn, huh? Remember when he was rolling around on the sofa? You just encouraged him, scratching his belly like he had done something great."

Internally, Dane breathed a sigh of relief. Nicole took it as the joke it was. "Okay, fine, I'd be like having a second kid if we had a kid. But,

I've got time to straighten out since we're not having kids anytime soon, right?"

"No, I don't think we're in any state to consider kids, yet." Nicole played with the ring on her left hand. "After all, we've barely discussed marriage, and I won't have kids unless I'm married."

"Well, I don't need to be married to have kids, but I do think I need to get myself together before I could ever consider it beyond a joke. You're right, you know?"

"Right about what?"

"Christine. I do need to talk to her. I need to hear her out for my own peace of mind and to move forward in some way. Unfortunately, I know if I can run away from her, I will. Don't know what to do about that. Ideas?"

"Give me some time to think on it. For now, let's get back to the car, so we can get this young man to the park to play with his friends." Nicole glanced down at Haydn. Dane smiled and nodded.

***

Dane yawned and sat up from the couch, as she heard the front door open. Leaning over, she tried to see Nicole and Haydn as they came in, but she knew it was impossible. Haydn bounded into the living room seconds later.

"Hey, there, little guy!" Dane greeted the pup as she leaned down and picked him up. He nuzzled her immediately, and she rubbed him down.

"I wish you greeted me that enthusiastically." Nicole smiled as she entered the living room.

"Well, maybe if you were half as enthused to see me as he is…"

Nicole chuckled and went in for a kiss. Dane returned the show of affection, while Haydn wiggled out of her arms. She made sure he ended up dropping on the sofa rather than falling the long distance to the floor. With her hands freed, she wrapped her arms around Nicole's waist.

"Since we don't have anything planned and it's Saturday, what say we just go upstairs and never come back down?" Dane suggested with a lewd grin and a wiggling of her eyebrows.

A teasing smile lit up Nicole's face. "And leave your darling Haydn all alone?"

"We'll leave some water out for him and just open a whole bag of food. He'll be fine." Dane laughed.

"No, I don't think that'll work."

"Why not?"

"Because, you have a play date scheduled in a couple of minutes."

Dane's brow wrinkled. "I do? Didn't know Luke and Thomas were coming over today. I would've planned something. Maybe we can play *Guitar Hero* or something."

Nicole chuckled, apparently amused that Dane felt the need to organize activities when her nephews came over. Nicole tried to explain why organizing a house visit wasn't necessary and, intellectually, Dane understood. When Luke and Thomas were at the house, they almost never did what Dane planned. But, the look in Nicole's eyes, something like pity, told Dane this wasn't the play date she thought it would be. Nicole's eyebrows curled up slightly and green eyes sparkled, wetter than usual. Dane was about to ask about it, but the bell rang.

"Is that them?" Dane's smile covered a slight twist in her stomach.

"Baby, it's not who you think it is," Nicole said softly, taking Dane's hand.

Dane squinted a bit, studying her lover. "What do you mean? Is it somebody for you?"

Shaking her head, Nicole glanced down a bit. "No, I'm sure it's for you. It's just not your nephews."

"Oh?"

"Don't be upset, but you said you wanted to deal with this when you wouldn't be able to run. You don't really have any place to go in the house." Nicole seemed to apologize, and that's when it hit Dane.

"Nick, you didn't," Dane begged, glancing over at the door.

"You asked for my help." Nicole moved to the door to let their company in.

"If I ask you to shoot me, you gonna do that, too?" Dane huffed, upset by the presence of the person at the door, the idea of speaking to her, the idea of listening to her, and the fear.

Dane hated the fear inside of her; it was one of the things that kept her from speaking to Christine. She worried her mother's explanations might make sense, and Dane would then find out that she truly was disposable and unworthy of love. She also feared she might just forgive her mother, which seemed unthinkable. *How can anyone forgive abandonment and silent consent to torture?* Her guts dropped at the thought she might.

The spite she held in her heart for Christine seemed right to Dane, like she should feel it. If the contempt vanished, how would she feel? She doubted she'd like it. She *should* feel vindictive toward her mother. She deserved at least that much.

Dane flopped down on the couch and took a deep breath to calm her nerves. Her hand went through her hair, as she heard Nicole open the door and greet her mother. A second later, Christine was in view with a large tote bag in hand. Christine offered an awkward smile. Dane pretended not to see.

"Christine, please, sit." Nicole motioned to the sofa before turning to Dane. "I'll be outside in the backyard with Haydn if you need anything."

Dane nodded, and her heart screamed out 'Thank you!' because her mouth refused to work at the moment. Nicole nodded like she got the message, and took them in with soft emerald eyes. She called for Haydn, who yapped happily while following her outside. Dane watched them leave before looking at her mother.

"So...Guess Nick called you out here, huh?"

"Of course. She suggested I come with conversation pieces, which I thought was a very good idea." Christine jostled the bag in her hand a little.

Dane nodded. "She's full of good ideas." *Like this, because I damn sure don't have anywhere to go.*

"She's a good woman."

"That she is."

"Well, I decided to bring some things to show you that I haven't ignored you for your whole life as you seem to think." Christine pulled out two shoeboxes and some loose objects. She placed them on the coffee table, before she sat down on the sofa.

"Yeah, believe it or not, pretending I don't exist counts as fucking ignoring me." Dane glared down at Christine. "You don't even have any fucking proof that I exist!" There wasn't a single photo of her in the Wolfe home. Her childhood room was about as big as a prison cell, especially compared to everyone else's rooms, and had been turned into an office when she was sixteen. God only knew where the hell her original birth certificate was. Sometimes, she was shocked they hadn't locked her in the attic and fed her fish heads.

"I thought you might say that, which is why I was very careful when I packed the things I would bring," Christine explained as she opened the top box. She pulled out a small photo album and opened it. "This is you at a day old." She pointed down to the baby picture.

Dane blinked and turned her attention to the photo. She inhaled sharply. She had never seen pictures of herself as a baby. She assumed none existed. Reaching out, she ran a finger down the pristine picture. She had chubby cheeks and her complexion had much more of a red undertone to it than now. Big grey eyes had an almond shape to them and her hair seemed much blonder back then.

"You might not want to hear this, but you looked a lot like Michael. He had blond hair when he was born, too, but yours was curlier. Just like his, yours became darker and straighter as you got older."

"Where…where did you get this?" Dane asked in a breath. Running a shaky hand through her hair, she tried to calm herself down. Unfortunately, her heart wouldn't listen and beat so fast she feared it would explode.

"I paid for it. The hospital…they offered and I paid. No one…no one visited after you were born and Russell went on a tear about…you know…" Christine sighed, causing her shoulders to slump and a shamed blush colored her cheeks.

"About me being a bastard and everything. Yeah, I know. It's one of the more important messages I got from my childhood," Dane grumbled. She took the picture out of the sleeve in the album. "I'm keeping this." There was no room for argument or negotiation.

"Um…yes, of course," Christine replied with a slightly scrunched up expression, like she couldn't understand why.

Dane didn't expect Christine to understand. Hell, she barely understood. But, she'd never seen herself as a baby and now, there she was—tiny, pudgy, one eye partially closed wrapped in a hospital issue baby blanket. *I was a baby. I really was a baby.* There were days as a mixed up teen when she felt like she had just come into existence at that age, like she was never a baby, never born. She'd just materialized. She'd felt confused, unloved, unlovable, and completely alone in the world.

"I have other things from when you were a baby…" Christine reached into the box and pulled out a pair of tiny shoes. "This is your first pair of baby shoes."

Dane inspected them with an arched eyebrow and felt a ping inside of her. "Hard to believe my feet were ever this small." She was rather tall and with her height came pretty big feet.

"You were actually pretty tiny. The smallest out of the bunch, now that I think about it. You were barely five pounds. Your brothers and sister were almost eight pounds each. You were also the shortest labor.

You were out in six hours, like you couldn't wait. Sometimes, I wish you had."

Dane rolled her eyes. "You don't get to choose when you come into this world and you don't get to choose who you come out of."

Christine sighed and flipped the page of the photo album to a very small Dane with her arms wrapped around a huge, black Great Dane. Blocking Dane's little legs was a small beagle, clearly rubbing against the child.

"I guess this is when you developed your love of dogs," Christine said in a low voice. A small but sad smile ghosted across her features.

"Oh, the Briarmoors. I bet they took this picture of me with their dogs. Jupiter used to act like I was his pup or his pet or something. He'd actually nudge me places he wanted me to go, like corralling me or something. He'd stare at me when I was supposed to eat and make sure I ate everything on my plate. Wouldn't let me leave the table until the plate was clean. And Tumble, that's the beagle, he used to hate it because we played together all the time and he was too little to take me away from Jupiter. How are Henry and Lynn?" Dane tried not to think of them, had forgotten a lot about them, but they were always in the back of her mind, again making her feel unlovable and abandoned.

"They're fine. They're still collecting dogs."

Dane nodded. "I figured as much. They were nice people."

A blond eyebrow crawled up Christine's head slightly. "They were? They refused to see you by the time you were seven and you think they were nice people?"

"Wasn't their daughter. They didn't have any obligation to me. I used to call them my mom and dad. Got creepy, I guess." Dane shrugged.

Dane ignored the brief frown on Christine's face at her admission. She had called Lynn and Henry mom and dad, because she'd been stupid enough to think that was who they were. It explained why she spent so much time with them. They made sure she didn't think that for long, though, and didn't call them that for long.

Dane's jaw tensed for a second. "Who wants a kid that isn't yours claiming you, after all? You and your husband didn't even want a kid that was yours claiming you."

"Dane, it wasn't like that..." Christine tried to object, but her mouth just trembled and no words came out. She scanned the floor as if it could tell her what she should say. Anything Christine said to justify the amount of time Dane had spent with Henry and Lynn would only be excuses, lies, and other bullshit.

"No? Well, let's see, you dumped me on the Briarmoors from the time I can remember until the point they didn't want to see me anymore. I remember you'd leave me at their house for days. If they didn't return me, nobody in the Wolfe household came around to ask for me. Henry and Lynn were tired of raising a kid that wasn't theirs, tired of listening to me claim them as parents, and tired of you guys trying to put one over on them. I was your responsibility, not theirs, and they knew that. Did you think you could just take advantage of the new, young couple on the block?" Dane snorted and rolled her eyes.

"It wasn't like that."

Dane glared her. "No? Did you ever wonder how I knew I was your daughter and how I knew I was Russell's daughter, or how I knew about the stupid DNA tests? Henry and Lynn told me. Sometimes on purpose and other times I'd overhear things. They used to argue how it wasn't right that you guys were just tryin' to pawn me off on them and trying to quietly disown me. They didn't know what to do. Wasn't my fault, they'd point out, but they didn't know what to do. In the end, they washed their hands of your whole mess. So, yes, *they were nice*."

"I didn't know they told you..." Christine muttered, shaking her head a little. Again, she glanced away, maybe taking in what she'd just learned or just at a loss.

A snarl curled onto Dane's lip. "There's a lot you don't know. You show up here with your little box of keepsakes and bullshit, and I'm supposed to fall all over you and cry or some bullshit? The fuck outta here with that bullshit. You want to know why they were nice? They fed me whenever I was at their house. They watched TV with me. They let me play with their dogs. They read me stories. They hugged me and every now and then, they actually reassured me life would be fine. So, yes, *nice*. Next bullshit move, *Mom*." Never had the title mom sounded so much like fuck you.

Christine looked away and sniffled, like she'd cry. Dane scowled tightly. If this woman dared to shed a tear in front of her, Dane would literally throw her out of the house, weak leg be damned.

Christine regained her composure with a deep breath and turned her attention back to her daughter. "I didn't know you held them in such high regard."

"Yeah, tends to happen when a person says a fucking word or two in your general direction, you know. What you don't seem to grasp is that they didn't have to do anything. They were just our neighbors. They didn't have to watch me at all. You fucking gave birth to me and ignored the shit out of me. You never even tried." Dane pointed down at Christine, condemning her with a simple finger.

"Of course I tried! Like you said, I gave birth to you. I had a connection to you. I tried, I tried..." Christine covered her face with her hands and sniffled again. "I just...I didn't want to lose my husband."

"Yeah, and you had three perfectly good kids. No need to love the defective one." Dane folded her arms across her chest.

Watery brown eyes stared at her and Dane just wanted to slap the woman. How dare Christine play the victim here? Like she was supposed to feel sorry for Christine. *What the hell is wrong with this woman?*

"I never saw you as defective," Christine whispered.

Anger flared in Dane's chest, unable to take the lies. "You never saw me at all! Where were you when he was beating the shit out of me? Huh? Where were you then? He was more important. I get that. Don't sit here and fucking lie to me like it wasn't that way. I was easy to give up. I wish you would just admit it."

"It wasn't easy," Christine growled, standing up from the sofa. "It wasn't easy, and I was never completely able to let go. I used to stand outside your room for hours, while you slept, and just stare into the room, stare at you. I would hide nearby when you played the piano—"

"And do absolutely nothing when *he* showed up and beat the shit out of me for touching the goddamn thing." Dane threw her hands out, resisting the urge to reach out and strangle Christine.

Dane had it with Christine. She couldn't bear to listen to the whining and the denial. There was no justification for what happened to her.

"Dane, I care about you," Christine declared and something inside of Dane shattered. "I care about you and I never completely let go."

Tilting her head, a smirk curled onto Dane's face enough to make Christine actually step away. "You care about me? You care about me?" Dane chuckled. It sounded dark to her own ears and the way Christine's eyes widened, she imagined it sounded worse to Christine. "You wanna know how much you care about me?"

Christine gulped. "What do you mean?" her voice quivered.

"Remember when I was fifteen and I 'moved out?' You remember that?" Dane asked, smiling now.

For a second, Christine's voice failed her and she nodded. "Of course I remember." The response was low, nervous.

Dane's smile was a grin now and it hurt her face. "Yeah, well, what you don't know is that I hadn't really moved out. I wanted to see how long it would take before someone at least filed a missing person's report or called my school or asked around about me. But, no one ever did. I was fifteen and gone for a fucking year and no one looked for me. Better still, it happened only a year after I damn near died from that cocaine overdose and not one person in our household gave a shit. So, what the fuck am I supposed to think?"

"Dane, I kept track of you. I knew you were all right."

"Kept track? All right? Ha!" Dane glared at the woman in front of her and pointed at her. "You have no fucking clue. I was homeless for over a year. I lived in a van with the goddamn drummer from the band I was playing in. The only reason I stayed in school was because I had a music teacher there that took an interest in me. He pushed me through, helped my stupid ass graduate. While you were 'keeping track' of me, did you know I was pretty much a functioning alcoholic? Or how about my coke habit? Did you know if I had a choice between eating and snorting, I'd snort the livelong day? Did you?" Dane slapped her hands together.

Christine jumped back and blinked in shock. "I...I..."

Dane shook her head and her finger. "No, you didn't know that. Let me enlighten you about what happened while you were 'keeping track' of me. I was playing in a band and had been playing with them for two years. They were some random college dropouts, but just as fucked up as I was. The drummer, we called him Animal, lived in a fucked up van. We were pretty tight, so when I told him I needed some place to stay, he offered his van. It was either that or the fucking park, so I picked the van. Just in case you're wondering, he didn't touch me or anything. Wasn't that kind of guy. Always said I was too young for him. Not that it mattered since I had already been fucking girls for years," she said, just to get a reaction.

Christine gasped, first at the mention that Animal might've touched Dane and then at the revelation of how long Dane had already been intimate with women. Brown eyes dropped to the floor as Christine obviously tried to process the information. Dane didn't want to give her a chance to catch up, just yet. Christine needed to understand, she hadn't done shit for Dane and no amount of excuses would ever change that.

"Yeah, living in the van wasn't too bad. We really only slept in it and that was during the day. At night, we had clubs to play and parties to hit. Most of the time, Animal'd sleep while I was at school and then I'd sleep when I came from school. It wasn't so bad, but it was still living in a van. It was fucking cold in the winter, though. Hard to sleep. Sometimes, we just got high to stay awake through it all or just deal with it. One night, we got high, way high. So fucking high I didn't realize until the next day that this motherfucker Animal had actually OD'ed. I had spent the night with his dead body and was too fucking high to realize it. Probably coulda saved him if I wasn't so fucked up, but in the end, all I could do was call 911 and call his family. Did you hear about that?" Dane barked, glaring hatefully at her mother.

It took all of Dane's willpower not to cry, not to go back to that day, and not see Animal's pale face staring at her. No, Christine didn't have a goddamn clue and she needed to stop acting like she knew what had happened.

Christine's chin trembled, and she reached out for Dane before wisely dropping her hand. "Dane, I didn't…"

Scoffing, Dane rolled her eyes. "You didn't know? No shit! And no one bothered to ask, on that freezing cold day in the middle of February, why the fuck the cops brought me home. They wanted all this fucking information and then insisted on driving me home. But, I know how it was. Everyone just assumed I did something stupid while I was gone for the year. You know, it was in that moment, I decided not to live at the house anymore. Sure, I stopped by every now and then to give you guys grief, but I was done. It was back to the streets."

"Back to the streets? You continued living on the streets, even after all that?"

Dane shrugged and then shook her head. "It wasn't much of a big deal. By that time, people were starting to recognize my talent. Called up Bryan, got him to get into the scene, and before you know it, we had a band. *Destined for Nowhere* was hot by the time I was seventeen, and I had saved what money I could, so I had a little, crappy studio apartment. Before that, well, was always good with women. Whatever I needed, they were always happy to provide, as long as I kept 'em happy."

"So, you basically began prostituting yourself?" Christine asked in a whimper.

"Not so much, no. It was more like a symbiotic relationship. I enjoyed being with them and probably would've done it even if I didn't need stuff, but I did need stuff and they needed stuff, too. It was a wild time and it didn't really change when people started loving the band.

But, you know all of this since you were 'keeping track,' right?" Dane scoffed as a mocking smile overtook her face. "But, I've monopolized the conversation. You were gonna tell me how much you loved me or whatever the hell it is you came here to do. Tell me how much you care or some bullshit like that, right?"

Christine sighed and rubbed her face with her hands. "All right, I will admit that I've done a piss-poor job in keeping track of you. I thought I was doing all right, but you've proven me wrong. Nothing I can do will make up for it. Nothing."

"Glad you know," Dane huffed. *Okay, now what?* She wracked her brain for something else to say, but came up short. She'd vented and made Christine very aware she didn't know half as much as she thought she did. *Maybe there's nothing left to say.*

"Then, can we start from scratch?" Christine asked with big eyes and a trembling bottom lip. She looked down for a moment and kicked at imaginary dust.

"Don't know. What's the point?" Dane turned her mouth up.

"Dane...I realize that nothing I can say will undo the damage done, the years of neglect, ignoring you, and then pretending I could somehow make up for it with music lessons, an expensive violin, and...a guitar."

"What made you think there was any way for you to undo things? You gave me away to the neighbors, then the cook when the neighbors gave me back, refused to acknowledge I existed, and watched the entire household abuse me in every way possible. You thought music lessons and a couple of instruments would fix that? Really, what the fuck were you thinking? How fucking stupid is that?" Dane knew if looks could kill, the one she gave Christine would've put her on trial for murder.

Of course, as much as Dane loathed admitting it, the few tokens her mother had thrown her way in life had stuck with her. She considered it was those gestures that festered and burned more than she believed they should. She still had those first instruments from her mother. The violin was lovingly resting in a case alongside the guitar in Dane's music room, which used to be Nicole's den. That violin had lived through tough times, but no matter what happened, Dane always made sure she had it with her.

Tears began to gather in Christine's eyes, and Dane wasn't sure if she should feel horrible or satisfied by that reaction. She didn't want Christine to cry, but she did want the woman to realize things didn't happen just because she deemed it so. Wounds that were decades old

S.L. Kassidy

didn't seem to mend either.

"I don't know what to do. I don't want us to be the way we are anymore." Christine sniffled as she wiped her eyes. It didn't occur to Dane to offer her a tissue.

"How we are? We're strangers," Dane said. *Christine acts like there was something between us to even be considered a relationship.*

"I wish we were. It would be so much easier if we were just strangers. Instead, we're at this point where if I don't do something, I know I may never see you again. I know and acknowledge I'd be much poorer for it. In the past, I would've lied to myself and said that I could live with that, but I can't. I can't lose any more family. I've already lost so many people. I just can't lose any more family. I just can't." Christine bawled, shaking her head.

Dane's face scrunched up as she considered Christine and her words. She wondered who the 'so many people' were. Yes, her mother had lost her parents at an extremely young age; neither of them lived to see her first birthday. But, other than that, Dane couldn't think of anyone. Hell, even her mother's grandparents, who had raised her, were actually still alive. Curiosity won out.

"What do you mean?"

Christine took a deep breath and collected herself. Sniffling, she turned her attention to Dane. "I think it would be best if I showed you."

Dane arched an eyebrow. "Showed me?"

"Yes. Come, I think this will be the best for you to gain some understanding of me, as I have gained some understanding of you."

Dane sighed and put her hand through her hair. She didn't really want to gain any understanding of Christine. Again, it only made it seem like Christine was full of excuses and wanted to play the victim. But, Dane was still curious.

She shrugged and motioned for Christine to lead the way. Christine nodded and marched to the door. Dane called out to Nicole that she'd be back later. She wasn't even sure if Nicole heard her, but she wanted to see what Christine was so anxious to reveal.

The car ride was silent and much longer than Dane anticipated. Almost half an hour after they took off, they pulled up to a cemetery. Dane continued to just follow Christine's lead and didn't ask any questions. They marched through the garden of headstones and memorials before coming to the site her mother wanted. Dane looked down and read the stone. It belonged to "Harun Miller. Beloved son and brother."

"Is this your father's grave?" Dane guessed.

Christine nodded. "This is my father. It took a lot of work to find that out since my grandparents would never even say his name around the house. It wasn't until I saw my birth certificate that I had a name to go by. He and my mother were married, I assume. She had her name down as Miller on the certificate, and my family name was down as Miller, too. I doubt that made my grandparents very happy. I never knew that was my last name until I saw it on the birth certificate."

Dane nodded. "They kept a lot from you?"

"Pretty much any and everything about my father, they kept from me. Before I saw my birth certificate, the most I knew about him came from some photos I found in my mother's old bedroom. She had them hidden away under a floorboard in her closet. There were love letters, too. It was clear from the language that he loved her dearly. In one letter he talks about how happy he is that she's carrying his baby. He seemed like he was overjoyed, and he hadn't even met me yet." A sad smile graced Christine's face.

Dane almost felt compassion for her mother. Instead, she consciously decided to feel sorrow for a man who never got a chance with the daughter he obviously wanted. Of course, had he lived, Christine's grandparents would've tried their damnedest to keep him from seeing Christine.

"Do you know how he died?"

"Drunk driving. Unfortunately, he was the drunk one." Christine sighed. "He was lost without my mother, I suppose. She died so unexpectedly, and he took it badly. Plus, he was fighting with her parents over me and he just got so depressed. I managed to find and speak to his friends, and they said up until that time, he'd never drank. His friends said that he had been so happy with my mother and with me. They made it seem like God had wronged my father when my mother died, and I think my father actually took it that way. His friends said he changed completely after that and they understood why, because he had loved my mother so thoroughly, to lose her was too much for him to bear. Not being able to have me was salt on already festering wounds. I wish I had known him, and I wish I had treated his legacy to me with much greater respect." She focused directly on Dane.

Dane put her hand through her hair. "Okay, so you obviously weren't ashamed of him. Just me."

"It wasn't shame. Not at first. The reason I took your picture when you were a baby, even after Russell openly showed his disgust and contempt for you and swore that I had cheated on him, was because I was actually proud and happy of how you looked. I wondered 'was my father's skin this tone at one point?' I met his family once...when I started looking for him."

"They were my complexion or something?"

"No. From who I met, they were a shade or so darker than you are. They knew who I was right away. They showed me a few pictures and gave me some basic information about him, but beyond that they didn't want anything to do with me."

Dane's brow wrinkled. "Why not?" She would've thought his family would be happy to have the kid he was so heartbroken over. Christine was a little piece of him still here. *What the hell is wrong with people?*

"They blamed my grandparents for his death. They said he never would've started drinking if they had just treated him with respect and had they not tried, and succeeded might I add, to take me away from him. My grandparents made his life hell, I didn't even need them to tell me, but they did, in great detail. My grandparents did everything they could to keep my father away from my mother, and they didn't stop harassing him when my mother died. For his family, my grandparents were behind the wheel of the car the night he died. It was so clear that even twenty years after the fact, they were still crushed by his loss. They didn't want to know me because of them. They said I reminded them of how my grandparents treated him, and my presence only reminded them of what they lost and how they lost it. I was crushed..." Christine sighed, shaking her head. "I could actually understand their reasoning, but I couldn't hate my grandparents because they were the only parents I had known. I felt so lost..." She shook her head again and wrapped her arms around herself briefly.

Dane sighed and rubbed her temples. She thought she understood what Christine hinted at. But, as much as she understood it, she was glad it changed nothing inside of her. She didn't feel forgiveness, but she also didn't feel more resentful.

"They ignored you and you ignored me. You probably could even empathize with my situation, but you were scared to lose the people that had always been there for you. Why risk it all on a kid who looked kinda like the folks that threw you away, huh?" *It makes sense, but it didn't make sense.*

"That's a horrible way to put it, but unfortunately, rather accurate," Christine confessed with a nod.

Sighing, Dane looked around for a second. "Why is it different now? You say you don't want to lose any more family. How do you know you haven't already lost me? Even if you haven't, if you get closer to me, don't you just lose Russell?"

"Honestly, I feel much more secure in my relationship with Russell now than I did when you were born. Yes, we had already been together for a long time, but now we've been together decades, children, grandchildren. I was by his side for many of his less than stellar moments, and I stood by him through his stroke. He may never accept you, Dane, but I don't think he'll reject me for reaching out to you."

"And if he did?" Dane couldn't, and wouldn't, even consider putting herself out there, only to be dropped like a hot brick. Besides, apparently she was only worthwhile now because Russell didn't have the options he once had. No matter what, she was a last thought to Christine.

Christine rubbed her forehead. "I wouldn't reach out if I planned on letting go again. I wouldn't do the unforgivable twice, especially after suggesting we start over. Dane, I brought you here, to this spot that I haven't shared with anyone, to let you know how serious I am."

Dane blinked in surprise. "You haven't shared this with anyone?"

"You're the first person I've brought here. The first person I've told about what happened between my father's family and me. Sometimes, I come out here to think, and I feel close to my father. I talk to my dad. He knows all the dark, depressing details of my life. I'm sure he's ashamed of me wherever he is. I tried to lead a good life, but what I allowed to happen to you and between us…He and my mother didn't care what I looked like. They were happy to have me for the short time they did. I should've been more than happy to have you."

"Can't call you a liar there," Dane grumbled, scratching her head.

"I knew at the hospital, after you got hit by the car, if I didn't do something, I'd be more dead to you than my own parents are to me. The very thought made me physically ill. I couldn't even get excuses to be near you with Nicole by your side. She takes better care of you than I ever have."

"She does," Dane said without hesitation. It was the truth. "Not that it's a hard thing to do, considering."

Christine nodded and smiled, taking the snap in her stride. "I'm happy for you. You deserve a good life. I just want to be a part of your life in any way that you'll have me."

Her hand went through her black hair as Dane sighed. She didn't know what to do and decided she didn't want to deal with all of the information for the moment. Turning around, she started back toward the car while fighting off the weary sensation that crept through her body. This was all so draining. Her mother silently followed behind her.

The ride back to the house was as quiet as the ride to the cemetery had been. Dane spent most of the time looking out of the window, trying to make sense of the world, to make sense of Christine and what she should do. There was so much. She had baby pictures, mementos, memories of neighbors who had been parents for a short time, and now information about her mother's other family. It all just swirled together, and she couldn't figure out what it meant or how she should feel. When they came to the house, Dane was the only one to get out of the car. She wasn't surprised, figuring Christine had her own thinking to do.

"Is it all right if I call you sometime soon?" Christine asked in a low tone.

Dane scratched her head. "Honestly, I have no idea. Don't know if I'll be willing to talk or not." This wasn't some great odyssey that led to some emotional epiphany. While they had both learned a great deal, Dane didn't feel any different toward Christine.

"So, it would be the same as before?" Christine's voice cracked. Her eyes held the usual fear, but now there was a spark of hope, too.

Dane shrugged. "I guess. Take a chance. See what happens." Maybe she did feel different. Maybe she'd pick up. She didn't know.

"I will," Christine promised.

"Then that's pretty much it. Today we learned some things about each other. I just need to see where I'm going to take this."

Christine nodded. "I understand."

That seemed to be a good enough farewell for them. Dane strolled into the house as her mother drove away. Haydn was yapping at Danny's feet the second she stepped through the door. Nicole wasn't far behind him.

"How'd it go?" Nicole asked with a small smile.

Dane scratched her head. "Not sure." She wrinkled her nose a bit.

Nicole nodded. "Well, I made dinner if that helps."

"It helps a lot. A hug would help a whole lot more."

"I think I can do better."

Dane smiled as Nicole embraced her with loving arms and then planted a passionate kiss on her lips. In that moment, Dane felt her world right itself. Sure, she still had no clue what to do about her mother, but it didn't seem pressing. It could wait.

***

"Were these the things your mother had in the bag?" Nicole asked, as she and Dane settled on the couch after dinner. The mementos Christine brought over were still spread out on the coffee table.

"Yeah. You didn't look through it while we were out?"

"I had other things to do, like make sure dinner was ready and Haydn needed a walk."

Dane nodded. "I can see how you didn't have time to snoop. Well, we can snoop together. She didn't get to show me much before I went off on her."

"I heard. No one came looking for you when you were gone for a year?" Nicole asked, sadness in her eyes. Her hands actually trembled, and Dane took them into her own to get them to stop.

Dane wasn't surprised Nicole had heard. She'd probably been yelling, even though she didn't mean to. She was just so sick of her mother and all of that other bullshit. She locked eyes with Nicole. She wanted Nicole to understand how serious her words were.

"Nope, but that doesn't matter, Nick. What I went through doesn't matter. I survived, I made it through, and I'm here now to share my life with you. That's what matters. If I had to live through all of the bullshit, all over again, to be in this moment, you know I would." She truly would. Nicole let her know she wasn't unlovable. There wasn't something wrong with her and not all people were assholes wanting to abandon and ruin her.

Nicole gave her a soft smile. "That's sweet of you, but I would've preferred you have a normal, functioning childhood, even if it meant that our paths would have never crossed."

"Can't change the past, Chem. I'm doing better now. Let's just leave it at that. Hey, you wanna see something to cheer you up?"

"What?"

Dane reached over onto the coffee table and picked up the photo she'd claimed. She held it up for Nicole to see. Emerald eyes widened and Nicole gasped.

"Is that you as a baby?" Nicole cooed in both awe and disbelief.

"According to my mom, that's me. I can't believe I had so much blond hair."

Nicole's eyes remained wide as she stared at the photo. "You were so small."

"Again, according to her, I was tiny. I told her I'm keeping this picture. This is the first time I've ever seen what I looked like as a baby."

Nicole shifted her body to cuddle into Dane. "That's a shame. Do you want to go through and see if she had more pictures of you as a baby?"

Dane nodded and leaned forward, picking up the photo album her mother had flipped through. There were a few more pictures of her as a baby and some pictures of her as a toddler, but it still seemed like too few pictures that someone would have of her child, even if it were her fourth.

"Hey, do you have pictures of you as a kid?" Pictures and stories of a normal childhood, her beloved's childhood, would cheer her up.

Nicole regarded her with a curious expression before nodding. "I have some, but my parents kept most of those. Let me go get the album."

"I'll get you some cookies then."

Nicole didn't object to that offer. They went their separate ways and met back up at the couch. Nicole settled in against Dane again and gave Dane the photo album to keep her hands free for the cookies.

"So, let's see what we have here." Dane cracked open the book. The first page held candid shots of Nicole's parents fawning over her as a baby. "You were a lot lighter when you were a baby."

"My eyes were also blue when I was a baby, according to my parents."

Dane felt her brow furrow. "I guess it's possible. I didn't know eyes changed color, but then again, I never would've believed I started out as a blond."

"You didn't really start out blond. You just had a lot more of it than you have now." Nicole ran her hands through Dane's hair. There were faint strands of blond highlighting ebony locks and Nicole always seemed fascinated by them. Dane didn't mind.

Dane chuckled and turned her attention back to the album. "Wow, do you have the chicken pox here?" There was a little toddler covered in telltale sores, lying on a couch and looking absolutely sullen with mittens on her hands.

Nicole ate a cookie. "Oh, God. My mother said I was so miserable. She tried everything to make sure I didn't scratch, but nothing worked. I was in tears most of the time and gave myself a fever. In the end, I remember the only way to keep me from freaking out was having her hold me and read me a story. It's just about the first thing I remember in life."

"Sounds nice."

"It wasn't for me. I was so itchy," Nicole wailed.

"I don't remember having the chicken pox. But, I don't remember a lot of my early childhood. Oh, what's this one?" Dane flipped the page. "Where are your teeth?"

Nicole chuckled as she focused on the picture of her smiling and missing her two front teeth. "They fell out, as baby teeth do. I wonder what you looked like when you lost your teeth."

Dane scratched her head. "I don't remember not having front teeth. Hey, this one? You look cute in a tutu!" A massive smile lit up her face, as she focused on a new picture.

Nicole reached for another cookie. "Oh, I was six here. I swore I was going to be a dancer. So, my mother and father signed me up for lessons. This was my first recital and they were in the front row. I took a jump, landed wrong, and sprained my ankle so badly I never wanted to even look at dancing, so forget doing it." She tittered.

Dane laughed a little, too. "I never would've guessed you were a ballerina."

"Yeah, for like five seconds. This is where I really shined." Nicole pointed to the next picture of her as a little girl holding a baseball bat. "I was great at softball. I played first base. My mother always worried I'd get hurt. My dad practically had to tie her down to keep her from running on the field if I collided with an opponent at the bag, or had a ball hit at my head. It was a great time."

"I never played a sport." The pictures made it look fun, though. *Did most kids play sports? What else did I miss out on?*

"That's all I did as a kid, outside of school. Softball, tennis, I ran track for a little while, swimming, and just about anything I could do. Keep going through the book, I'm sure I have more pictures of sporting activities."

There were plenty of pictures of Nicole playing sports or being active in some other way. Her family was also in many of the pictures, not just her parents, but her cousins, her aunts and uncles, and her grandparents were also featured. There were birthday parties, holiday gatherings, and simple family meetings. There were so many smiling faces and embraces of all types. Dane guessed that was what a normal family photo album looked like. It was very different from the one that her mother left. She was happy Nicole had such an amazing childhood.

***

Dane lay in bed, staring at the ceiling and gently caressing Nicole's arm. Nicole was asleep, her head resting against Dane's shoulder. Dane thought about her mother and found she was still uncertain as to what she would do about Christine. She didn't feel forgiveness moving within her, but she also didn't feel a new wave of bitterness rising. It was like she was the same...but, not quite.

Talking with Christine, telling her mother about herself, and learning more about her mother had done *something*. Unfortunately, Dane couldn't figure out what that something was. The acknowledgement of that something helped her make a decision. The next time Christine called, she'd try to speak to her. She'd probably still hang up in the end, but it was a step closer than where they started out.

Dane knew, despite her mother's wishes, they'd never be able to start over brand new. Too much had happened in her life that she knew a mother was supposed to shield a child from for her to just wipe the slate clean. But, it was like Nicole often told her, walking around with that weight on her, carrying that acridity, and finding it necessary to be malicious wasn't doing her any good. She needed to try to move forward.

"I have to try. Get better. Be better," Dane told herself. "Be the bigger person."

Dane felt like she'd resolved the issue, but she was unable to fall asleep. She let thoughts of Nicole and the photos they had gone through play through her mind. She couldn't help wondering what a normal childhood would've been like, growing up with normal, loving parents.

"Would I have stuck with piano and violin more if I had parents that showed up at recitals? Would I have actually tried to play a sport if they suggested it? Would I have stayed off drugs, gone to college, maybe actually tried to make a career out of something?" Dane sighed. Of course, she didn't have any answers and she'd never know. But, as she looked down at Nicole, she thought having parents that cared and paid attention obviously helped.

***

Kathleen Cardell was busy at work and was disturbed by a call from her assistant. She was about to bark at him, but he informed her there was a delivery for her. Curious, she allowed it and was surprised to find a flower delivery coming into her room. The beautiful arrangement was put on her desk, and she tipped the delivery guy. She studied the flowers and sighed.

"I wish clients would listen when I say don't send me gifts." Kate shook her head. She reached for the card with the bouquet and her eyebrows drew in as she saw the card was addressed to both her and her husband. Picking up her phone, she called her husband. "Raymond, sorry to disturb you, but I have a gift here for both of us. Do you want to come see the card or should I read it to you over the phone?"

"What sort of gift are we talking about?"

"An array of flowers. It's very nice, actually. Not very elaborate, but still nice. It's almost elegant," Kate replied with a smile as she looked at the flowers once more. They were definitely eye-catching, and she could tell that some thought went into the arrangement.

"Hmm...I think I want to see this."

"All right."

Raymond was in the office less than a minute later. His green eyes went right to the flowers and then to his wife. Kate shrugged.

"These are for both of us?" Raymond asked, as he pointed to the flowers.

"According to this." Kate held up the card.

"Who are they from?"

"Let's see." Kate flipped the card open, as her husband stood by her side. They were surprised by the message and who sent the card. "What do you think this is all about?" she asked, staring at the card as if it was in another language.

"I don't know what to make of this, but I have to say, the girl is full of surprises," Raymond replied with a smile.

"She can't buy my approval." Kate snorted with a curl on her lip and tossed the card down on the table.

Raymond chuckled and shook his head, but he didn't say anything else. He took his leave to get back to his work. Kate decided to do the same. Before doing so, she glanced at the card again. The message was simple: *Thank you for raising a wonderful daughter and being exceptionally good parents. ~ Danny.* A small smile actually settled on Kate's face, as she turned her attention back to her computer.

S.L. Kassidy

Band-Aid

"HEY, BABY, DO YOU know what you want to do with the boys this weekend?" Nicole flopped down next to Danny on the sofa. Danny was showering attention on Haydn, playing tug of war with a rope they had purchased from a pet store. She went so far as to growl every now and then, as she pulled on the rope, just to hype their pup up even more. He growled back.

Grey eyes went to Nicole, even though Danny did not let go of the rope. "No, no clue what I want to do with them. Why, do you have an idea?"

Nicole smiled. "I think so, but I want to keep it a surprise. Okay?"

Danny shrugged and Nicole giggled while kissing Danny on the nose. Nicole had an idea she was sure Danny would enjoy with the boys. After all, Danny didn't have much of a childhood. She had an inkling Danny had never done what she had in mind, which was why it needed to be done as far as Nicole was concerned. *There's no reason for Danny to do without, even if she's in her twenties now.*

***

Thankfully, it was still unseasonably warm when the weekend came around. It wasn't summer weather, but it was still nice enough for Danny to wear her favorite jean shorts. Nicole had to fuss, though; it was her job as Danny's partner.

"Sweetheart, please, put on some pants. I don't want you to get sick," Nicole said, eyes locked on bare, caramel legs.

"You said we're going someplace casual. This is casual." Danny motioned down to her usual attire, a plain jersey on top of a t-shirt and tattered shorts that fell just below her knees. The chain from her wallet dangled at her side, falling to the end of her shorts.

"I know, but summer's over, baby. Can you change into something before the boys get here?" Nicole practically begged. She grabbed

Danny's hand and ran her fingers up and down her lover's arm to hopefully help change her mind.

Danny smiled. "Nice try. I'll be fine. It's like, 70 degrees out there or something." She shrugged. "I'll be fine, Chem. I used to wear shorts in the snow."

Nicole nodded and conceded, because it was true. Besides, she had only seen Danny sick once and that was due to Danny's complete negligence toward herself rather than the weather. She let the matter drop as Luke and Thomas arrived.

"All right, time to go," Nicole announced, as soon as the boys were through the door.

"Go? But, we want to play with Haydn!" Luke gave her a sour face, wrinkling his nose at her.

"He's not here, buddy. We're going someplace he can't come, so he's with his Aunt Mina." Danny motioned to the door.

Adam's face scrunched up. "Where are you guys going?"

"It's a surprise. Don't worry, we'll be back by six," Nicole promised with a reassuring smile. She didn't want to waste time with Adam and his separation anxiety today. They needed as much time as possible for her surprise.

Farewells were said as Nicole ushered everyone out of the house, clearly in a rush and with a bag slung over her shoulder. She had made sure Adam brought the boys over before noon. They'd have time to enjoy as much of her surprise as possible, or they could have enough time to find something else to do if her idea was a flop. They drove off before Adam was even at his car.

"Nick, where we going?" Luke bounced in his seat as best he could with the seat belt securing him in place.

"Yeah, where?" Thomas bounced as well, staring out of the window, trying to figure out the great mystery.

"It's a surprise," Nicole replied with a gentle smile. She knew that in less than five minutes, they'd ask her that question again. She didn't mind.

"Do you think all kids suffer short term memory loss?" Danny joked after the question of where they were going was asked roughly once every two minutes, meaning they heard it at least fifteen times before both Danny and Luke figured out where they were headed.

"Hey, this is the way to the zoo!" Luke beamed, showing he actually had an extremely good memory. Adam told Nicole it had been over two months since he took the boys to the zoo. He also said they hadn't seen much because it started raining. She hoped they'd have better luck.

"We're going to the zoo? I love the zoo!" Thomas threw his hands up and grinned.

"Well, that's good. We're going to try to see the things you guys missed the last time you were here." Nicole had questioned Adam a little about their last trip to the zoo, but not enough to tip him off. She wasn't sure if Adam would blab the surprise or not.

"Cool!" Luke declared.

"I wanna see the penguins!" Thomas said.

Nicole smiled. "Then we'll see the penguins." She turned her attention to Danny. "Anything special you want to see?" Delight danced through her entire being. She was sure she was preening, probably glowing, because she was so certain she had done something good.

Danny shook her head. "Don't know what's here. I've never been to the zoo before."

Even though Nicole expected that, it still troubled her heart. Her stomach dropped a little and her happy aura faltered briefly, but she took a deep breath to settle herself. The whole point of the trip was to let Danny experience something that she should've in childhood, she reminded herself. *I'm going to show my baby a damn good time then*.

"Daddy said he used to go to the zoo all the time when he was little. You was never little?" Luke asked with childish innocence that Nicole thought was adorable.

"'Course not! Dane's too big to be little." Thomas motioned to their aunt with one hand.

Danny laughed, while Nicole focused on finding parking. Luke didn't argue with his brother, busying himself with staring out the window. Nicole didn't want to think about Adam getting to go to the zoo all of the time as a child, while Danny had never been. That thought was knocked out of her mind when her girlfriend saw how much parking cost.

"Holy crap! Ten dollars to park the car? Are they nuts?" Danny practically shouted with her eyes wide as she stared at the price. "You're actually going to pay this crap?"

"I have to. There's no other place to park and even if there were, it'd be too far for the boys to walk," Nicole argued.

Danny grunted in response, but didn't say anything else. Nicole paid for parking, and they each grabbed a boy's hand as they went to the entrance. Nicole paid for their tickets, took a couple of maps, and they embarked on their journey.

"This place is huge," Danny said as she unfolded her map. Smoke-colored eyes seemed to shine as she scanned the map. Nicole smiled when she noticed the look in Danny's eyes.

"And we have until five to see as much as we can. So, onto those penguins." Nicole smiled down at Thomas.

"Penguins!" Thomas threw his hands up in the air again.

They hurried to the penguin exhibit and found Thomas was too short to see over the railing and bushes used as a divider. Danny picked the child up and put him on her shoulders. He cheered as he watched the penguins playing, and Danny's eyes sparkled as she tried to take in the dozens of penguins, swimming, sliding, and going in and out of burrows. She took Nicole's free hand for a moment and their eyes met.

"I've never seen penguins in real life. They're cute." Danny grinned.

"We've got a lot more to see. I hope you have a good time." Nicole squeezed her lover's hand.

"I'm sure I will. This is cool," Danny said, almost as if she was surprised and she'd never considered going to the zoo.

Nicole smiled when Luke insisted on seeing the lions next. Thankfully, the African Safari exhibit wasn't too far. The boys cheered as soon as the lions were in view. Danny's mouth dropped open in awe. The look would remain on her face all day.

"What else is there? I wanna see other stuff." Danny grinned with childish glee, holding Nicole's hand and squeezing tight.

"If we walk around this exhibit, we'll see a lot of other animals from the African plains," Nicole replied.

Danny nodded and hobbled off with Thomas on her shoulders while holding Luke's hand. Nicole hoped no one thought Danny was kidnapping the boys considering how fast she moved with them. Nicole rushed off after them, not wanting Danny to hurt herself.

They made it to an exhibit where they got to pretend they were on safari, riding a slow roller coaster through a makeshift Serengeti. Thomas squealed when he saw the giraffes and did the same when he saw the elephants. In his enthusiasm, he accidentally hit Danny in the head a couple of times since she insisted on keeping him on her shoulders. Luke was fascinated with the hyenas and their 'laugh.' He spent the whole trip trying to mimic it. Danny was speechless.

"Nick, those were real zebras," Danny whispered as the ride ended.

Nicole couldn't help chuckling. "Yes, baby, those were real zebras."

"And leopards," Luke chimed in.

"And wildebeests, Nick. They were actually real." Danny practically bounced on her heels.

Nicole wasn't sure what to do about her girlfriend's giddiness. *I feel so bad Danny didn't get a chance to do this as a child, but it's magical to see her first time.* It was special to not just share this moment with Danny, but with the boys, too, even though they didn't know exactly how amazing this day was. It was just great that all of the Wolfes were enjoying themselves.

They went into the insect house next, since it was close by. Luke and Thomas weren't quite drawn to the bugs and pulled the couple through the house quickly. Danny had to see as much as she could in fast forward, not nearly as revolted by insects as most people were. A couple of times, Danny actually wandered away from them, almost putting her face on the display glass. The boys tugged her away from the window just as quickly.

Nicole was quite happy with how fast they went through. She wished they had gotten through the Old World monkey house as rapidly. She couldn't understand how the smell of the monkeys didn't keep everyone out of there.

"This is so cool," Danny whispered, as they moved through an outdoor wolf exhibit. She'd had to put Thomas down for a while, but he was content with holding Nicole's hand.

"They spelled our name wrong." Luke scowled as he pointed at the sign with the animal names and basic information on the animals and their habitat.

Nicole chuckled, while Danny grabbed the child up into one of her playfully rough hugs. She corrected Luke; while Nicole made sure Thomas had a clear view of the wolves. When they left, Danny grinned widely once more.

"Happy to have seen your spirit animal?" Nicole asked, bumping her girlfriend with her hip.

Danny only nodded. They continued on, stopping for breaks as Danny's and Thomas' legs got tired at about the same time. They ate lunch after a couple of hours and went shopping for a few souvenirs while some exhibits were still fresh in their minds. Nicole made sure to purchase a t-shirt with wolves on it for her beloved. They all got matching shirts of parrots in different colors, because they all liked the parrot exhibit.

They took in a few shows, which Nicole paid for, even though Danny protested. Of course, the protests didn't last long as they got to touch dozens of reptiles, saw the tigers being fed and watched snakes being milked for venom. The boys were interested in it all, and Danny forgot to blink at certain points.

They ended the day at the children's zoo where they got to pet and feed what most would consider farm animals. Thomas wasn't open to being that close to the creatures, and neither was Nicole. So, she hung back and took pictures, while Luke and Danny touched everything they could. Nicole made a mental note to get them some hand sanitizer before they touched anything else.

Thomas was up for a pony ride, as well as a camel ride, and a llama ride. He also wanted to sit on a rhino statue and a turtle on the way out. Nicole got plenty of pictures as they basically shut the place down. They hit a gift shop again on the way out.

The excited conversation all the way home was about how cool the zoo was. Nicole was not nearly as animated as the Wolfes were, but she joined in because she'd had a great time, too. When they pulled up to the house, Adam was there, waiting.

"We went to the zoo!" Thomas beamed as soon as he was out of the car. He charged his father and tried to tell Adam about the trip, but all anyone could understand was the word zoo. Adam smiled and nodded, looking a bit confused.

"It was Dane's first time!" Luke said as he went over to his father.

Adam's brown eyes went wide, and he looked at Danny. When he saw Danny, it seemed that he remembered who she was and what she had been through. His gaze softened and he seemed somewhat sorrowful for her circumstances. Glancing at Danny, Nicole could tell that she wasn't moved by her older brother's expression.

"Did you two thank Dane and Nicole for such a fun day?" Adam asked his sons, hands on their shoulders.

The pair went back to their aunt and her partner. There were thanks and hugs all around. Danny and Nicole made sure the duo had all of their souvenirs with them as they got into their father's car. Adam didn't drive off immediately. He stared at Danny, his eyes slightly wet.

"I'm sorry you missed out on so much stuff as a kid," Adam said softly.

Danny waved him off. "You don't know what I really missed out on," she said and then turned her attention to the boys. "Bye, guys. I hope you come back next weekend."

"We will!" Thomas said, waving goodbye already.

"Let's go to Fun Land," Luke said with a bright smile. It was an amusement park geared toward small children.

"We'll see, buddy," Dane replied. There were more goodbyes before Adam eventually drove away.

***

Nicole and Dane sat down for dinner after they made sure Haydn had food in his bowl. Nicole's dear friend and coworker, Mina, had been kind enough to bring the pup back to them, so they didn't have to make the trip. They were also happy to hear that Mina had walked him before bringing the dog home.

"So, how was your first trip to the zoo?" Nicole inquired, as if she didn't know. The little smirk on her face told the whole story.

Dane grinned and decided against holding back. She wanted Nicole to understand how amazing the whole day was and how much she appreciated it.

"It was great! Don't think I don't know why we went there, too. Thanks for trying to give me bits of a childhood, angel. You're one of a kind. I really appreciate this," Dane reached across the kitchen table and held onto her partner's hand. "You're the best."

Nicole shook her head. "You deserve normal things in your life, just like anybody else. There's no reason that you've never been to the zoo as a child. That's just a shame. How about we go to the aquarium when we have the boys again?"

Dane shrugged. "I've never been, but it sounds cool. They got sharks?" She watched a lot of nature programs now, finding herself curious about the natural world, and sharks seemed very interesting.

Nicole nodded. "Several species."

"Cool! I look forward to it."

S.L. Kassidy

Antibodies

"SO, WHAT ARE WE doing now?" Mina asked as she and Nicole wandered down the street. They were supposed to be at the gym.

"I want to get Danny a promise ring," Nicole replied. *Why is this such a hard concept to grasp?*

Mina's face scrunched up. "Why?"

"To let her know she's important to me and I'm working toward bettering myself for marriage just like she is." It took a lot of self-control not to say *duh*. There was no need to be rude. She was just anxious and a bit upset, but not with Mina.

Mina arched an eyebrow. "And you need a ring to do that?"

"That's generally how a relationship works. You have a ring, do you not?"

Mina waved it off. "A wedding ring and an engagement ring, but because I'm actually married. Last I walked down crazy-relationship road with you, you ended up in a domestic partnership that you don't want to call a marriage, and now you want to get an engagement ring that isn't an engagement ring."

Nicole sighed. "Maybe I should've just brought Clara."

Mina scowled. "Ouch. I'm losing best friend status over asking questions and being me?"

Nicole sighed again and realized she was being hard on Mina. She was bothered, though, and couldn't take it out on the real person it was directed toward. She took Mina's hand and smiled at her for a second.

Mina chuckled. "So, now you want to tell me what's up?"

"Yeah, I'm sorry. It's just, Danny's mother came over a couple of days ago, and I'm a little messed up over it."

"Why are you messed up over it?"

Nicole scratched her head with her free hand. "Mina...I don't think either of us will ever be able to really imagine what Danny's life used to be like, but imagine thinking for twenty-five years of your life that no baby pictures of you existed."

Mina took a moment and stared ahead of them. Her brow furrowed and her braids shifted slightly. She glanced at Nicole and shook her head.

"I don't even know how to feel about that," Mina said.

"I know. It seems like nothing to us. Somewhere out there, we both know there's a ton of pictures of us that no one even looks at anymore, but there are tons. The idea of no baby pictures is something we can't even fathom, but this was Danny's reality up until a couple of days ago."

Mina shook her head again. "I don't even know how to take that. How do you not take pictures of a baby? Shit, I took pictures of my first car when I got it."

"There's so much in Danny's life that's like that. I wish I could tell you."

Once more, Mina shook her head. "You don't have to. So, the hunt for a complementary ring for a complementary promise?"

"More than that. All of Danny's life, she's been told you're not good enough, you're not worth it, and you can be thrown away. I need her to know she is worth it, she is good enough, and I would never throw her away."

Mina nodded. "You'll need a hell of a great ring to say all of that. Unless, of course, there's more."

"I don't want to make a grand gesture out of it. Danny's best days are when we do something normal and completely boring. I figured I'd cook for her and play some of her favorite jazz music while we eat."

"She really is a cheap date."

"One of the many things I love about her. Sort of like you being crabby and mistrustful, but Shawn keeps you around," Nicole said smiling.

Mina laughed and lightly pushed Nicole. Nicole laughed, too, and they were fine again. Mina always reminded Nicole of her cousins on her father's side, the ones closer to her in age.

"What kind of ring would Danny wear? She doesn't really wear jewelry, right?" Mina asked.

"She doesn't own any jewelry beyond her piercings."

"Maybe you should get her a promise eyebrow ring."

Nicole laughed again, but didn't respond as they came to the first store. They walked in and went right to the ring display.

A sales rep appeared in front of them. "May I help you ladies?"

"Just browsing for now," Nicole answered.

"Anything in particular?"

Nicole thought on it for a moment. Did she have anything in mind? She glanced down at the plain promise ring on her finger. For a brief second, she considered getting something that matched her ring, but then thought better of it. Danny deserved a unique ring that fit her personality.

"I don't really have anything in mind right now," Nicole replied.

"All right. Feel free to call me if you need anything," he said.

Nicole nodded, her eyes focused on the rings. Mina looked them over as well. She pointed to a couple, but they didn't speak to Nicole. They weren't good enough for Danny.

"You think she could pull off a guy's ring?" Mina was looking at several men's bands.

"I don't think it would look particularly attractive on her if it's too big. She has long, graceful fingers. She used to play piano, after all."

"So, her fingers are too good for these?" Mina teased.

Nicole only snorted. Nothing really caught her eye, and they ended up leaving without making a purchase. There were several shops, though. Surely one would have a good ring.

***

Dane growled and resisted throwing her game controller. Instead, she pushed back on the sofa. Terri gave her a sideways glance while flashing a teasing grin. Dane made sure to focus on the television, even as it reminded her that Terri had won, yet again.

"Your mind's not on the game," Terri said.

Dane only snorted. She knew it was obvious. She was losing so badly each time they played, she might as well just sit on her controller. She probably should've told Terri to find something else to do with her afternoon, but she really wanted a distraction. She wanted someone who wouldn't look at her and wonder if she needed to talk. Unfortunately, Terri proved to be the wrong candidate. Well, there were worse choices. Had she invited Crow over, she'd have had a therapy session on her hands right now.

"So, what's going on? Trouble in paradise?"

Dane snorted. The last time Terri had seen her upset, she and Nicole had been having a little communication trouble. But, that was months ago. Everything was all right with them, now.

"It's nothing like that," Dane replied. *It is my damned mother. No, Christine. It was Christine.*

"You want to talk about it?"

"Nope. Just want to kick your ass in this game." There was nothing to talk about because she didn't have a freaking clue how she felt about it. Hell, she didn't even know what *it* was.

Terri gave a soft grunt and they started up a new game. Dane was mostly button mashing. She couldn't really focus like she wanted to.

Was Christine the problem? Dane had lived her life with this ghost hanging over her. It bothered her, yes, but not like this. This was raw, new. It didn't make any sense. Why was it new? *Because she's playing with you now. Before, you knew where you stood, and now you don't have a fucking clue about anything.*

"Dude!" Terri threw her hands up.

"Huh?" Dane turned to her.

Shaking her head, Terri scowled. "You're not even trying! You stood there while I walloped you. Now, what's going on?"

Dane scratched her head. "I honestly don't know. I don't know what's going on. There's just something on my mind."

"What something?"

Dane rubbed her forehead. "That's just it. I don't know."

She couldn't make sense of it, even if she tried. Was she more hurt? Less hurt? Did she care more or less? No, she was just confused.

"You wanna talk about it?"

"I can't really talk about it. I don't know what it is. It's bugging me, but I don't know why."

Terri sighed and gave her a little half-smile. "I wish I could help...or at least get a better fight out of you."

Dane shook her head. She didn't know what to say and didn't really have a comeback for the tease. Thankfully, she didn't have to think of a smartass comment, as she noticed Nicole's car pull into the driveway.

"Guess that's my cue."

"You don't have to leave, you know?" Back when Terri first started hanging out with Dane, Nicole hadn't been too happy with Terri being there when she came in. Of course, that was because Nicole thought Dane and Terri were going to get together, which was pretty crazy. Since then, Terri didn't like to stick around too long when Nicole showed up.

"I know, but you need someone to talk to, and I think she'll have better luck if I'm not here."

Dane couldn't really argue with that and it was the best excuse Terri ever had for leaving right after Nicole showed up. She might as well let Terri have this one. She walked Terri to the door just as Nicole opened it. Terri greeted Nicole and bid farewell to Dane in the same breath. The door shut before Dane even realized Terri was on the other side of it.

"She seemed like she was in a hurry," Nicole said as they watched Terri drive away.

"Yeah, she wasn't having much fun with me." Dane shrugged.

Nicole studied her. "Why? You two aren't fighting, are you?"

Dane grinned. "I think that was the problem. We weren't fighting."

For a moment, Nicole's forehead wrinkled and then she smiled. "I get it. Why weren't you fighting?"

"Yeah, my mind wasn't in it." Dane ran her hand through her hair. Before Nicole could ask questions, she decided to redirect the conversation. "You were gone much longer than usual. Everything okay?"

"Everything's fine. How about you?"

"Yeah, I guess." She put her hand through her hair. Noticing green eyes on her, she quickly dropped her hand. "Uh...why the bags?" She nodded down to the grocery bags in Nicole's grip. Usually, Dane handled the grocery shopping.

"Oh." Nicole smiled. "I'm going to make you a nice dinner."

Dane blinked. "Why?"

"No reason." Nicole disappeared into the kitchen.

Dane decided to leave her girlfriend be. Returning to the living room, she turned off the game and picked up her writing pad. She might be able to sort herself out through music. Writing a song might be the way to go. If she couldn't get lyrics, she'd just pick her guitar and try to get the music.

***

Nicole hummed as she worked in the kitchen, trying to keep up with Danny's light strumming. She had poked her head in on Danny, not too long ago, and saw her struggling with a blank page on her writing pad. Now, she was trying something that sounded almost like the blues, but was a little too up-tempo.

"Something's bothering her," Nicole muttered. She saw it in those grey eyes the moment she'd entered the house. At first, she thought something happened with Terri since Terri left so quickly, but then again, Terri always left minutes after she came in.

Now, she knew it was bigger than Terri. Danny was stuck on her music. She couldn't write lyrics and everything she played had that same weird blues-rock quality to it. She stopped abruptly every couple of minutes, let out a frustrated sigh, and started playing something else that sounded very much like the thing she'd just stopped playing. This was probably about Christine.

"Maybe she'll talk about it over dinner. I don't want her to carry this around with her." Nicole sighed.

After she put the food on, she was tempted to go talk to Danny, but decided to wait. Danny seemed to be trying to work through it on her own, through her music. She might be able to do it, even if the music told a different story.

So, while waiting for the food, Nicole went to take a shower. She didn't say anything to Danny when she went through the living room, and Danny didn't look up from her guitar. After her shower, Nicole decided to dress up for the occasion, if only to lift Danny's spirits and it'd be fun. She donned one of her little black dresses and made her way back to the kitchen. Danny looked up from her guitar that time. Nicole smiled at her.

"Uh...you going somewhere?" Danny asked.

Nicole laughed. "I have a date."

"You do? Lucky dog," Danny said with a lopsided grin.

"I suppose. Hopefully, I'm not stood up."

Danny ripped off of the couch and limped up the stairs, probably going to change. Nicole took the time to make them plates and set it up pretty. She poured fruit punch into the wine glasses. Glancing out, she wanted to see if Danny was on her way. The coast was clear, so she went to a drawer and pulled out the little ring box she'd stashed there earlier. She smiled and secured it by her chair as she heard approaching footsteps.

"Hope I'm not late," Danny commented with a smile, as she stepped into the kitchen.

Nicole smiled back. "Of course not." She took in Danny's appearance. Danny had on beige shorts with a white shirt and a dark blue vest. "You look kind of fancy," she added with a smirk.

Danny smiled back. "Says the woman in a dress."

"I wear dresses all the time."

"Yes you do." Danny's gaze went to the table. "Now, to what do I owe the honor?" Danny asked, as she moved over to the nook.

"It'll explain itself as it goes along," Nicole answered as she sat down.

Danny nodded. "This about my mother?"

Nicole sighed, wishing Danny hadn't jumped right into that. She'd like to have a fun, good dinner, before they approached that elephant in the room. "You tell me, is it?"

Danny shook her head. "I can't really figure it out. She makes me crazy." She made a show of circling her ear with her index finger.

"How so?"

"That's just it, I don't know. I don't know how I feel about her, or her visit, or her pictures, or whatever the fuck else. Nick, I just don't know, and I don't know what to do. It makes no sense to me. How can she make me this nuts?"

Nicole reached across the table and took Danny's left hand. Danny squeezed and took a deep breath. Nicole waited. Danny needed time and she'd give her that. They ate in silence for a while.

"I like your orange chicken, especially with these beans," Danny said, after swallowing one of several forkfuls.

"I thought you'd like it this way." Nicole enjoyed playing around with meals when she got a chance to.

There was a beat of silence. "Why'd she share her father with me?"

Nicole wished she had an answer for that. She wished she had any answer for Danny when it came to Christine. Nicole had already fumbled this once. She had no business tackling it again, not that she had any business tackling it the first time.

"I don't know, love," Nicole whispered.

"Why can't I just hate her? Why?"

"She's your mother, love."

Danny snorted. "My mother. Ignored me for twenty-five years. How can she be a mother? My mother?"

"Well, in a biological sense." Nicole wasn't sure what else she should say.

"I don't even want to think about this crap. I feel like I should just think of her as a stranger I just met, but there's so much crap under the bridge with us."

"Well, maybe that's all the more reason to let it go. How can you move forward if you allow yourself to be chained down by all of these things in the past? I know it might seem like she's emotionally manipulating you to get back into your life, but maybe she does just want in on your life. Do you want to punish her and deny her? That's your right. Or do you want to know her? That's also your right."

Danny nodded and then turned her attention back to the meal. Nicole sighed. *I want to tell her something to make this all better, but is there anything like that?* She doubted there was. So, she ate quietly with Danny.

"Baby, I need you to know, no matter what's going on with you and Christine, I'm here," Nicole said.

"I know, Chem. Hell, I'm very aware of that, actually. The fact that you've stuck around after getting to meet the madness that comes with the Wolfe name...Just know, I don't doubt you're here."

Nicole smiled a little. "I really wish I could help."

Danny shook her head. "Don't worry about it. I'll figure it out, maybe. This thing with Christine has been going on for my whole life. I don't expect this to clear up with one visit. I guess, I just didn't expect to feel so bananas after one visit either."

Nicole nodded. Danny probably didn't expect her mother to be able to affect her much anymore. This probably just went to a deep desire for Danny to have a mother, or even just a parent figure.

"Sorry I'm not a better dinner companion."

"I'm quite fine with it. I want you to talk to me about these things. I want to know what's on your mind, like when I tell you what's on mine. That's never a bad thing. Ever," Nicole said.

Danny nodded. "I'm getting the hang of it."

"Take your time. I'm here."

Danny nodded again. There was a little of the meal left, but Nicole felt like this was a good time to introduce her gift. Reaching down, she picked up the little box from its secured spot on the floor.

"Love, I have something for you."

"Yeah? More than just this awesome dinner?"

"Much more. Not too long ago, you made me a promise. I would like to make one of my own." Nicole held up the box.

"Nick..." Danny breathed. "You don't have to."

"No, I do. You're not the only one in this relationship, you're not the only one who has to improve, and you're not the only one who wants this to work as best it can. So, this is my promise to you. I, too, want to do better for you. I have to work on myself as well. I want to support you at all times, and I have to know when I'm supporting and when I'm pushing, because I don't want to push. I want you to know and believe in your heart, I'm always going to be here for you." Nicole removed the ring and held it up. It was a gold band of an infinity knot.

Danny swallowed, but didn't move. Nicole needed to wait. She wanted to see how Danny would wear the ring. Nicole wore hers proudly on her left hand, even though it was just a promise ring. She knew Danny had a love-hate relationship with her left hand and also believed their relationship had a long way to go. Would she be comfortable wearing the ring on her left hand?

"I knew you'd do this, and I know I said I'd just accept whatever you give me..." Danny took a deep breath. "But, this is still so amazing to me. I sit here and I actually wonder 'why does she want me?'"

Nicole smiled. "We fit, baby. I want you for the same reasons you want me. I've never met anyone like you. I've never had someone support me the way you do. And, everything you do is just so cute." She giggled a bit, wanting to lighten the situation a little, hoping to relax her love.

Danny chuckled a little and finally plucked the ring from Nicole's hand. She eased it onto her left hand and turned it. She smiled at Nicole, who couldn't help grinning, widely.

"I think it's too big." Danny said.

Nicole burst out laughing. "We'll put a catch on it."

Danny wore her ring. She wore Danny's. The idea was heady and beautiful, like the woman across from her. She grabbed Danny's hand and held firm. She'd be there for Danny because she wanted to be there. She'd support Danny, even when she was quite troubled. She'd love Danny through it all.

S.L. Kassidy

Treatment

DANE WAS HOME ALONE and Haydn asleep, so she didn't have any distractions from the boredom she surprisingly felt. Boredom wasn't something that typically hit Dane, since she enjoyed being sober and domesticated. Sometimes, she just figured she had gotten all of her excitement out of her system when she was a party girl. But most of the time Dane conceded she was always rather boring. Large amounts of cocaine fueled with alcohol, ecstasy, and a raging libido had made her seem more exciting than she was.

She remembered when she used to get urges to do things. Exciting people didn't have the urge to do something, because they were typically already doing something, she reasoned. So, maybe it was all of the drugs and sex that had made her seem lively once upon a time.

"No, that can't be," Dane argued with her brain, shaking her head.

Before the world had lost its luster and then gained a whole new shine, she had been more vivacious than she showed signs of recently. She used to go to clubs every night and not just the clubs she played. She went anywhere there was good music. She saw movies, walked in the city, and played music wherever she could, not just clubs, but anywhere. The rhythm of the world beat through her, poured out of her, carried her, moved her, and she shared it in any way she could with all the people she could.

"No, I wasn't getting into gun fights, but I wasn't boring. Hell, the last few dates me and Nick have been on were with Luke and Thomas. And those were because I had a shitty, nonexistent childhood. I owe my angel more than that. I need to take care of her like she does me," Dane said, as if saying it aloud would make it happen.

Nicole appreciated their little routine. Dane did, too. But, sometimes, she was all too aware Nicole wanted more. She was supposed to be rededicating herself to her lover. They had agreed to work on their relationship and they were getting stronger every day, but Dane wanted more. In order for that to happen, she needed to do more.

She wanted Nicole to never doubt her affections or her intentions, as Nicole had done some months ago. They hadn't had any real trouble since then, but she knew better than to take that for granted. Being in a relationship, she'd learned there were great times and there were low times.

She laughed. "Nick'd be tickled if she knew the full extent of my naiveté as far as this relationship stuff goes."

Being with Nicole was her first, and only, long-term relationship and she planned to keep it that way. She'd had two girlfriends before Nicole, but the second things went wrong, the relationships were over. She hadn't been with either of them for longer than a month, while she had been with Nicole for over a year; as friends, they had been together for a year and a half.

"If I want to be with her another year and more, I need to stop acting like a lump," Dane muttered, scratching her head.

Dane started on some romantic plotting. She was rather good at coming up with little romantic evenings, so she had ideas for a date quickly. *Nick must be the inspiration for this weird side of me I never thought I could have.* She got moving; figuring tonight was as good as any for a date, especially since Nick didn't have class.

***

Dane was dressed in a nice way, not formal, but not casual. She had on black cargo shorts with a sky-blue polo shirt and a midnight-blue vest. She knew Nick would catch on just from seeing her, but it was still a surprise.

She heard the key in the door at a little after five thirty in the evening, and she ushered Haydn into his crate. He'd be upset to be in the container for the rest of the night, but if she kept the den dark, he'd sleep most of the time. She exited the den, as Nicole entered the house. They came together without words, embracing tightly before kissing on the lips.

"Baby, why are you almost dressed up?" Nicole asked with a delighted smile. Her emerald eyes shined.

"Take a guess," Dane replied with a smile of her own.

Nicole gave a little giggle. "Do I have time for a shower and to change before date night officially begins?"

Dane laughed. "It's not official until you're ready."

Nicole kissed her on the cheek before making her way upstairs.

Dane took the time to dim the lights and put on some smooth jazz. She cleared the coffee table to set up dinner there. She felt like the living room was a more intimate setting than the nook in the kitchen. The dining room table would always be too large for them alone.

She made sure to put the plates close together, so she and Nicole could sit as close as possible. She had a flameless candle, just wanting to test it out to see if it compared to regular candles. Lastly, she went upstairs to the spare bathroom and put a brush through her hair a few times while thinking about Nicole putting her fingers through the inky mane.

"Hopefully, I do get a little of that. Love Nick's hands in my hair," Dane purred as she finished up. She rushed back down to the living room, wanting to be there before her girlfriend. She gave the whole scene a final look as she heard Nicole descending the stairs.

Dane's mouth went dry and fell open when Nicole came into view. The redhead was wearing one of her many dresses. It was a deep wine-colored cocktail dress that displayed Nicole's cleavage in a tasteful manner and made Dane almost drool. It didn't help that Nicole had on a silver necklace with a simple teardrop charm that dipped into the valley of her breasts. It all but beckoned Dane's eyes.

"Danny, are you okay?" Nicole's impish smirk told Dane that Nicole had dressed in that manner just for her slack-jawed reaction.

"Huh?" Dane couldn't function beyond the idea that she could reach out, right now, and feel bare breasts, bare *magnificent* breasts.

"Maybe I should change," Nicole said with a teasing glint in her eyes.

"Don't you dare," Dane hissed. Her hand was already halfway moving of its own accord toward Nicole, and she pulled it back.

Nicole snickered. "Down, Big Dog. Date first. You've got to earn the right to touch," she teased, wiggling her hips just a bit.

"What?" Dane whined.

A smirk curled up one side of Nicole's face. "You got me to dress up, baby. You have to let me enjoy this for a little while."

"Fine. If you insist, but I'm peeling you outta that thing later."

Nicole only smiled, but the spark in her eyes promised Dane could do just that. Dane wasn't sure if she'd be able to make it through the whole date, knowing what would happen at the end of the night. She wanted to get to the end already. Taking a deep breath, she settled her inner passion. *Gotta show Chem a good time first. That's only right.*

She led Nicole over to the coffee table, earning an arched eyebrow from Nicole. Dane flashed a grin that got Nicole to ease herself down to the floor, which was where Dane wanted her. Unfortunately, she didn't have the good manners to flash Dane. *I'm turning into such a little perv.* Dane groaned mentally.

"Oh, lamb chops." Nicole smiled as she looked down at the meal.

There were lamb chops, potatoes, broccoli, and carrots. Dane hoped it tasted as good as it looked. Nicole dug right in.

"Oh, my God, this is so good," she cooed after swallowing her first bite.

Dane smiled shyly, just to tease her lover a bit. Nicole giggled at the expression and tugged at Dane's pant leg to get her to sit down. Dane eased herself down to Nicole's level and put her hand on Nicole's bare knee. She savored the soft skin under her calloused fingertips, unable to stop the smile that settled on her face. Nicole reached out and took Dane's hand into her left hand.

"This is so sweet of you."

"I do my best." Dane gave a slight shrug before she began eating, a little upset she had to let go of her girlfriend to do so. They ate silently for a little while, exchanging glances and smiles.

"It tastes very good," Nicole said, partially through the meal.

"Thanks. I wanted to try something new. I like lamb when you make it, so figured I'd try. Obviously not the same thing, but pretty good for a first go, eh?" Dane thought Nicole made it better, but it was always good to try new things.

Nicole nodded. "Very good. You're really good at cooking."

"Well, that's to be expected since I was somewhat raised by a cook," Dane shrugged. Well, she spent a few years around a cook, watching him work anyway. "Besides, not hard to follow a recipe. Directions always make it easier."

"Stop acting so smug," Nicole giggled and playfully swatted at Dane.

Dane grinned. "You like me smug, angel, and you know it."

Nicole chuckled, which let Dane know she was right. They went back to eating. Nicole closed her eyes every few minutes and swayed to the music. There were a few low moans that let Dane know her girlfriend appreciated the food, along with the music.

"How do you like the flameless candle? Doesn't really touch me the same way regular candles do." Dane motioned to the candle that somewhat illuminated the table.

Emerald eyes glanced down. "I agree with you. But, it's nice to see it in action."

The meal finished and Dane moved as quickly as she could to clear the table. Nicole enjoyed the music until Dane returned with dessert— one chocolate ice cream sundae with rainbow sprinkles, fudge, and whipped cream. As Dane grabbed the spoon, Nicole knew what was coming and leaned forward. Green eyes fluttered shut as the cool, rich chocolate touched her tongue, and she practically hummed.

"I'm gonna make you make that sound later tonight," Dane whispered and her lover moaned louder.

"Promises, promises," Nicole teased.

"Nick, trust me, the neighbors are gonna complain about the noise."

A blush rose to Nicole's olive-toned cheeks. Dane smirked and made her eyes promise that her words were the truth. They spilt the sundae, giggling and moaning throughout. Dane again cleaned up the mess. When she returned, Nicole patted the empty space on the couch next to her, and Dane wasted no time accepting the silent invitation. She pulled Nicole into her lap. Nicole laid gentle, passionate kisses to her lips. Dane returned each wonderful show of affection, but she didn't let things go beyond that.

Glancing at the clock, Dane checked on the time while Nicole began caressing her sides. Dane moved the hands just as sweet lips laced her neck with precious kisses, but Nicole wasn't to be denied. Dane's stomach fluttered with each touch of those adoring lips. She purred from the attention, and she forgot about stopping the exploring hands. Just as she was about to surrender to the burning affection, she remembered why she was resisting. She pulled away.

"Baby, you're going to give me a complex if you don't kiss me back," Nicole said as if she was joking, but there was some truth to it.

Dane smiled and caressed her lover's thigh. "Chem, you know if I start kissing and touching you, I'm not stopping. There's more to this night, before we get to fall into bed and wear each other out."

Emerald eyes blinked. "More?"

"Yup, more. Up to driving us to the movies?"

"Movies?" Nicole echoed with a scrunched up face.

"Yeah, movies. Standard date night, angel. Dinner and a movie."

"You're serious? You want to go out for a movie? Not watch one on TV, but to an actual theater?" Nicole asked in sheer disbelief. Their usual movie date consisted of sitting on the couch and finding something to watch, because Dane didn't usually want to go out.

"Yes, and you need to drive."

Nicole seemed incredulous to the idea, but climbed to her feet. Dane put on her sneakers, while Nicole put on her shoes and grabbed a jacket. She also grabbed a hoodie for Dane, which let Dane know her girlfriend was concerned about her wearing shorts to the air-conditioned movies.

"I'll be fine, Chem. You know it takes a lot for me to get cold." Dane wasn't sure why, but it was always like that. She could take a lot of punishment as far as the outside environment went.

"Just humor me, baby."

Dane could only smile. Arguing was never worth it; she wouldn't win.

***

The couple arrived at the multiplex just in time. Danny already had the tickets, so Nicole didn't know what movie they were going to see until they got to the exact theater. She gasped when she saw.

"Danny, I thought you said you'd hang yourself with the shoelaces you don't have, before you'd see this."

"Honestly, my wish upon a star is that they'd used the money that went into this and made something worthwhile, but you wanna see it. I'm okay with that."

Nicole laughed. The movie was called *Wish Upon a Star*. It was a romantic drama. Pretty much a standard chick flick, but it had gotten good reviews.

"The things you do for me." Nicole wrapped her arm around her girlfriend's waist.

Danny shrugged as she led Nicole to seats in the corner, by the wall. Danny undoubtedly wanted a surface on every possible side of her for when she inevitably fell asleep. Plus in the seat by the wall, Danny didn't have to worry about people hitting her damaged leg and knee.

"You want snacks?" Danny asked.

"No, I'm good from dinner and dessert. Let's sit."

Danny's face scrunched up for a moment, but she did as suggested. They eased into their seats, just as the coming attractions started. A few minutes into the movie, Danny was already curled into the corner. Nicole smiled to herself and took Danny's hand, holding it tightly. Grey eyes glanced over at Nicole. Danny tried her best to be engaged by the movie, but thirty minutes in, she was nodding off.

Nicole believed Danny watched movies like she listened to music. Yes, some of the commercial stuff was good, but more often than not Danny thought the commercial stuff was too clichéd. Clichés bored Danny. She'd sooner watch an indie movie or a foreign film. She was a bit of a snobby artist in that regard. Not that Nicole would ever begrudge Danny her art. Danny's appreciation for music allowed her to appreciate so much in life and made her curious about so many things. Art made Danny and that was enough for Nicole.

Nicole didn't bother Danny while she enjoyed the movie. Her attention went to her girlfriend as she felt gentle fingers on her knee. She glanced at Danny, who focused forward, as if she weren't doing anything inappropriate. Nicole decided to ignore her despite the small jolts taking the short trip from her knee to her pleasure center. When those curious, questing fingers slipped under her dress to her bare thigh, she grabbed her lover's hand.

"No, Danny," Nicole hissed in a low tone, definitely not looking to call any attention to them. She wouldn't allow Danny to fondle her in a semi-crowded movie theater just because she was bored.

"What? Nobody's paying attention," Danny argued. She nodded ahead of them. The closest people were four rows up, and they were paying attention to the movie.

"Don't," Nicole ordered with a stern look.

Danny snorted and turned to look up at the wall. Nicole actually felt guilty. Her lover had planned a nice date night for them and brought her to this movie. Danny was quite right that no one was paying attention to them. Still, the idea of Danny touching her intimately in public was disconcerting. *The fact that I'm considering it, though, is even more troubling. How does she affect me this way?*

Glancing at her pouting girlfriend, Nicole wondered how often Danny had fooled around in public. Danny had more than likely done much more than making out or innocent groping and wouldn't have minded if anyone saw. Of course, that didn't make it right.

Nicole tried to stay focused on the movie, but continued to feel terrible for scolding Danny, which she didn't understand. She never made it a point to do more than kiss a partner in public and would've reprimanded any partner that tried for more. Of course, none of those partners were Danny. Things were always different when it came to Danny. She wanted to try new things, daring things. It didn't feel cheap to her like it would have with anyone else. *And Danny thinks I'm the one who bewitched her.*

Nicole was surprised to find she felt like a coward. She was scared someone would see, but she felt a little thrill at the thought. She wanted to be a little mischievous. Danny made her feel that way, because Danny would never purposely hurt her or humiliate her. This wasn't Danny trying to show ownership over her either. This was just Danny adding a little spark to what was obviously a very dull moment to her.

Nicole scanned the theater to make sure the coast was clear. Everyone was locked onto the screen. Nicole put the hoodie on Danny's legs, before making her move. Danny looked down, probably wondering what on Earth Nicole was doing. Nicole's fingers slipped onto Danny's bare knee, causing the guitarist to gasp and tense.

Danny's head snapped to the side to look at Nicole, who continued watching the movie. She felt Danny relax and carried on with her tender petting. Eventually, her fingers slipped from the knee to the thigh, but Nicole couldn't bring herself to do more than caress her lover's thigh. Danny didn't seem to mind, quietly mewing contently with her eyes closed. That seemed to be enough for Danny throughout the film.

"You've got a little naughty streak in you, don't you, my little nice girl?" Danny purred in Nicole's ear as she helped Nicole up. The credits rolled on the screen in front of them.

Nicole smirked. "I'm the perfect angel."

"You're perfect all right."

"Sweet talker."

Danny smirked. "I hope you know I now plan to use that naughty side."

Nicole wondered what her lover meant, but didn't have long to ponder it as Danny squeezed her ass. Nicole jumped and squealed, before slapping her girlfriend's hand away. She glared at Danny, who had the nerve to look innocent. Nicole practically pulled Danny out of the movie theater before she did something even more embarrassing.

***

The drive home was playful with Nicole trying to tell Dane how good the movie had been, while Dane halfheartedly attempted to grope her. There was plenty of laughter until they parked in the driveway. Dane got very serious.

"Danny, what are you doing?" Nicole asked as Dane came up behind her. She wrapped her hands around Nicole's shapely hips.

"Standing here, kissing you," Dane whispered, purposely tickling Nicole's ear with her breath. She peppered Nicole's delicious, elegant neck with wet kisses. She purred as Nicole moaned.

"Not outside," Nicole weakly protested. It was dark, but with the streetlights and neighbors' lights, anyone from across the street could see what they were doing.

"Then you'd better get us inside quick." Dane nibbled a sweet earlobe.

Nicole moaned again making Dane shudder. Nicole fumbled with her keys, but hurried to open the door as a tan hand stroked a full breast.

"Danny," Nicole groaned.

"I got the door." Dane kicked it shut. Her other hand slid from Nicole's hip to her stomach.

"Gotta...gotta..." Nicole was close to panting already, as Dane manipulated all her right spots. "Lights. Turn out lights..."

Dane nibbled her lover's neck for a second. She knew Nicole wanted to turn out the living room light, which they often left on when they went out at night. They had to turn it off now, because if Dane had her way, they'd definitely be too worn out to do anything beyond sleep.

"You get the lights. I'll check on the pup," Dane said.

A nod and a moan were the only responses, when Dane kissed her shoulder and squeezed her breast at the same time. Briefly, Dane considered just having her way with her angel on the floor, right in front of the door. But, she had other plans for Nicole that really needed a bed or her ass would be sore, so she reluctantly released the redhead and somehow managed to stop kissing sweet flesh.

Nicole gasped in surprise and then rushed off to turn out the lights. Dane peeked into the den and saw all was quiet. She opened the door to Haydn's pet carrier. While he'd sleep in the crate, he preferred his pet beds; he had two—one in their bedroom and one in the corner of the den. If he woke up and saw the cage open, he'd explore and then return to the den because he had trouble climbing the stairs on his own.

Dane checked to see where her girlfriend was and smiled to see Nicole was inspecting the kitchen for whatever reason. Dane hurried up the stairs, wanting to be the first in the bedroom to set up for the naughty mood Nicole seemed to be in.

Nicole's actions in the movie, though pretty tame, had surprised Dane. She tended to think of her girlfriend as an angel. It limited what she thought about doing, sexually, with her lover. It often seemed like whenever something popped in her mind, she quickly dismissed it, because she didn't want to soil her seraphic lover. Now, she wanted to see what she could get away with. Her idea wasn't too outrageous, but beyond what she had done with Nicole.

Kicking her shoes off, Dane made sure they were out of the way. She piled the pillows in the center of the bed and pulled back the blankets. She stripped down to her sleeveless t-shirt and boxers. Dane jumped into bed, just as she heard Nicole's footsteps on the stairs.

"Baby, you in here?" Nicole said, as she opened the bedroom door.

"Just waiting for you, Chem," Dane purred.

Nicole blinked a couple of times as she set eyes on her lover. "You're going to sleep?"

Dane chuckled. "No, I'm not. I'm watching you strip for me."

Nicole's eyes went wide. "Strip?" she yelped.

"Yes, strip. Come on, love. You seemed all naughty at the movies and now you're all shy. What happened to the playful vixen who felt me up in the movies?" Dane smirked.

Nicole bit her bottom lip, obviously considering the request. Dane wasn't sure if she'd go through with it. They'd never really done anything like this before. In the past year of being physically intimate, they hadn't explored much variety. Dane never suggested anything really new because she didn't want to chance offending her lover. Besides, Dane was content with what they had.

To Dane's surprise, Nicole smiled and put a hand on her shoulder strap. Dane groaned and wiggled slightly before the redhead did anything more; the sheer thought of what was to come soaked Dane. As Nicole slowly slid her shoulder strap down, Dane had to fight down the temptation to touch herself. She had never done that with Nicole watching, and she was not sure if that'd be too much on the minor boundary push.

So, she sat there as Nicole eased down her other shoulder strap. Dane groaned as the dress continued to cling to her lover. Nicole heard the noise and was emboldened, smirking at her captive audience. She added a little hip movement as she pulled the dress down, revealing her red lace bra. Dane feared her eyes might fall out of her skull with how wide she opened them, but she didn't want to miss a thing.

"Good God, woman," Dane whispered. *How the hell could something this simple make me this freaking hot?* Lap dances with actual strippers hadn't turned her on this much.

"You like what you see so far?" Nicole asked with a smoky gaze and sexy smirk.

"You know I do. Keep going, please." *God, please.*

Nicole nodded, and slowly the dress was gone, revealing smooth, olive-toned skin and leaving her in red lingerie. Dane was surprised by how rapidly her heart beat. Nicole just made everything inside of her flare, burn, and erupt without even touching. Nicole's very existence set Dane ablaze.

Nicole kicked her heels off when Dane beckoned her with a single, crooked finger. The redhead smiled and confidence sparkled in her eyes as she got on her hands and knees and stalked up the bed in a way that a cat would've been proud of. Dane wasn't sure how she didn't peak on the spot. When they were face to face, Nicole was the one that initiated a kiss between them, and Dane was the one that broke it.

"You're wearing way too many clothes." Dane's fingers caressed creamy biceps. Nicole was so soft to the touch. Dane just wanted to keep touching her, always, forever.

"Says the woman in an undershirt, bra, boxers, and possibly panties under the boxers," Nicole countered.

"Details, details." Dane's hands moved to Nicole's back. She toyed with the lace for a moment, moving her left hand to fondle and squeeze her girlfriend's breast. Nicole moaned and arched into the touch.

"Danny..." Nicole whispered the name like a desperate plea.

"Feels nice." Dane popped the bra hook. She used both hands to ease the bra off and stroke Nicole's heavy cleavage. "Better now."

Nicole gasped loudly, as Dane kneaded her freed bosom. Leaning down, Nicole captured Dane's mouth at just the right time because she screamed as Dane tugged the twin peaks with just the right amount of tender force. The neighbors definitely would've heard if Nicole hadn't released the sound into Dane's mouth. It tasted delicious. Nicole pulled away and tugged at Danny's t-shirt.

"Take it off." Nicole panted the request.

Dane's hands refused to leave the wonderful treasures they were engrossed with. "Can't. You have to."

"Sit up."

"Bossy. Like it."

Nicole just pulled at the shirt. Dane sat up more and Nicole yanked off both her shirt and the simple, very unsexy sports bra. Dane barely noticed because as Nicole settled back against her, she realized how close her mouth was to both gems her hands caressed. She wasted no time catching a pink pearl between her lips and ravishing it with a wanton tongue. A loud moan escaped Nicole, and she arched into Dane's fervent attention.

Dane groaned as she felt more of Nicole. Her free hand stroked any bit of delightful flesh that it could find before settling on Nicole's beautiful ass. She had plans to do sinful things to that ass, but Nicole suddenly tensed, so Dane beat a hasty retreat. She didn't want to make Nicole uncomfortable, even though she couldn't understand why Nicole tensed. No matter. There were more wealthy areas to visit on the blissful bounty before her, especially if the slickness on her thigh meant anything.

While Dane's hand wandered, Nicole writhed on top of her. Moans, mews, and heavy pants escaped them both, filling the room. Nicole's head dipped and she began kissing whatever piece of Dane that she could get to. She released a long groan, as Dane's roving fingers slipped by her waistband and dipped into the jackpot. Nicole gripped Dane's shoulders and bucked against the welcome fingers.

"Oh, God, Danny..." Nicole held on tighter. She seemed to come to her senses slightly and realized that something was different. Emerald eyes locked onto grey orbs. "Is it okay like this?" she asked in a breath.

Dane nodded. "Leg's fine. Don't worry. I want you here, like this. You like this?"

"I need more."

Their underwear needed to go. Dane was loath to move, considering that worrywart Nicole would try to change positions on her to protect her lame leg. She knew that was why they almost always had sex with her on top. Nicole left Dane in charge, so there was less of a chance of Dane's leg being pained. Well, there was also the fact that Nicole enjoyed Dane on top; she liked Dane's weight on her.

Nicole had to climb off of Dane in order to take her panties off. Dane quickly rid herself of her boxers...and the panties underneath. Briefly, she worried Nicole would lie down beside her, but the redhead was right back on her as soon as she was naked.

"Take me, baby," Nicole begged as she clung to her lover.

The breathy words made Dane's entire body burn up. Nicole's short nails dug into Dane's shoulders as Dane plunged into her. Dane exhaled loudly through her nose, as her mouth went back to the tempting breast, kissing, nipping, and sucking all over the gorgeous globe. Her other hand occupied the lone hill.

Moments later, Nicole was doing most of the work, her body moving as if she was possessed. Her head dropped down to Dane's neck and she showered the area with wet kisses and nibbles. On several occasions the nipping of teeth registered to Dane, before the sensations clouded her mind more.

Dane began meeting each of Nicole's movements with a hard thrust of her fingers. Nicole yelped before letting those turn into long moans as Dane curled and twisted her fingers. Nicole's hands tried drifting over Dane's body, but Dane could feel the telltale signs that she was almost at the tipping point. Nicole was in between a kiss and a nip before ecstasy washed over her. The next thing Dane knew teeth sank into her shoulder. She moaned as Nicole stilled and released her shoulder.

Nicole panted and nuzzled Dane's neck. Dane didn't move, giving Nicole a chance to gather herself. But, she also didn't remove her fingers. Once Nicole's breathing evened out, Dane began gently toying with her breast again. Nicole moaned and began moving. Dane slowly followed her lover while dragging her tongue along Nicole's chest, tasting the sweat that started to build.

They both moaned and grunted uncontrollably, rolling against each other. Nicole's hands moved all over Dane, as if she didn't know if she wanted to caress, cling, or fondle Dane. Somehow, her hand burrowed in between Dane's legs, and as her body moved more frantically, she rubbed Dane as best she could. It felt so good, but Dane did her best to focus on Nicole.

Dane was surprised when she was suddenly seeing stars, pulsing wildly from Nicole's attention. Just beyond those heavenly sensations, she felt Nicole fluttering around her fingers again. The feeling made her growl. When she returned to herself, she felt Nicole leaning against her and breathing heavily.

"One more?" Dane asked in a whisper. Her voice couldn't go any louder. Nicole usually was good for three, but she had to coax the third one out.

Nicole let out a long sigh. "No, I don't think I could survive another one. You?"

Dane shook her head. "Good. Sleep?"

Nicole could only nod. Dane eased out of Nicole and wrapped her arms around the redhead to let Nicole know that she wanted Nicole to stay there. Nicole understood, and they moved enough to lie down, Nicole on top of Dane with her legs spread, so they were at Dane's sides. Dane pulled the covers over them.

"You did good, Danny," Nicole said before sleep claimed her. Dane fell asleep with a smile on her face.

***

The couple woke up after a few hours. Nicole had been moving around, until she accidentally caused Dane to stir. Dane groaned a complaint that was silenced with a gentle kiss. Their eyes met and Dane smiled.

"That was fun," Dane commented.

"Yes, it was," Nicole agreed.

"We definitely need to switch things up more often."

Nicole nodded. "You're right. We tend to make love the exact same way, no matter where we're doing it. This was a great change."

"Yeah, you learned to be brave, and I learned you're a biter," Dane laughed. *Which is awesome information.*

Nicole gasped. "Did I hurt you?" Her voice was filled with concern, but something more. She sounded ashamed and embarrassed.

"Nah. Only actually bit me once. I've had worse. You should've told me you bite. I don't mind," Dane tried to assure Nicole, hugging her tightly to make sure Nicole knew everything was all right. She would've bet her left leg that her lover blushed, but she couldn't see in the dark room.

"Really?" Nicole somewhat squeaked in surprise.

Dane caressed Nicole's shoulder. "Really. Bite me whenever the urge comes. I want you to be able to let loose with me, Chem, like at the movies." She wanted Nicole to be comfortable around her and try new things.

Nicole gulped. "I'll try. I just don't usually do some things in bed, and I don't want you to think I'm weird."

Dane laughed. "Trust me, angel, nothing you do or want done in bed will seem weird to me. I promise you that. I want you to be happy and fulfilled in every way, including sexually. Okay?"

"I want the same for you, so tell me when you want to try new things, okay?"

Dane nodded and kissed Nicole's forehead to seal the promise. They settled back down for sleep. Goodnights were said, a few sweet kisses exchanged, and then all was quiet. As they drifted off, Dane hoped things would get interesting between them. She wanted Nicole to trust her with everything.

ACE

NICOLE THOUGHT ABOUT HER date night with Dane and the passionate ending. She was quite happy they'd changed their routine, even slightly. During the talk they had in the middle of the night, Danny had given her permission to explore a side of herself she had never felt comfortable with—the desire to bite a lover during sex. It wasn't something that came up often, but every now and then she did get the urge, especially with Danny.

Nicole always thought the urge was weird, sometimes even wrong. Danny didn't make her feel that way, though. So, she'd like to explore it a little bit. She'd also like to let Danny give in to her urges.

The idea made her blush. Danny jokingly called her naughty, and that's how she felt with her inappropriate actions and thoughts. She wanted to be a little naughty, but she wasn't too interested in doing it at home. For some reason, the house didn't seem like the right place to try new things. She wasn't sure why, but she felt like they needed to get out for her to explore this new adventure.

That thought actually worked to her advantage. She wanted to get away for a little while. She was still interested in showing Danny things she had never had the chance to experience. She wanted to take Danny on a short trip for her to get a feel for vacations. If Danny had a good time, they'd be able to go on longer trips.

Nicole sat at her desk, supposedly working, as she surfed the Internet and planned a little jaunt for them. She wasn't sure what Danny would want to do on a trip, beyond visit a club with good music. She made sure to keep that in mind, as she also searched for things she'd like to see and do. She found several choices and noted what they'd do on a three-day vacation.

"Hey, Nicole, ready for lunch?" Mina stepped in, narrowing her gaze immediately. Mina's chocolate colored eyes practically pulled Nicole from her computer.

"Gimme a second, Mina." Nicole held her hand up momentarily.

"What? No, I'm not letting you work through lunch." Mina huffed and moved closer. She unabashedly looked at Nicole's computer screen. "Oh, not working. Are you planning a trip? You really think Danny will go for all of this?"

"She will. She likes the outdoors. In fact, if I call her right now, she's probably in the park with Haydn. It'll be fun and it'll be new. I doubt she's been out of the city before. At least not to some place like this."

Mina nodded. "Is it going to set you back some?"

"No, it's not really expensive. I've gone on more expensive weekend trips with partners in the past."

Mina chuckled. "Yeah, but you weren't footing the bill then."

"Which is why this is no great expense to me. I've saved a lot of money from not having to pay for those vacations."

Mina laughed again. Nicole finished up and they left for lunch. She couldn't wait to tell Danny about their mini-vacation.

***

Dane put the finishing touches on dinner with Haydn bouncing around her legs, looking for attention and scraps. She let him have a couple of bits of chicken, but nothing more than that. He whined when the pieces of chicken cutlets stop coming.

"No, your food's over there." Dane pointed to his food dish in the corner. Haydn whined more. "No, I wasn't supposed to give you those cutlets in the first place. You have premier food that I'm sure any other dog would be more than happy to eat, so stop bugging me. Hell, I might've even eaten your food back when eating was a luxury for me."

Haydn wasn't impressed and whined more while standing up on his hind legs. He was learning that doing cute tricks got him treats. She resisted the urge to reward him, but he got to try Nicole as she wandered into the kitchen. Nicole had just finished showering after coming in from work. Haydn jumped at her, and she bent down to pet him. He whined and moved against her, almost frantically.

"What does he want?" Nicole sighed.

"Chicken. Isn't he transparent?" Dane shook her head.

"Extremely. We're spoiling him, aren't we?"

"Probably. Tell him no. Already gave him some."

Nicole directed Haydn to his dish. She put up with a lot of whining from him, but eventually he got the hint and slinked over to his dinner. She washed her hands and sat down to dinner with Danny.

"Oh, chicken parmesan. What possessed you to make this?"

Danny pointed to Haydn. "He barked at everything that looked like a bird today, so I figured we should have chicken tonight."

Nicole smiled. "Good choice. So, what did you do today?"

"Had a few lessons and took the little man to the park for a while. Everything okay with you?"

"Yeah, it was a nice, quiet day. I booked us a little trip."

Dane's eyes widened. "Trip? Where? When? Why?"

Nicole chuckled. "You got all of your questions out of the way?"

"I don't have to ask who. So, what trip?"

"Just a little trip upstate. We can see the leaves change color and do a little canoeing if you want. I thought that might interest you. There's horseback riding, a few night spots with live music, some hiking if your leg is up to it, and an odd art festival during the weekend I want to go, which is next weekend."

Dane nodded. "But, why?"

"I want us to go on a trip together, and I want us to use this trip to...be a little naughty, I guess," Nicole confessed with a blush.

A shiver raced down Dane's spine and she had to fight down the heat spreading through her. She took a moment, wanting to make sure her voice didn't sound different when she could finally speak. "Naughty can be fun. How much will it cost?"

Emerald eyes blinked and Nicole's forehead creased a little. "You don't have to worry about cost."

"I can pay, Nick. We can use some of the money Christine gave me."

An auburn eyebrow arched. "Christine gave you money? You mean from when your father tried to get you to pay him back for being alive?"

Dane shook her head. "No. Different money. Since she's decided to prove she doesn't hate me and she wants to be part of my life, she gave me a trust, like her other kids. It doesn't have as much money as those trusts, but it's money. Don't know what to do with it."

Nicole's face scrunched up. "Danny, when did she do this?"

Dane shrugged and scratched her forehead. "Yesterday, I think. Not really sure. I found out yesterday, anyway. I was gonna tell you after I talked to her about it and found out what the hell she's up to, but she hasn't called in a couple of days."

Nicole laughed. "The phone works both ways, sweetheart."

Dane threw her head to the side a little as she scoffed. "Ain't calling her."

"Of course, you're not. How did you even find out about the account?"

"Statement in the mail, along with an ATM card. You think she's trying to buy my affection? I kept thinking that yesterday."

Nicole sighed and thought about if for a moment. "I'm not sure I would say that, but I'm not sure what it could be. She might be trying to make amends, but if she was doing that then she'd give you the full trust. I don't understand your mother, and I've given up on trying."

"That makes two of us. But, you know, the money's there and I know she won't take it back, so I might as well use it to show you a good time. Hell, I used it to buy Haydn a new toy today. Don't wanna use it on me, but I'll definitely use it on you."

Nicole smiled. "I can tell you've thought this out, so I won't fight you on it. We can go half on the trip."

Nodding, Dane gave her girlfriend a smile. "Gotta get you a card for the account, too."

Nicole held up a hand. "Danny, you don't have to."

"I know I don't have to, but I want to. I have access to your accounts, so now you can have access to mine."

"Yes, you have access, but you don't have a card," Nicole pointed out.

Danny nodded because it was true. Typically, if she really needed to get money, she'd ask Nicole for her card and then return it as soon as possible. She sensed a compromise coming on.

"I take a card and you take a card?"

A smirk worked its way onto Nicole's face. "Now, you're learning, baby."

Dane laughed, even though she was fully aware she was completely and totally whipped. Not that she minded in the slightest. Honestly, she wished her mother would stay out of her life and leave her alone. She didn't want money, even if it wasn't a large amount. She could take care of her family on her own, but the money was there. She figured she could put it to some use.

After dinner, the couple planned out their trip. They decided to go by train because Dane had never taken a real train trip; the closest she had come was taking the subway. They chose the activities they'd do, provided they made it out of bed; the trip was about being a little naughty. They also agreed not to tell each other how they'd be naughty, but they were limited to one surprise each. They needed to be able to walk, after all.

***

"This is so cool." Dane stared out of the window of the train. She wished she had taken a train ride through the state sooner.

"I'm glad you're enjoying it." Nicole patted her lover's knee.

"Wish we could've brought Haydn with us. But, I'm glad Mina could watch him again."

"She loves the little guy. I'm surprised she hasn't gotten a dog, yet. Her husband doesn't seem to mind."

"Who could mind the little guy? Haydn's great!"

Nicole chuckled and nodded. "I don't understand why he was the last pup in the box. I don't get why he wasn't interacting with any of the people that wanted to adopt them."

"Don't wonder about it. We got an awesome dog out of it."

Nicole smiled and nodded, as Dane focused out the window, watching the country go by. She had left the city a few times, but only to go to other cities, and she always went by plane. She had never seen so much forest, or farmland, or cows.

"Chem, check out the cows," Dane accidentally shouted.

Nicole laughed. Dane realized how childish she must've sounded and appeared, so she dialed her excitement back. Silently, she noted she wasn't acting like a grown woman on vacation with her sexy girlfriend. But, when Nicole smiled at her and those green eyes shined with delight, Dane knew it was all right to be awed by these things.

"First time seeing cows in real life?"

Dane nodded. "I'm a serious city gal. No cows roaming the parks or bridges I haunted. I've seen horses before."

"Good, since we'll be riding one. You sure your leg is going to be okay?"

"If not, I'll tell you. I want to do it. I rode a few times, when I was really little. I told you about the Briarmoors, right?"

There was a nod from Nicole. "The neighbors who practically raised you for the first few years of your life. I'm glad they did a few things with you."

"Me, too."

"You never get upset that they, well...I suppose...didn't keep you?"

Dane had thought about the couple often throughout her life. "Sometimes, I used to get pissed, but I've always understood why they didn't. I'm sure my life would be very different if they had kept me. But, since I can't be sure I'd have met you, I'm glad they didn't keep me. I'm all about you, love."

The words got the expected flattered smile and blush. Nicole gave Dane a kiss for the statement and snuggled into her.

***

They rented a car and Nicole drove for the short trip from the train station. The hotel was just as nice in reality as it was online. It was next to a golf course that was somewhat popular, so the place wanted to be extraordinary to attract out of town people. It wasn't far from the lake that also made the town a popular tourist spot.

Dane got the bags, but only to pass them to a bellhop. Nicole checked them in and ignored the disapproving look from the woman behind the counter when she saw Dane and Nicole had a single room. The couple went to their room without saying a word to anyone.

"I wonder if that chick knows her face is bad for business," Dane said.

Nicole laughed. "I doubt it, but we don't have to look at her anymore and we'll ignore anyone who looks like her. We don't have to give them the time of day. We're on vacation."

"That we are. What should we do first?" Dane asked, while scoping out the room. It was cozy with a great view and even a terrace that looked out on the sparkling lake. "Glad the room doesn't look out on the golf course." Since neither of them played, golf didn't hold much appeal, and even Dane had to admit looking out onto the lake was romantic.

Nicole stepped over to her girlfriend and wrapped her arms around Dane. Dane kissed the top of her head and allowed her fingers to knead the small of Nicole's back.

"It's early enough for us to get in a short hike around the lake before dinner," Nicole said.

"Sounds good," Dane agreed.

"But, you have to wear pants and a jacket," Nicole said, putting her index finger up.

For a moment, a frown marred Dane's face, but Nicole kissed it away. Another kiss got Dane out of her shorts and into some cargo pants that Nicole had packed for her. Nicole held out a black bomber jacket.

Dane's face scrunched up. "Since when do I have a jacket like this?"

"I just bought it. The weather is colder up here, and your usual jacket isn't going to cut it. Besides, you can use this in the winter. It's large enough that you can put your other jacket under it, so you can layer."

Dane would've liked to be angry. She still wasn't comfortable with Nicole buying her clothes and such. She still had to get used to being loved and taken care of, as Nicole did for her. Much of the time, she felt like Nicole was babying her, but for once, she just felt the sweetness of the gesture.

"Baby, you okay?"

Dane blinked, realizing she had zoned out. "I'm fine. Just, I think I'm starting to get it."

Nicole's brow furrowed. "Get it?"

Dane shook her head. She didn't get it enough to explain it yet. She smiled and grabbed her lover into a tight embrace. She sighed when she felt Nicole's weight against her.

"Love you so much, Nick."

"I love you too, Big Dog," Nicole replied.

"Now, let's go make a little hiking," Dane remarked.

Nicole chuckled. "Was that a super obscure Monty Python reference?"

"The fact that you got it means it's not super obscure."

Nicole didn't argue that. When they were both ready to go, they marched down to the shore. They walked around the area, watching the people on the lake. There were plenty of boats, including canoes. Dane definitely wanted to give that a try.

"Canoeing looks fun," Dane noted.

"Yeah, there's supposed to be a stream or river that leads into the lake. So, we can start there and then end up in the lake. It should be fun," Nicole replied.

Dane nodded in agreement. After walking around the lake, they found a hiking trail into some nearby woods. They held hands as they slowly walked through the area, taking in the sight of the orange and yellow leaves. They paused a few times, whenever they came to rest areas or rocks large enough to sit on.

"This is pretty. Never really stopped to look at just the leaves before," Dane said, before taking a swig of water from the bottle that she was in charge of. She passed it to Nicole for a drink.

"I used to watch the leaves change with my mother. Sometimes, my father would take me camping during this time, too, and I'd look at the leaves. I like seeing the change." Nicole sighed contently.

"That's cool. It's great that your parents did so much stuff with you. The most I can remember doing in the fall is going trick-or-treating once."

"The Briarmoors?"

Dane nodded. "Yup. Lynn took me when I was six. She dressed me as Mozart. She thought it was hilarious."

"I would've loved to have seen that. Are you still in touch with them?"

"No, not really, but Christine said they still live in that same house. I can't really remember if they took pictures, but we can try to see if you want." Of course, she'd rather not. She hadn't seen the Briarmoors since she was a child. She'd rather forget them. It was easier, but now they proved harder to forget than earlier in her life. She wasn't sure why.

A bright smile lit up Nicole's face. "And you can show them how you turned out. I'm sure they wonder about you."

"You and your rosy outlook. We can go one day, though. I'd at least like to thank them for being so cool to me when I was younger. Owe them that much, I guess." Maybe that was true.

Nicole handed Dane a bag of trail mix to snack on. They walked until the sun started to set, making sure to take it easy and not tire out or harm Dane's leg. They made it back to the lake in time to watch the sun spark the water with brilliant orange, before it disappeared behind the tree line.

"Breathtaking," Nicole whispered.

"Second most beautiful thing I've seen today." Dane put her arm around Nicole's waist.

"You are such a sweet talker."

"Gotta play to my strengths."

Nicole chuckled, but didn't argue. They went out for an early dinner, and even went to a small club, if only to put up a front for each other that they weren't eager to get back to their room and bone each other's brains out. They managed to keep up the illusion for an hour, before Dane took Nicole by the hand and led her back to the car. Nicole wasted no time driving them back to where they wanted to be.

***

They had barely gotten into the hotel room when their mouths collided. Danny pinned Nicole against the door, seemingly forgetting about the fact that they each got one surprise during the trip. Danny obviously just wanted to get right to the event.

"Baby," Nicole hissed as Danny's lips moved to her neck. Danny didn't stop until Nicole pushed her away. Danny made a whimpering sound in protest.

"Wha?" Danny said in a daze.

Nicole shook her finger at Danny. "We're being a little naughty, remember?"

"Pretty sure fucking you against the door for all in the hall to hear is naughty." Dane realized what she said, shook her head and frowned. "Wait, hell, no. We're not giving people in the hall a show, even if it's just an audio show."

Nicole chuckled. "Besides, we agreed that tonight would be my naughty night."

Danny sighed. "Okay, you're right."

"I know I am. Now, go take a quick shower and when you come out, sit on the foot of the bed while I get ready."

Danny nodded and did exactly as commanded. She took quite possibly the fastest shower in history and when she came out, she sat on the edge of the bed. Nicole was surprised she wore pajamas, just a tank top and shorts, but was pleased with that.

Nicole disappeared into the bathroom with a small bag. She took a shower, too, hoping to relax herself to be able to go through with her surprise. She was a little nervous as she went into her bag of tricks. Dressing was easy after she reminded herself that Danny would never judge her, and Danny would definitely enjoy what she had on. Walking through the door and into the room proved much harder. She had her somewhat shaking hand on the doorknob and took a deep breath.

"It's Danny. She'll like this. I want to do this and she'll like this. I've always wanted to dress sexy and not feel like it's an obligation," Nicole told herself.

In the past, she wore lingerie because her lover had expected it. Danny really didn't expect anything of her in regards to intimacy. The musician happily took whatever she offered without any demands, to the point that they had practically been making love the same way for almost a year.

"No more of that," Nicole told herself, as she turned the doorknob.

Stepping into the bedroom, Nicole saw that Danny still patiently sat on the bed, listening to R & B playing low on the radio. Smoke-colored eyes grew wide as they landed on Nicole. The openly awestruck, appreciative, and admiring gaze from Danny gave Nicole confidence, making her feel like she was the sexiest woman in the world. The expression also caused a warm tremor in her belly.

"I love that dress on you," Danny whispered.

Nicole smirked. She wore a white dress that clung to her torso, flared out at the waist, and fell just below her knees. She often wondered why Danny liked her in the simple dress, but she didn't question it. As long as Danny continued to look at her like that, she'd continue to wear the dress.

"You always love this dress off of me," Nicole smirked.

"It does look damn nice on the floor. May I take it off?" Danny entreated, voice still low.

"Well, since you asked so nicely."

Nicole sauntered over to her lover and Danny took a moment to just look at her. There was reverence in her gaze and Nicole doubted anyone had made her feel as beautiful as Danny did without even saying a word. Once the staring was done, Danny worshipped her with her hands, lightly touching Nicole's arms from her wrists to her shoulders. Her fingers gently caressed Nicole's neck, chin, and cheeks before going back down to her neck. The trail went to her cleavage, where Nicole let out a small moan as Danny palmed both breasts and seemed to enjoy the weight of them in her hand.

"Danny..." Nicole breathed out the name as her hands went to Danny's shoulders to keep her upright. "You'll ruin the surprise."

"You mean, you standing here in this hot dress and those sling-back heels isn't the surprise?" Danny asked in disbelief.

"Of course not. I dress like this too often for this to be the surprise."

"Then maybe I should get you out of this and we get to the surprise." Danny's hands drifted to Nicole's stomach and paused there for a second before moving to free her girlfriend from the garment.

As the dress fell from Nicole's shoulders, Danny got a glimpse of what was hidden beneath. Danny gasped as she saw the silken edge of the pearl white corset. Once the dress was at Nicole's waist, Danny's mouth was gaping. She pulled the dress down more and made a strange, strangled noise when the dress hit the floor.

"Oh, my God. Oh, my God. Those are...and these aren't..." Danny couldn't speak. Her eyes were glued on Nicole's legs.

"You like my stockings and garters?" Nicole asked with a smirk. She knew her lover would assume she had on panty hose, which was what she typically wore.

Danny looked up at Nicole with wide eyes and her mouth stuck open. Her expression definitely answered the question. Nicole leaned down and kissed the corner of her girlfriend's mouth.

"I like this surprise," Danny said in a low voice.

"It gets better," Nicole promised, hoping her heart would stop hammering against her ribs. She was about to suggest something that boyfriends had asked of her, but she refused because it seemed sleazy to her. But, she was curious why her boyfriends had wanted to do it.

"Better?" Danny echoed in a breath. "Might not survive better." Her voice trembled. She was such a visual person, which Nicole thought was a little strange for a musician.

"I'm sure you've seen much more exciting things."

Ebony locks swayed, as Danny shook her head. "Nothing's more exciting than you. You're it for me, angel. Maybe it's because I love you so much, but you could read me the dictionary in a turtleneck and I'd be turned on."

"Baby, there you go again with sweet talk." Nicole leaned down and kissed her on the cheek. She didn't pull away. "I'll keep the heels on."

Danny gasped. "No kidding?"

"No kidding. You like that?" This was something else that had been requested of her by past lovers. Nicole didn't get the fascination, but this was the perfect time to explore it.

"Uh-huh." Danny swallowed.

"Anything else you want me to keep on?" she whispered.

"The corset can stay. Can I...?" Danny reached out, hands exploring her lover's torso.

"Yes, this is the end of my surprise."

"I fucking love surprises," Danny murmured before shooting up off the bed and capturing Nicole's mouth with her own eager lips. Nicole moaned as Danny pulled her as close as possible while continuing the passionate kiss.

Nicole could barely fathom the fire burning inside of her. It helped her understand why Danny reacted to her lingerie, even though she was certain Danny had seen sexier sights in her short life. None of Nicole's past lovers had ignited the raw, carnal, erupting, yearning ardor like Danny did. She craved and ached for her partner for the first time in her life.

Nicole could barely control herself as she reached down to Danny's shorts and yanked them off of her hips. Danny wiggled out of them and kicked the shorts away. She moved her hands from Nicole long enough to get out of her tank top. Danny was now naked and Nicole backed her up to the bed, so they could get comfortable.

"On your side, okay?" Nicole said in between kisses.

Danny nodded and allowed her lover to ease her down onto her left side. Nicole followed her, making sure to keep the kisses going. Once they were down and facing each other, Nicole's hands leisurely roamed her girlfriend's body. Danny purred as Nicole's fingers kneaded her breast.

"Uh, that's so good, angel." Danny moaned loudly.

"You like that? Hmm…" Nicole focused on the flesh at her fingertips. "What would happen if I pull it?" She didn't wait for an answer and gently tugged on the chocolate brown peak. She didn't usually do anything beyond massage Danny's breasts because, in the past, she had her own nipples tugged and it mostly just hurt.

It certainly didn't hurt Danny if her loud moaning meant anything. Emboldened by the sounds, she twisted the gem between her fingers and moaned herself when Danny arched into her. She placed a soft kiss to Danny's mouth that turned into a serious, passionate embrace.

"You feel so good," Nicole whispered as they broke for air.

"You too." Danny's hands caressed Nicole's toned belly and thighs. "I wanna…" Her fingers traced Nicole's waist.

"Go ahead."

Nicole's eyes fluttered shut as Danny's fingers crept into her panties and touched her soul. Determined to pleasure Danny, too, her fingers found the source of Danny's fire and stoked the flames higher. They were quickly moving in tandem, loud moans filling the room with the smells of their love. The noises increased in volume, and Danny lifted her leg to give Nicole better access as she crested.

As Danny came down from her wave of bliss, Nicole threw her leg over Danny's hip as she got closer. The musician knew what was happening and pushed into Nicole with more passion. Nicole screamed as she peaked, while Danny placed gentle kisses to her cheeks, chin, and neck.

"You okay?" Danny asked in a quiet tone. Nicole could only nod. Danny smiled and peppered a few more tender kisses to her lover's face. "No more?"

Nicole made a noise, which Danny understood. Long, graceful

fingers eased out of Nicole, causing her to whimper. She then gently removed her fingers from Danny. She kicked off her shoes, as Danny covered them with the blankets.

"Help me take the corset off," Nicole said in a low voice.

"Don't gotta ask me twice." Danny did as requested. She also happily helped her girlfriend out of her garters and stockings.

Once Nicole was naked, they cuddled close. Danny kissed the top of Nicole's head while she caressed Danny's sides. She tilted her head for Danny to kiss her lips and after that, they settled down.

This is wonderful. Nicole doubted she could ever do this with anyone else she had ever dated. *Danny is so special to me*. Not only that, but Danny made her feel special and secure. For once, she was comfortable with exploring herself beyond the idea that she liked both sexes.

"Hey, Chem."

"Yes?"

"This is just a break, right?"

Nicole laughed. "Yes. Round two in a few minutes." It was a promise she kept.

***

The couple didn't rise until noon, but they were able to get breakfast at a nearby waffle place. They could hardly believe how famished they were. They ate waffles, pancakes, sausage, fruit, and a half dozen scrambled eggs between the pair of them.

"Do you think we'll be able to do that again?" Nicole asked.

"Oh, yeah. We got a good sleep, good food in us, and it's not like we're about to jump back into bed. Should we go canoeing or to the art festival?" Dane shoved some waffles into her mouth. Syrup oozed out of the corner of her lips.

Nicole reached across the table and wiped her mouth. "You can be so messy. How about we save the art festival for tomorrow? It'll give us something to talk about on the train ride in the morning."

Dane chuckled. "My sweet angel, if I've done things right, an art festival will be the last thing on your mind."

"Still, baby, we have to do something with our Sunday. We're not going to be in bed all day. We could've done that at home."

Dane smirked. "You're the one that felt like we were defiling the house with our naughty behavior."

S.L. Kassidy

Nicole laughed, but didn't argue. They finished their massive breakfast and then walked it off around the lake. Once they no longer felt like they weighed twice as much as normal, they rented a canoe. They ended up going right out on the lake because Dane definitely wouldn't have been able to carry a canoe to get to the inlet.

"This is cool," Dane said, as soon as they were on the water. She sat in the front of the boat. "Thanks for suggesting this, Chem."

"Well, I know how into the outdoors you are. I used to do this with my dad all the time, when I was little. We haven't done it for a few years now, though, because we're both always busy. I should talk to him about going camping again. If only for a few days. You'd like it."

"No heat, no running water, no real bathroom, and sleeping on the ground exposed to the elements? Pretty sure I did that before I met you."

"I'm sure camping is a completely different experience than sleeping in a park."

"You're probably right. One day we can test your theory." Dane glanced back to see her girlfriend smiling. She wondered what camping would be like, but she was sure she'd enjoy it just because Nicole would be there.

They were quiet for a while, taking in the grand scene before them. The lake water was sparking as the sunlight hit it, and it seemed like magic. Dane reached behind her, wanting a connection to her lover. Nicole wasted no time taking her hand and squeezed. They slowly moved toward each other after securing their oars.

"This is so peaceful," Dane said, as Nicole rested her head against Dane's shoulder.

"Maybe we should've gone horseback riding first."

"Nah. We'd have thrown up that huge breakfast."

Nicole laughed. "Yeah, we would've. Horseback riding should help us work up an appetite for dinner, anyway."

They drifted on the lake, curled up together. They didn't say anything, even as they started back to the boat rental place. They walked away, holding hands.

"Nick, this trip was a great idea," Danny declared with a grin. They took their time walking back to the rental car.

"Oh?"

"We're both more relaxed and we're closer. You feel it?"

Nicole smiled and nodded. "That's why I was able to do what I did last night. I've had lovers ask me for a lot of things that made me feel uncomfortable or dirty. Sometimes I even wondered if they saw me as some kind of whore. But, I never feel that way with you, and even though you don't ask for a bunch of sexual things from me, I want to give them to you."

Dane was touched and leaned down to place a kiss to her girlfriend's crown. "That is a special gift, angel. I'll never abuse that trust," she vowed.

Nicole offered her a small smile. "I know you won't."

"And tell me if I ever do anything, in bed or otherwise, that makes you uncomfortable." Of course, she had purposely held off on plenty of things to make sure not to offend her girlfriend. But, sometimes, she felt like she'd failed.

"I will."

An ebony eyebrow arched. "Will you?"

Nicole's brow furrowed. "What do you mean?"

"Talk about it later when we're not out in the open like this."

Nicole nodded, definitely not wanting to discuss their sex life outside. So, they went about their day.

***

"You look really comfortable on that horse," Nicole said to Danny. They were out on a trail, slightly ahead of the group of other riders.

"This is something I've done before. My knee isn't really comfortable, but it isn't throbbing either." Danny leaned forward a bit to pet her horse. "He's a good horse, too."

"I'm glad he's taking care of you. I haven't done much horseback riding. I prefer to do my own running in sports."

Danny laughed. "I need to see you play something."

"You name it and we'll play, if your leg can handle it."

Danny scoffed. "So you can beat my ass? You know I don't play anything beyond instruments." She smirked. "And you," she added in a whisper.

Nicole blushed and looked around to make sure no one else heard. Everyone else had their attention focused elsewhere. Danny chuckled at Nicole's paranoia, and Nicole reacted childishly by sticking her tongue out at the musician.

"Is that an invitation?"

Nicole yelped and put her tongue back where it belonged. She blushed deeper and her lover laughed again. To punish Danny, Nicole didn't talk to her for about five minutes. That only tickled Danny more if the smile on her face meant anything.

"We should take more trips together." Nicole reached over to pat her lover's arm.

Danny chuckled. "The silent treatment might be more effective if you could last longer than Bach's Little Fugue."

"Keep it up and I'll keep being mad at you," Nicole threatened, even though it was clear she couldn't uphold that. "But, seriously, we should go on more trips. I'm really enjoying this time with you, doing these types of activities."

"That just means we should go on more dates before anything else, but this is fun and I'd like to do it more often. I've been able to realize a lot about being with you already. I want this to last forever. I want to love you forever; I want you to love me forever; and I want to let you love me forever."

Nicole was speechless. While she was used to Danny saying sweet words from the heart, these words were different for some reason. They were more than emotions shared. They seemed to be deep thoughts and beyond. This was an epiphany that Danny shared with her.

"Baby...before this...did you think we wouldn't make it?" Nicole quavered. She almost didn't recognize her own voice.

"What? No, of course not!" Danny grabbed for her lover's hand and giving it a reassuring squeeze. "I never thought that. But, there's always been this part of me that's pulled away from you because I'm wary of you wanting to take care of me. I dunno, I felt like you were babying me or something." She shrugged.

Nicole's brow furrowed. "I'm not trying to baby you. I just want to make you happy in any way that I can."

Danny smiled a little. "I know. And I know you do it out of love, and now I feel like I can accept it openly, without any second thoughts or underlying emotions. This vacation helped me realize that, and I think I'm more open and ready to accept this from you."

"I'm glad," Nicole whispered with a small smile.

Danny smiled back. They were able to ride holding hands for a few more minutes. Nicole definitely felt closer to her lover now. They definitely needed to go out more, be it for trips or just dates.

***

The couple returned to their room after enjoying dinner and hitting a couple of clubs. They were more under control, but still quite amorous. Dane's hands leisurely wandered all over Nicole, her mouth on Nicole's in a slow kiss, and she slightly ground against Nicole's backside while the redhead opened the door. They stepped in and let the door shut.

"Sweetheart," Nicole breathed out the term of endearment. She broke the kiss, so Dane kissed her neck.

"Yes?" Dane whispered in her love's ear.

"I know it's your surprise tonight, but can we go slow? I want slow tonight."

"I will go as slow as you like, my dear."

"And showers first?"

"Of course. You go first."

Nicole went to wash off the grime of the day while Dane checked on her surprise. She felt more comfortable with the idea, now, after admitting to Nicole that she was going to let her in more. She wanted them to be able to share everything with each other.

"Slow should fit this perfectly," Dane told herself while securing her surprise.

Nicole exited the bathroom smelling like lavender; Dane loved it. Nicole wore a robe, so Dane suspected her girlfriend had a minor surprise for her, even though it was supposed to be her night. That idea didn't bother Dane at all, and she went to take her own shower. When she returned, she wore long, baggy, mesh shorts and a tank top.

"Uh...Danny, are we just going to sleep?" Nicole asked, her eyebrows drawn in close.

Dane couldn't really focus on the words her lover said, because Nicole was posed on the bed in a silk, champagne-colored teddy, with her back bowed so that her breasts were on display. Dane practically leaped on the bed, vigorously attacking Nicole with her hands and mouth. Nicole moaned and clutched Dane's shoulders tightly, holding her in place.

"You feel so good, angel. Smell good, taste good," Dane muttered as she rained wet, butterfly kisses on Nicole's neck and bare shoulders.

"I love your mouth on me, baby. I love my fingers in your hair. So soft, so beautiful." Nicole sighed as she combed through thick, ebony locks.

Dane didn't say anything, filling her mouth with her girlfriend's delicious skin. She also occupied her hands with Nicole's wonderful cleavage, gently kneading and twisting each lovely globe. Nicole moaned again and pulled Dane closer.

Nicole jumped.

"Baby?" Nicole's hands left the sanctity of Dane's hair and meandered down her body. She moved to explore the curious item that had nudged her thigh.

Dane tried her best not to squirm. She wanted to give her lover a chance to discover the new terrain. Nicole's hands were slow, but steady, as they traversed her body. Dane gasped and arched into the curious hands that lingered on her breasts. Leaning over, she nipped and kissed whatever she could reach of Nicole without moving much.

"Sweetheart, is that...?" Nicole's hand drifted to the inside of Dane's thigh.

"Uh-huh," Dane replied with what she hoped was a sexy grin but suspected was a slightly dopey smile. Underneath the haze, she was glad Nicole thought her rare goofiness was adorable.

"Oh, God!" Nicole sounded quite surprised, as she discovered their new toy. A tiny whimper escaped her.

"I guess it's safe to assume you like my surprise," Dane whispered before nipping Nicole's earlobe.

Nicole shivered. "Yeah." She licked her lips. "Forget slow."

A lump formed in Dane's throat. She could see so much trust in those deep, green orbs. She wanted to give Nicole everything she possibly could: all her worldly possessions; all of her love, devotion, and talent, and pleasure that no one else could.

Swallowing to drive down the lump, Dane was surprised by how strong and assuring her voice came out. "Okay. I need you to not hold back then." She wanted to give Nicole everything, but she wanted everything in return. She wanted Nicole to let loose, show her true self, and give in to everything she had inside of her.

Nicole nodded her vow and the mood in the room shifted. Things were suddenly more intense, and Dane felt like she engulfed Nicole, as if they merged into one. Nicole seemed to feel the same and had to hold onto Dane after Dane practically tore their clothes off.

Dane gave Nicole a hard, fervent kiss. It was different from their usual kisses, but the emotions underneath were more than familiar. Clutching on to Dane tighter, Nicole massaged the musician's back, as Dane led Nicole to the head of the bed. By then, Dane was fully on top of Nicole, propping herself on one elbow while her hand rubbed up and down Nicole, getting lower with every pass.

"Danny, please," Nicole hissed, breaking their kiss. She arched, causing the toy to press against her. Dane hissed as the toy pushed back against her.

"You want me?" Dane asked, as if she didn't know. Her right hand eased down between Nicole's legs, and she hissed again when she felt just how much her lover wanted her. "Dear lord, Nick." Her fingers couldn't stop caressing Nicole.

"Baby, please. I need you so badly. I want you so badly." Nicole sat up slightly to pepper Dane's body with wet kisses. Each touch of her lips was like a touch of heaven.

"You sure?" Dane wanted to melt into Nicole, be one with Nicole, and never separate again.

"Come on, Big Dog. You know you want to. You have me begging." Nicole ran her tongue along Dane's collarbone, causing the musician to quiver.

"Oh, God, Nick. I need you, too. I need to make you feel good. I need to have you," Dane growled.

"I'm all yours. Every single inch, every part, anything that makes me who I am is yours. Do with me what you will." Nicole tried to pull Dane close to her. Any closer and they would've been one being, which would've been totally fine by Dane.

Dane gazed into emerald eyes, seeing deep into Nicole's soul. Taking a breath, she pushed, linking them together. Nicole moaned, and her nails bit into Dane's copper-toned, tattooed back. Dane hissed and pushed more, touching deeper, making her lover moan more. Emerald eyes closed in surrender, giving herself to the loving pleasure of Dane.

"Nick, angel, look at me, please. Look at me and keep us connected."

Nicole nodded. "Just don't stop."

"Can't. Won't. Love you."

Green eyes locked on Dane again. She smiled and placed a gentle kiss to Nicole's lips, as she started with a tender motion. With each moan from Nicole, Dane dug a little deeper. She wanted to touch all of Nicole, to return all that Nicole had offered to her.

Soon, looking at each other was impossible, but it didn't matter. Dane could hear Nicole's spirit in the sounds that grew more licentious with each stroke. She could feel Nicole's love and desire in the bite of her nails, as they clutched her back and tried desperately to pull her closer.

Nicole began kissing Dane's shoulders, neck, ears, and anywhere else that her mouth could reach. Dane roared in response and drove her hips just a little harder.

"God, Danny, yes," Nicole screamed, arching off the bed to meet each thrust that was a little more powerful than the last.

"You going to heaven, angel?" Dane panted. She knew. The toy pressed against her enough, but the thing really getting to Dane was Nicole's reaction to the experience.

"Take me there, baby. Take me there," Nicole panted.

Dane had no choice but to obey. Her mind was enthralled by the smell of Nicole's arousal, her soul delighted by the feel of her lover's hands, and her own body possessed by the sounds Nicole made. Even though Nicole had been the one to offer herself to Dane, it was Nicole who was in complete control.

Dane adjusted their bodies to allow Nicole to experience more. She pushed herself up on both arms, and Nicole locked her legs around Dane's waist. Using her legs, Nicole pulled Dane closer, and the musician growled as she fulfilled Nicole's silent demand. Faster and deeper called forth more moans and scratches.

"Oh, God, Danny," Nicole screamed so loud Dane was certain the entire hotel heard. They certainly heard when Nicole bit down on Dane's shoulder.

"Fuck!" Dane shuddered and collapsed on her girlfriend.

The next few seconds were a complete blur. Dane lost herself in her lover, totally unaware of anything beyond the pleasure of taking Nicole to the edge and then falling off herself. The sensation of fingers gently rubbing her back and tender kisses to her sweat-covered neck brought Dane back to herself.

Dane sighed. "Chem, love, that's never happened to me before. You're a-fucking-mazing."

Nicole giggled. "Does that mean I'm amazing to fuck?"

A tired grin conquered Dane's face. "Damn right. Even though, this definitely didn't feel like fucking."

Smiling, Nicole gave her another soft kiss to the neck. "No, we made love here. I think we always make love, baby, no matter how we do it."

Dane couldn't disagree with that. "Yeah, that was one of the reasons why I wanted to try it like this, just to see if using a toy with you would be different and special like always, which it was. Speaking of like this, I can't possibly go again after you literally knocked me out."

"Don't worry. You're not the only one that can't go again. I'm probably going to be a little sore since I haven't...well, your fingers are great and all, but they're not this big."

Dane laughed when she noticed her girlfriend was blushing. "No, they're not."

Dane moved enough to lift off of Nicole and slid out of her lover, earning moans from the redhead. Dane rolled over onto her back, and Nicole wasted no time cuddling into her side. Dane made as few movements as possible to get rid of her toy. She tossed it on the floor.

"So, what other reasons went into you picking this surprise?"

"Well, I figured since you've dated both men and women, you'd appreciate the change. I know you like penetration, too. Won't lie. I also wanted to show you my skills with a strap-on." She liked to think she was damn good.

Nicole chuckled. "You're very skilled. I'm guessing you've used it before."

"Not gonna be stupid and tell you how many possible times, but I've had chicks that only wanted me with the dildo. I've had chicks that wanted some crazy things from me, which is why I always try to tell you that you can do whatever you want with me. First off, everything about you turns me on, and it'd be a pleasure to do just about anything with you."

Nicole nodded. "I think I bit you pretty good." She massaged the area she'd sunk her teeth into.

"Good. Bite me all you want. The bite was what did it for me, that and knowing *I* made *you* let go. Shit, that was probably what knocked me out. It was mind blowing to know I could make you feel so good that you let loose and bit me."

"It felt so good." Nicole shuddered in remembrance. "So, nothing in bed squeaks you?"

"Now, I didn't say that. I'm willing to do anything with you, but there have been things that squeaked me. Every now and then, I'd run into a woman who'd want to call me Daddy in bed." Dane groaned at the thought.

"Daddy?" Nicole echoed in disbelief. "I can't even imagine that. Did you let them?"

"Yeah. Worse than that were the women who wanted me to call them Daddy. With my father issues, they really didn't know what they were asking of me," Dane sighed, shaking her head.

Nicole had to sit up a little to look her lover in the face. "You called them Daddy?"

Dane shrugged. "They had the beds and the food. After I left home,

I'd do anything for food and shelter. Calling some woman Daddy was better, by far, than being beaten by my actual father. Being numb had helped."

"That's true," the lawyer conceded and settled back down.

"Does anything in bed squeak you?" Dane had noticed that, during sex, whenever her hands drifted toward Nicole's ass, her girlfriend tensed. She hoped to learn why.

"Several things," Nicole admitted in a small voice.

Dane put her arm around her lover's shoulders and pressed her closer. "You don't have to tell me all of them. I only gave one, so that's all you need to do. It's something we can take time to discover about each other."

Nicole nodded. "Is there something you want to know about?"

"Uh...why do you get scared if I touch your butt when we make love?"

Nicole's brow furrowed, and her eyes looked downward for a moment, focused on the crumpled linen. "Oh. I didn't realize. But, that is a valid question. Back in college I had a jerk boyfriend, which shouldn't be a surprise."

"What did he do?" Dane caressed her lover to help keep them both calm. She doubted this would be a pleasant story for either of them.

"He always wanted to...well, let's just say he was fascinated with my ass and wanted to do things to it. I didn't want that and told him so, but still, it was a frequent conversation with him. One night, while were in bed and I was on top, he grabbed my ass, which was fine, but then, the next thing I know, he's trying to stick his big, fat finger some place it wasn't wanted. I practically flew off of him."

Dane bit back a frown and nodded. She supposed that made sense. She could understand why Nicole tended to want the bottom whenever they were in the missionary position. Yes, Nicole might like the feel of Dane on top of her, but she was literally protecting her ass, too.

"What an asshole! No pun intended," Dane said.

"He was. We broke up that moment," Nicole replied.

"You should've broken his goddamn dick and fingers! Stupid prick."

Nicole smiled. "Thanks for the righteous indignation. I appreciate it. I've actually never told anyone that before. It felt good to tell you."

Dane's fingers danced across Nicole's skin. "Glad you shared and you felt safe enough to share. I want us to be able to share stuff like that."

"I want that, too. I want us to be confidants and to trust each other not just to tell each other stories of the past, but also to share thoughts, dreams, and everything."

Dane smiled. "Definitely want that. So, first things first, trust that I will never, ever, ever stick my fingers anywhere without your permission, especially somewhere like your ass. I mean, who the hell does that?" She rolled her eyes and snorted.

Nicole chuckled and kissed her lover's shoulder. "Thank you for that. And, just for the record, you have permission to touch me all you want, everywhere, because I know you'd never do anything to make me uncomfortable like that. If I ever told you no, I know you'd stop."

"Damn right." Dane pulled Nicole closer. "And just so you know, you can touch me anywhere you want, ass included. I thankfully have never had anybody try to go there by surprise."

"They were too busy calling you Daddy," Nicole said, earning a laugh. "And just so you know, I'm never going to call you Daddy."

"Thank you, sweetheart!" Dane kissed the top of her head. "I'll never call you Daddy either."

Nicole laughed and then yawned. They were both fading, so they kissed each other goodnight and fell asleep. Hopefully, tomorrow would be just as great.

***

The next morning, Nicole blushed and Dane laughed when they left their room at the same time as the couple next door to them, who inquired which one of them was Danny. Dane admitted it and earned a high five from the guy. Nicole almost passed out from embarrassment. Somehow, she recovered enough to carry on with their day.

***

"This is an art festival? Guess I now understand the saying 'I don't know art, but I know what I like.' I don't like this," Danny remarked, as she and Nicole walked around the park. They held hands, ignoring occasional looks from others attending the flea-market disguised as an art fair.

Nicole smiled. "You're so judgmental about art. You're the same with movies and music, too. Are you like this with books?"

"I'm not judgmental. I know about music, like you know law or chemistry. So, I know when music is a piece of someone or some bullshit produced to make a quick buck. That's how I feel about movies sometimes, and other times I can enjoy commercial junk just like anybody else. This is amateur art, probably full of heart and soul, but still not that great."

Nicole laughed, but nodded. The art was subpar, but she didn't expect much from a small-town art festival. There might be a couple of diamonds in the rough, but they were buried deep in a vast desert of mediocrity. Still, they walked around for a couple of hours.

"That was damn near painful," Danny said, as they finally left the art festival.

Nicole laughed. "It was pretty bad. I honestly thought it would be better since it's an annual event."

"Maybe some years are better than others." Danny offered a supportive smile.

"Thanks for that. Let's go get some food."

"Sounds good to me."

They had an early dinner and retreated to their hotel room. They didn't bother pretending they wanted to spend their last night hanging around outside. They wanted to be together, alone.

"What should we do?" Danny whispered before placing several caring pecks to Nicole's wanting lips.

"Combine our surprises?" The very idea made Nicole quiver. *I really like exploring things with Danny.*

"You have the best ideas," Danny purred.

Nicole attacked Danny's tongue with her own. Dane moaned, and their hands groped wildly, almost as if they were trying to tear each other apart. They frantically removed each other's clothes, moving around the room with no direction in mind. Danny ended up against the wall, hissing against Nicole's lips. She grabbed Nicole by the back of the head, and kept her close until their lungs demanded otherwise.

"What do you want, baby? The whole outfit? Pieces?" Nicole was panting.

"Whole thing. Wanna peel you out of that corset." Danny shuddered.

"What else do you want to do?"

Grey eyes searched Nicole's face, trying to figure out what she meant. "To you?"

"Yes, baby. What do you want to do to me? What can I expect?" Nicole kissed Danny sweetly on the mouth.

Danny groaned. "Wanna do crazy things."

"Like what?" Nicole was certain they had different ideas of crazy; her sex life had been much more vanilla than Danny's. But, she wanted to know and she wanted to try.

"Taste you," Danny breathed.

"Nothing crazy about that. I want to taste you, too." Nicole placed wet kisses on Danny's neck and chest. "What else?" She peppered her lover's cleavage with tender nips. Danny moaned loudly.

"Take you on your knees."

Nicole's knees shook at that confession. They had never done it in that position before. They hadn't made love in very many different positions, at all, which she knew was her fault. She always wanted Danny on top; the weight, the skin contact, the everything drove her wild. The *feel* of Danny was the ultimate aphrodisiac for Nicole.

"What else, sweetheart? Tell me more." Nicole's mouth continued to drift across Danny's breasts.

"Make you ride me," Danny panted.

"You've thought this out. Let's work on your plan."

Danny nodded and managed to break away. Nicole hurried to her bag while Danny went to her own. Nicole knew whoever was ready first was going to have control, but she also knew she had zero chance at being first. She had more to put on.

She knew she was beat when strong arms wrapped around her middle and pulled her close. She hadn't even put her dress on. She felt Danny's new piece against the small of her back and groaned at the thought of what Danny wanted to do with it. She practically melted into her lover's front.

"Put on your shoes, baby," Danny whispered. Her tongue traced the shell of Nicole's ear.

Nicole felt like her breathing was louder than a thousand drums. She wasn't sure if she would be able to slip her feet into her shoes, because her legs were like wet noodles. But, she felt Danny, holding her up, supporting her, so she was able to complete her ensemble for the most part. The dress remained in the bag.

"So fucking sexy." Danny moved long hair to one side, exposing Nicole's neck to her kisses. Her hands caressed all over Nicole's corset-covered torso.

"I thought you wanted the whole outfit," Nicole panted, wanting more of everything her girlfriend had to offer.

"This is more than fine," Danny practically growled in her ear. Nicole would never be able to wear her panties again.

Danny led Nicole over to the bed and sat her down. Nicole's heart sped up, and she bit her lip in a moan, anticipating Danny's tongue on her. *Danny loves the way I taste.* The reverse was also true. Their sexual compatibility was wonderful, just a small piece of why Nicole was certain they were soul mates.

Danny settled in between Nicole's legs and kneeled before her. Light kisses tickled the inside of Nicole's thighs, while fingers stroked her stocking-covered legs. Nicole panted as ecstasy raced through her.

Nicole licked her lips. "Baby...."

"Yes, angel? You need something?" Danny looked up, and Nicole, gasping, locked on to her grey eyes. Whenever they gazed at each other like this, it was like their spirits intertwined. Nicole had never felt like this with anyone. She was certain her life was richer, graced by Danny.

"You. Only you. Forever." She ran her fingers through Danny's hair.

Danny gave her a lopsided, amorous grin. "You have me. I'm wrapped around your little finger, my queen. Let me serve you, worship you, and be all you ever need."

Nicole could only let out a long breath. *Dammit, Danny! You're so good with words.* Danny was very talented with her mouth, and Nicole longed for that talent. She got what she wanted, as Danny removed the barrier between them. Nicole felt...everything.

Danny moved one of Nicole's legs onto her shoulder, groaning as the stockings slid across her flushed, dark-caramel flesh. Nicole threw her head back as soon as she felt the deep reverence of her lover's blessed mouth. Nicole moaned so loudly it would've made her blush if she was of sound mind.

"Yes, my beautiful, sweet, generous love," Nicole breathed, tangling her hands in Danny's lovely hair.

Danny simply drank in more of her, tongue gliding against Nicole. Nicole moaned again and tightened her grip on Danny's ebony locks, pulling her closer. The musician murmured contentedly, as she adjusted her mouth, touching Nicole in different spots—all the spots she liked. A whine, long and heavy, escaped Nicole.

The noise seemed to echo through Danny, and she moved with more purpose. Nicole cried out; it felt like her girlfriend's mouth, tongue, and hands were everywhere. Soon, Nicole had no control over her hips, and she ground against Danny's face as though the movement would take her to heaven. In the end, Danny's skillful tongue made her soar, sliding inside and moving just right.

"Danny!" Her hands crushed Danny's head to her. A brilliant, white light flooded her vision, and she lost track of herself as well as time.

"You okay up there, angel?" Dane whispered, as if she was scared she might shatter Nicole.

Nicole mewed and stroked Danny's scalp. "Perfect."

"Not perfect yet. Up," Danny ordered as she climbed to her feet.

Nicole wasn't completely recovered, so she wasn't entirely sure what Danny meant. Danny didn't bother to explain. She took hold of Nicole's hips and moved her further back onto the bed. Nicole allowed her lover to manipulate her body, turning her over and pulling her up onto her knees.

"Is this all right?" Danny murmured. Her hips were rocking already, her addition caressing Nicole intimately. Nicole bit her lip, whimpering, and nodded her head. Danny had to swallow around a lump her throat. "I need you to tell me yes."

"Yes, it's fine," Nicole answered in a breath, pressing herself back against Danny.

"Good. Angel, you look so fucking gorgeous like this. My queen, dressed all in white. So pure, pristine, like the perfect snowflake as it drifts from heaven." Danny seemed to recite the words like a prayer. Her hands lightly traversed Nicole's legs and back. Her fingertips made Nicole whimper, and she pressed back into her girlfriend again.

Danny threw her head back when she felt Nicole rub against her, and she let loose a deep, low bellow. Even that odd sound sent shivers through Nicole, and she pushed into Danny more. Danny's hands wandered, as though she needed to feel as much of Nicole as humanly possible. Nicole whined with desire.

"Baby, please. I'm ready. So ready." Nicole glanced back at the musician.

Danny nodded, even though her lover could not see. Glancing between them, she saw the accessory was coated in Nicole's essence. Her new pick was ready to play her greatest, most beloved instrument. Danny's chest heaved, as one hand steadied Nicole and the other caressed her torso.

"Danny!" Nicole cried out, and Danny gave them what they both wanted. Nicole moaned, as Danny eased gently into her.

"Just tell me when you want more," Danny said, even though she always seemed to know when Nicole wanted more.

Nicole only moaned more, wondering how Danny could zap her of all her thoughts and make her body feel as if it was made of pure bliss. Danny licked her lips, eyes half closed, bent into Nicole's every sound.

"You like this. Those loving screams and begging purrs. Best music ever. Gotta play more," Danny panted, thrusts getting a little more powerful with every move.

Nicole couldn't formulate a response and only wantonly pushed her hips back. Their sweat-drenched bodies slid and slapped together. Danny growled. She looked down between them, witnessing their combined movement, seeing their connection. It was quite a sight as Danny moved with even more purpose.

Danny wrapped her arm around Nicole's waist and eased her fingers to the space that'd really make Nicole sing. Ecstasy flooded Nicole's system and she shouted her lover's name to the heavens for all the stars to hear. Danny called her lover's name to the sky as well. Euphoria enveloped them, as they collapsed into the mattress, Danny stretched over the lawyer's back.

They lay there quietly for what seemed like an eternity. Nicole thought that might've been the end of things, but then she felt long digits undoing the laces of her corset. She whimpered as soon as the piece of lingerie was gone. Nicole's chest heaved, as Danny's hands began to knead her aching beasts. Suddenly, those lecherous hands were gone and so was the pressure against her back. Nicole panicked, scared, frightened Danny had left her, vanished.

Nicole twisted around to see Danny making herself comfortable against their pillows. Their eyes met, and Danny smiled at Nicole in invitation. For a moment, Nicole was lost, and then she remembered what Danny wanted from her. Nicole didn't move.

"You okay with this?"

Nicole flashed her lover a confident smile. "More than okay."

"Then get on. Let's see what you've got," Danny teased her.

Nicole gave her a glare as she turned around. The glare didn't last long, as she took in her lover's long, lean body along with her accessory. She groaned at the sight and thoughts of Danny's proficiency with that attachment.

"You think highly of yourself, huh, baby?" Nicole crawled over to her girlfriend.

"Oh, you don't wanna know what I'd be endowed with if I had one of these, but we can definitely pick out some we'd both like." Danny looked like she was about to say something else.

Nicole quickly pressed a finger to her girlfriend's lips. "Your mouth isn't doing what it should be."

Danny nodded in agreement. Nicole was right on top of her and there were so many things she could've been kissing. Hardened nipples dangled right in front of her face. Wasting no time, she popped a gem into her mouth, moaning at the taste.

Nicole almost fell over when she felt those warm, tender lips engulf her. Maintaining her balance, she moved to lower herself onto the musician. Danny had to sit up more to follow her treat. She groaned as she felt Nicole's weight on her.

"Fuck." Danny's hands automatically went to tempting hips. "Shit, move, baby, move," Danny begged.

Nicole didn't need to be told twice, especially since that was what she desired and required. Her hips rolled and they moaned together. Danny tried to sit up a little, to press closer. Nicole was moving on her, in front of her. Danny seemed to forget how to get up. Her hands roamed over Nicole, her eyes fixed on bouncing breasts.

"God, baby, so good," Nicole moaned.

Danny only grunted, eyes straying to the high heels on her lover's feet. Nicole was riding her while wearing high heels. There were no coherent words. Nicole certainly didn't help when she increased her speed.

Bronze hands clutched Nicole's waist, urging her on. Nicole moved faster than Danny would've thought to thrust. She pushed her hips to meet Nicole's downward strokes, almost keeping up. Danny's body was about to burst.

Nicole let out a boisterous groan as strong, wanting hands pressed her down. She did not need the encouragement. Danny's hands moved on to Nicole's ass. As soon as her fingers gripped appealing flesh, Danny seemed to realize her mistake. She pulled her hands away and totally lost the rhythm of their soulful dance.

"Dammit, Danny, don't you dare stop." Nicole grabbed Danny's hands and placed them squarely back on her ass.

"Fuck." Danny groaned and wasted no time meeting her lover's movements, squeezing Nicole's ass.

The level of trust that Nicole just showed her seemed to be exactly what Danny needed. Nicole watched as Danny's eyes actually rolled up in the back of her head right before her body exploded. She collapsed onto Danny.

"Baby, you okay?" Nicole's voice was low and rough.

"No…you killed me, but it's cool. Keep moving."

"Sweetheart, I couldn't move if I wanted to. I died right after you did." Nicole chuckled.

"Oh, cool." Danny wrapped her arms around her lover. "Stay here."
"I have to. I can't move." The confession got a laugh out of Danny.

***

In the middle of the night, Dane woke up for no reason. She looked down at Nicole, who was pressed against her, sound asleep. As she drifted back into oblivion, she thought about the differences between fucking around, like she used to, and making love with Nicole. Both involved pleasure, ecstasy really, but only Nicole touched her physically, psychologically, emotionally, and spiritually. *I'll never give this up.*

Cast

NICOLE COULDN'T BELIEVE SHE was standing in *Brooks*. Mina used to drag her to this place. They'd built plenty of fond memories in this upper class bar. Now, Nicole would have to add one weird memory.

She had agreed to play Danny's little game. The musician wanted to see if she could pick Nicole up, as a stranger. She had tried to talk her girlfriend out of the role play, telling Danny there was no way she'd ever go home with someone she'd just met at a bar. But, Danny wanted to try. Besides, it was just a little harmless fun and they'd agreed to shake up their routine a little.

Nicole wanted to see what her girlfriend, a woman who had never needed to approach a female, would come up with. Danny was good with words, when she wanted to be. If nothing else, Nicole figured the lines her lover fed her would be worth it.

The venue Nicole picked might make it a little harder for Danny to work. Besides, if Danny was going to attempt to take her home, it might as well be from some place Nicole would be comfortable in, a place she might actually hang out.

Why would Danny wish to see if she had the skills to pick up women? According to Danny, she'd never needed skills; women just fell in her lap. Why did she need pick-up skills with a steady and committed girlfriend, a partner to grow old with? Nicole would ask Danny about it later, but for now, she was content—and maybe a little curious—to see how things played out.

After scanning the lounge, twice, to see if Danny was around, Nicole decided to have a drink. She rehearsed her story once more, in her head. She didn't want to stammer or hesitate when Danny finally did come to her. *This is so silly!* She sipped her glass of white wine and declined several offers from gentlemen trying to buy her something stronger.

"Excuse me, but does that taste good?" a very familiar voice asked.

Nicole turned around to see just what she expected—a tall, scruffy and grungy woman with untamed, ebony locks and a mischievous glint in her grey eyes. She was dressed in jean shorts despite the fact that it was the middle of November. Scars from aged injuries marked her legs. There were scars on her left hand, too, but they were faint.

Nicole managed a smile. "Is that some kind of pick-up line?" She chuckled. *I expected better, my dear.* She'd also expected Danny to dress better. Danny was fortunate girls fell in her lap before and that she now had a committed partner.

The laugh was light, melodic. Grey eyes sparkled. "Not that I know of. I'm serious. I saw the way you were sipping from your glass. Let's just say, what I saw made me curious about what the drink tastes like."

Nicole arched an eyebrow. "Why not just order some to find out? It's just the house wine."

"That'd be a great idea, but I don't drink."

Nicole played along, and her eyes bugged out. "You're in a bar and you don't drink?"

The faintest hints of a smile played at the corner of full lips, as if the woman were trying her best not to burst out laughing. "I'm here on business."

Nicole couldn't help the skeptical expression on her face. "Business?"

"Don't look so shocked. I'm not lying. I actually have business here and, no, it has nothing to do with fashion."

Nicole chuckled at the little joke. *Good that she knows how ridiculous she looks.* "What business, if I may ask?"

A small, but bright smile lit up the caramel visage. Nicole noted the smile highlighted cute features and brought out the bronze undertone of the face. She had to resist the urge to reach out and caress the slightly chubby cheek.

"I'm a musician. I'm supposed to be meeting my band's manager. Don't think he's here, though." Grey eyes scanned the establishment once before settling back on the redhead.

Nicole nodded. "A musician? It suits you." She gave the confessed musician another once-over.

"Because I look like a punk?" She gave Nicole a leveled look.

Nicole blushed. "No...I didn't mean that."

The musician chuckled and waved off the apology. "Calm down. Just messing with you. I'm Dane. What's your name?" The tall woman extended a friendly hand.

"I'm Nicole," she replied and shook the offered hand. "Dane's an unusual name, especially for a woman. Is it a stage name, by any chance?"

"Nah, it's my given name. Given to me by me, but it's what I've gone by all my life. Is Nicole some kind of stage name?" Dane countered with a small smile.

Nicole laughed. "No, and I hope you meant that in a good way."

Dane smiled. "Trust that I did. So, what is it you do, since you know what I do?"

"I'm a lawyer." Nicole didn't want to get into what type of law, and she made sure to keep her face neutral.

"Cool. Do you have a card or something? I might need a lawyer if I ever find myself on the wrong side of the law." Dane chuckled.

"I'm not that type of lawyer. Besides, there has to be a less obvious way for you to try to get my number." Nicole smirked.

An ebony eyebrow lifted. "Get your number? But, your card would have your business number." Dane's hair pushed forward a bit with her wrinkled forehead.

Nicole snickered and struggled to remain in character. "Yes, it would, but you'd be able to call me."

A hand went through short, ebony locks. "I guess. But, it'd be for business. That's what a business number is for. I wouldn't call your business number for anything beyond business."

That's cute and probably true. "What type of music do you play? You said you're a musician, but you didn't specify."

Dane shrugged. "I play all types. But, mostly rock. Different types of rock, but rock just the same."

"Do you make a lot of money doing that?"

There was another shrug. "Make enough. Do you make a lot of money being a lawyer who doesn't get people out of jail?"

Nicole laughed. "I make enough, thank you very much."

"Guess you would, hanging out here and all. You being stood up, too?" Dane asked casually.

She didn't really come off as flirting. It was like they were having a normal conversation. *Does Danny not know how to flirt?* She supposed it made sense because Danny never had to pick up girls. *Even when she was a teen, though?* The lawyer scanned the lounge. "Yes, I suppose I am. I was supposed to be meeting someone, but she didn't show up."

"Her loss. A good friend?"

Nicole froze for a moment. She hadn't thought that far ahead. She was enjoying herself, somewhat, but wasn't very interested in creating so many details. She was a lawyer and a chemist, not a fiction writer.

"My best friend." Nicole managed a smile. "I'm sure she had a good reason for not being here. She'll be upset when I tell her I met with a musician. She's interested in music, too."

"Does she play anything?"

"Beyond the bodies of musicians, no," Nicole laughed at her own memory. "Maybe it was just because we were crazy college kids at the time. She certainly isn't that way now."

Dane nodded. "And what about you?"

Nicole's smile transformed into a guarded expression. "What about me?"

Dane smirked. She had purposely asked that question in an ambiguous manner. "Are you interested in music?"

Was she purring? "Oh." Nicole felt her cheeks heat up just a little. *Maybe she does know how to flirt a little bit, the little sneak.* "Some. I mostly like classical. I'm a huge Mozart fan."

"A lot of people are." It was clearly a struggle for Dane to not roll her eyes.

Nicole frowned. "And what do you like?"

Dane chuckled and opened her mouth to respond, but they were interrupted. The bartender seemed to come out of nowhere and cut between them. He put a drink down in front of Nicole, causing her to scowl again.

"I didn't order this." Nicole still had plenty of wine left.

"No, but the gentleman at the end of the bar wanted you to have it. He was very insistent." The bartender walked away as quickly as he'd arrived.

The disdain didn't leave Nicole's face and she pushed the drink away. She didn't look down the bar, knowing that would only encourage the guy. Apparently, he didn't need encouragement. He marched down and rudely planted himself in between Nicole and Dane. He didn't even deign to glance in Dane's general direction.

"Excuse me, but I just had to come down here and meet the most beautiful creature to ever grace this place. My name is Evan," he introduced himself, leading with his left hand to show off an expensive watch, unaware of smoke-colored eyes rolling behind his back.

"Hello, Evan," Nicole said through clenched teeth. "It's a pleasure to meet you, but I am engaged in a conversation with my friend." She motioned to Dane with her free hand.

He regarded Dane as if she were some kind of insect. Dane's gaze narrowed at his back as he returned his attention to Nicole. What he surely believed was a charming smile worked its way onto his face. He looked like a predator, and Nicole was the chosen prey.

"You know, you deserve better than this house wine. I know some good restaurants where we could get better wine, a meal, and to know each other." His confident smile gleamed with perfect, pearly white teeth.

"While that might sound like a good idea to you, Evan, I am currently engaged in a conversation with my friend." Nicole purposely chose those words, as she rested her left hand against her cheek. Her promise ring was clearly on display; she'd refused to remove it for the silly night of semi-mindless role-playing.

Evan refused to glance at Dane again. "You can talk to her whenever you want. Dinner with me is a limited time offer." He smirked as if he had just given her an offer she couldn't refuse.

Mentally, Nicole groaned. *I'd forgotten guys like this exist*. Evan gave her a whole new appreciation for Danny.

"Well, could you go somewhere so we can let that offer expire?" Dane remarked.

Nicole held in a chuckle while Evan scowled. He adjusted his body just enough for Dane to see the look on his face. Dane didn't seem moved by the expression. Snorting through his nose, he turned to glare at the musician. He actually had to look up to her. His eyes proclaimed her unworthy of his presence.

"Look, little girl, you're out of your league. There's no way this beautiful woman would give your punk ass the time of day. So, why don't you go back to your parents' shack and just fuck yourself?" he suggested, quite loudly, obviously wanting the whole bar to see him put Dane in her place.

Nicole was about to end the farce, if only to keep Danny from decking the guy. But, Dane just smiled. Evan's scowl deepened, and he snorted through his nose once more. *Was he part horse?*

"Pretty sure a woman this classy doesn't have time to put up with someone like you," Dane calmly replied.

"I could buy and sell you. You don't know anything about class. In fact, here's fifty bucks." He pulled out a flashy money clip, thick with cash, and waved a fifty-dollar bill in her face. "Go buy some class."

"Funny, was gonna tell you the same thing, but you might be right." Grey eyes went to Nicole. There was a twinkle there that Nicole couldn't put her finger on, missing a joke Dane seemed to want to let her in on. Dane sighed dramatically. "I am clearly out of my league. I mean, there's no way I could do something better than pulling out a wad of cash to convince this pretty lady that I could show her a good time and treat her right. Right?"

Evan puffed out his chest in victory. "Glad you see it my way."

"Of course." Dane quickly snatched the fifty from him. "I'm going go buy some class now."

Nicole wondered what Dane was up to and felt her stomach tighten as the musician actually walked away. Her throat went dry, as Evan turned back to her, his predatory smile in play once again. *Danny, please. What the hell are you doing?*

***

"Gotta love places like this," Dane muttered to herself as she walked deeper into the lounge where a guy was playing the piano. She figured she could get him to give it up for a second. She lightly tapped him on the shoulder.

"Yes?" Glancing over, he frowned a bit. "I don't take requests," he informed Dane in a snotty tone. *Of course, the downside to places like this is that everybody has a fucking uptight attitude.*

"No? I was hoping you'd loan me your instrument, so I can make this douche bag look like the douche he is...well, more so than he's doing himself." She nodded toward the bar.

He glanced back at her. "You play piano?" The skepticism in his voice was almost tangible.

She smirked. "How about you loan me this seat and find out?"

Curiosity obviously got the better of him, as he relinquished the bench to her. Dane sat down and took a moment to check on Nicole, who was a couple of yards away. Nicole's body language displayed her disgust. She was clearly ready to flee Evan's presence, as he leaned in close to the lawyer. Dane's nostrils flared, and her hands played on their own.

Mozart poured from her fingertips until emerald eyes found hers. She was glad her fingers went for a song with a dramatic beginning, as it took Nicole only a few precious seconds to spot her. Once she was sure she had Nicole's undivided attention, and Evan was watching her with murder in his eyes, she eased into a Chopin nocturne. It was hard not to smile when Nicole seemed to float toward her on the music. Evan stomped behind Nicole.

"Dane, that's beautiful," Nicole whispered, as if her voice would somehow diminish the melody.

Dane smiled. "Wish I could take credit, but Chopin wrote it. He's no Mozart, but you know." She shrugged. She winked at Evan, who appeared ready to pop a blood vessel.

"No, but you're playing it. And it sounds like heaven." Nicole shut her eyes and seemed to let herself go in the music.

The smile on Dane's face grew. Evan growled. There was nothing he could do without causing a scene and ending up the fool. He stormed off and Dane finished playing the composition. People actually applauded when the music ended, but Dane didn't really register the sound. Her focus was squarely, solely on Nicole. Emerald eyes opened, sparkling as they gazed down at her.

"Thanks, man," Dane said to the stunned pianist, as she climbed to her feet. He stood at her right with his mouth agape. She was about to pat him on the shoulder, but considering how stiff he was, she didn't want to chance pushing him over.

"That was marvelous," Nicole said.

"Marvelous?" the pianist scoffed, regaining his wits just in time to defend Dane, who really wished he'd keep it to himself. "Divine is closer to the truth." He stared at Dane in awe. "You're incredible."

A smirk settled on Dane's face as she focused on Nicole. "You hear that? I'm incredible. Made a fan. That's gotta be worth at least the first three of your numbers."

Nicole laughed and grabbed a nearby napkin. "Do you have a pen?"

"As a matter of fact..." Dane went into her pocket and pulled out a pen. She handed it to the redhead and Nicole quickly jotted down something on the napkin.

Dane looked down at the napkin and grinned when she saw a complete number staring back at her. When she looked back up, she found the space Nicole had occupied was empty. *What the hell?* Nicole was walking away. *Where the hell is she going? I thought I did all right.* Dane fully intended to chase her down, but the pianist grabbed her wrist.

"Hey, take your hands off of me," Dane growled. Leveling a glare at man, her wishes were quickly fulfilled.

"I'm sorry. I just wanted to talk about your playing."

"Later, man. Can't you see I'm trying to score?" she replied in a huff. She had thought she was close to her goal and only needed to seal the deal. It turned out she was wrong.

***

"I can't believe you're not going home with me. You gave me your number. I played the piano for you!" Danny argued while she and Nicole strolled to Nicole's car.

"I told you before we started this that I don't have one-night stands and I don't go home with people I meet in bars, no matter how classy the bar is. So, no, I wouldn't go home with you."

"But…but, you gave me your number and it's not your business number." Danny ran a hand though her hair and squinted, clearly confused. Her brow furrowed adorably.

"Danny, getting a number doesn't mean a girl will go home with you. It just means she wants you to call her to set up a date. You can get to know each other through conversation, not sex," Nicole said as they entered the car. She didn't start the engine.

"What?" Danny scrunched up her face.

Nicole laughed. "Baby, you are too cute sometimes. Your rock god status has totally screwed with your perception of dealing with women."

Danny let out a long breath and threw her hands up slightly. "I know, which is why I wanted to see if I could pick a girl up the normal way and I did. You gave me your number."

Nicole regarded Danny out of the corner of her eye for a second. *Wow, does she really think a number gives her all access to a girl's pants? Of course, if Danny thought that, it was probably because that had been her experience. I suppose I should set her straight, not that it matters.*

"One, in your mind it doesn't seem to count as a pick up unless I go home with you and we have sex. I'd hate to see your reaction if a girl went home with you and just wanted to talk. Two, it hardly qualifies as normal once you sit at a piano and play Mozart and Chopin. Three, you cheated by playing one of my favorite piano concertos, even though I never told you what it was."

Danny scoffed. "All right, Miss Lawyer Pants. You're right about number one. I don't see what was wrong with sitting at the piano, though. To impress a girl, you're supposed to use whatever you have at your disposal. That Evan jackass tried to use money. I just happen to have piano skills and there happened to be a piano nearby. That was fair. Hell, if I could've pulled a piano out of my pocket, I would've. It was a coincidence I played your favorite. It was the first thing that came to mind."

"Uh-huh." The skepticism practically oozed from Nicole's entire form.

Danny sighed, scratching her forehead. Grey eyes stared down at the floor. "So, I didn't do so good, huh?"

"No, baby, you didn't because you cheated," Nicole admitted bluntly, but then she reached over and took Danny's hand in her own. "But, you don't need to pick up women. You have one already. One who loves you, is devoted to you, and will do everything in her power to make you happy."

Danny smiled. "You're right. Guess I don't need to pick up girls." They were silent for a moment and Nicole was about to drive off.

"You didn't have fun tonight, did you?" Danny's voice was low, as she eyed the floor.

Nicole sighed. "I didn't really like the reason we went out tonight and that might've soured me to the whole idea. I didn't like the role-playing, even if I was playing a younger version of myself. Or maybe it was because I *was* playing a younger version of myself."

"You were really good, though. You stayed in character through Evan."

"I know. Maybe I don't mind role-playing, but still, I don't like the idea of you wanting to practice picking up women. You have me. Also, the idea of pretending not to know you is lost on me. I mean, maybe this could be fun, but there were pieces of it that I didn't like. Is that all right?"

Dane flashed a bright smile. "Yeah, it's fine. I want you to always tell me if you don't like something. The you that you were playing had just started as a lawyer?"

Nicole nodded. "I wasn't happy with it, but I wasn't jaded by it yet either. What about you? You didn't drink, so obviously this was a recent you, but you looked scruffy and spoke of being a musician." They had decided to play different versions of themselves since Danny had been adamant about wanting to pick Nicole up. *Which, I guess I should be flattered by. She didn't want to pick up any other woman. She wanted to see if she could pick me up.* Now that Nicole thought about the idea, it was kind of nice.

"Yeah, this would be me after the incident, but I went to my uncle's house and cleaned up a little bit. I'm always a musician, and I did have a manager. Every now and then, I'd toy with the idea of going back to music and think about contacting him, but I obviously never did. Hell, for all I know, poor sap could still be looking for me."

"Why not just get in touch with him?"

"Because that would mean talking to him and I really don't wanna do that. He's an asshole." Danny laughed. "So, you really didn't like this?"

Nicole shook her head. "Sorry, baby. I wouldn't mind going to *Brooks* or any other place with you, but I don't want you to try to pick me up. There's nothing sexy about it to me, even if you did manage to put a big goon in his place."

"Speaking of the big goon..." Dane pulled the fifty dollars from her pocket.

Nicole laughed. "I can't believe you actually took his money."

"As they say, don't flaunt it if you're not gonna give it up. I thought I might need it to bribe the pianist. But, anyway, I think I can make this up to you. Wanna go to your favorite jazz club and pretend to be madly in love?" Danny gave her one of those monstrous grins that Nicole couldn't resist.

"Sounds like the role I was born to play." Nicole started the car with a grin.

Scab

BABY, WHAT THE HELL?" Nicole entered the living room, frowning as soon as she caught sight of her lover. Danny was on the couch in her pajamas...or street clothes, as it was sometimes difficult to tell the difference. She was stuffing her face with potato chips, with Haydn lying on her legs. The dog was fast asleep.

"What? What did I do?" Danny inquired with a furrowed brow.

"You're not ready for one, and you're spoiling your appetite." Nicole snatched the chips from her girlfriend.

Danny's expression didn't clear and she whimpered, reaching out for her salty snack. Nicole gently slapped her hand down, earning another whimper from the lounging woman. Danny pouted and rubbed her hand pathetically, clearly trying to gain some sympathy. Nicole only glared harder.

"Why are you harassing me, woman?" Danny whined.

"Because you're not dressed and we need to get going. Come on," Nicole urged, putting her hand out to help Danny off of the couch.

"Come on?" Danny hopped up and ran her hand through her hair. "We going somewhere?"

Nicole frowned. "Baby, I told you we're going to my grandparents' house for Thanksgiving." *Why is she acting like we haven't discussed this at length?*

"Uh-huh." Danny nodded, even though the cloudy look in her smoke-colored eyes said she clearly had no idea what Nicole was going on about.

"Danny, today is Thanksgiving," Nicole deadpanned.

A caramel face scrunched up. "But, it's Thursday."

"Yes, Thanksgiving is always on a Thursday." Nicole said. *Either Danny lost brain cells to her years of drug use or her childhood was messed up to unfathomable levels. How can she not know when Thanksgiving is?*

Danny scratched her forehead. "What? That's crazy. Who has a

115

holiday on a Thursday? People have to work the next day."

"It depends, but most people get Friday off. Now, go get dressed, so we may leave. I don't want my mother to beat us there."

Danny laughed. "That means we're really late, huh?"

"Yes, and I detest being late. Now, come on, get dressed." She pointed upstairs.

"Is it okay if I wear shorts? We're not going to be outside or anything, right?" Danny was marching toward the stairs.

"Wear whatever you like. They're used to you by now, and there'll be heat on so you won't get sick."

While Danny disappeared upstairs to put on a proper outfit, Nicole straightened up and got Haydn ready for travel. Danny returned, wearing crimson, knee-length shorts, a matching vest, and a black button-down shirt. Her usual chain dangled at her side.

"Didn't brush your hair, huh?" Nicole teased.

"Like you said, they're used to me by now. I only brush my hair for you and special occasions." Danny paused then rushed back upstairs. Upon her return, her ebony hair shone like obsidian and her blonde streaks shone.

Nicole smirked. "Suddenly, it's a special occasion."

"My first Thanksgiving with my wonderful girlfriend and her kick-ass family. Damn right it's a special occasion." Her monster grin put the sun and all of the stars to shame.

Nicole's heart fluttered as she approached her lover. She ran her hands over the vest, savoring the soft, smooth material. She placed a tender kiss on Danny's willing lips.

"Maybe we could be late?" Danny proposed with a sly smile. She even wiggled her eyebrows a little.

"No, we can't be late, especially not for that. God, I don't even want to imagine showing up to a family function after rolling around our bed. So, come on, let's go enjoy dinner and we'll pick up on this when we come back."

Danny sighed dramatically. "Fine. But, you owe me."

Nicole chuckled and went to the kitchen to grab a dish out of the fridge, while Danny took a bouncing Haydn out the door. She put the pup in the backseat and took the food from Nicole, to hold on her lap.

"This the mac and cheese I made?" Danny asked, pointing down to the pan in her lap.

"Yes. We always bring at least one side dish, I told you."

"Why didn't you make potato salad? I love your potato salad."

116

Chuckling, Nicole shook her head. "You just had it two days ago."

"But, it's freaking delicious!"

"That explains why you ate the whole bowl. In a day."

"Trying to say I'm fat?" Danny looked down at her stomach, which was blocked by the mac and cheese.

"I'm trying to say that you ate a whole bowl of potato salad in a day. It's not healthy."

"Says the woman that sat right next to me and ate a freaking bag of cookies! Whole bag of cookies."

"One of us goes to the gym, though."

"Yeah, and the other one of us walks Haydn every day."

Nicole laughed. "You still need to watch what you eat. Besides, other than walking Haydn, you don't get much exercise."

Danny nodded since that was true. She glanced out the window and was quiet for a long moment. "Hey, Chem, why don't you visit your dad's family as much as your mom's?"

"They live farther away." Nicole shrugged. "The drive takes almost four hours. I don't have much time to do that anymore."

"Makes sense. Do you see them a lot?"

"Not as much since we've all grown up and got jobs and families."

"You miss them?"

"Of course I do. We're all so close. They were my first real friends. We all had a blast together." Nicole sighed thinking about her cousins on her father's side. She'd love for Danny to meet them.

Danny smiled a little, even though they both knew she didn't comprehend. Nicole believed Danny would eventually understand. Danny was adapting to things she had only recently experienced, and she seemed to enjoy those things, for the most part.

***

Nicole and Dane were the second set to arrive. Good, Dane assumed she was out of trouble. After all, they weren't late. Again, who made a holiday for a Thursday anyway? Dane handed the macaroni and cheese pan to Kimber, who helped her mother finish up in the kitchen. Nicole and Dane walked into the kitchen anyway, needing to see Nicole's grandmother. The couple greeted Alicia, who hugged both of them and then shooed them out of the area with a wave of her hand.

"Go bother your papa." Alicia pointed them in the direction of the living room.

Nicole giggled, but pulled Dane toward the living room. Nicole's grandfather was the sole occupant of the room. Dane thought that was odd since there was football on. Typically, that was the Bat signal for male members of the family, and her, to gather in the living room.

"Hey, Papa. Where's Jarred and Philip?" Nicole leaned down to hug Benito, who was sitting on the sofa.

"They got sent on a drink run. Apparently, the kids can't drink beer," Benito laughed.

Nicole's brow wrinkled. "Grandma didn't think of that?"

"There was some miscommunication between your grandma and your auntie. So, Katrina ended up picking up the wrong stuff." He shrugged.

"So, we're going to have double beer and no juice?" Nicole chuckled.

Benito laughed and shrugged again. "It happens sometimes." He turned his attention to Dane. "Come on and sit down, Danny. We'll get your football lesson in while you're here."

Dane cocked an eyebrow. "While I'm here?" She looked at her girlfriend and rubbed her forehead, trying to remember whatever she might have forgotten. "I'm going somewhere else?"

"Nowhere to my knowledge." Nicole shook her head. "Papa, what're you talking about?"

Benito's face scrunched up. "What? I figured you both would only be here for a couple of hours, like almost everyone else. You do have to go see Danny's family. It's Thanksgiving, after all."

"So?" Dane asked with a wrinkled brow. She didn't get the connection between the holiday and her family. Even if her family wasn't full of assholes, she didn't see why they'd have to go see her family, too.

"So, you should be going to see your family." Benito said. Dane wasn't following.

"We're not going to see her family, Papa," Nicole said.

His face twisted just a little more. "Oh. Do they live far from here? What made you two decide to come here then?"

"They don't live far. We don't need to see them. Now, let's watch some football," Dane declared with a grin.

The frown that conquered his face let Dane know they damn sure wouldn't be watching football anytime soon. In fact, the hard look in his eyes made her wonder if she was about to be thrown out of the house and never allowed to darken the door again. Nicole taking her hand didn't help put her at ease like it was supposed to.

"You don't see your family on holidays?" Benito's voice boomed and he climbed to his feet. He almost seemed to glare down at her, even though she was much taller.

Dane stood her ground. "No. And I don't want to. To hell with them." Her lover squeezed her hand, but she wasn't sure why. It could've been a scolding, but she doubted it since Nicole was staying out of anything involving the Wolfe family, unless her assistance was requested. But, Dane also doubted it was support since she was talking to Nicole's grandfather.

"What kind of attitude is that? You dismiss your family and think you can just come in here to join ours? We wouldn't take someone who doesn't know how to respect family. What do you think, you can worm your way in here and then take Nikki from us, have her abandon her family like you've abandoned yours?" Benito's voice rose with each word until he was practically screaming.

The shouting drew a crowd, which should've been expected, but the house had been practically empty five minutes ago. It seemed at some point, while the couple was with Benito, the rest of the family showed up. They didn't come in the room, but stood on the outskirts, bewildered if their expressions meant anything.

"I'm not trying anything. Don't wanna take Nick anywhere either," Dane replied calmly.

"Like I believe that! What kind of woman doesn't see her family on Thanksgiving? I don't think you're the type of person I want my granddaughter seeing," Benito said, and shades of Kathleen started to peek through his typically affable demeanor.

"Papa!" Nicole protested.

"That's not your decision." Dane leveled a stony glare at Benito. If she wouldn't bend to Kathleen, who she had to deal with more often than Benito and who was definitely closer to Nicole, then she wouldn't bend for this abnormally cranky old man.

The response got a growl from Benito. "But, it is my decision to have you in my house and if you're going to be disrespectful, you can leave!" he bellowed, pointing to the door. His face was bright red.

"Benny!" Alicia rushed over to her husband. "You can't just kick Danny out."

"I just did! This woman doesn't respect family. She's just like every other loser Nikki's brought home, and I didn't put up with them, so I won't put up with her," Benito said, as if his word was law.

"Papa, you don't even know why Danny doesn't want to see her family!" Nicole replied.

Dane scoffed. "Like they don't want me around and shit like that." Not that it mattered.

Benito looked like he had an epiphany as soon as those words left her mouth. "So horrible your own family doesn't want you! I won't let you corrupt Nikki and then steal her away from us!"

"Papa, it's nothing like that! You're judging Danny without knowing all the facts!" Nicole said.

"Oh, really? Enlighten me," Benito scoffed.

"It's not for me to say, Papa," Nicole replied.

All eyes went to Dane, including a set of beautiful green ones. She had to say something. Nicole needed her to say something. There was no way they'd make it as a couple if she wasn't allowed in Nicole's grandparents' home. Nicole would stop coming just to spite them, and Benito would turn out to be right—she'd have taken Nicole from her family. Dane couldn't live with herself if she did that. Swallowing, she opened her mouth, but nothing came out.

Dane felt Nicole squeeze her hand. Her heart sped up a little and she wondered why it felt like an eternity had gone by. Taking a deep breath, she opened her mouth again.

"I'm not close to my family. Don't wanna be either. They're happy to be rid of me. My father doesn't claim me, and ever since I can remember...he...he beat me." Dane scratched her head and turned her eyes to the floor. "Beat me badly. Beat me just for existing. Beat me because his day sucked. Just beat me. My sister and one of my brothers eventually did the same. My mother ignored me, pretended I never existed, and so did my oldest brother. They never helped me. They just let the rest of them beat me and blame me for everything wrong in the house. So, you want me to go spend holidays with that?" Dane's voice was raw, almost a growl. She had to talk around a lump in her throat and her hands shook.

Dane wasn't sure why she felt so emotional. She was done with her family. But, she supposed it was because she didn't talk about what they did to her. That was buried in the dark graveyard of her mind, but there was always the possibility of those memories coming up out of those coffins. *I wish they'd just stay dead. They don't matter. It doesn't matter*. This was once her mantra as a teenager.

Dane felt Nicole squeeze her hand and then her girlfriend engulfed her in a powerful hug. She returned the embrace automatically. Her head dropped, and Nicole was the only thing in existence, the only thing around her, the only thing that mattered. *It doesn't matter. It doesn't matter. It doesn't matter.*

"It's okay, sweetheart," Nicole whispered, fingers running through Dane's hair.

"I know it is. You're here," Dane replied. *Nicole is the only thing that matters.*

"I'll always be here."

The family thankfully dispersed and went about their business. Dane was happy for that, knowing her own family would've stayed around until the end of the affectionate moment to see if there would be more drama or even bloodshed. Even Kathleen walked off before the hug was over. It was as if they realized they were intruding and did the polite thing, the humane thing. Only Benito remained in the living room with the couple.

Dane's eyes went to Benito as he sat down on the couch. He locked eyes with her. She was now aware they weren't done. Pulling away from Nicole, Dane smiled down at her girlfriend.

"Why don't you go help the women folk while me and your granddad clear the air?" Dane spoke into Nicole's ear.

Nicole pulled away just enough to study Dane's face. "You sure?"

"Yeah. I think this can be salvaged." After all, Benito actually liked her. They had just had a misunderstanding, which she had learned was easy to fix thanks to her time with Nicole.

"You can do this alone? I don't want to leave you if you really need me."

Dane offered her a small smile. "Angel, I'm a big dog. You said so yourself. Gotta let me off the leash every now and again."

Nicole chuckled and nodded. She hugged Dane once more before turning to leave. Dane had to resist the urge to slap Nicole on the ass because she was certain that was inappropriate to do in front of her lover's family. So, Nicole walked away unmolested, and Dane turned her complete attention to Benito as she ran a hand through her hair.

***

Nicole went into the kitchen and found "the women folk" putting the finishing touches on dinner. Jody was taking drinks and minor groceries out of a plastic bag on the table with several more resting on the floor at her feet. Nicole bent down to pick up a sack and immediately looked into her cousin's eyes.

"Nikki..." the teenager obviously had questions.

"Jody, I can't talk about Danny's family situation. You'd have to talk to her about it," Nicole said.

"Sweet pea, did you know about Danny's troubled family?" Alicia asked.

"I don't know all the details, but I do know her family did awful things to her and would continue doing terrible things to her if she were around them." Of course, Nicole did know some major details. They disturbed her so greatly she tried to bury them until Danny was ready to talk, which might be never. Sometimes, never suited Nicole just fine, but eventually Danny would need to get all of the abuse off her chest.

Kathleen scoffed and shook her head. "I'm not surprised her father abused her."

"You know her father?" Kimber asked.

"Unfortunately. He's not the best of men. In fact, there are times when I'm sure he's the lowest of the low, worse than a beast. But, just because Danny's from unfortunate circumstances doesn't mean I accept her for you." Kate wagged her finger. "If anything, her family situation makes her less acceptable. She's clearly not normal and possibly unstable."

"That's not fair," Katrina argued.

"Danny's not unstable. And what is normal, anyway?" Nicole asked.

"You say this now, but you know that the abused tend to grow up and be abusers," Kate said.

"Danny is *not* an abuser." Nicole actually growled at her mother. She didn't want anyone to put that out there. Danny was already scared something like that could happen, just because she'd been beaten so much in her life.

"Kate, don't stir up Nikki. You shouldn't speculate on Danny's behavior if you don't know anything about her. She's not her father and you shouldn't judge her by his actions. He is him and she is her." Alicia pretty much ended the argument before the holiday was ruined.

Kate sighed. "Nikki, I just worry about you, especially you being with a Wolfe. A cast off Wolfe who doesn't seem to have any goals in life, or direction."

"Mommy, Danny's nothing like that, and I've asked you several times not to talk about her like that. I know you worry, but Danny's a good person, she's finding herself after having a lot happen to her, and I love her."

"And that says it all, so let's get back to enjoying our family and having Thanksgiving dinner," Alicia said.

They all silently agreed Alicia was correct. They went to work to prepare everything for Thanksgiving. Nicole was surprised Jody stuck around since she was usually wrist deep in some piece of outdated technology minutes after entering the house. But, from the way Jody kept looking at her, Nicole was aware that her cousin had questions. Nicole wasn't going to tell them anything about Danny's home life; that was on Danny to share if she so desired.

***

Danny sat on the sofa with Benito. They were the only ones in the living room. Benito had turned the television off, but said nothing for a few minutes that seemed like forever.

"Danny, first off, I'm sorry I shouted at you and judged you like that. I do like you. You seem to be Nikki's perfect match and you make her happy."

"Thanks. I do my best, What you did wasn't cool."

He sighed and shook his head in shame. "No, it wasn't. I'm sorry, but I'm sensitive and paranoid about family. I understand you a little better than everyone else, though."

She arched an eyebrow. "What do you mean?"

"I grew up in a house where my father beat my mother. He never touched us kids, but he beat the shit out of her on a daily basis. If it was too hot, too cold, cloudy, he'd beat her. They say if you grow up in house like that, you're likely to grow up to abuse people, too. That always scared the shit out of me, that one day I could become that bastard," he growled.

She swallowed. "Have you ever felt like a monster? Or there's a monster inside of you?" For a long time, she'd believed there was something wrong with her and then sometimes she'd feel sick inside. She was certain there was a monster in there and it wanted out. She used to think other people could see it and that was why her family treated her the way they did. She fought down the monster and demons with drugs, alcohol, sex, and music, but they always seemed to be gnawing at her heels...until recently. While the demons were still there, she felt like the monster...it was shrinking. Maybe one day, it'd vanish completely.

"Yeah, I felt like there had to be a monster in me because he was a

123

monster and he was my father. And I felt weak because I couldn't stop this man from hurting my mama."

Dane nodded. She knew that feeling all too well. Sometimes, she'd wish she'd just die instead of feeling so helpless and weak. She wanted to tell him, this man who might understand, but she couldn't. It'd be revealing too much of herself, like standing before him in the nude. Only Nicole could see her like that.

"I promised myself I wouldn't be like him ever. I don't even speak Spanish because of him," Benito said, which earned a raised eyebrow. "He'd scream at her in Spanish. Sometimes, when I was much younger, hearing it would give me flashbacks."

She nodded. She used to get flashbacks, too. The nightmares were worse, but she didn't have them as frequently anymore. "So, what happened?"

"We grew up, moved out. She stayed and he kept beating her. We told her to leave. Hell, we—my siblings and I—we offered our homes to her, but she refused."

"This story doesn't end with someone killing someone else, right?" she asked because that damn sure wouldn't make her feel any better.

Chuckling, he shook his head. "Thankfully, God saw fit to take care of that bastard young, so my mama still had some life left to live."

"Did that monster in you ever come out?"

"No. Nothing beyond just being angry, which was mostly directed at him anyway. I never laid my hands on anyone. Before realizing I was my own person that had nothing to do with him, I vowed I wouldn't be like him. When I met Alicia, I knew I *couldn't* be like him. I could never raise my hand to her in anger. I love her way too much and when Kate was born, I knew I could never touch her in anger, either. I cherish the family I made with Alicia. This family is everything to me, which is why I flipped out on you."

Dane nodded. "You want to protect this wonderful family you made, which makes sense to me. I know family is important to you because that's passed on to Nick. I want to be better for her. Before, I knew there was a monster in me, and I tried to drown it in alcohol, drugs, and shit like that. I wanted to forget it was there or suppress it, but not anymore. I don't need those things anymore, and I don't do them anymore thanks to Nick. When I'm with her, I don't even feel like there's a monster there, and all I want to do is make her happy."

He smiled. "That's good. It's great you got off of drugs, too. My brother used those to cope and it almost killed him before he went into rehab."

Dane nodded again; pleased he was not upset with the fact that she used to be on drugs. She knew everything was all right when he turned on the television. Football appeared on the screen and Benito's sons-in-law seemed to come out of nowhere. They all greeted Dane in friendly ways with smiles and handshakes. They, thankfully, didn't ask about her family, and they all just enjoyed the game.

***

Dinner was served earlier than Dane expected. Apparently Kimber's family and Katrina's family had to go to their husbands' families. They sat at the dining room table as they had during the Easter dinner. Dane thought that was a little funny; it was like a television show.

Things got even funnier to her, but not like a joke funny. It was just weird to Dane. They went around the table and everybody stated what they were thankful for. She supposed she could get used to such closeness, but it'd take some time. Eventually, all eyes went to her.

"Danny, do you want to say something?" Nicole took Danny's hand and squeezed. Dane smiled.

"Um...sure. I mean, I'm thankful for tons of stuff. I'm thankful just to be alive and to be here with the woman I love and share my first Thanksgiving with her wonderful family. I haven't had a normal Thanksgiving in almost twenty years. So, thank you for this."

The family clapped for her and her smile turned into a grin. They said grace, which Dane expected. They ate a grand Thanksgiving dinner. Dane enjoyed it, smiling through the whole meal. Nicole smiled, too, as conversation flowed and happiness seemed almost tangible.

"You okay?" Nicole asked her lover in a low tone.

"Yeah, love this, though. Your family's great."

Nicole smiled, beaming at the compliment. The expression, of course, made Dane happy. It was a good day, but it was a little overwhelming. Dane just wasn't used to all of the friendly chatter and sincere questions, especially from multiple people. Dane sat out much of the conversation.

When the main meal was done, the family left the table. Dane found a corner to be alone in, sitting by the stairs near the front door. She curled up by the wall and closed her eyes for a moment. The peace was fleeting as she felt a presence. Opening her eyes, she was greeted by the sight of a chubby, smiling face.

"Hey, Wayne." She gave the baby her own bright smile.

Wayne's deep, umber eyes shined with delight. He wasted no time climbing on her since she was on his level. Danny didn't have much interaction with Wayne, because he was usually napping while she played with his siblings. According to Nicole, Wayne was a nighttime baby, who liked to hang out late and then sleep all day. Danny had been around him enough to know he liked her hair, so she watched his hands.

"Hi." The baby hit her in the shoulder. She wondered if he normally greeted people in such a manner.

"So, Wayne, do you talk?".

Wayne didn't respond as his eyes went straight to her hair. He put his hand up and petted where she knew her blond streaks were the thickest. Seconds later, he tugged her hair.

"Ow, dude! Your grubby little mitts. Gimme that," Dane said, pulling his hands away.

Something about holding his tiny hand in her much larger paw made her feel warm on the inside. She rolled his fingers around on her own before she even realized what she was doing. Her eyes drifted to his hand as he giggled.

"You have long fingers, little man. That could be good for you when you get older. Grow up and play piano. Girls love it. They love musicians really. Doesn't matter what you play. But, you have to play it well. If you play like crap, they'll treat you like that every chance they get." Wayne giggled more and then grabbed Dane's nose with his free hand. "You won't be getting me, boyo. I don't swing that way, but I can totally help you. I'm not too smooth when it comes to talking, but if you play music, you don't have to talk. And if you sing, it's even better."

Wayne laughed and let go of her nose. He caressed her cheek gently and she hummed. Suddenly, he grinned and curled into her chest. She hummed again and he snuggled closer.

"I get it. You like singing, too, huh? Well, for girls, it'll be different. Some might like you singing in a metal style, which I do very well. Others might like soul. I can do that, too. But, a lot of them like when you sing real soft, only for their ears. Like this." Dane cleared her throat. She began singing in a tender, soothing tone. "You start out really low, so she has to sit closer. Cradle her so she knows you really chose her. Look deep in her eyes and tell her no lies and that she makes your soul stir."

Wayne yawned and his eyes drifted shut. Dane glanced down at him when he settled and smiled. She continued singing.

***

"Uh-oh, look who's holding the baby." Katrina grinned as she glanced over by the stairs. Her mother, sisters, and most importantly, her niece turned to see what she was talking about.

"Danny," Nicole squeaked.

"She looks pretty comfortable with a baby, too," Kimber said, while Kathleen frowned.

"And Wayne fell asleep on her. Too freaking cute." Katrina snapped a picture of the moment on her phone. Danny must've spotted the movement because she looked up just in time to see the flash.

"Wha?" Danny blinked a few times, blinded by the bright light. Suddenly, her eyes were wide and she seemed to panic. Rushing to her feet, she held onto Wayne. "I didn't do anything. He just crawled on me and fell asleep."

Katrina smiled softly. "Calm down, Danny. It's fine."

"You sure? I really didn't do anything," Danny insisted, practically shoving the child into his mother's arms. Katrina's brow furrowed as she accepted her son.

Nicole rushed over and went to Danny, wrapping her arms around Danny. "Baby, calm down. Aunt Katrina isn't Sharon. She doesn't think you would do anything to harm Wayne. She doesn't think you hurt him."

"Sharon?" Katrina echoed and then shook the name away. "Doesn't matter. Danny, I definitely don't think you'd hurt Wayne. Hold him and entertain him whenever you want."

"Really?" Danny sounded incredulous with heartbreaking wide eyes.

"Really. Danny, my niece trusts you with her heart, and you're obviously taking good care of her. I don't think you'd hurt my son based on how you treat my niece. Not to mention my other kids adore you," Katrina said.

"Uh…" Danny wasn't sure what to say.

"You're good with kids. And you look good with a baby in your arms," Katrina smiled.

Danny blushed a little, and Nicole pulled her a little closer. Katrina got ready to leave. Kimber and her family did the same. Danny and Nicole hung out for a little while longer, but when Haydn started whining, they both were all too aware that it was time to go.

"Bye, Grandma." Nicole hugged Alicia. She turned to Benito. "Bye, Papa. Thank you for being big enough to admit your mistake."

"It's no problem. I shouldn't have jumped all over Danny like that." Benito hugged Nicole and then shook Danny's hand. "Keep taking care of my granddaughter."

"Doing my best, sir."

***

The day ended well and the couple cuddled together in bed. Nicole felt closer to Danny and she knew it was because Danny cared enough about her to reveal parts of herself to her family. She planted a gentle kiss to Danny's jaw.

"What was that for? Not that I'm complaining." Danny pressed Nicole into her side.

"It was for being you. Thank you for not freaking out on my grandfather."

Danny shrugged. "It was no big deal. I know he's just protective of you. Besides, it worked out."

"Which is great. And you know you did look good holding Wayne. Were you singing to him?"

"Yeah. He liked it."

"You think...you think you want children to sing to?" Nicole asked in a low voice.

Danny shrugged. "Still haven't thought about kids, Nick. Maybe I could handle one, though. But, I'm not sure since all the kids I interact with go home at the end of the day."

"Don't think too much about it, sweetheart. Thank you for today, though."

"No, thank you for today. It's been a long time since I've had a good Thanksgiving. Not since the Briarmoors."

"You had Thanksgiving with them?"

"Only once. It was good, even though I don't remember a lot of it. I was really little, but it doesn't matter. I liked today."

"Well, I hope there are many more good Thanksgivings in our future, as well as other holidays."

"I like the sound of that, too."

Aloe

"WHERE ARE WE GOING again?" Dane asked, as they jumped into Nicole's car. Haydn was already asleep, so he was locked up in his crate until they returned.

"*Blank Slate*," Nicole answered for probably the tenth time. It was amazing she had not sighed yet.

"I still have no clue what that is. Sounds like a date rape drink or something." Dane chuckled.

"I told you, it's like an arcade, but more mature."

"How can an arcade be mature?"

An auburn eyebrow arched. "Asks the woman who practically bit my head off when I suggested that video games were for teenagers?"

Dane didn't have a retort, so she pouted instead. The expression earned her a sweet kiss on the cheek, which turned the pout into a smile. Dane decided to just wait and see what this mature arcade was like.

"Mina and Clara are meeting us there?" Dane asked.

"Yes, they'll meet us there."

"With their partners?" Not that Clara seemed to have a steady person in her life or that Mina was likely to take her husband out with the group.

Nicole scoffed. "You know you're the only partner allowed to hang out with us. It's a girls' night."

"I guess it's good they think of me as a girl for these things. Your grandfather thinks of me as one of the boys."

"That's just how Papa is. I'm glad he's so accepting, but his mind still separates couples into male and female. I've been his baby girl all my life, so I'm obviously the female. That leaves you to be the male. Does it bother you?"

Dane shook her head. "Doesn't bother me at all. Glad he still likes me and accepts me. I like your family. I like your friends, too. I mean, how cool are they to take you out because school's over?"

Nicole smiled brightly. "They are good people, aren't they? They've always been supportive, especially Mina."

"Even when she accidentally takes advantage of you?"

"She doesn't do it much anymore and before she did it because she respects my intelligence and opinion. She's not bad."

Dane smiled. "I know. I like Mina." Mina was always there for Nicole, and for them, when they needed something. Dane knew that was more than most people could ask for.

"And Mina likes you, which is another reason you're always invited out when it's just us girls. Mina likes hanging out with you. Clara, too. They like you."

Dane had nothing to add. She liked her lover's friends, but found it a little odd they invited her out with them. They were a close trio and sometimes she felt like she was intruding, even though they invited her and were always friendly. She went along, though, because it made Nicole ridiculously happy.

Nicole pulled into the large parking lot where bright lights proclaimed the dark building *Blank Slate*. When they got out, Nicole scanned the lot, searching for her friends or their vehicles. It was dark, so Dane wasn't sure if Nicole saw anything or not. Nicole eventually took her hand and tugged her toward the entrance of the "mature arcade."

"We can wait inside if they're not here at the door," Nicole said.

Dane nodded and allowed her girlfriend to lead her to the door. Dane was surprised they had to show identification to get in. Briefly, she wondered if she had photo ID.

"Should have my driver's license," Dane muttered to herself as she opened her wallet.

"Baby, I told you to make sure you had photo ID." Nicole sighed.

"Did you? Because you were saying a lot of things while wearing a towel. I will confess, I didn't hear much beyond the sound of your breasts bouncing." It didn't help that Nicole slipped on a blouse that hugged her torso and complimented her cleavage to the point Dane almost drooled.

Nicole laughed. "You're awful."

Dane smiled, especially since she'd found her driver's license. They flashed their IDs and, after close scrutiny of Dane's license, they were allowed in. They found Mina and Clara waiting, as they descended the stairs.

"Well, it's about time." Mina grinned.

"I had to get Danny to put pants on." Nicole, obviously, had not considered how that sounded.

Mina smirked and her eyes sparkled with mischief, even in the dark. "Did we interrupt your own little, private 'school's out' celebration?"

Nicole blushed and Dane came to her girlfriend's aid. "She meant that one literally, Mina. I was gonna wear some basketball shorts, but the clothing Nazi here wouldn't let me." Dane jabbed her thumb at the redhead.

"What?" Clara said incredulously. "It's in the teens out there. You could've gotten sick."

Dane shrugged, but Nicole appreciated the backup. "That's what I said."

"And you were right." Clara laughed. The others chuckled a little, too.

***

"Danny, I can't believe how much you suck at pool." Mina laughed, as she bent over the pool table they were all crowded around.

Danny only shrugged and smiled, but the expression didn't reach her eyes. Nicole moved closer to her lover and wrapped her arms around Danny. Moving her pool stick to one hand, she used her free hand to take Danny's left hand. She gently stroked the scarred extremity with her thumb.

"I used to be better at pool. Haven't played in a while," Danny said. Nicole waited until her friends were focused completely on the game before she brought up the topic with her lover.

"Is your hand bothering you?" Nicole asked, in a low tone, as she continued to caress her lover's hand.

"Not really, but it's limited, especially with stuff I don't do regularly. It's not bad, but I'm gonna keep sucking at pool for the night." Danny's slight smile showed she didn't have a problem with reality.

Nicole nodded and held on to her girlfriend until it was her turn to shoot. She made a little show of bending over for Danny, knowing grey eyes watched her intently, and wiggled a little before demonstrating her billiards skills. Danny whistled as Nicole pocketed a ball, but Nicole was sure the sound was directed at her ass and not her skills.

"Nikki, don't start being perfect now," Mina groaned. "Give me a chance to win once."

Nicole smirked. "I don't think so. I like winning and I need to show off to my hot girlfriend." She earned some surprised looks from her friends as she knocked another ball into the side pocket.

"Is my dear, sweet, angel a pool shark?" Danny put her hand on her chest as if she were scandalized.

"Damn near," Mina grumbled, frowning at the table.

Danny laughed, but Nicole had a good time displaying her pool prowess in front of her lover. Of course, her swagger caused her to mess up because she tried a trick shot. She cursed under her breath and went to stand by her lover, as Clara went to the table to shoot.

"Are you all pool sharks?" Danny asked, as Clara cleared the table. "Maybe I should just fetch drinks or something," she quipped with a smile.

They didn't take up her offer and Danny stayed for a few more games. She was the worst player amongst them, and Nicole felt bad that her baby had barely sunk any balls. But, Danny seemed to be having fun, smiling through the whole thing. She even joked about her bad playing.

"How about we go see if some bowling lanes are open?" Clara said, once the game was over.

"There's a bowling alley in here, too?" Danny had already seen the arcade part when they walked through rows of new and classic video games to get to the pool tables.

"Just a few lanes. Let's go see if we can get one." Nicole took her lover by the hand and pulled her away. Her friends followed behind.

They were given a number and directed where to watch for notice that their lane was open. They had a few people ahead of them, so they went to kill time at the air hockey tables. Danny had never played.

"Sweetheart, seriously, you've never played air hockey before?" Nicole asked as they stood at a table. It was clear her lover had no clue what to do because she didn't even know how to hold the mallet.

"Nope." Danny grinned.

"Why not? You've been to an arcade before, right?" Nicole inquired.

"Yeah, but I always play the video games, pinball, and junk like that. Never played anything requiring more than one person."

"Of course," Nicole laughed. "I'll take it easy on you until you get the hang of it."

Danny laughed and they began playing. She showed signs of getting the hang of air hockey after a couple of games, just when it was time to go bowl. Nicole figured they could go back to hockey after bowling.

"This bowling alley is really...neon." Danny squinted a bit as she tried to take it all in. The lanes were dark, but there were plenty of lights, including the pins that glowed yellow, pink, and orange. Markers on the lane were all the same colors.

"It's supposed to make it feel like a club," Nicole replied.

"Although, it makes no sense for them to make the bowling alley look like a club, when the upstairs is an actual club," Clara shook her head.

They all grabbed balls as they piled onto their lane. Mina put their names onto the screen, and they got started. Danny proved to be much better at bowling than pool or air hockey.

"Yo, she is kicking our asses! Can I win at something?" Mina playfully complained, as Danny picked up another spare.

"Serves you right for putting us up there in age order," Clara huffed, folding her arms across her chest. She was the first to go because of that order.

Mina only smiled, having the nerve to look innocent. Clara sucked her teeth and rolled her eyes before taking her turn to bowl. Mina made a mocking face at her back.

"Don't think I don't know what you're doing, Mina. You're such a child sometimes," Clara said.

"I'm a child says the woman being petulant over having to go first," Mina countered.

"I'll get us some drinks to calm Mina down," Nicole proposed. "You want anything, Big Dog? Some ice to cool your hot streak perhaps?"

Danny stuck her tongue out at the redhead. "Soda's fine. Hurry back."

Nicole nodded and trotted off to the nearby bar. The bar was surprisingly clear, so she ordered quickly. While waiting for the glasses, a distinguished looking man stood next to her. She glanced at him, but didn't pay him any mind. So, of course, he started talking to her.

"Hello," he said with a smile.

"Hello," she replied to be polite.

"Here by yourself?"

"Not hardly. And just so you know, asking a woman a question like that is quite creepy." To her surprise, he laughed. *Why is that funny? It's the truth.*

The creep smiled. "Maybe you could help me with that. I could ask you a series of questions and you could tell me if they're good or not."

She had to push down the urge to vomit. "I don't think my *girlfriend* would like that," she smirked. She hoped that would get him to leave her alone.

"I'm sure your friend won't mind you going out to dinner with a handsome guy," the creep said, still confidently smiling.

"Considering the fact that she put a ring on it, I think she would mind." She waved her hand in front of his face for him to see her promise ring. The bartender snickered, but was obviously trying to avoid laughing.

The creep blinked hard as he took in the ring, and his confident expression fell. He had the nerve to glare at her.

"You've got to be kidding me. You're a dyke," he huffed; quite offended by her if the look in his eyes meant anything.

"Yes. In fact, I think speaking with you might have been the cause of my lesbianism. I'm sure it happens a lot around you." She didn't like his attitude. How dare he insult her after coming onto her. All she'd wanted was to get her drinks, return to her friends, and enjoy her night with them. The bartender snickered again and didn't bother to hide it that time.

The creep growled, but didn't get the chance for a retort. The bartender stepped back over with Nicole's order, coming between Nicole and her unwanted admirer. The bartender winked at Nicole.

"I'd quit while I was ahead if I were you, buddy. I'm pretty sure the tall one is her girlfriend, and she could probably snap you in half." The bartender warned the creep, nodding to the trio on the bowling lane. He didn't look pleased with that information. Nicole took the chance to escape, having already paid for the drinks.

***

It was Nicole's turn to bowl. Dane and the others looked over to the bar, ready to call her back to them. They all stopped when they saw a guy talking to Nicole.

"You're not going to go punch him in the face or something, are you?" Mina asked the musician.

Dane scoffed. "Don't need to. Nick's mine." She didn't have to go all peacock over some guy. She wasn't that insecure. Now, if he touched Nicole, then things might change.

Mina opened her mouth, possibly to argue. But, her mouth closed with a pop as Nicole briskly walked away from the guy. Obviously, she expected her friend to just put up with the guy, which Nicole would've done in the past. Returning to the group, Nicole put the drinks down on a small table.

"Is it my go?" Nicole met their stares with a curious expression.

"Yeah," Dane answered.

"Nicole, was that guy at the bar hitting on you?" Mina asked.

"I'm sure he thought so, but he was really pathetic." Nicole grabbed her ball.

"Usually, you'd let the guy talk your ear off," Mina said.

"There's no reason to listen to him ask me out since I'm happily in a relationship with Danny." Nicole rolled her first ball.

Mina smiled and walked over to Dane. She quickly gave Dane a handshake, silently thanking her. Dane wasn't sure what the thanks were for, and didn't ask. It was clear Mina didn't want to talk about it. Dane let it go and focused on bowling.

After bowling, Dane wandered away from the group. They were at an arcade and she had to play certain games: pinball, a fighting game, and some racing games to be exact, or she'd feel cheated. She lost track of time.

"Baby, here you are. We were wondering where you wandered off to." Nicole stood next to Dane's seat.

"Wanted to play some video games while we're here." She shrugged and saw Nicole nod out of the corner of her eye.

"So, you can drive a car in a video game, but I'm the chauffeur in real life?" Nicole tittered.

"Trust me, if you saw my last couple of games, you'd probably not want me next to the car, never mind in it, and you'd never think of me driving, ever again."

"Does your leg really bother you that much?"

"I'm not sure how to explain it. Sometimes my leg and foot press harder than it feels. Other times, they don't respond as much as I think they are. It's weird." She supposed it was the nerve damage, but she couldn't be sure. They were silent for a few seconds. "Wanna play?"

Emerald eyes blinked. "Play?"

"Yeah. Have a race with me." Dane tilted her head toward the empty chair to her left.

Nicole shrugged. "What the hell. After all, you played a bunch of games with me."

Dane smiled and nodded. Nicole eased into the seat next to her, and Dane put several tokens in the machine. Nicole picked a car and they began racing.

"What the hell? The steering for this car is awful!" Nicole complained as she crashed into a wall. She hit the steering wheel with the heel of her hand before hastily trying to get back on track.

Dane laughed until her car flipped. "Son of a bitch!"

"Is the steering on your car just as bad as this?"

"The steering's loose on all of these, but the thing killing me is that the damned gear shift isn't right."

"Gear shift? You're driving a stick?"

"Always do."

"How do you know how to drive a stick? Hell, who even taught you to drive? A friend?"

"Kinda. The crew I hung out with as a teen just gave keys to people, despite their age or if they had a license. I had driven dozens of times before I was fifteen. At night, drunk, and high."

Nicole scoffed. "God really does protect fools and babies."

"I guess I had double the protection back then. I don't know how I never had an accident. Anyway, when I was old enough, I went out and got my license because, for some reason in my head, it was worse to be stopped and not have a license than it was to be stopped and be totally intoxicated on all types of shit." It still made no sense to her, but it did make sense, somehow.

Shaking her head, Nicole chuckled just a bit. "Only you, baby. So, how did you learn to drive a stick? Just by observing?"

"Knew a few people with stick shifts that showed me what to do when they were sober. Guess they realized they didn't want people fucking up their rides. Of course, they showed me a lot more when they were drunk and tended to mess up their rides on their own."

Nicole nodded. "Did you ever own a car?"

"Nah. Never needed one."

"Or wanted one?"

Dane laughed. "That too. Video game cars are more than enough for me."

Nicole giggled and they continued racing. She was as bad at racing as Dane had been with air hockey, but they played on. Eventually, Mina and Clara found the couple and joined the races. Clara was surprisingly talented, but she admitted she played such games with her son.

"I think you practice this video game thing," Mina accused Clara after she won several races. The group rose from their seats, ready to do something else.

"I need to practice," Nicole said.

"You did crash a lot." Dane put her arm around the redhead's waist. "We can practice at home."

"Please, when you two go home, we all know you won't be practicing video games." Clara smirked.

"Practicing baby making if anything," Mina joked.

"No more drinks for Mina," Nicole stated.

"I only had one," Mina protested.

"And that's all you're going to have since you need to drive home. I'm not calling Shawn to come get you, and you know Clara will leave you sitting in your car to teach you a lesson," Nicole pointed out.

Mina had no response to that, so Dane assumed it was true. She couldn't believe someone as nice as Clara would leave one of her best friends. But, Mina smiled, so Dane assumed it wasn't a big deal. The friends seemed to be enjoying each other. Mina even led them off to Skee-Ball.

They didn't drink any more liquor, which was really the only thing that made the place "mature," aside from the fact that only adults were allowed inside. Dane supposed the dim atmosphere and club music helped, but she didn't consider those things mature. Clara did say that there was a club upstairs, so that might've been the thing that made it mature, but she didn't see why that should affect the arcade. She stopped thinking about it as they moved on to the next activity.

***

"Did you have fun?" Nicole asked as she and Danny prepared for bed. They had come home late that night...or early that morning, depending on who was asked.

"Yeah, it was cool. I still feel a little weird hanging out with your friends. I mean, you don't hang out with Crow or Terri," Danny replied from the bed, rubbing lotion on her arms and legs.

Nicole was in the bathroom, going through her own skin care regime, which was much more intense and extensive.

"You're right, but they want to include you. They want to show their approval of you. You're the only person I've ever been with that they ask me to bring around. Plus, they like being around you. And, for the record, I don't hang out with your friends, because you don't hang out with them when I'm around. Crow's invited me places before, and Terri only comes here because all you two do is play video games. So, it's not really weird. Do you want me to tell my friends to stop because you feel uncomfortable?" Mina and Clara would probably be a little hurt if Danny didn't want to hang out with them. They really did like her.

There was silence for a moment. "No, you don't have to. If you don't mind it, then I'm okay with it. Just tell me if it ever gets annoying to you to have me around when you want to be with your friends."

"I doubt it will, but I'll keep that in mind."

Nicole had joined Danny in bed, the lights were out, and the couple settled in against each other. They exchanged a few kisses.

"Today was a good day," Danny whispered.

"We'll have a few more like this since I have a free month as far as school is concerned," Nicole replied.

"Does that mean you'll play video games with me?" Danny looked so hopeful.

Nicole laughed. "Well, I do want to stop crashing so much."

That response put a smile on Danny's face. She fell asleep with that smile lighting up her features. Nicole couldn't help herself and tenderly kissed her sleeping girlfriend.

"I think we'll do a bit more than play games while we have the time." Nicole spoke to the air; but Danny continued smiling, as if she approved of Nicole's plan.

Sling

IT WAS NEW YEARS' Eve, and Dane found herself inside her home on the holiday, for the first time in a long time. She didn't mind. In fact, she had been the one to push for it. Nicole hadn't fought her very hard when she mentioned staying in. The redhead had seemed somewhat relieved by the suggestion.

Dane wondered if Nicole was as exhausted as she was from the passing holidays. Christmas Eve and Christmas had done Dane in. The shopping leading up to those holidays had definitely helped in tiring her out. This was her second Christmas with Nicole, but her first with Nicole's family. It was Dane's first time shopping for more than one person, which was nerve wracking itself, without the additional worry of wondering if everyone would actually like what they received. Dane had freaked out several times during the month of December.

She doubted December really troubled Nicole, beyond having to worry about her and the fact that she freaked out throughout the month. Nicole was used to spending the holidays with her family and shopping for her family. Dane was willing to bet it was last New Years' Eve that made her angel eager to stay home more than anything else.

"What do you want to do to ring in the New Year?" Nicole plopped down on the sofa and quickly, she cuddled into Dane. The musician wasted no time wrapping her arms around Nicole and pulled her closer.

"What did you have in mind?" Dane nuzzled her lover's soft neck. Taking a moment, she breathed in the soft, light scent of Nicole's body lotion. Just underneath that, she picked up the delightful aroma that was all Nicole and made her neck very tempting. She placed several light kisses to the area.

Nicole giggled. "Hot chocolate."

Dane blinked and pulled back to look at her girlfriend's face. "Hot chocolate? Are you serious? It's New Year's."

A small smile lit up Nicole's features. "I know, but I'm in the mood for hot chocolate with lots of whipped cream." She licked her lips at the thought of the sweet drink.

Dane laughed. She should've known her lover was serious. She still couldn't understand how, out of the two of them, *she* was the pudgy one. Nicole's sweet tooth ruled her. Dane guessed that going to the gym paid off, even though that idea was definitely not enough to get her in a gym.

"At least I know this break from tradition isn't because we got drunk last year," Dane said.

Nicole chuckled. At the last New Year's celebration, Nicole had half a glass of champagne and Dane had only had a sip. That sip had completely scandalized Nicole, who seemed to think Dane even being around alcohol would cause her to flip out. Dane understood; New Year's had come so shortly after she had abandoned Nicole only to return high, drunk, and injured. For a long time, Nicole didn't seem to want her to even look at alcohol. Dane had obliged for the most part.

"You know, I was so tempted to give you white grape juice," Nicole admitted with a guilty expression.

"I was surprised you didn't. I expected you to do something like that," Dane replied with a shrug. "I would've accepted it," she added in a low voice before kissing Nicole's temple. She would've done anything, as long as Nicole stayed with her.

"I know you would've. I want what's best for you, but I don't want to control you. I definitely don't want to baby you, like you thought I was doing."

Dane nodded. "I wouldn't have took that as babying." While she had some trouble figuring out how to let Nicole take care of her, something like alcohol, she would've understood was a reaction to her overall bad behavior. Dane deserved that reaction.

Sighing, Nicole shook her head. "Sometimes, it's hard to tell which I'm doing, especially now that you pointed it out, but I knew then that would've been way too much. Especially since you told me that you could handle one glass."

"Not to mention I didn't care about the glass after we got to the other tradition." She wiggled her eyebrows.

Nicole giggled, but blushed at the same time. "That's actually why I was happy you said we should stay in. I've never been so happy to cancel on Mina before."

"That's why I wanted to stay in, too!" Well, it was one of the reasons, anyway.

Last year, the couple had gone out with Mina and her husband. It was actually pretty fun. They went to an upscale bar, had plenty of conversations with people, and even danced as much as Dane could before her knee throbbed. They did the countdown while watching the ball drop. They toasted, which was when Dane had her sip of champagne. They shared a New Year's kiss, and moments later, they found out they probably shouldn't celebrate the New Year in public.

The kiss started out simple enough, just a gentle press of their lips. Dane had even pulled away slightly, but Nicole hadn't been ready to let her go. Dane wasn't one to argue and stayed in place. Her eyes fluttered shut, and she forgot they were in a crowded bar. Nicole must've done the same, because seconds later their mouths were open and their tongues were caressing each other. Once Dane's hand drifted to Nicole's breast, the whole place erupted into cheers. The couple jumped away from each other as if poisoned.

Nicole blushed, but Dane got thoroughly pissed off. In the past, she wouldn't have cared about putting on a show, but this involved the woman she loved. Nicole was sacred to Dane, and nothing they did was for the entertainment of others. They had left shortly after the kiss and never returned to that particular establishment.

"So, hot chocolate or do you want something else?" Nicole asked.

"Nah, hot chocolate is good. Are we going to have the little marshmallows in it, too?" Dane pinched her thumb and forefinger close together to show the size of the marshmallows.

"Of course." Nicole laughed.

"Just hurry back. The ball's gonna drop soon."

Nicole nodded and went off to make their drinks. Dane had to find a channel that aired the ball drop. She found one showing musical acts before the big moment. The noise must've reached the den because Haydn rushed out, even though he had been asleep. Showing that pets sometimes took on the characteristics of their owners, Haydn moved along with the music as if he enjoyed it.

"Is that our little man up past his bedtime?" Nicole returned to the living room with two mugs of hot cocoa.

Dane made space on the coffee table for their drinks. Nicole put the mugs on top of the coasters. She sat down on the couch and cuddled into Dane. Haydn came over to inspect the beverages, but grew disinterested when he pressed his nose on the hot cup. Whining, he went back to the music, and his owners laughed a little at his accident. They turned their attention to the television and found Haydn blocking their view, because he kept jumping up.

"Hey, down in front," Dane called to the energetic pup. His head popped up every few seconds.

"Let him tire himself out. We're not really watching the show." Nicole rubbed Dane's stomach to keep her relaxed.

Dane didn't argue with that. Haydn certainly did tire himself after a few minutes of constant moving and jumping. He went to have some water and put himself back to bed in the den. His owners couldn't help laughing at his quick exit.

"He left at the right time," Dane stated, as the ball appeared. The camera focused on the crowd below the ball. They all appeared to be having a good time in the freezing cold. Dane reached for her hot drink, took a sip, and ended up with a whipped cream mustache.

"You look silly." Nicole giggled and leaned in, running her tongue over Dane's top lip.

Dane's eyes drifted shut briefly, and she moaned. "You keep that up and we won't be counting down to the New Year."

Nicole tittered. "Not much of a threat."

Dane definitely couldn't dispute that and didn't try. Nicole reached for her own mug, sipping her hot chocolate. The countdown began when they had gotten halfway through the warm beverage. They stopped drinking to save something to toast with. Once the countdown was under five, they turned to each other. Staring into each other's eyes, they gently touched mugs as the host on television wished the viewers a happy New Year.

"Happy New Year, baby," Nicole whispered.

"Happy New Year, angel."

Nicole held up her mug to make a toast. "To a lifetime of peaceful New Years with you and may this year smile good fortune on us as the previous year did by giving us the strength to carry on together."

"I'll drink to that," Dane said, and they touched mugs again before taking drinks. "To years of enjoying each other, loving each other, and always being there for each other."

Nicole smiled and tipped her mug to that. They finished off their hot chocolate quickly and turned to each other for the reason that they'd stayed home. Nicole leaned in for the other New Year's tradition, capturing Dane's lips with her own. The kiss wasn't nearly as scandalous as the one they had shared a year ago, but they still preferred it without an audience.

"You taste like chocolate," Nicole said, as they broke for air.

Dane couldn't help laughing. "Gee, I wonder why."

"While I like chocolate, I like you more, so we have got to do something about that."

Before Dane could ask a question to play along, Nicole was on her again, kissing her deeply. Dane moaned from the swirl of Nicole's gifted tongue, which seemed intent on getting rid of the chocolate residue inside of Dane's mouth. She felt like she had to play catch, trying to stroke Nicole's tongue with her own, but Nicole didn't seem interested in her tongue. Dane cursed the fact that they needed more air and had to pull away.

"Do I still taste like chocolate?" Dane was certain she knew the answer, but she wanted to see how her lover would respond.

"I should check to make sure you're all clear."

Dane had hoped that was the answer. Nicole was on her again, hitting her with enough force to give the idea that Nicole wanted her to lie back. She eased down onto the sofa, not wanting to lose contact with her lover's wonderful mouth. Nicole followed, making sure the kiss wasn't broken. Dane's hands wandered Nicole's back and caressed her shoulders, while trying to pull her closer. Nicole moaned into Dane's mouth and her hands roamed Dane's sides. Again, the need for air broke them apart, and Nicole shifted her body to get comfortable on top of Dane.

"This is why going out is overrated." Dane kissed her girlfriend's cheek.

"Damn right," Nicole concurred and placed a small peck on her lover's chin. She playfully nipped the area, dragging her teeth down Dane's chin. Dane held onto her tighter and rubbed her back again.

"You are so goddamn sexy," Dane whispered, as her hands worked their way underneath Nicole's tank top.

Nicole only smiled and started another kiss. She moaned into Dane's mouth, as Dane's hands fondled her breasts. Sitting up, Nicole rid herself of the top, and Dane filled her hands with wonderfully bare cleavage.

"This is quite possibly the best start to any year, ever in the history of the world," Dane decided, before taking a pebbled nipple between her lips, which meant no more talking for her.

"Happy New Year to us," Nicole moaned, holding Dane's head to her chest.

S.L. Kassidy

Ice Pack

NICOLE SIGHED, READY FOR the day to be over. She was stuck at work, which seemed to go on forever lately. Shades of her former work life were peeking out, people pestering her for help when she had her own piles of work. Her parents tended to keep folks at bay, but only when she had school. When she was out of class, she was on her own. Much of the time, she no longer had a problem sending people away, but occasionally there were those who really did need help, and she felt obligated to help them.

Making matters worse, she wasn't looking forward to driving in the snow that was being predicted. She hoped she'd be home before the snow started. She partially got her wish—it started snowing as she was on her way home. Her phone rang, and she answered it on speaker.

"Hey, baby," Nicole greeted her lover. *I wonder what my sweet, precious pup would do if she knew I have a violin concerto as her ringtone.*

"It's snowing. You headed home?" Danny asked.

"I'm in the car as we speak."

"Okay. Don't wanna distract you on the road and everything. Take your time and be safe, okay?"

"I will. See you in about an hour. Love you."

"Love you, too."

The call was disconnected, and Nicole focused on the street ahead of her. Shivering as she drove on, she sucked her teeth as she realized the heater wasn't working as well as it should. With one hand on the steering wheel, Nicole checked the vents that were within arm's reach.

"Great, just great. Another thing to make this week annoying," she grumbled. Between her stacks of work, her coworkers bothering her, and now having to ride home cold with almost blinding snow, Nicole was done. By the time she pulled up to the house, she could see her breath and could barely feel her fingers. She glared at the snow, which lightly covered the front yard. A sigh of relief escaped as soon as the warmth in the house engulfed her.

The patter of paws caught her ears and Haydn was in front of her within seconds. He was getting big, looking like a "real dog," as Danny had put it. He was still very much a puppy, though—a happy puppy.

"Hey, little man," Nicole smiled, scratching behind his ears. Haydn barked, which was more like a chirp. He rubbed his head against her arm before moving deeper into the house, pulling her by the end of her coat.

"Just in time." Danny exited the kitchen and went to help Nicole out of her coat.

"Just in time for what?"

"Hot chocolate."

Nicole cooed. "I love you."

Danny laughed. "I know you do, but what about that hot chocolate?"

"Just what I wanted."

"Kinda figured that. It's on the counter in the kitchen. I'm going to go run us a bath. Sound good?"

Nicole grinned. "Excellent." *Danny has to know how amazing she is just for these things.*

With her coat hung up and her briefcase out of Haydn's reach, Nicole went to enjoy the hot, creamy, sweetness that was cocoa. A single sip helped melt away the stress of the day. Haydn bouncing around her legs helped too. He was such a jovial little guy that his just being there brightened her day.

"You want a snack, Haydn?" The pup barked, probably because he had come to learn what the word snack meant.

She and Danny kept snacks for Haydn in a jar, but they had a system to make sure they did not overindulge him. They each only gave him one snack, so no matter what he only had two snacks maximum. She held the treat out for him.

"Okay, Haydn, let's see if that expensive training school paid off. Roll," she commanded, and he yelped before rolling over several times. She smiled. "You are too cute, Haydn. Here you go." She put the snack on the end of his nose, as Danny had taken to doing. He balanced it for a second before eating it.

Laughing, while Haydn went to have some water, Nicole made her way upstairs carrying the hot chocolate still in hand. She wanted to take a quick shower before soaking in the tub with Danny. Finishing her drink, she stripped and cleaned her body as fast as possible.

***

Dane prepared the bath in the main bathroom, complete with bubbles, bath beads, and candles. She had to go get the dock for the music, and she put to use a new item they'd purchased—a gate for the stairs. Since Haydn was growing, he found it much easier to get up the steps and make a nuisance of himself.

"Maybe I should crate him," Dane considered, but she shook that away. He'd whine loudly if he were locked away while the lights were still on in the house, and he had so many more things to explore.

Returning to the bathroom, Dane started some classical music. She checked the temperature of the water and was about to go get her lover when Nicole walked through the door only wearing a towel. They smiled at each other.

"Looks like you started without me," Dane said as she pulled her lover to her.

"No, just wanted to wash away the grime of the day."

"Did it work?" The tired look in her girlfriend's beautiful green eyes told her all she needed to know.

Nicole offered her a sigh and a half-smile as an answer. Dane unwrapped her from the towel and helped her into the tub. Dane got in behind and Nicole settled her back against Dane's chest. She began massaging Nicole's back.

"Damn, angel, you're tense here, all knotted up," Dane said.

Nicole groaned. "I hate work."

"Tough day?"

"Tough week and it's only Wednesday. I'm not sure if I'll be able to make it through the rest of the week." She shifted, so that Dane could get to just below her shoulder.

Dane worked on her girlfriend's back and kissed Nicole's neck. "You'll be fine, Chem."

Nicole sighed and shook her head. "This is going to be a long month." They were silent momentarily. "I was thinking of taking a couple of days off."

A smile settled on Dane's face. "I'm all for that. You've got tons of days, right?" She didn't want Nicole to get in trouble.

"I do. Hey, want to take a vacation?" Nicole twisted around slightly to look Dane in the eye.

Dane startled at the out-of-the-blue suggestion. "Did you just think of that?" It sounded so spur of the moment.

"Well, not really. Of course, it's been on my mind since our first trip. I figure if I'm going to take off a couple of days and then ask you to cancel some appointments..." Emerald eyes twinkled.

Dane pretended to gasp in shock. "You want me to cancel appointments? Why, I never!" She laughed.

Nicole chuckled, too. "Is that too much to ask?"

Scoffing, Dane pecked the end of Nicole's nose. "Of course not, Chem. I'll shuffle whatever I need to if it means going on a trip with you. Where do you want to go?"

Those enchanting eyes shined again. "Skiing."

Dane's eyebrows knitted close together. "Skiing? I've never been skiing before and don't know if I can." She knew she could barely run on her leg, so she wasn't sure how her leg would hold up skiing.

"So? Baby, I know it's uncertain with your leg and everything, but we shouldn't let that stop us from going. We go for a few days, and you can find out if you can ski. If you can't, we can do a bunch of other things." Nicole smiled.

Dane laughed. "Guess you're right about that. You have a place in mind?"

"Yeah, I've been there before. We can rent a little cabin. Four days sound good?"

"Sounds great. Do we get to surprise each other again?" Dane asked, grinning and waggling her eyebrows.

Nicole smiled, too, and purred. "Yes, but only one surprise again. I don't want to spend the whole trip stuck in the cabin."

Dane pouted. "You make it sound like a bad thing. Is making love with me such a chore?" she sighed.

Nicole kissed the expression away. "Making love with you is always a grand experience. I don't want the trip to be only about that. I want to have some fun with our clothes on as well as off. I like you enough to want to spend time with you doing other things."

Dane grinned and sat up a little straighter. "Sounds promising. Sure you can arrange this before you have to go back to class?"

Nicole scoffed. "Arranging it is easy. Getting the days off might be tricky."

"What? Just tell your parents you need time off to fuck my brains out," Dane joked.

"That would guarantee I never get another day off. My father would probably faint if I even said the word fuck in his presence and meant it in a remotely sexual way."

"Then I guess he'd die if he knew what you do to me."

Nicole chuckled and wrapped her arms around her lover. Dane returned the embrace, caressing Nicole's back. The redhead sighed and relaxed, which caused her partner to smile. Dane looked forward to taking another trip and began thinking on what to surprise Nicole with.

***

"You didn't want to take the train again?" Dane and Nicole were on board a plane, flying north.

Nicole's hair bounced as she shook her head. "The train ride before was because you had never traveled by train. Now, I just want to get to our cabin and hit the slopes!"

The musician only smiled. She had been on an airplane several times before so she was nowhere near as excited as they moved closer to their destination. She held Nicole's hand the whole flight. They both ignored stares and glares from a few people who obviously didn't approve.

After landing Dane made sure to stand at her full height and glower at everyone who dared to stare and disapprove. Suddenly, several eyes found the floor interesting. Nicole grabbed their overhead bags, but Dane took them from her immediately. They had one other bag to pick up before Nicole drove the rental car to the cabin. She smiled as she stopped by the main office to get their card keys for the cabin.

"I know you thought it would be like a cabin in the movies, but I definitely couldn't get something like that on such short notice." Nicole pulled up to the little rental. There were other small cabins within view, but far enough that no one would be high-fiving Dane if they ran into neighbors in the morning.

"Your dad doesn't own a cabin or something? I thought he was all outdoorsy and junk."

"He is, but he prefers camping."

Dane shrugged as they began unloading the car. The thick snow crunched under their feet and Nicole felt the chill through her coat. She hurriedly opened the front door, pleased to feel the heat on in the unit.

"Oh, this is cool." Dane took a look around.

The cabin was small, but had all of the essentials. There was a kitchen area that Nicole had paid extra to have fully stocked for the four days they'd be there. The living room was cozy with a fireplace and cushy carpet as well as a plush sofa.

"Thank God it doesn't have one of those moose or deer heads hanging on the wall or a bear skin rug." Dane sighed in relief.

Nicole laughed. "I checked about that when I called, all too aware that you wouldn't have approved having dead animals or representations of dead animals as decor."

Dane went to inspect the bedroom and bathroom. "Babe, is this a Jacuzzi?" Dane called from the bathroom, the grin evident in her voice.

"Yes, it is," Nicole chirped, but, she burst Dane's bubble. "Put the bags down and let's go. We still have a few hours of sunlight to burn, so let's go skiing."

"Skiing?" And now the grin became a pout.

"Yes, we'll get in the hot tub when we come back."

Dane walked out with an adorable pout on her face that Nicole kissed away. The show of affection worked and Danny was smiling when Nicole pulled away. She dragged Dane out the door, so they could hit the slopes.

***

By the time Dane got her skis on, she realized she didn't like skiing and knew she wouldn't be able to do it. She was uncomfortable just standing in the damned things, and she wasn't even sure that was because of her leg. She kept that to herself because Nicole wanted to ski, and she'd be damned if she was going to ruin something that her girlfriend wanted. She couldn't really move, even with Nicole coaching. Grunting, she decided to go it alone, so that her partner could enjoy the couple of hours of sunlight that was left.

"Angel, you can go ahead. I can figure this out on my own." Dane wobbled and lost one of her ski poles. If Nicole would leave, she could just take the skis off and stop troubling her leg and knee.

Nicole smiled softly while retrieving the pole. "I'm not leaving you, baby. Skiing is the secondary reason for me suggesting a trip up here. The primary reason was to spend time with you. So, I'm not leaving you."

"But, you'll miss your chance to ski."

Nicole continued to smile. "Weren't you listening to me?"

Dane smiled back. *Why try to fight?* She turned her energy to trying to figure out how to at least stay on her feet with the skis. It took over thirty minutes for Dane to feel comfortable standing on her skis and by then her knee throbbed. She managed a shuffle to move, and Nicole acted as if it was the greatest thing Dane had done in the history of history. She threw her arms around Dane and kissed her chilled cheek.

"Now, to get you on the bunny slope." Nicole patted Dane on the shoulder.

"I get the feeling this isn't going to involve the type of bunnies I'm thinking of."

"You better be thinking of cute, little baby rabbits because any other bunny will involve you sleeping on the couch for the rest of the trip," Nicole countered with a mock glare.

Dane let out a loud laugh. "Of course, cute, little baby rabbits! You know I love animals!" She threw in a monster grin for good measure.

Nicole smiled, letting Dane know everything was all right. They slowly made their way to the bunny slope, where Dane promptly embarrassed herself by falling on her face every single time she tried to ski. After the fifth fall, she just laid in the snow. Her knee and leg were happy for that.

"Hopeless," Dane huffed.

"You're not hopeless, baby. This is just your first time. You're doing fine. How's your leg feel?" Nicole helped Dane up for the fifth time.

Dane didn't want to admit her leg ached from being forced to stand in the unforgiving, unbending ski boot. "I'll live."

Nicole smiled, as if she expected that evasive response. "And your clothes? Are you warm?"

Nicole had practically dressed Dane before they left, because Dane had never been in so much snow before. The city had snow, but not feet worth of it. She layered Dane's outfit in ways Dane hadn't imagined, mostly because Dane layered by style rather than necessity now. She had also forced gloves and a funny—in Dane's opinion—hat onto her, which Dane had fussed about, but was now happy for.

"I'm good. You?" Dane asked, just to be sure since Nicole got cold so much easier than she did.

"I'm fine. Ready to try again?"

Dane couldn't resist the twinkle in those emerald orbs. So, she tried again until she didn't fall. But, by then Nicole had lost any chance she had to actually ski. Yet, Nicole was grinning, as they made their way back to the cabin. Dane wasn't sure how the hell she had managed that one time of not falling. She didn't consider moving a very short distance of a few feet "skiing" as Nicole seemed to. Still, she wouldn't say anything to ruin Nicole's good time.

"I see you limping," Nicole pointed out.

"I'm fine," Dane grunted.

"Fine?" Nicole arched an eyebrow.

"Not totally fine considering I'm soaked," Dane complained, pulling at her clothing, which now clung to various parts of her body.

"Is that because of me?" Nicole teased, wiggling her hips while opening the cabin door.

Dane groaned. "Don't point that thing at me unless you want naughty things done to it, you little minx."

"Maybe if you're good, I'll let you touch it." Nicole turned around to wink at her lover.

Well, now Dane definitely was soaked. She didn't understand the how or why, but one well-placed look or move from Nicole turned her on more than the dozens of women she had been with that would've done anything—no matter now degrading or crazy—to please Dane. *Does being emotionally attached make such a huge difference?* She wasn't sure for other people, but for her, all signs pointed to a giant, flashing yes!

"You go get out of those wet clothes, and I'll make us a snack and get some ice for your leg." Nicole smiled as the heat greeted them from inside the little cabin.

Dane was going to argue; after all, she was the housewife. She was supposed to prepare the meals. But, a stern look from her girlfriend stopped her words. Not to mention, she really did want to get out of her wet clothes as soon as possible.

Peeling herself out of all of her ski clothes, Dane took a hot, ten-minute shower. She put on her pajamas, since she doubted Nicole would want to drive anywhere in the dark and in the snow. She rejoined her lover just in time to not be able to help with the snack.

"Grilled cheese? Yum!" Dane grinned.

"I made tea with it if that's all right," Nicole said.

"Of course, it's all right. Wanna watch a movie?"

Nicole nodded. "After I take a shower and you ice that knee."

Dane did as ordered. Nicole disappeared into the bathroom for about fifteen minutes. Dane's leg felt better by the time her lover sat next to her, smelling lovely and wearing her pajamas. They cuddled on the sofa while enjoying their sandwiches and tea. Dane picked a movie they had already seen, but that they had enjoyed. When they were done with their snacks, Dane threw away their paper plates. Two hours later, the movie was over and it was close to dinnertime.

"Want me to make something?" Dane offered.

"No, baby, I got it," Nicole said, as she stood up.

"You sure?"

"Positive. It's your vacation, too. Take a break from the things you usually do. Listen to some music. Hell, write some music. Enjoy yourself."

Dane smiled and nodded. She went to retrieve her guitar—she rarely left home without it—along with her notepad. Parking herself back on the couch, she strummed a few chords before Nicole was back in the living room.

"Want me to light a fire?" Nicole nodded to the fireplace.

"Yes, please. Are we going to drink wine, too?"

Nicole chuckled. "Only if you want to, baby. Is that something you saw on TV or is that a real life thing?"

"I saw it once between Henry and Lynn—the Briarmoors. They kept me one time, and I guess they'd planned a date or something, but they kept me anyway. Anyway, Lynn put me to bed in my room."

Emerald eyes were so wide Dane was scared her girlfriend would lose them to gravity. "You had a room? You were there so much that you had a room? God, baby." A muffled gasp escaped Nicole as she covered her mouth with her hand.

Dane waved it off. "It's okay. They were cool about it. Anyway, I got put to bed. She even read me a story, probably to keep my little butt in bed. Didn't work. I heard 'em talking and wanted to know what they were doing, so I crept my little body downstairs and saw them sitting by a fire with wine."

A teasing grin spread across Nicole's face. "Do I even want to know how this story ends?"

"This is probably my only cute little kid story, so yes, you want to hear how it ends." Dane playfully puffed out her cheeks.

Nicole giggled. "Oh, a happy ending then?"

"Yeah." Dane smiled a bit. "I was six when this happened, but I remember it so clearly." She took a breath and it was almost like she was back there. "I was a quiet kid. I'm talking ninjas could've taken lessons from me. So, I managed to get real close to them. Could've touched Henry with my fat little finger, and then Lynn saw me as she was leaning in for a kiss. Damn near jumped out of her skin."

Nicole chuckled, her hair bouncing as her shoulders shook. "I can imagine, since you should've been in bed."

"Yeah. I got scared for a second because Lynn looked mad when she looked at me. I damn near pissed myself."

"Hey, I thought you said this was happy."

Dane laughed. "It is. Lemme finish. So, I was scared out of my mind and then out of nowhere, they both laughed and hugged me. I got a cookie, another bedtime story, and a great memory."

"Wow that is a cute story. I wish you had more of them." There was a moment of silence as Nicole seemed to struggle with her thoughts. Her eyes searched the floor, and she started working on the fire.

"Chem, you okay?"

"Yeah, you enjoy your time. I'm going to go check on dinner."

The redhead rushed off, leaving Dane confused. She ran her hand through her hair. *Did I say something wrong?*

***

Nicole finished up in the kitchen, avoiding Danny for almost twenty minutes. *She actually stayed with the Briarmoors enough for her to have a room in their home?* Nicole couldn't wrap her mind around it. *But, if they kept her so much, why did she miss out on so many things from childhood? Were they just babysitting?* If they were, she didn't understand why they had made a room for Danny. But, she didn't have the answers and she wouldn't get any hiding in the kitchen. She didn't want to bombard Danny with these questions, though.

She went back to the living room with a plate of lasagna for Danny, one for herself, and some toasted bread. She went back in the kitchen for beverages. She placed those down and sat quietly to eat.

"Hey, angel, did I do something?" Danny asked in a low voice, eyes on her plate.

Nicole blinked. "Did you do something? Why would you ask that?"

"Because you stopped talking, and you walked out. Was there something sad in the story that I didn't realize? You know, sometimes I don't realize something's sad because I don't know any different."

"Oh, baby, no!" Nicole shook her head. "It was a cute story, like you promised. But, it just made me curious. You don't talk much about your time with the Briarmoors. Why? I didn't even know they existed before your mother brought over those pictures."

Dane nodded, but there was sorrow in her slate eyes. "Guess I'd just rather forget it all, the bad and the good, from when I was younger. I mean most of the good I missed out on, anyway. My memories start at four, and I think I smoked most of those away. Besides, what good does it do to remember them? They're still gone. So, you...you got quiet because you wanna know more about Henry and Lynn?"

The nod was so slight that Nicole was barely aware she'd moved. Danny had to have seen it, though, because she smiled. She caressed Nicole's leg. "Anything in particular you wanna know?"

Nicole let out a sigh before she realized it. There was so much she wanted to know, but she didn't want to trouble Danny. Besides, she doubted Danny could answer some of her questions. "No, just tell me some things about them," Nicole requested with a small smile.

Danny nodded and began eating. Nicole did the same, knowing her girlfriend would get started at her own pace. Before that, though, Danny had to let her know how "freaking delicious" dinner was. Nicole laughed, but took the compliment.

"I don't really know what to say about Henry and Lynn. They were just the neighbors, but I found myself often at their house. Henry sometimes watched cartoons with me, while Lynn would read to me. They fed me snacks and dinner. They helped me with homework and stuff. One of the last things that they did for me, before sending me back to the folks, was go to a parent-teacher conference for me."

"They went?" *Wait, they cared enough to go to parent-teacher conferences, but never threw her a birthday party? I don't understand. Who are these people? Maybe they did and Danny doesn't remember.* She doubted that, though.

Danny nodded. "Yeah, they were the ones that cared. My grades had dropped really bad. It sucked at home. By then, Michael and Rachel were beating on me, too, and saying horrible stuff. Rachel was convinced I didn't belong in the house. Russell had moved onto doing some bad stuff, too. Hitting me with his hands wasn't enough, cursing at me for just existing, and making me feel like I was the worst thing to ever happen to anyone. I was getting into liquor cabinets and drinking already. It was just really bad. My teacher at the time wasn't really sympathetic to my plight. She was really disrespectful to the Briarmoors. She had the nerve to ask who they were when they came up. And when they told her they weren't my parents, she was a real bitch." Danny's face twisted into a sneer.

"So, what happened?"

Danny shrugged. "She told them she couldn't discuss me with them, because they weren't my legal guardians. They were pissed because that was total bullshit. I'm sure it was one of the many reasons they returned me."

"Baby, don't say it like that. You weren't some broken instrument returned to neglectful owners. You were a child with large, adult-sized problems. I'm sure they had good reasons for..." Nicole wasn't sure how to say it without sounding callous. But, these people didn't sound like the type to "return" a child. Something more must've happened.

Danny smiled a bit. "Thanks for trying, Nick, but it's cool. It hurt for a long time, feeling abandoned again, but when I got older, I was able to let go by reminding myself that I wasn't their kid, and they did more for me than any other people on Earth—until you. They didn't owe me anything."

"That's true." Sometimes, Danny surprised Nicole with how mature her thinking could be, even when her actions were very immature.

"But, anyway, I had good times with them for the short time they had me. Got my love of dogs from them, definitely. They came to a couple of my concerts. Played a few games with me. Henry was the first to find out I suck at sports. Couldn't catch a ball to save my life."

Nicole smiled. "They sound like good people."

"They were." And that was the end of the subject.

Nicole was fine with Danny not talking about the Briarmoors anymore. While they were a bright spot for her lover, they didn't seem to have been a constant source of good, only being in her life for a short period. If that was enough for Danny, then it would be enough for her.

"This was good." Danny sopped up her last bits of lasagna sauce with a piece of bread.

"You want seconds?"

"Nah. That'll just put me to sleep and I have miles to go before I sleep." Danny smirked.

"Quoting Robert Frost now, are we?"

"You know you like it."

Nicole giggled flirtatiously and batted her eyes at Danny, just to tease her a little. The heated look that ignited in those smoky orbs caused a fire in Nicole's belly. She didn't even taste her food as she finished. She took care of the trash, returning to the kitchen to get them a treat. She could hear Danny strumming her guitar.

When she went back to the living room, she discovered Danny was singing softly to herself. She paused to listen, even though she couldn't make out the lyrics. Danny glanced up just as Nicole was about to lose herself in the music.

"Babe, what is that in your hand?"

Nicole smiled. "This is a little treat for both of us. I think it works after your little story." In her hands, she held a half glass of wine for each of them.

"You trust me enough to have wine?" The question was a tease. While Danny didn't usually drink, she indulged in small amounts on very special occasions. Nicole had only recently learned to live with that and not feel like her lover was going to transform into a raging drunk.

Nicole gave her lover a sexy smile. "Just a sip."

"Oh, gonna want way more than a sip." The look in her eyes went from burning to supernova, and Nicole almost lost control of her legs.

"Come sit by the fire." Nicole sat on the rug. She put Danny's glass down where she wanted her partner to sit.

Danny didn't need to be told twice. She was up in a flash and in the spot just as fast. Nicole smiled and tipped her glass to Danny who mimicked her actions. They reached out to touch their free hands, and Nicole's pinky caressed the top of Danny's hand. They quietly sipped the wine for a few moments.

"This is sweet," Danny said, possibly referring to both the wine and the moment.

"It is," Nicole agreed.

"But, I've had my sip and I don't like the glass. I need something more substantial."

Nicole wasn't sure what her partner meant, but the way Danny rolled the word substantial on her tongue made her heart beat a little harder. Danny turned to take Nicole's wine glass from her, setting it down an arm's length away. She then made short work of Nicole's clothes. It all happened so quickly that Nicole could only make squeaks of protest.

"Baby, what are you doing?" Nicole whispered, even though she could guess. After all, not too many activities required her to be naked.

"I need a better glass. You're perfect," Danny whispered before showering Nicole's torso with tender kisses.

Soft murmurs escaped Nicole's mouth. "Perfect for what?"

"Perfect for my wine," Danny replied as if it was obvious.

Nicole's brow furrowed. The gentle kisses continued, as Danny began moving Nicole's body, positioning it just so. Nicole allowed it, wondering what Danny was about to do. When Danny finally pulled away, Nicole sat with her arms behind her, causing her chest to jut out. Her legs were straight out and pressed as close together as possible.

A smirk settled onto Danny's face. "Ready?"

"For what?" Nicole answered in a breath. She hoped it involved her lover relieving some of the pressure building inside of her.

Grey eyes sparkled as Danny's smirk grew. She grabbed her glass of wine and then slowly poured a little over Nicole's collarbones. A small amount of the liquid pooled just below Nicole's waist, where her legs were locked together. Wasting no time, Danny lapped up the wine, drawing out small moans from Nicole.

Nicole felt herself getting hotter and hotter. She couldn't believe Danny was actually sipping wine from her body. No one had ever proposed such a thing, and she never considered such a thing. *But, goddamn, it feels so good!*

"God, baby, I think you need more than sips," Nicole panted. She knew she needed more.

"I drink at my own pace, Chem."

Nicole groaned as her girlfriend kept pouring and kept licking. She was certain she'd explode, as Danny's tongue worked all over her torso. Danny's talented tongue drifted over her collarbones, the valley between her breasts, all around her breasts, and down by her bellybutton. Nicole began to squirm, wanting more. Danny pulled away and held Nicole's legs.

"Baby, please," Nicole begged.

"Stop moving or you'll spill my wine. I won't have anything to drink, and I'll have to stop." Danny pinned Nicole with her gaze.

Nicole gulped, but stopped wiggling. Panting, Nicole did her best to stay the way Danny put her, so that Danny wouldn't stop. Tongue and lips continued on, blazing across her wanting flesh. She wasn't sure how she didn't go out of her mind with desire and need, as her lover's mouth drifted lower.

Danny slurped and licked the wine resting in between Nicole's legs. Nicole shuddered and whimpered, fighting to keep the pose and not open her legs. *But, it's so hard and I'm hotter than this damn fire!* Still, she remained as Danny had put her and was rewarded with Danny gently prying her legs open.

"Oh, look at this. More wine," Danny remarked with a smile.

"Baby, please. I want you so much. Love me like only you can," Nicole implored, breathing heavily through her mouth.

"Only me. Like the sound of that." With that, she dived into her partner, going right to where Nicole needed her.

Nicole wouldn't have thought her back could bow any more than it was, but she found out that wasn't true as soon as Danny's lips touched her most intimate area. As Danny's mouth worked her magic, bringing her pleasure higher and higher, Nicole had to move, adjust, or she would've gone mad.

Curling more into herself, Nicole tried to hug Danny's head to her. It was awkward, and she actually lost contact like that. Whining, she allowed Danny to push her down to the floor, and she moved her legs onto Danny's shoulders. Danny reached up and put a couple of sofa pillows under Nicole, who didn't care about that. She only cared about Danny touching her. Nicole whined for her lover, who went back to work immediately.

Nicole clawed at the carpet, as Danny's tongue glided through her, making her burn all the more. Her heart raced, and her mind succumbed to the sweet attention. Passion rose until, finally, she could only explode. Letting loose a loud cry, she dropped to the floor with a thin layer of sweat covering her body as if to cool down the dying flames.

Danny pushed herself up and smiled while gazing down at her. Nicole's heart raced again, as the fire in the hearth danced and highlighted her lover's copper tone. She looked like something from another world.

"You're the angel," Nicole said with reverence, reaching up and caressing Danny's slightly chubby cheek.

Danny smiled. "Then you're the sex goddess, my little vixen."

"Vixen? I've gone from an angel to a vixen."

"You're both." Danny leaned down and nuzzled Nicole's neck. She placed a couple of gentle kisses, earning a few whimpers from Nicole, who wrapped one hand around Danny, hugging her close.

"It was wonderful, sweetheart. Is there nothing those fingers and that mouth can't do?"

Danny didn't reply, just continued to nuzzle Nicole. Eventually, Nicole had to let Danny go and lie down on the floor. Danny fetched a blanket to put down and then followed Nicole's lead, pulling Nicole to her. They stayed there, quietly, just enjoying their existence together.

***

The couple cuddled close in bed that night, fighting off sleep in favor of plotting out their full day tomorrow. The best they could come up with was skiing and shopping. Dane wasn't looking forward to more falling or her leg hurting, but she wanted Nicole to get some skiing in.

They fell asleep, and Dane woke up to the smell of breakfast. Her stomach rumbled in approval, and she was about to get up, but Nicole appeared in the doorway. She held a tray, but Dane didn't know what was on it. She was distracted by what her girlfriend had on...or what she didn't have on. All Nicole wore was a pair of lacy panties.

"Nick, what are you doing?" Dane asked, eyes glued to her lover's cleavage.

"Aside from putting a spell on you, I'm serving you breakfast in bed," Nicole answered with a coquettish smile.

"Spell?" Dane mindlessly echoed. *I don't think God made a more perfect pair of tits.* She wanted them in her hands and her mouth, yet again.

Nicole smiled as she sashayed over to the bed and set the tray in front of her dazed lover. "Waffles, scrambled eggs with cheddar cheese, some fruit, and apple juice."

Dane heard the words, but they didn't really register. Her eyes were stuck to bare breasts, and her ears were halfway invested, just in case. She definitely wanted her sense of touch and taste to get involved.

"Should I put on a shirt?" Nicole asked with a teasing smile.

Dane blinked. "You'd better not! Be a crime against nature to not let those hang free. Matter of fact, can you not wear shirts or bras when we're in here?"

Nicole chuckled. "No, I don't think so."

Dane's face fell into a pout. "But, why?"

"Because, I'd like to have a conversation with you and have you actually look at my face."

"I'll get there eventually."

Nicole laughed, but she didn't make a move to cover up. Instead, she turned to the food and broke off pieces of the waffles. Making sure the bits were thoroughly saturated with syrup, she brought the fork to Dane's lips and fed her breakfast. Dane moaned as she took in the food.

Breakfast was spent with Nicole feeding both of them from one fork. Had it been anyone else, Dane would've found the whole thing weird and disgusting. Some things weren't meant to be shared, regardless of where her tongue had gone earlier. But, with Nicole, that never even occurred to her. Everything she did with Nicole seemed perfectly normal and natural.

"Nick, have you ever done this before with a lover?"

"Breakfast in bed?"

"Well, that, and sharing one plate and one fork?"

Nicole smiled a little. "Only you, baby." She seemed to think on it for a moment. "It would've been weird with anyone else. I don't know why, but with you, it seems fine. Everything with you seems fine."

Dane grinned. "That's how I feel, too. I've had a few people try to feed me in bed and it's always creepy to me. Hell, not too long ago, I'd have thought you were babying me. But, I've grown a little and I'm so connected to you, so in love with you. God, Chem, I love you so damn much that I'm willing to try skiing again." *I might die trying it, but shit, it'll be worth it just to see her smile.*

Nicole laughed. "That's good enough for me, but I don't want you to hurt your leg or your knee if it's a problem."

Dane shook her head. "It's not a problem. Now, go put some clothes on before I throw you down on this bed and don't let you up until we have to leave."

The redhead obviously wanted to go skiing, because she rushed out of the room with the empty tray in her hands. Dane laughed and got out of bed to prepare for the day.

Once they were properly cleaned, groomed, and bundled, they started for the slopes. Dane convinced Nicole to go off on the real hills by basically saying it embarrassed her when Nicole saw her fall. It was partially true, but Dane really didn't care about falling.

Dane fell often in the fresh snow, but she made it down the bunny slope a couple of times without killing herself. She considered it an accomplishment, but it bored her, as most sports did. She didn't mind watching a variety of sports, but participating in them never struck her like it did with most people. Plus, her knee and leg were already sore, and she didn't want to make those worse.

"There might be something else to do," Dane muttered. Looking around, she spotted something in the distance she'd like to try, but she wouldn't get the chance just yet.

"Hey, baby, ready to grab lunch?" Nicole asked as she came over.

Dane opened her mouth, about to say they had just had breakfast, but her stomach growled. She felt a blush burn her cheeks, but it was almost impossible to tell thanks to the scarf Nicole forced her to wear. Besides, the cold, crisp air made much of her skin a dull red.

"Is it lunch time already? Seems like we just got out here."

Nicole laughed. "You didn't hit your head while you were out here practicing? We've been out here for three hours."

"Three hours? Get the hell out!" Dane declared in disbelief. "It doesn't seem like that long." *I've been busting my ass for three hours? No wonder my leg feels like it's ready to shatter.*

"I'm sure it hasn't. Did you have fun?"

Dane shrugged. "I guess. It was all right, but I probably wouldn't do this on my own."

"No? I thought you'd have fun outside and in the snow."

"I am, but still not something I'd do on my own."

Nicole accepted that with a nod and didn't press Dane. They returned to the warmth of their cabin and showered. Nicole went to make lunch, while Dane sat with her guitar. She played a soft melody, even as Nicole joined her with their lunch, tuna sandwiches on toasted bread with lettuce and tomatoes.

"So, anything you want to do, now that I've got skiing out of my system for the day?" Nicole asked.

"Wanna build a snowman?" Dane inquired as if it were the most normal thing on Earth.

A gentle smile highlighted Nicole's wonderful features. "Sounds like fun."

They finished lunch, re-bundled, and made their way outside. The road and walkway had been shoveled, but there was more than enough space in the back for them to make a grand snowman...if Dane could get the mechanics of rolling the snowballs together.

"Okay, so this small thing is the start of our snowman?" Dane asked, as Nicole packed together a snowball in her hands.

"Yup. We'll roll it in the snow until it gets bigger and it's going to be the base of the snowman. You get started on the middle part," Nicole replied before bending down to gather more snow on her snowball.

Dane nodded and followed her partner's lead. It never occurred to her that this was how snowmen were created. She thought they were like sandcastles, not that she had a great understanding on the process of creating sandcastles either.

"Is this big enough for the middle?" Dane asked after her snowball grew several times its original size.

Nicole looked up from her task. "Perfect! Now, you have to put your middle on my bottom."

A lewd smile spread across Dane's face, even though her scarf hid the expression. "There's a dirty joke in there, but I'll stop short of telling you what I want to do to your bottom."

"Just for that, you can lift the middle and put it up here." Nicole patted the top of her giant snowball.

"Fine. So bossy." Dane's part wasn't huge, so it wasn't a great hardship for her to move it or lift it.

"You like me bossy."

Dane could only smile. Gathering her snowball in her hands, she grunted as she lifted the thing and piled it onto Nicole's snowball. Nicole was already busy on the head.

"What do we do for eyes and stuff?" Dane asked, scanning around.

"Go look around for rocks—and sticks for arms," Nicole replied.

Dane nodded and hunted for items to give their snowman features. She found some pebbles for the eyes and nose, which she and Nicole both placed on the snowman's face. Dane then fetched some sticks for arms and stones that she thought made really good shoes. Stepping back, they admired their handiwork.

"He's a handsome fella, eh?" Dane asked with a grin.

"Impressive for a first snowman," Nicole commented.

"Yeah. Let's make another one."

Nicole laughed, but she agreed. Dane could sense there was something different about their second venture, but she wasn't sure what it was. It didn't stay a mystery for long, though. While she was busy working on her part, she felt a snowball break against her back. She heard suspicious giggles coming from her girlfriend.

"What the—" Snow slapped Dane in the face as she turned to question Nicole. "Oh, you're so going to get it," she growled.

Nicole giggled more and pelted her lover with a couple more snowballs before Dane began retaliating. The snowball battle was epic if anyone asked Dane. The stuff of legends. It wasn't nearly as rough as the drunken scrapes she used to get into with her so-called friends, which seemed like a lifetime ago. She ended it by "killing" their snowman.

"Danny, you'd better not!" Nicole's warning was cut off, as Dane slung Nicole over her shoulder and quickly dropped her onto their poor snowman.

"And the winner by a KO!" Dane threw her hands up. She reveled in her victory while ignoring the throb of her knee. She'd just take a painkiller when they got inside. She refused to let her leg spoil her fun.

Emerald eyes glared frozen daggers at her. "I hope that was worth getting in the hot tub with me."

Dane's whole face fell. "What!"

Nicole laughed. "I wish I had my phone right now." She had left the device in the cabin. "I just wish you could see your face!"

"That's not funny, Nick!" Dane huffed, and then she dived onto Nicole. They rolled around in the snow, laughing and throwing snow at each other.

***

Nicole wasn't serious about the hot tub threat, considering it'd be just as much a punishment to her. The couple hopped in right after they came in from the snow war. Nicole watched Danny go to the kitchen and get a couple of painkillers before she went to start up the hot tub. Danny sighed in relief the moment she sank into the water and grinned as Nicole eased in next to her.

"That was fun, even if you did murder our snowman," Nicole teased as she settled against Danny.

Danny gasped in feigned shock. "I murdered the snowman? He was totally your casualty! You crushed him!"

"You threw me on top of him, you brute!" Nicole turned to slap Danny very lightly in the shoulder.

Danny laughed. "Pretty good for someone on one leg, huh?"

Nicole only smiled. She didn't want to encourage Danny to do something that could lead to her injuring her leg and knee more than they already were. The last thing they needed was for Danny to think it was all right for her to try to lift Nicole.

"How's your leg, baby?" Nicole reached down and massaged Danny's knee.

"The painkillers are working. Nothing hurts. Plus, being in the hot tub is doing some work on it, too," Danny answered with a comforting smile. She didn't appear to be in any serious pain.

"This feels so good." Nicole cooed, as she moved so she was sitting on Danny's lap, facing the musician. "But, this feels so much better."

"It'll feel even better when you kiss me."

"Let's test that theory."

Their lips met as soon as Nicole was done speaking. Slowly, they moved against each other, just tasting each other. Hungry for more, they opened their mouths at the same time and moaned as their tongues greeted each other with fervor. With the first stroke of their tongues, Nicole wanted more.

Nicole's hands moved on their own, going to Danny's cleavage. Danny purred into Nicole's mouth. That was all the encouragement she needed. Her hands kneaded warm, plump flesh while she made sure to keep Danny's mouth busy with her own. She'd have her way with Danny now. Probably not the most appropriate punishment for being dumped on a snowman, but she didn't care.

As her hands continued to massage Danny's tempting breasts, the musician clutched onto Nicole's hips. Nicole refused to allow herself to be pulled along Danny's thigh. As a signal to stop and to get Danny's mind on her own pleasure, Nicole tugged at one chocolate peak. Danny moaned loudly; Nicole knew but couldn't understand that Danny enjoyed the rough treatment.

Once Danny ceased to pull on her, Nicole moved one of her hands between them. She discovered there wasn't much space for her to truly touch her lover. Frowning, Nicole pulled away.

"We're getting out."

Danny's brow furrowed. "What? Why?"

"Because I have to have you this very second or I'm going to explode," Nicole declared quite seriously.

Danny didn't need to be told twice and got out of the tub as fast as she could. She wisely wrapped herself in a towel before Nicole had to tell her to do it. Nicole followed, taking a quick second to let the water out and wrap a towel around herself. She rushed to the bedroom, eyes on the bed, only to discover it was empty. She narrowed her gaze a bit and frowned slightly, confused as to what was going on.

"Sweetheart?" Nicole called. *What part of "this very second" did Danny not get?*

"Right here." Danny popped up from the far side of the bed.

"What are you doing?" Nicole resisted the urge to jump Danny while she was on the floor.

"Getting my surprise since it is my night."

Nicole sucked her teeth; she'd forgotten all about their surprises. They had agreed that Danny would go first, since Nicole had gone first on the last trip. Right now, Nicole didn't give a damn about surprises.

"Must you do this now? I want you," Nicole practically whined. It took all of her willpower not to stomp her foot.

"I know. And I wanna try this." Danny climbed to her feet. She held up her bounty, which appeared to be silk scarves.

Nicole felt her brow wrinkle. "You want to tie me up?" Internally, she congratulated herself on not yelping.

"Not exactly. I figured we could use them, but they could just be a blindfold for one of us...or something a little more. You can use them on me. I don't mind," Danny explained in an almost shy tone. Grey eyes even wandered to the floor a couple of times.

"Danny, you want me to tie you up?" Nicole wasn't sure how she felt about the frisson that raced down her spine.

"Only if you want to. It's just something to try. Besides, you seem like you're in a dominating mood tonight," she said with a teasing smile. It would seem that Nicole's obvious nervousness rid Danny of hers.

"Honestly, it's never crossed my mind to restrain you, ever. Is this something you want?"

"It's just something to try," Danny answered, stressing the end.

Nicole knew she didn't have to do anything that she didn't want to. She nodded and decided not to think on it. It was something to try. She trusted Danny, and Danny trusted her. Hell, it might end up being good, like the other surprises.

She marched over to Danny with determination in her step and took control of Danny's mouth. Hearing Danny moan sent another frisson through her and that one didn't confuse her. Without breaking the kiss, she took the scarves from Danny and held them in her hand.

Nicole backed up to the bed with Danny silently following her. They made their way to the center of the bed without breaking their embrace. Nicole removed her towel with her free hand and also took care of Danny's towel. She moaned loudly into Danny's mouth when their nude, still wet bodies touched.

"Just touching you shouldn't turn me on so much," Nicole muttered, pulling away for air briefly. Once she had enough oxygen, she rained kisses down on whatever part of Danny she could touch.

"Welcome to my world, except just seeing you, hearing you is enough to make my blood boil, my heart race, and make me turn into a puddle."

"Let's get you into that puddle then," Nicole purred, pushing Danny back against the pillows. Danny didn't resist, even when Nicole took charge of her hands. "We'll try one scarf," she whispered.

"Whatever you want, angel," Danny breathed.

A smile settled on Nicole's face, as she loosely tied her lover's wrists together. She honestly didn't see the point, but Danny wanted to do it, and she wanted Danny to have fun. There was no other person on Earth that she trusted enough to do these things with.

"Don't pull loose, okay?" Nicole cautioned.

"I'll try, but you could've done this tighter." Danny rubbed her wrists together.

Nicole shook her head and picked up where she left off, kissing Danny and pressing their bodies together. Danny groaned, as Nicole caressed her intimately. They kissed almost lazily, savoring the taste of each other.

"I want more," Nicole hissed.

"Take whatever you want from me, Chem." Danny's chest heaved; she seemed desperate.

Nicole began kissing and licking her way down Danny's body. When she got to her lover's torso, she remembered Danny was fine with being nipped and bitten. While she didn't plan to bite Danny a bunch, she wanted to indulge and knew Danny would oblige her.

She nibbled as she got to the swell of Danny's breast; her hand massaged the other. Danny wiggled and made the sweetest noises, as Nicole raked her teeth down the heaving mound until she got to the peak. Her lips, tongue, and teeth occupied the pebbled nipple until she was sure she'd leave a mark.

Danny writhed underneath Nicole, which sent pride through her. She had to fight down a snicker, as Danny tried her best to get a grip on Nicole's head, but found it impossible with her hands bound. She could tell the tie wouldn't last long, so she needed to work quickly or calm her partner down.

"Hey, sweetheart, I want to savor you." Nicole moved her attention to Danny's unmarked breast.

"Dammit," Danny growled, but her thrashing ceased. "Stupid scarf," she muttered.

Nicole chuckled before going back to work. She nipped and kissed the base of the precious hill, drawing out whimpers and purrs from her girlfriend. Her hands drifted, slowly and softly caressing Danny's sides. Dragging her teeth across plump caramel flesh, she took one good bite, which caused Danny's back to arch. A smile settled on Nicole's face without her knowledge; she was pleased with the reactions she drew from her girlfriend.

"You like when I bite you?" Of course, the bites weren't extremely hard, but they were satisfying on her end. She liked them even more if Danny drew pleasure from them.

"Feels good. Plus, it feels good for you, so it feels even better for me," Danny panted.

Nicole nodded before continuing to love as much of Danny's form as she could. Her hands touching, rubbing, and lightly scratching along Danny's body. Her mouth moved down slowly, delighting in the delicious terrain. Each taste drew cute little noises from Danny, which rippled through Nicole causing shivers of pleasure.

By the time she got to her main destination, Danny was moving again, bucking like a wild horse. Nicole paused briefly, but it was enough for Danny to calm down. Glancing up, she locked eyes with pleading grey orbs. Nicole smirked at her.

"Please, angel. Please, my sweet, beautiful cherub," Danny implored.

"If you can still sweet talk me, then I must not have done something right."

"Doing everything right. Keep doing," Danny begged.

Nicole didn't need to be asked twice. Kissing Danny's navel, she dipped lower and felt Danny desperately trying to put bound hands in her hair. Purchase was nearly impossible without breaking the silk bond. Nicole ignored the struggle, focusing on her goal of tasting Danny's soul.

The initial sweep of her tongue drew a moan from both of them. Nicole was certain Danny was made of pure nectar. There was no other way for her to explain why she needed to take in every drop of her partner. Her tongue and lips relished all that Danny gave and caressed Danny to gain more. The loving was leisurely, but deliberate.

"Nick, need…need…" Danny's legs spread open, revealing her whole being to Nicole. Her arms moved, loosening her tie enough to give her hands freedom. Fingers instantly went to Nicole's hair, racing through auburn curls and massaging her scalp.

Nicole's response was to attack with more zeal, trying to drink in more of her dearest love. Danny's grip on her head and the tremble in Danny's thighs told Nicole that she had pushed her girlfriend to the limit before Danny cried out, convulsed wildly, and collapsed on the bed in spread eagle fashion. Nicole moved to rest her chin on Danny's pudgy abdomen.

"You okay?" Nicole asked with a gentle smile.

"Who the hell's stupid idea was it to use this damned scarf?" Danny replied with an exhausted laugh.

"I honestly don't see the point."

A tired half-smile worked its way onto Danny's face. "There's a point. You're actually looking at it. The frustration of not being able to touch you the way I want to makes the buildup and end result that much more powerful."

An auburn eyebrow craned. "Oh, really? Let's test that theory." She reached for the other silk ties. Danny moaned in anticipation.

***

"So, skiing again?" Nicole teased her lover, who shuffled through the room to get dressed.

Dane scoffed. "Can barely stand up on my own two feet. Damn sure can't stand on skis."

"Or speak in complete sentences?"

Dane only snorted, not having the vocabulary to wage any sort of warfare against her girlfriend. Nicole hadn't taken just her passion last night, but her knees—*even the bad one*—and her mind. It had taken her almost ten minutes this morning to remember how to get out of bed. Thank God Nicole brought her breakfast in bed again, and fed her, or she would've starved to death while trying to figure out how to work the fork.

"I know what we could do," Nicole chirped.

Dane glared. "Stop being so cheerful. I'm sure you're not the first person on Earth to give someone six orgasms!" Dane still wasn't sure how she lived through the night.

"No, but it was the first time I did it for you," the redhead replied with a pleased smile on her face.

Dane shrugged, unable to argue that. "What do you have in mind?"

"Snow tubing."

Nicole said those words as if they should mean something to Dane. She was certain her bewilderment showed in her eyes, because her angel gave her one of those sorrowful smiles that told her she'd missed out on another thing as a child. Nicole didn't bother to explain, grabbing Dane to help her get dressed.

Nicole's energy helped revitalize Dane. Once they were dressed, bundled for warmth and to keep dry, they headed just beyond the slopes. Dane was so happy to pass up the slopes, because she was sure

S.L. Kassidy

her leg wouldn't be able to last another day on skis. Dane knew what Nicole meant the second she saw what a snow tube was and couldn't stop the grin that spread on her face.

"I've always wanted to try this." Dane had planned to do it later if Nicole had wanted to go skiing again.

"Well, let's get to it then. I haven't done this in at least fifteen years."

They spent the whole day snow tubing and then sledding. Dane couldn't believe how fun it was. She definitely preferred those activities to skiing. She knew where she'd be tomorrow while Nicole got in her last runs down the slopes.

"Danny, you ready to get going?" Nicole called, as Dane zoomed down the hill on her rented sled.

"One more ride," Dane replied with a grin.

Nicole only smiled, and Dane got her last ride—three times. Her growling stomach kept her from going for a fourth, and she realized they hadn't eaten lunch. That was more than enough to get her moving.

"Had fun?" Emerald eyes sparkled, as Nicole asked that question. She was clearly pleased with herself.

Dane grinned as big as she could, even with her scarf in the way. "You know I did. This whole trip has been great!"

"I'm glad you feel that way, even though I know your leg was bothering you before."

"It's okay, angel. I don't want my leg to slow either of us down. This was fun."

Dane's grin coaxed a smile out of Nicole. They made their way back to the cabin and stripped. They showered and ended up in the hot tub once more. There was heavy petting and kissing, but nothing further. Afterward Nicole worked on dinner, which they ate together in the living room. Once that was done, Dane got her guitar and played a few songs, while Nicole seemingly vanished.

"Oh, my God, are you Dane?" an oddly excited Nicole asked from behind her lover.

Dane was almost scared to turn around and discovered that she had a reason to be frightened when she caught sight Nicole. The redhead was dressed in black stockings with a short black skirt that barely went to mid-thigh. A torn, red t-shirt clung to her torso.

"Uh...is it Halloween?" *Please, let it be Halloween! Because if this is going where I think it is, I'm not for it!*

Nicole laughed. "Halloween in January? Someone would have some explaining to do."

Dane hoped her face didn't look as horrified as she felt. She didn't want to hurt Nicole's feelings, but this was too much. "Someone still has explaining to do. What the hell are you wearing?"

"This is my surprise. I wanted to try role-playing again, but not as myself."

Dane arched an eyebrow. "And you are?"

"A fan that's managed to get to meet the goddess of rock."

"I was afraid of that. No, just no. I won't even pretend to put you on the same level as a groupie," Dane stated in the sternest voice ever.

"No?" Nicole's face fell and instantly broke her girlfriend's heart.

"God, Chem, don't look like that." Dane jumped to her feet. She rapidly took Nicole in her arms and caressed the side of her face. "I'm not saying no to role-playing. I had fun when we did it before. It's just the role that you picked to play. I can't…No, I *won't* treat you the way I treated those girls. You're way too precious to me, angel."

Nicole pouted. "But, I thought we could do anything together."

"We can, but I can't treat you like that. You're the most important person in the world to me while those girls meant absolutely nothing to me. I was using them and they were using me. I can't treat you that way. I just can't." She leaned down and placed a sweet kiss to Nicole's crown.

Nicole sighed and looked down for a long moment. "I'm sorry for making you uncomfortable."

"I'm not. I want you to come to me with things like this, but I also want to be able to admit if I can't do it. I want you to be able to do the same. It'll be worse if we start something and then realize one of us is forcing the situation to make the other happy."

Nicole nodded. "You're right, sweetheart. I do want to try this pretending-to-be-someone-else thing, because it seemed interesting and fun as long as I didn't have to pretend to be me and you weren't trying to learn how to pick up women. This was the best I could come up with because I didn't know what you'd want to be."

Dane smiled. "We can do the role-playing thing, but let's talk this one out first. Never want to treat you like I did those girls, even if it's just pretend. It's nothing against you. So, can you change and then we talk?"

Nicole smiled and rushed off. Dane decided to make hot chocolate to help her lover feel better. When Nicole returned, they had a long conversation with their delicious beverages.

"I guess our surprises weren't so great this time," Nicole sighed.

Dane put her arm around Nicole's shoulders. "What? It happens. Besides, we talked it over, which gets us almost the same as a surprise. Plus, this vacation totally kicked ass and we have one more day to play in the snow!"

Nicole laughed. "You really like the snow, huh?"

Dane grinned. "Yes. Yes, I do."

"I'm glad."

"Thank you for this, angel."

"Same to you, sweetheart." They leaned over and exchanged a beatific kiss that tasted of chocolate, love, and promise.

Gauze

This chapter is dedicated to Beck for inspiring it.

DANE WAS ON THE computer in the house library, looking up things about the museums in the city. She never imagined there'd be so many, but now she was interested in visiting several. She had originally been looking up a renaissance exhibit one of her students had mentioned, something she thought Nicole might enjoy. Now, she had discovered several "somethings" she was sure her partner would love.

"Well, what would I like, too?" Dane asked the air. She was fully aware Nicole enjoyed things all the more when Dane was clearly having fun, too.

Having never been the type to go to a museum, not even one devoted to music, Dane was at a loss. She wasn't even sure about what type of art she might like if she went to an art exhibit with Nicole. Running her hand through her hair, she decided to do research.

"Thank you gods of the Internet," she chuckled.

She began looking through different art forms and reading a little about the periods they were from. She scanned through some of the more famous pieces from each time period and read up a little on those, too. She didn't study much anymore, but the idea that she was studying for a date tickled her.

Surprisingly enough, studying helped her decide where to take Nicole. Now, she just had to find out when was a good time. Even though Nicole wasn't back in school yet, her hours at work had become more erratic as she, her coworkers, and parents fell back into old habits.

"Speaking of that," Dane said as she glanced at the time. "She should've been here by now." Getting up from the desk, she made her way to the nearest phone. "Hey, Chem, where are you?"

"Hi, baby. I'm still at work." The pout could be heard in her tone. "But, I was just packing up to leave." Now, a smile certainly shined through her voice.

"Okay, good. So, I was wondering if you're free this weekend."

Nicole laughed and Dane realized just how ridiculous it sounded for her to ask that question. They'd probably have a better chance of going on dates once Nicole went back to school, but then Dane would also have to get herself in the mood to go out.

"Am I free this weekend? I don't know. My girlfriend might be planning something," the redheaded vixen remarked in a low, almost seductive purr.

"Forget about your girlfriend. I'm talking about you and me, sweet thing." Dane held in a snicker.

"But, my girlfriend's so sweet," Nicole cooed.

"Not better than me, baby. I could do things to you that your girlfriend never dreamed about."

"Oh, yeah? Like what?" Nicole demanded with a laugh.

"Oh, like take you to the Museum of Classical Art on Saturday, if you're interested," Dane replied with a smile.

"The Museum of Classical Art?" Nicole echoed as if she didn't know what that was.

"Yes, you wanna go?"

"Yes. Please, yes." There was that smile in her voice again.

"Told you I could do things for you that your girlfriend never dreamed of."

"Be careful what you say about my girlfriend. She's very tall and can probably beat you up," Nicole teased.

"Bet she's not that tough. I could probably take her on with one hand and not break a sweat."

Nicole laughed. "I doubt that."

They ended the conversation on that note. Dane took the time to see what else the Museum of Classical Art offered, beyond classical art, and was surprised to find that it was basically a museum dedicated to the classical period. Some of the things listed on the website seemed interesting.

"I guess I'll know how interesting they are when I see them in person." She looked forward to the visit.

***

"Are you sure we have to leave this early?" Dane groused while pulling on her bomber jacket over her other jacket. It wasn't really early, but earlier than she thought they'd leave.

"Yes, that museum is huge and we'll want to see a lot." Nicole grinned, a sparkle in her eyes.

"When was the last time you were there?"

Green eyes glanced up at the ceiling, as Nicole thought about it. "Almost ten years. I'm long overdue for some culture," she giggled.

"Guess that makes two of us, since I've never been."

"No, you have your music to make up for it. You've had much more culture than I have. Now, let's get going. I'm sure you'll like the museum. It was awe inspiring the last time I went."

Dane shrugged and laughed a little, as she followed Nicole out the door. They didn't have to worry about Haydn since Dane's nephews had volunteered to take him for the day. Actually, Adam wanted to see what it was like to have a dog and to get an idea if the boys were old enough for the responsibility. Dane was more than ready to put Adam back on her shit list if he messed up with their pup.

"You act like the museum will close before we get there," Dane teased. Nicole fumbled her keys, as she unlocked the doors for the car. "Calm down, Chem. Nobody should almost drop a simple button to open the car."

"I just want to see as much of the museum as possible, because I know it'll be a while before we return."

Dane smiled. "You said we."

"Of course, I said we. We're going to go together again, right?"

The musician nodded. "Wouldn't have it any other way."

***

A stream of people filled the museum, when the couple arrived. Danny paid since it was her date idea, which earned her a sweet kiss on the cheek. Nicole linked arms with Danny and proceeded to grab a map to help them on their journey.

"So, where would you like to begin? They have art and artifacts from all over the world here, most of it from ancient times." Nicole grinned.

"Is it broken up by country?" Danny asked, looking around the place like an over-stimulated kid. She seemed a little amazed by how big the museum was.

"No, it's split in many different ways. Some things are grouped by country, but there are also mediums, tools, designs, items, and such."

"I guess they're talking about 'classical' in a broad sense," Danny muttered, running her hand through her hair.

Nicole laughed a little. "Yes, I'm sure it is in the broad sense. Classical meaning before the medieval period, I suppose. What do you want to see first?"

"Doesn't matter to me. I'm following you."

"How about we start with ancient weapons and work our way further in? Hopefully, we'll go all the way around and come out through an exhibit on ancient Egyptian tombs."

"So...it's art in the broad sense as well?"

Nicole chuckled. "Stop being so picky. Do you want to start with ancient weapons or what?"

Danny smiled. "Sounds cool."

They set off to their left and entered a chamber displaying all types of weapons from ancient times. Each one had complex, complicated designs on some section of the weapon. They both paused at display after display, studying the artifacts and reading any little tidbits of information that were around.

"How long do you think it takes to do something like this?" Danny asked after a long stretch of silence between them. They stared at a collection of swords with designs, along with precious metals and gems, on the scabbards, hilts, and blades.

"I have no idea. I've never had to create something like that," Nicole laughed.

"Smart ass." Danny smiled and clutched Nicole's hand just a little tighter.

They continued on, eventually coming to a section with silk kimonos. Again, they paused at every display, which also had combs and hair accessories in cases with the robes. By the time they made it to the next exhibit, Danny held Nicole just a little bit closer.

"You're really enjoying this, aren't you?" Nicole asked her.

"Oh, yeah, this is cool. I mean, I'm actually into history and stuff. Usually, it's just the history of some kinda music, but coming here is making me see things a little differently. This is an art museum, so I expected paintings and stuff, but we haven't seen a painting yet. Art is more than I thought and I realize I should look at art the way I look at music. Maybe even look at the world as art, like I look at music," Danny tried to explain, but she ran a hand though her hair before she was even done. "Or something...I dunno."

Nicole gave her a teasing smile. "You do know music is art, right."

Danny laughed. "I know. I just never bothered to look at art really beyond music. Maybe because I play music. I dunno. Music always touched me, but something about seeing how vast art is…it's touching." She tugged Nicole closer to her, wrapping both arms around her waist.

"I'm glad you're looking at it that way. I can't really appreciate the art that way, but it's interesting to hear the way your mind works," Nicole replied as they moved on.

Danny's face scrunched up. "How do you appreciate art?"

It was Nicole's turn to look bewildered and stumble through what she hoped would sound like an explanation. "Well, first, there's the respect for anyone who can create art in all forms since I can't do anything that could feign being art. But, then, there are just things that are pleasing to the eye or capture the imagination, like everything we wondered on how they did that. The dedication, love, and just all around work that goes into pieces leaves me in awe."

"You're quite elegant when you put your mind to it." Danny grinned as they moved on.

Nicole smiled. "Well, how about you use your words and tell me what you like about art?"

"It depends on the art. This stuff has opened my eyes, but it doesn't speak to me beyond being beautiful. I'm not sure why, but that's just the way it is right now."

Nicole accepted that and they continued on. They made a game out of trying to explain why a certain item appealed to them. They held hands and giggled, getting weird looks, which they ignored.

"That explanation was worth at least ten points," Danny said, as they finished looking at a fresco from ancient Rome.

Nicole scoffed. "Don't try to add rules of points. The most you can get is two points and saying, 'it's great because they're doing it hard' isn't close to being worth ten points."

"But, they were and that's why I liked it. In fact, gonna do that to you later," the musician said in a sing-song voice.

Nicole scoffed. "Keep cheating and you won't be doing anything to me for a good, long time."

The pout that instantly appeared on Danny's face put a smile on Nicole's face. She kissed Danny's cheek and they moved onto the next fresco. Grey eyes went wide.

"What is up with porn in ancient Rome? They didn't have kids back then or something?" Danny wondered aloud.

Nicole laughed. "It wasn't considered porn back then. Ancient Rome had different morals and values compared to today."

"Yeah? Think I'd like ancient Rome."

Auburn hair swayed, as Nicole shook her head. "You'd never survive. No guitar."

Danny couldn't help chuckling. "I'd invent the guitar. That's in my soul. Besides, they had to have something guitar like."

Nicole laughed. "You'd invent the guitar? I'd love to have seen that."

"Well, you'd have to be there or I couldn't exist there." Danny squeezed her hand and earned a smile from Nicole.

"You're such a charmer."

They moved on, eventually going into a pottery hall. Some of the cases only had shards, but for the most part, there were full pieces. They admired the images on the pottery as well as the pottery itself.

"It's like two pieces of art in one," Nicole said.

"So, to make pottery, you need to know how to draw, too? Seems too much." Danny shook her head.

Nicole gave her girlfriend a teasing smile. "Says the woman who plays six instruments, composes her own music, and writes her own lyrics."

Danny stuck her tongue out. "Well, we can't all do simple stuff like practicing law and being master chemists."

Nicole smiled and they continued on. They practically cooed when they saw the porcelain artifacts. Danny quickly straightened up when she realized the noise she made. Of course, that made Nicole laugh.

* * *

The couple made their way to a food court inside the museum. Nicole grabbed a table, while Danny went to get their lunch. Nicole managed a space by the museum's glass wall, which offered a view of a closed exhibit—a garden of statues. She smiled as she looked into the assortment of figures.

"That would've been nice to walk through. Maybe in the summer we'll come back." Nicole sighed.

"Missed me so much you had to start talking to yourself?" Danny eased their meals down onto the table. She pushed a basket of chicken fingers and fries in front of Nicole and sat down in front of her slices of pizza with toppings.

"No, I was delirious with hunger because it took you so long," Nicole countered with a grin.

Danny laughed. "Not my fault everybody in the place decided to eat lunch right now."

Nicole only smiled before they turned their attention to their meals. The redhead had to put a dash of salt on her fries. Her chicken needed hot sauce, and both items were covered in ketchup. Danny used the hot sauce, sprinkling a few drops on both slices of pizza.

"What's all that on your pizza?" Nicole asked, as she broke one chicken finger in half and began eating.

"This one?" The tip of the slice was already in Danny's mouth. Nicole nodded and her girlfriend finished her bite before answering. "Hamburger, sausage, and extra cheese."

A grimace tore through Nicole's face. "You're just trying to develop heart disease, aren't you?"

Danny smiled. "It's a throwback to when I never knew when I'd eat again. A slice with a bunch of toppings was filling, but it was also like having something different when I ate, unlike if I kept eating burgers or tacos."

Nicole's heart clenched. "Every time I forget that you were homeless, not once, but twice in your life, it sneaks back up, and I feel so bad for you."

"Don't, angel. It's the past and it wasn't all bad. Now, what the heck is this thing out here?" Danny nodded out the window and took a huge bite of her pizza.

"They call it the Sculpture Garden. It's a park of statues on display with flower arrangements."

While chewing and swallowing, Danny nodded. "Is it open?"

"No, it's closed for renovations. According to the map, they're changing the design and they're adding new artifacts. I've never been through it, but it's supposedly a very popular exhibit." Nicole finished off one of her chicken fingers.

Danny twisted her mouth up. "When does it reopen?"

"This summer."

Danny tilted her head, like she was thinking, and then ate more of her pizza. "Want to come back?"

Nicole smiled. "I was hoping you'd say that."

"So, it's a date?"

Still smiling, Nicole nodded. "Of course."

Grey eyes shined, and Nicole felt her heart swell. She was happy Danny was enjoying the museum as much as she was. In fact, Danny pulled Nicole on after she practically inhaled her pizza. She shared a bit with Nicole, who was curious about the peppers, spinach, and olives all over Danny's second slice. Thankfully, Nicole was done with her meal.

"Where are we headed now?" Danny asked, as they started walking.

"Asks the person tugging me," Nicole remarked with a teasing smile.

A blush rushed to bronze cheeks. "Sorry. Um...so, where to now?"

Nicole studied the map. "We're headed toward the Chinese terracotta figures. We've watched a few shows about those. It'll be nice to see them in real life."

"Oh, yeah. They were cool on TV."

The couple was awestruck by the terracotta figures. They went back to their little game, explaining why they liked certain items. It was easier to do with statues than anything else.

"I love this expression. He looks so fierce." Nicole pointed to a terracotta soldier to their left.

"I'd run in terror if I ever saw any of these guys," Danny replied with a light laugh.

"No, you'd do that weird thing where you sort of reason with them, if they were going to attack you," Nicole countered with a smile of her own.

An ebony eyebrow arched. "What? What weird thing?"

"You don't fight, baby. I've seen you talk your way out of several conflicts by pointing out why fighting wouldn't solve anything, or pointing out why the person is an asshole and then walking away. Have you ever even been in a fight?"

Danny laughed. "And if I haven't? You'll leave me because I'm not a fighter?"

"No, but I would judge you," Nicole joked.

"Well, I'll just judge you right back!" Danny stuck her nose in the air.

Nicole rolled her eyes. "You can't judge me. I've had my fair share of scraps."

Danny's jaw dropped. "What? You in fights? No way! Your mom would've tanned your hide good the second you looked like you were going to fight somebody. I know she wouldn't let it happen twice."

Nicole laughed. "My fights happened during sporting events. My mom could only watch in horror. What about you?"

"What makes you think I have ever had a fight or that my mom cared?"

"I know the answer to the latter, but not the former. Have you ever had a fight?"

Danny shrugged. "More than my fair share. Never saw much of a point in fighting, but get me high or drunk enough and I forget any of the few rules I had in life."

"Of course." Nicole shook her head.

Danny smiled a bit and they went back to focusing on the art. As they moved onto another exhibit, the younger woman glanced at the map. Nicole did the same, if only for an idea of what to look forward to. They went through a hall of coins from around the world and studied the details that even went into currency.

"This place fucking rocks," Danny whispered to Nicole, who giggled.

"Agreed," Nicole concurred through her titters. They moved on.

***

It took a while, but they eventually made it to the part of the museum that Dane had expected—paintings. Of course, they weren't exactly the type of paintings she was familiar with.

"No Da Vinci?" Dane asked, looking for something familiar.

"No, sweetheart, this is before his time. Think of it like us being in a museum about the Baroque era of music, and someone asking where's Beethoven or where's a piano." Nicole softly patted her lover's hand.

Dane smiled and nodded; that made perfect sense to her. "Somehow, that helps me appreciate things a little more."

Nicole gave her an impish smile. "Glad I could help."

They studied the paintings. The color had faded on some or there were blank spaces, but the museum had done something amazing with the damaged paintings. Next to any of the damaged work, there was a smaller, redone version of the piece done by young artists. Those artists weren't famous by far, but their styles and talent spoke loudly through their work.

"This is so cool." Dane wanted to see everything at once, but also desired to study each piece—old and new, ancient and contemporary—individually.

"What is it, Danny? You look so...enraptured," Nicole whispered, as if afraid that she'd disturb Dane.

"This is incredible. All of this is so incredible, and I never knew. Never bothered with it, but it's all so...beautiful," Danny replied in pure awe.

"Why do you say that?"

"I can visualize the painting being done. I could play painting. The different colors and the strokes are like notes, pitches, tones, and even melody. The picture itself is a song, a mood, a statement from the mind, body, and soul."

Nicole was silent for a moment. "Danny, you win."

Butterfly Closure

DANE WHISTLED AS SHE hustled around the hotel room, setting things up. She hooked her iPod to the dock connected to the radio and clock. She blasted her favorite metal songs and jammed along on her own guitar. Standing on the bed, she rocked out until there was a loud, demanding knock at the door.

"Yo!" Dane called while marching to the door. "What's up?" she added before looking through the door's peephole. "Whoa, she's hot," she muttered, then opened the door.

Standing before her was a gorgeous, but clearly upset redhead. Her eyebrows were drawn together and a vein in her forehead popped up slightly, but the fury seemed almost hot to Dane. *There's something magical about an angry redhead*. There was something more about an angry redhead wearing wealthy clothing.

The woman was dressed in a black skirt suit that teased the public by complimenting her figure exceptionally well. The skirt fell right above her knee, but there was a slit to give a clue about her thighs. Surely, the skirt would ride up when she sat down and call all to peek at the peep of thigh that would have to show. Her curves seemed to beckon eyes and hands. Added to that, she had on a tight, lime-green, button-down shirt, with three buttons undone, leaving her mouth-watering cleavage exposed.

"My face is up here," the testy redhead huffed, motioning with her hand from her breasts to her face.

Dane's eyes managed to move from lush, begging breasts to a tense, yet lovely face. "The view's just as good," she remarked with what she hoped was a charming grin.

A frown cut across olive-toned features. "Do you mind turning your god-awful music down? Some of us have business meetings to attend in the morning," she said through gritted teeth. Emerald eyes glared as hard as the stones they were colored from.

"Wouldn't call it god-awful or even regular awful. You look like you're still in a business meeting…" Dane trailed off and held in a laugh. Taking a breath, she continued. "A sexy business meeting," and then the snickers escaped.

"Is that supposed to be cute?" the fiery redhead demanded with a glare.

"No, you're…" The snickers were now chuckles.

Emerald eyes glared at Dane seriously now. "Goddamn it, Danny, how is this supposed to work if you don't take it seriously?"

"Sorry, sorry, angel. I'm good." Dane swallowed her laughs and took a calming breath. "Okay, now where were we? You know, what? Screw it. Lady, you're hot as hell and burning me up. Do you want to come in and give me something to do other than listening to music?" She smirked and wiggled her eyebrows.

Nicole scowled. "Dammit, Danny, stick to the script!" she huffed, pushing her lover's shoulder slightly.

Dane laughed. "It's like a bad porn! Just get in here!" She snatched Nicole into the room and slammed the door behind her.

"Danny!" Nicole reprimanded her girlfriend, glaring at her even harder than before. "You're supposed to stick to the script!"

Dane tossed her hands up. "The fact that we even have a script is preposterous! This is stupid! Sheer insanity! We're no good at it! If we're not doing something that makes the other uncomfortable, then we're sitting down and approaching it like a homework assignment, complete with written work." Dane grinned big, which was just to prevent her from laughing at the sheer absurdity of the whole matter. "Can't we just fuck?" She pouted, poking out her bottom lip.

Nicole continued frowning and stomped over to the bed to sit down. She also turned off the loud metal music pouring from the iPod dock. Dane remained on her feet and tried her best to read Nicole. The stony, frustrated expression was new and cut her to the bone. Dane felt like her stomach was suddenly upset and grinding against her other organs, especially when Nicole decided to look off to a wall instead of at her. *Shit, I messed up.*

"Angel, I am so sorry! We can start over and I'll do it right! I'll follow the script and everything!" Dane kneeled before her sweetheart, wanting and needing to make everything better. She put a hand on Nicole's knee, caressing her gently.

Shaking her head, Nicole sniffled. "No, you don't want to do it and I won't force you."

Dane offered her a sad smile and continued petting her knee.

"Look, angel, this role-playing thing just isn't us. Even when we sit down and plan it, it's still weird and not natural for us. Don't tell me you didn't feel like a goober just now."

There was a sorrowful smile. "I did. But, what are we going to do to keep our sex life interesting?"

Dane's brow furrowed. "Interesting? Nick, our sex life is plenty interesting."

"We had sex in the same position for a year because of me! I don't want to make that mistake again and bore you."

Dane smiled softly and climbed up on the bed. Wrapping her arm around Nicole's shoulders, she pulled the redhead to her. Nicole embraced Dane around the waist, which let Dane know they were somewhat okay. She still needed to do damage control, though.

"Sweet, sweet angel, first, I need you to know I'd never leave you over sex. I'd gladly forsake sex for the rest of my life if it meant I could be with you just as long. Next, we won't get bored. If things started to slow down between us, we are both highly skilled in seducing each other. We'll just do that. It's something we are good at."

Nicole sniffled a little. "But, what if that eventually gets boring or predictable?"

"Well, we have a lot of other alternatives and things we haven't tried yet. We can even do research to sate the nerd in you. I just can't do a role-playing thing where we actually sat down and wrote a script. I'm not an actor and this is crazy. That's forcing it, love, and this is supposed to be fun."

Nicole nodded and curled closer to her lover. "You're right. We did force it, but it seems like it would be so interesting to pretend to be other people or just did other roles."

"We don't have roles, Chem."

"What? Aren't you the housewife?" Nicole teased, pulling away just enough to flash her an amused grin.

Dane chuckled. "Okay, you got me there. Wanna play around with that?" She felt like she could play the role of a housewife from the 50s. That might be fun.

Nicole's eyes narrowed as she thought on it. "Maybe when we go back home. I shouldn't have asked you to come on this trip. I'm supposed to be worrying about work, but you being here makes me think about personal stuff."

"It's okay. You thought getting away would be the perfect chance to try this out. Not like you could pretend I was some rocker and my music was bothering you from home while you were trying to unwind from a meeting. It'd just be weird."

"You're teasing me, aren't you?"

"I am. Sorry. I'm glad you brought me along, though. I can still help you relax." Dane rubbed Nicole's shoulder.

"How?"

Dane opened her mouth to respond, but a knock at the door interrupted her. A wide grin took over her face. Leaning down, she placed a gentle kiss to Nicole's forehead.

"You'll see right now," the musician promised.

Nicole's brow wrinkled as Dane went to the door. She smiled reassuringly at Nicole before opening the door. Standing in the doorway was a room service cart and a smiling hotel employee.

"Your room service order, miss," he smirked at her. He clearly knew what Dane had in mind and looked just a little envious if she read the spark in his dark brown eyes correctly.

"Thanks. Just leave it here," Dane said as she pulled out some bills to tip him.

"Oh, okay," he agreed while pushing the cart away. He stepped away from it and accepted the money. He glanced over at the bed, spotting Nicole. He turned back to Dane, giving her a quick wink as he grinned. "Good luck." He quickly made himself scarce.

Dane laughed. "I wish I'd tipped him more."

"What's that?" Nicole asked, nodding toward the cart.

"This is..." Dane grinned almost lecherously and removed the cover off the food. "A cure for boredom." She licked her lips.

An auburn eyebrow arched. "A cure?"

"Oh, yeah," Dane said with a wolfish grin, as she selected a bowl to show Nicole.

Nicole yelped happily. "Chocolate covered strawberries."

"Figured that'd get your attention. But, there's more." Dane pulled out a can of whipped cream.

Nicole smiled. "I guess we won't be bored tonight."

"Not if I have anything to say about it."

Nicole's smile curled in a sexy manner and then suddenly dropped. "Wait, you had this planned. Did you ruin our role-playing on purpose?" Her eyes narrowed, targeting Dane.

Dane scrunched her face up. "No! I didn't think I'd get a case of the chuckles. Was gonna use this stuff in the role-playing. You know, like 'oh, my room service just arrived. Maybe you'd like to share with me' or something. Why waste it, even though the role-playing didn't work out?"

Nicole was silent for a moment. "You make a point."

Dane smiled widely. "Good, then let's get this party started."

She rushed over to the bed. Nicole giggled as Dane settled next to her and took the strawberries from her. Nicole opened her mouth, all too aware of what Dane planned. The musician wasted no time feeding one large berry to her lover. Nicole moaned as the smooth chocolate and sweet juice burst in her mouth.

"Good?" Nicole could only nod, and Dane leaned in close to whisper to her. "I'll make you moan so much louder than that."

That statement alone made Nicole moan loudly. She was silenced with another strawberry. When she was done, she fed a strawberry to Dane. It was so good! Moaning in delight was really the only option. Dane had another bright idea, as Nicole pulled the fruit away. Dane ducked her head and licked Nicole's fingers. The redhead yelped and jumped a little before somewhat glaring at Dane.

Dane gave her an innocent grin. "Just getting the strawberry juice off your hand."

Emerald eyes narrowed. "A likely story."

"Should I not have done it?" Dane purposely pouted, even though the burning gaze in her lover's eyes told it all.

Nicole practically tackled Dane to the bed, pinning her with sweet lips. Her mouth controlled Dane's, and Dane loved every second of it, moaning and purring against Nicole's wonderful tongue. It was like Nicole's mouth danced against hers, moving to some beat that Dane couldn't catch, could only revel in. The kiss only stopped for Nicole to snatch Dane's shirt off and fling it away as if it were the vilest item in existence.

"What about the strawberries?" Dane panted as Nicole caressed her bare sides. She had foregone a bra since it was a given she'd soon be nude.

"Later. Right now, I really need us to be naked." Nicole peppered loud, wet kisses against Dane's collarbones and the tops of her breasts.

Dane moaned and arched into the touch, grabbing fistfuls of the lawyer's jacket. "Agreed, but I'd like to point out if you did this every now and then, I'd never be bored."

Nicole didn't ask any questions. She sat up and just peeled her suit jacket off while Dane attacked the buttons of her shirt. Nicole went after her pants. Dane decided on a surprise attack to show Nicole she wasn't boring either. She slipped her hand underneath Nicole's skirt. Dane actually gasped.

"You naughty, little minx. Where the hell are your panties?" Dane slid her middle finger through pure bliss.

Nicole hissed and then managed a taunting grin. "Wouldn't you like to know?"

"Part of me does, but most of me just wants to slide into you and never leave. Can I live inside of you?" Dane moved faster through the slickness, adoring what she'd built up in her love.

"Please," Nicole whimpered, gripping her shoulders tightly.

Dane couldn't deny either of them, easing inside. Nicole moaned as her hips moved with Dane's hand. Dane was mesmerized by the movement and put her other hand on Nicole's hip, just to feel her move.

"Angel, you're so perfect," Dane mumbled, inhaling Nicole, trying to take her all in.

"Only to you." Nicole kissed Dane on the lips.

"That's all that matters," Dane whispered, thrusting a bit harder. The ease with which she moved amazed her, and she glanced down, wishing she could see what she was doing, wishing she could see how much her angel relished her touch. But, feeling it was more than enough, cutting into her heart and soul, making her more and more in love with Nicole.

"Oh, God, baby, that feels so damn good. It's like heaven, it's like everything." Nicole dropped her head to Danny's neck. Soft kisses turned to nips as the pressure built. They served as warnings for Dane that a bite was coming shortly.

"Let it be everything. Let it be all. Let go, angel. It's okay. I got you," Dane promised, as her thumb made circles around Nicole's pleasure center. She hissed a bit, enjoying the feel of what had to be rapture as far as she was concerned.

Nicole practically cooed as she sank her teeth into Dane's neck. Dane moaned right along with her, loving the flutter around her fingers. Nicole's teeth dug in deep, stifling a cry that escaped her, but thankfully not breaking Dane's skin. Her nails, blunt as usual, still bit into Dane's back and even that was worthy of a moan.

"God, Danny," Nicole breathed as she released her neck.

When the convulsions halted and Nicole was slumped against her, Dane slipped out with care. Her fingers missed her version of heaven, but she could go back anytime. She locked eyes with half-open green orbs and smiled before slowly licking her fingers clean. Nicole whimpered.

"Tastes better than any nectar from the gods," Dane smirked. She was certain she could get drunker off of Nicole's essence than any other drink on Earth.

"That's not fair, Danny. I was in charge, and you just flipped it around," Nicole griped in a low voice.

"Didn't hear you complaining five minutes ago, sweet angel," Dane replied with a proud grin.

"Shut up." Nicole laughed. "Now, I do believe I said I need us naked and you totally messed that up, just like you messed up our role-playing," she scolded Dane, but it was clear from the smoldering look she gave Dane that the musician wasn't in any real trouble.

Dane forced a pout while keeping a growl down. *Dammit, she's so sexy. I don't know how anybody could have let her go.* "I didn't mean to. What're you gonna do to me for messing up your precious role-playing scene?"

Nicole put her finger to her chin, "thinking" on things for a moment. A clear spark went through her eyes and she got up. Dane whimpered while trying to keep down the throbbing going on below her belt.

"Calm down. The night's young and you need to take your pants off before you get into more trouble," Nicole ordered.

An almost inappropriately toothy grin conquered Dane's face. "This is a nice change from telling me to put pants on."

"Those pants better be off by the time I get back to that bed."

"You being bossy is so goddamn sexy." Dane wasted no time wiggling out of her already opened pants. *I love this woman!*

***

Nicole went to the closet, where their bags were for the short weekend, working trip. She went into Danny's bag, knowing Danny had packed a few things for her "rude rocker" persona. She plucked out a couple of the red silk scarves and hurried out before she had time to consider what she was doing.

The sight of Danny lying naked on the bed, waiting for her, greeted her. Her heart thumped heavy in her chest as she realized what she was doing. She almost dropped the scarves.

"Angel, I'm ready for you."

"Danny," Nicole whimpered. *Can I really do this? This is crazy. She makes me crazy.*

Grey eyes locked on Nicole. "No, baby, don't hesitate. Keep going. I need to be punished because I ruined the night you carefully planned, and then I took the lead when you were clearly in charge. Now, come on, Chem, teach me a lesson."

Nicole nodded, still not in the same place mentally as she was a minute ago. But, Danny's reassuring voice was enough to move her forward. She eased onto the bed and straddled Danny's waist. The musician was clearly eager, reaching for her already.

"Don't touch." Nicole caught Danny's hands. "Bring both hands up to me."

Danny obeyed while clearly fighting down a grin; the twinkle in her eyes betrayed her. Nicole was happy that Danny kept the grin at bay because she was trying her best not to feel awkward and self-conscious. She tied Danny's wrists together, making sure the scarf was tight enough that Danny couldn't get free.

"Does it hurt? It's not too tight?"

"The throbbing between my legs hurts." Danny gave her a cheeky grin. Something about her response made Nicole want to up the ante instead of just calling the whole thing off. Maybe it was the daring, pushing look in Danny's eyes, a look that implored her to keep going. She couldn't stand the thought of putting disappointment there.

"Well, that could've been relieved a while ago if someone hadn't been so bad. See what happens when you behave badly, baby? Now, you have to wait." Nicole smirked and held up the other silk scarf. "Now, if you don't behave, I'll be forced to use this one. Maybe as a blindfold."

"I'll be good!" Danny promised. Since she was all about visuals, being blindfolded would be a good "punishment."

"Good."

Nicole eased off of her lover, earning a whimper from the tied musician. She smirked and moved slowly as she unsnapped her bra. A loud hiss echoed through the room, making it seem like Danny was in pain. Nicole's smirk grew as her hands went to unbutton her skirt. Danny's tongue snaked out, wetting her lips at the sight. Nicole wiggled out of her skirt, leaving it on the floor.

"Hmm...what should I do now?" Nicole pretended to think on it, putting a finger to her chin.

"Are you taking suggestions? Because I have plenty!"

"Yes, but you're being good or this scarf becomes a gag," Nicole remarked dryly.

Danny whimpered and nodded. She looked so helpless, but her eyes were blazing, daring, and begging all in one. Nicole turned her attention to the can of whipped cream and figured she needed to put it to use. Grabbing it, she moved onto the bed and leaned down to give Danny a powerful and passionate kiss. Danny made all of the purring sounds she loved and there was something about the idea of Danny not being able to clutch her that drove Nicole wild. Danny had to put her all into the kiss and work her tongue to give Nicole an idea of what she wanted. Nicole got the message loud and clear: I love you, I need you, and I want to feel you right now. When they broke apart, she straddled Danny's waist again.

Without saying a word, Nicole shook up the can and swirled the whipped cream around Danny's areola, burying the whole area including the nipple. Danny shivered a bit, possibly a mixture of the cold treat and anticipation. Nicole felt a shiver of her own, like lightning going down her spine and spreading throughout her whole body.

"Don't worry, baby, I'll take good care of you," Nicole promised and wasted no time making good on that.

"Please, I want you all over me," the younger woman said.

"I want that, too."

Danny purred as Nicole slurped up the whipped cream, giving the peak extra care. Her tongue played with the gem underneath the whipped cream, sucking on it like a piece of hard candy. The purrs grew louder, as Nicole treated the other globe to the same sweet torment. Soon, there was delicious whipped cream all over Danny's chest. When that was gone, there were red marks on Danny's breasts. She arched and wiggled, whimpering for more.

"Should I go lower?" Nicole pretended to muse.

"Please, baby. I've been so good! I didn't say anything or giggle or nothing," Danny whined. Of course, she had been too busy mewing in bliss and panting to say anything, never mind giggle.

Nicole smiled. "You're right. You have been good."

Moving off of Danny, Nicole put the whipped cream down and went to the foot of the bed. She settled between her lover's legs. She couldn't help admiring the view.

"You are so beautiful, sweetheart. My beautiful, kind, loving, partner. I love you so much," she whispered.

"Love you," Danny replied, lifting her head enough to see.

Nicole smiled before placing light kisses to the inside of dark thighs. She nibbled at the mouth-watering flesh a couple of times, but she didn't bite. Her tongue came out before she even got to where they both wanted her. They both moaned and shuddered when Nicole's mouth came to Danny's sweet spot. Her lips sucked and her tongue traced nonsense patterns, driving Danny crazy.

While Danny squirmed, she seemed to be trying to control herself to a degree. Nicole felt Danny's hands in her hair briefly, but that wasn't going to do much. She continued on her quest to taste Danny to her heart's content, even though she'd never get her fill. *I'll never get enough of Danny, ever. I get what she means about being with her forever, even if we never had sex again, but the sex is wonderful, too. I just want her to be happy.*

Danny moved wildly to the point that Nicole had to put a hand on the writhing stomach to keep her anchored to the bed. The fierce movement undoubtedly came from the fact that Danny's hands were tied, and she couldn't find purchase on anything. Just the thought of the tension building inside of Danny made Nicole's blood boil and her mouth thirsted for more of the musician. She moved with more intent, tongue, lips, and all seeking every inch and drop of her lover. She wanted all of Danny.

"Oh, fuck!" Danny shouted as Nicole's hand pinned her in place and Nicole had her way with Dane. She practically roared when Nicole scratched her belly slightly while simultaneously pushing a finger into the musician. "Goddamn it, Nick! Fuck!"

Nicole smirked because of the profanities flowing from her lover. They were almost as pleasurable as the passion flowing from Danny. Her mouth tried to drink all of Danny in, and her fingers caressed Danny to turn her inside out, which happened much too soon, in Nicole's opinion.

"Oh, goddamn it, Nick!" Danny hollered for the world to hear as her back bowed. She accidentally dislodged the adoring finger and moved away from loving lips.

Nicole sat up and watched Danny convulse with pleasure. She continued stroking Danny, drawing out her ecstasy. There was something about watching Danny come undone that touched Nicole in places that she didn't know existed until Danny became her lover. Those places belonged to Danny and no one else would ever know about them. By the time Danny was coming back to herself, Nicole had her wrists unbound and was holding her close. Danny looked up at her and grinned.

"Chem, that was so the opposite of boring!" Danny said.

Nicole mustered a soft smile. "I'm glad you liked it."

Grey eyes blinked and Danny shook her head a little to gather herself. "You didn't like it?"

Nicole's brow wrinkled a bit. She didn't really have time to process it, but she definitely didn't dislike it. "It was…weird. I mean, it was great. Fun. But, weird. I've never done anything like that before." She would've been scandalized if any other lover suggested it. Beyond this being with Danny, the fact that Danny hadn't wanted to tie her up helped. She was given control and she liked it.

"Like what? You tied me up before. You order me around every now and then. You go down on me almost daily. Aside from the whipped cream, you've done it all, angel. You may have only done it with me, which is fine with me, but you've done it. That's why you're my little vixen, too." Danny smiled and wrapped her arms around her lover.

"I…I liked it," Nicole whispered, as if she were confessing the worst crime in the world. It felt somewhat naughty, like the first time she had sex, natural, but naughty. She wasn't sure how to explain it.

"Well, then we'll have to do it more often," Danny declared as if it was the simplest thing in the world.

Nicole stared at Danny, trying to determine if she meant it. "Are you sure? It didn't bother you?"

"Of course not! I had fun! It's especially nice to see you let loose. Chem, babe, I'm all for having fun in bed and that's what we just did. If you like it and I liked it, then we should just do it. It's not like you tried to hurt me or anything. It was perfectly fine."

Nicole opened her mouth to disagree, but found she didn't have a reason to. It was fun, they both did like it, and of course she'd never try to hurt Danny. So, yes, they should just do it.

"Oh, and congratulations on your first role-playing," Danny said.

Nicole squinted a little. "What?"

"Chem, this would count as role-playing. You took the role of the dominant partner, even if it was only playfully. So, congratulations. Plus, you found something that we can play with more. Now, let's get some sleep."

Nicole smiled and kissed Danny in agreement. She suddenly felt drained. She knew the role-playing had taken a lot out of her, but she looked forward to doing something similar in the future.

"I love you so much, Danny. I love being able to explore myself, and us, with you."

"It is a fun ride. Now sleep," Danny insisted, eyes already closed.

Pressure

DANE WAS ON HER way out the door with Haydn as the phone rang. She sucked her teeth and the pup barked while tugging on his leash, as if trying to pull his owner toward the door. She chuckled and decided to give in to her dog's desire. *It's probably nothing, anyway.*

The caller left a message, so Dane played it after she and Haydn returned. "Dammit, Dane, where the hell are you? I wanted to tell you and not the voicemail. They're having a music festival at that old jazz club you like, to raise money. Apparently, they're trying to close the place down," reported the voice of Dane's best friend, Crow.

"Closing down an old jazz club I like? She'd better not be talking about *Melody*." Dane grabbed the phone to call Crow.

"Hey, Dane, I was wondering when I was going to hear from you," Crow said, answering her cell phone.

"Just got in from walking Haydn. What jazz club were you talking about that they're trying to close down?"

"Hmm...I think the name was *Melody*."

"Dammit! They can't close that place down. It's one of the oldest music clubs in the city." Dane threw herself onto the couch. Haydn followed her, jumping up on the sofa and laying his head in her lap. She scratched his ear to distract herself.

"I'm guessing that's the problem. Who wants to go to a boring old jazz club, except you and senior citizens?" Crow teased with a laugh.

Dane laughed. "Shut up! Damn, *Melody* is a nice place. Great music and good drinks with a very friendly atmosphere. They can't just close it down."

"Well, it's not gone yet, and they might save it. Go down there and check it out. It's not like you have anything better to do with your life."

"This is true. You at work?"

"Yes, so no, I can't come get you. Want to do it later?"

Dane thought it over. "Yeah. Nick has class."

"Aw, so Princess won't have a chance to miss you. How sweet."

"Shut up, Crow." She supposed that might actually happen if she managed to say it without chuckling. Once upon a time, Dane would've been able to say it without any humor attached and yet Crow was still her friend.

"I'll come get you at seven."

"All right."

They wouldn't go to the club until nine, more than likely, but if Crow was going to drive, they had to hang out. That was Crow's price and Dane didn't mind, well not anymore anyway.

"I'll try to have you back before your curfew, Cinderella."

"You're in a mood," Dane said. It wasn't like Crow to tease her with almost every sentence that left her mouth.

"Sorry. I'm actually nervous because I thought you'd be upset over the club closing. I figured it'd be on me to cheer you up, but you're taking it like a champ. Anyway, let me get back to work."

"All right. See you at seven." Dane disconnected the call and phoned Nicole right after.

"Hello, sweetheart."

"Hey, Nick. How you doing so far?"

"I'm fine. Work gets more bearable once school starts up. I oddly have less to do when I have to work and go to class than when I'm on break from school. How about you? Have you taken our little man out for his walk?"

"Just got back. He's sleeping on me now."

Nicole chuckled. "You wore him out. One day he'll learn that going to the park with you is meant to put him to sleep for the night. How are you doing?"

"I'm fine. Wanted you to know that if I'm not here when you come in, it's because I'm hanging out with Crow."

"Oh. You'll be out late?" Nicole sounded a little disappointed.

"Not really. Back by midnight, I'm sure." Crow had promised to have her back before her "curfew."

Nicole made a small noise that conveyed more disappointment. "Oh, all right."

"Chem, don't sound like that. It's just for the night. You can do homework while I'm out and then we can watch a movie tomorrow. Actually, we can watch a couple of movies since you don't have class tomorrow."

"You're right. I'm sorry I'm acting this way. I just like coming home to you."

196

Dane smiled. "I like being here when you ome home. I'm your little housewife and I love it."

Nicole chuckled. "You're a lot of things, but little isn't one of them. And you can't be housewife if you're not married to me."

"You got me there. So, we're good?"

"Yes, we're good. Enjoy yourself, baby. Tell Crow I say hi."

"I will."

They ended the call and Dane sighed. *Please, don't let them close Melody. God, that would fucking suck. Melody is fucking cool!*

***

"I don't get why this place is such a big deal," Crow said, as she and Dane pulled into a parking space on the city street.

"Crow, this is possibly the best jazz club in the city. It's an icon. A legend. They can't just close it," Dane huffed and hopped out of the car while it was still moving.

"Dude! I'm still parking." Crow barked the obvious, scowling at Dane.

"I don't care. I have to see." Dane rushed off down the street as best she could. Turning the corner, she saw there was a crowd outside of *Melody*. It actually made her breathe a sigh of relief. "Can they close this place with such a rocking crowd?"

Dane was about to go in, but she remembered she had come out with someone. Turning around, she returned to Crow. Dane could see the glaring frown in the dark and smiled sheepishly.

"First, you jump out of a moving car and then you leave me? Worst date ever!" Crow threw her hands up.

"Sorry," Dane apologized as she stood before her friend.

"Don't worry about it. I already called your Princess and told on you." Crow stuck her tongue out at Dane.

Dane's jaw dropped open and her eyes went wide. "You didn't," she kind of begged. *Nick will totally bust my chops for getting out of the car while it was still moving. Never mind the fact that I rudely left Crow at the car by herself at night.*

Crow had a good laugh. "I didn't, but I was going to if you didn't come back. How do you invite me out and then leave me behind?"

Dane put her hand through her hair. "Sorry. Got anxious. I really like *Melody*. I know you don't get it, but it's more than some jazz club, to me and to this city."

Sighing, Crow shook her head. "You are so weird when we're both sober."

Dane only smiled and offered her hand to her friend. Crow accepted and they marched off to the club. Finding that she still had some clout, Dane was let in after a trip down memory lane with several workers out front.

"You know them as well as you know the punks at our clubs," Crow said, as they walked in.

Dane smiled. "I'm a musician before a punk. Don't worry. Not gonna keep you here too long. I know you don't wanna be here." *Besides, I know who would love this place, and I'd rather be here with her than anybody else, especially if they're closing the old place.*

"Sorry, but this just isn't my scene." Crow eyed the crowd and her fingers fidgeted together. She undoubtedly felt out of place wearing her usual Goth gear. She looked lost in more ways than one.

"I know. Be cool while I go try to find some folks," Dane replied, and her friend nodded.

Dane found Crow a seat at the bar before going off to find a familiar face. She frowned as she drifted through the crowd of people she didn't know, people that didn't know her. She had been away from the scene for so long and away from *Melody* even longer. *And now it might be gone. I should've come here more when I had the chance.*

She shook her head free of those thoughts when she noticed someone waving in her direction. Weaving through people, she realized the person was the familiar face that she wanted to see. As she got closer, she saw more than one familiar face, which caused her to smile slightly.

"Bless my soul, Dane. We thought you died a long time ago," Jewel said with a laughing grin. She looked just as Dane remembered, except a little more mature.

Luck was tucked in close to Jewel, in a chair by the wall. He scoffed, dramatically throwing his head back. He looked bigger than she remembered, maybe a little buffer. His skin looked browner, richer, like he was healthier than she recalled. *Do I look as good as these guys?*

Luck looked up at her and smiled. "They thought you died. I figured you've done enough drugs to live forever since those didn't kill you."

"You'd know, Luck, since you did most of your drugs with me and with the way your hair looks I'd assume you're still doing 'em," Dane smiled. He actually looked like he stopped messing around with the drugs.

"Hell, I supplied you." Luck rose from his chair just enough to shake Dane's hand. "And don't try to crack on my hair. This shit is fly." He patted the side of his afro, which was really just his hair blown out and going in all directions. She assumed he had just taken out his braids and combed his hair all the way out.

Dane let loose a playful snort. "Yeah, just don't spread rumors of my untimely demise until I'm actually dead."

"You ain't got but two more years to live anyway, so we might as well start early," Fingers said from his spot in the corner. His dark face was hidden behind sunglasses and a fedora that was pulled down over his face.

She rolled her eyes. "I'm not the one that sold my soul, Fingers."

"Then explain yourself, demon," he demanded with a laugh. Fingers and others liked to say she was going to be one of those in the "twenty-seven club." They were convinced she sold her soul to the Devil for her musical talent and the Devil was due to collect when she turned twenty-seven. Maybe if she'd continued living how she had, they'd be right.

"Anyway, what're you doing here, Dane? You haven't graced these hallowed halls in years, and you disappeared from music for just as long," Jewel said.

"I hear you guys are getting shut down. I came to hear it straight up. Don't wanna worry about rumors, just the truth." The looks on the trio's faces were not encouraging. "Jewel, you can't be serious. This is history here." She gestured around them with one finger. "This is a part of the city's soul."

Jewel gave Dane a sympathetic look. "Calm it down, druggie. We're fighting it. The rumor actually made business pick up, so we won't need to sell, more than likely."

"Sell? You're being pressured to sell?"

"Considered it for a while," Luck admitted, glancing at the floor and then playing with the buttons on his bowling shirt. "But, we should be good now. This place is history, like you said, Dane. We've got to fight for it."

"That's good. Who's trying to buy it?" Dane couldn't imagine anyone who respected music, history, or historical landmarks would do such a thing.

Scoffing, Fingers pointed out ahead of them for a second. "Some office building people opening across the street. They want to turn the place into a parking garage. Can you believe that insulting shit? We're in a fucking building damn near a hundred years old, that's seen some of the greatest talent that jazz, the blues, and R&B has to offer, and they want to make it a fucking parking garage," he growled, disgust tugging the right corner of his upper lip. "Fucking disrespectful bastards."

Dane nodded. "That's a goddamn crime against history and culture. So, you're sure you're good?"

Jewel made a face, which again wasn't very encouraging. "We're getting there."

Dane frowned and put her hand through her hair. "Look, I gotta go. Gonna think on some things. Be back on Friday, okay?"

Luck shrugged. "We're here every day."

Dane nodded and shook their hands as a farewell. She went to pick up Crow, who appeared bored out of her mind. Dane noted the two empty glasses on the bar in front of her friend. *Hope she's not drunk.*

"Crow, you ready to go?" Dane noted that the bartender was making his way to Crow. She waved him off.

Crow turned around, and Dane recognized the unfocused, glassy look immediately. *Yeah, she won't be driving anywhere.* She gave Crow a smile, which Crow returned with a lopsided, goofy expression that could've been a smile if she tried harder.

"Dane, sweetie, glad you could join me. They have an amazing drink here that they're keeping hidden from the rest of us. Horrible people, the lot of them," Crow declared without slurring a single word. Crow became very articulate when intoxicated.

Dane laughed. "Oh, yeah. I forgot all about the A Train." It was an exclusive drink to *Melody*, named because it was accidentally invented while a band played Duke Ellington's famous composition "Take the A Train." She knew from firsthand knowledge how good it was.

"I would very much like another one."

"Maybe later. Right now we need to go to a club you like." Taking Crow some place that would keep her attention meant she'd drink less.

A bright smile lit up Crow's face. "I get to pick the club while hanging out with the famous Dane, goddess of rock and roll. How cool is that? Not to mention, the famous Dane, goddess of rock and roll, is my best friend."

Dane felt proud of that for some reason and smiled down at Crow. "You're my best friend, too. Now, let's get going."

Crow smiled brightly and nodded. Dane made sure to give Crow some support, but Crow wasn't so drunk yet that she needed the help. They left *Melody* and Dane followed Crow to get the night started.

***

Nicole heard Danny come in. She had been waiting up, reading on the sofa. Nodding off, she perked up instantly when she heard the door shut. Rubbing her eyes, she missed Danny's entrance to the living room, but she caught the musician smiling at her.

"You shouldn't have waited up," Danny said softly.

"Waited up? It's only 11:30," Nicole replied with a tired smile.

Danny decided against pointing out that it was late by their usual standards. Instead, she offered Nicole her hand and the redhead did not hesitate to take it. Danny led them upstairs, pulled back the covers, and helped Nicole into bed.

"You'll take a quick shower?" Nicole requested.

"Of course." Danny smiled.

Nicole smiled and settled into bed. She was drifting off when she felt the bed dip and Danny eased up next to her. Strong arms wrapped around her and she snuggled into her freshly showered lover. She automatically returned a kiss when she felt Danny's lips on hers.

"Nick, I've got something special planned for you on Friday. Gonna show you where I went today. You'll like it," Danny whispered; if Nicole was sleeping she did not want to wake her.

"I wanna see tomorrow," Nicole murmured, rubbing her nose in Danny's shoulder.

"No, I promised you movies for tomorrow. The surprise will still be there Friday."

Nicole nodded before sleep overcame her. By the next morning, she'd forgotten the conversation. Come Friday, she was surprised that they had a date.

***

"Chem, babe, you're not going to get ready? Figure we'd leave by eight." Danny marched into the living room. Nicole was curled up on the sofa with some cookies and a book.

Nicole looked up, her brow wrinkled. "What are you talking about? Go where?" As far as she knew, they didn't have any plans.

"My surprise. You don't remember?"

Nicole's forehead wrinkled, as she squinted and racked her brain. Nothing came up. "Remember?"

"Well, you were half asleep when I mentioned it. I have a surprise for you tonight. Go get dressed. You'll like it," Danny promised with a soft smile. She offered her hand to help Nicole off of the couch.

"Okay. How should I dress?" she asked, as she stood up.

"Regular. Just dress regular. Take your time. We can get there whenever."

Nicole nodded and went off to get ready. She took her time because Danny clearly had to get ready, too, since she was in her house clothes. She showered and dressed for a date, putting on a dark blue dress that fell right above her knees. She put on some light makeup and sling-back heels before going downstairs, knowing Danny would be waiting.

"Don't you look handsome," Nicole said as she caught sight of her girlfriend.

Danny was dressed in light blue jeans, without having to be told to put pants on. Her top was a black button-up shirt with a grey vest. Her hair was brushed back and to the left side. She held a rose swirled with red and white in her hand, like a flowery peppermint.

Nicole practically floated to Danny, accepting the flower and giving up a kiss. Danny melted into her and held onto her, even as she tried to pull away. She cooed against Danny's lips.

"You make me feel so wanted," Nicole whispered.

"You are wanted, sweet seraph. Now, shall we go?" Danny offered Nicole her arm.

"Is Haydn in his crate?" Nicole took the offered limb.

"Of course," Danny answered with a smile. "Now, let's go."

***

The one thing Dane detested about her injuries, beyond not being able to properly lift Nicole, was the fact that she didn't trust herself to drive. It meant Nicole had to drive everywhere. It always gave Nicole a chance to deduce a surprise. Dane suspected Nicole knew where they were going, even though they had never been there.

"You can park over there." Dane pointed ahead of them.

Nicole nodded and parked. Dane took Nicole by the hand and led her to *Melody*. They got in without a problem or a cover. Dane noted that green eyes scanned the large establishment, as they made their way through the crowd. They ended up at a table by the wall with a good view of the stage and sat down.

"What do you think?" Dane asked.

"I think this surprise is great! Where'd you find this place?" Nicole inquired.

"I heard about the drinks before anything else. It's actually an old jazz club. One of the oldest in the city, but what gets punks like me in initially are the drinks. They have a lot of exclusive drinks that taste just fucking amazing. Once I wandered in, the music made sure I'd never leave. The talent that's come through here is nothing short of breathtaking. It's blues night. So, gonna order the drink of the night, Heartbroken, and we'll listen to some blues."

Nicole nodded. "Sounds good."

"Oh, and just so you know, this isn't the surprise yet." Dane smirked.

Auburn eyebrows knotted together, but Dane didn't explain herself. They listened to the beautiful music the club was famous for. Nicole kept her eyes fixed on the stage, but her hand was wrapped in Dane's. Every now and then, when a piece got particularly emotional, there'd be a squeeze.

"Hey, Dane, didn't know you were serious about coming out tonight," Jewel said, as she and Fingers wandered over. Nicole turned her attention to the pair.

"Of course, I was serious. My girlfriend loves jazz, so I had to let her see this place. I figured I'd surprise her with blues night." Dane looked at Nicole. "Nick, this is Jewel and Fingers. They're jazz musicians and managers of this place."

"Pleased to meet you." Nicole politely shook both their hands.

"Dane with a single female that she calls her girlfriend? It's a pleasure to meet you. It's like meeting a unicorn," Jewel replied. "Nice to see her growing up some."

Dane rolled her eyes. "Don't you two have somewhere to be?"

"Just want to make sure you're ready. It's been a while and the place is packed," Fingers pointed out the obvious.

Dane scoffed and waved the pair off. Thankfully, they left without saying anything to give away her surprise. She looked at Nicole.

"I played here a few times," Dane said.

"I figured. They didn't pay you in drinks, did they?"

Dane chuckled, even though that was a good guess. "No, they didn't. But, this place became one of my little refuges from my usual scene. Really got outta my comfort zone here."

Nicole blinked. "You did? I didn't think you had a comfort zone when it came to music. You seem interested in it all. You seem good at it all."

"No, but thanks for thinking that." Dane felt her cheeks heat, which she covered up with a smile. "Jazz I knew, but the blues was new to me. Blues spoke to me, but mocked me as it spoke."

Nicole's brow wrinkled. "What do you mean?"

Dane didn't respond and turned back to the stage. Nicole did the same, squeezing her lover's hand. Nicole nursed her drink, taking small sips to avoid getting tipsy. After an hour, they got to Dane's surprise.

"Ladies and gentleman, before we get to the next scheduled performance, we have a special guest, and she's decided to grace us with her extraordinary talent. If you're a regular from a while back, then you're familiar with the extraordinary, wonderful stylings of Dane!" Luck announced.

Emerald eyes went wide as the audience applauded, and Dane climbed to her feet. Nicole watched as Dane made her way over to the stage, grabbing a guitar from Luck on her way up. She sat on a stool and settled the guitar against her.

"Good evening, people. Some of you might remember me, and some of you might remember this song I used to do here, whenever I popped up," Dane said into the microphone. "For those of you that don't know, the song is called 'Smile for Me.'"

The house lights dimmed, almost to the point of being off; things were considerably darker than before. Still, Dane's eyes sought out the only person that she wanted to hear her. *Nick, I know this is going to hurt, both of us more than likely, but I need you to hear it.* She strummed an eerie tune; her voice followed like a ghost.

> *"Hey, there, beautiful child, what are you doing with*
>   *tears in your eye?*
> *Hey, you, sweet child, you better never let them see you*
>   *cry.*
> *I know it hurts that life's so goddamn unfair.*
> *No, you're not invisible. They simply don't care.*
> *But, you definitely better not show them your tears.*
> *Then they'll know they got you, they'll know your fears.*
> *So, they don't know you, so they can't see*
> *You better put a smile on, smile just for me.*
> *You better never let them see you frown.*
> *Better smile, smile sweet, sweet child.*

And never ever let them know they got you down."

Dane strummed the guitar, hoping Nicole could hear what was underneath the notes, the lyrics, and the song. She could feel a difference from the last time she played the blues. It still mocked her, but there was something more. She couldn't put a name to it yet, but she felt it.

> *"Even when you're lying on that floor, bruised, bloody,*
>   *and hurt*
> *Even after you've been screamed on and treated lower*
>   *than dirt*
> *You better stand up before he sets foot out of the room.*
> *And you throw him a smile, even if it means doom.*
> *Let him know you're stronger, let him know you're there*
> *Look him in the eye, you could even stare.*
> *And you throw him a smile; you better never let him see*
>   *you frown.*
> *Better smile, smile sweet, sweet child.*
> *And never ever let them know they got you down."*

The guitar played its sorrowful melody, getting lower and softer, until it disappeared. The stage lights went out, as if she'd vanished with the music, leaving only the haunting memory of the song. For the first time, Dane actually felt like she hadn't vanished when the music stopped. *At least that little girl can smile for real now.*

***

Nicole practically curled into Danny as she came back to the table. Danny leaned down and placed a light kiss to Nicole's head. They sat silently for a while.

"May we leave?" Nicole whispered. She couldn't speak any louder. The song had stolen her voice.

Danny didn't verbally respond, but she got up and helped Nicole out of her seat. Danny nodded her farewells to her friends. They went out into the night air, and Danny started toward the car, but Nicole tugged her hand.

"No, let's walk around for a bit. Tell me about the clubs around here." Nicole wanted to know more about this Danny, the Danny who knew history, who sang the blues, and who broke hearts in ways most people didn't think about.

Danny smiled and put her arm around her girlfriend's waist. "There aren't that many left and the ones here are like *Melody*, really old. During the jazz age, this used to be the party district. By the time rock-n-roll was big, the parties started moving to the west side. *Melody* stays alive thanks to the popular drinks they serve, but they had such talent go through the doors. I mean, it's crazy some of the people who performed there."

"And then there's you. You surprised me, singing the blues," Nicole said, a small smile dancing on her face.

A sheepish smile made its way onto Danny's face, while her hand made its way through her hair. "Yeah, I'm no Billie Holiday."

Nicole laughed a little. "Your voice doesn't lend itself well to the blues," she agreed apologetically. This surprised her. Danny's voice lent itself well to all other genres Nicole heard her sing.

Danny smiled even more. "I know. Told you the blues mocked me. Shoulda been the one style of music I was good at when I was younger, but I just don't have the voice for it. So, it mocked me. Not so much anymore, though."

"No?"

Danny pulled Nicole close to her. "No. I felt different singing that song than I ever have. I don't have to sing the blues anymore. Before, it would pour out of me, even though my voice isn't good for it. But, now, I don't even think about the blues."

Nicole nodded. "Your guitar sounded like you don't think about the blues. Your voice, too. The lyrics made me sad, but your voice sort of reassured me that everything was all right."

Nodding, Danny leaned down and nuzzled Nicole briefly. "I hoped that'd be the case. So, are you all right?"

Nicole put her hand on Danny's arm and nodded. "I am. It'll always bother me that you were abused as a child, but life is better now, and we can't change the past."

Danny smiled softly. "That we can't, but life is *beyond* better. Life is wonderfully beyond description. You're wonderfully beyond description. Ready to go home?"

Nicole pressed herself closer to her lover. "No, tell me more about the clubs, the music, the history." She wanted to share this with her beloved.

Danny's smile spread, and she started up with the club they'd just left. Nicole hung on her every word, even when they returned to the car. Danny held Nicole's hand on the ride home, smiling and talking. Nicole couldn't help feeling proud.

"And just so you know, baby, I care," Nicole said.

"I never doubt that. You chase the blues away."

Suture

"BABY, ARE YOU READY to go?" Nicole asked, as she came downstairs.

"I've been ready to go," Danny answered while playing tug of war with Haydn. He was getting big enough to really overpower her if she wasn't careful. Of course, he probably didn't realize that.

"Did you call your brother? He should be here by now." Nicole frowned, giving her watch a glance.

The frown didn't last long when Nicole actually saw Danny's outfit. She held in a chuckle, as she took in the sight of Danny in a baseball shirt. Despite Danny's build, she didn't look quite right in sports clothing, even when she wore jerseys. *Maybe her style just suits her, even if it is slightly ridiculous.*

"I called him. I don't know where he is. Are we meeting your dad there?" She gave Haydn's rope a good yank and pulled him forward. He growled and pulled back, yanking her forward in return.

"Do you think he's upset we're taking the boys to their first baseball game? That's something most fathers would want to do with their sons. My dad took me to my first game."

Dane shook her head. "I don't think Adam cares about baseball. Sharon might just be giving him shit over it, as usual. I'm sure she's throwing a huge tantrum over the boys spending time with us."

Nicole nodded because that made sense. Adam didn't say much about the situation with Sharon, but the boys blurted things out as children often do. It didn't help that the boys liked running their mouths in general to Danny and Nicole. They talked about things their mother said about the couple, but they generally didn't understand most of the things they repeated. They did understand their mom really didn't like Danny or Nicole. Nicole hoped they never found out why.

"Are you looking forward to your first baseball game?" Nicole smiled as she curled up next to Danny on the couch.

There was a shrug. "Hope it's better live than on TV."

Nicole just laughed. Danny had watched a few baseball games with her on television, but had never made it to the end of one. She'd fall asleep, start writing, strum her guitar, play with Haydn, and do just about anything else to stop watching the game. Nicole was just happy that her partner would try to endure the games, because Nicole wanted Danny to watch with her. She doubted baseball would ever grow on Danny, but she was certain Danny would always try to watch with her.

"Have I told you I love you lately?" Nicole asked.

The musician smiled. "Not since last night."

"Well, I love you. I love you so much."

"Love you, too."

A few minutes later, Adam showed up with the boys, who were dressed in baseball jerseys and caps. They hugged Nicole around the waist and then rushed over to their aunt. Nicole turned her attention to Adam.

"I hope you don't mind us taking them to their first baseball game.

He laughed. "I told you, it's fine. I'm not a fan. I've already taken them to dozens of hockey games. Some baseball might make sure they don't grow up into crazy people wearing masks and beating people with sticks. "

She laughed. "I just want to be sure." *Does the whole Wolfe family hate baseball or is it just these two?*

"It's fine. I hope they have a good time. Call me when you get back, so I can come pick them up."

Nicole nodded. It was the first time that Adam didn't ask for the boys back by six, which she realized could've been the problem with Sharon and why they were late. Adam had admitted when Nicole first purposed the outing that he had no idea how long a baseball game was, so he'd just wait for Nicole or Danny to call him.

Adam left much easier than he had months ago when the couple first started taking the boys on their own. Nicole turned to see Luke and Thomas were now playing tug of war with the dog. Danny just watched, as Haydn pulled the boys little by little.

"Are we ready to go?" Nicole asked.

"Is Haydn coming, too?" Luke grunted as the dog yanked him and his brother a little more.

"There's no place for puppies to sit at the stadium. You can play with Haydn when we come back."

The boys charged out to the car with Nicole behind them. Danny put Haydn in the den, and they set off for the stadium. On the way, Danny put on some alternative rock for the boys. They played pretend instruments for the entire ride.

"Nikki, I was beginning to think you wouldn't make it." Raymond greeted the group at the front gate. There weren't a lot of people there, which led Nicole to believe that the game might've started already.

"Miss seeing my new favorite player? No way." Nicole greeted her father with a hug.

"And do we have three burgeoning baseball fans?" Raymond asked the others, even though he was more than aware of Danny's feelings toward the sport.

"It's gonna be fun! Nick said so," Luke declared with a grin.

"Yeah, she said baseball's great!" Thomas chimed in.

"She's right. Baseball is great, and I hear this is everybody's first game. So, let's make sure it's really fun," Raymond shouted with a grin that infected the boys with his enthusiasm immediately. They cheered and followed Raymond into the stadium as if he had lollipops in his back pockets.

Nicole took her girlfriend's hand and smiled at her. "Try to have fun, baby."

Danny shrugged. "I'll try, but honestly, being here with you and the boys is good enough for me."

"Smooth talker." Nicole leaned in and gave her partner a kiss on the cheek. Danny grinned widely at the small show of affection.

***

The first inning was barely over before Dane was ready to hang herself to escape the boredom of pre-season baseball. *It's worse than regular season baseball.* She didn't understand the dynamics of the game and didn't bother to try. Despite the number of games she had watched with Nicole, she didn't know the rules or the player positions or anything that was relevant. It just bored her so much. *Why couldn't Nick like football like the rest of her family?! I can get with football.*

She noted Raymond and Nicole seemed to be enjoying themselves, explaining the game to the boys. Nicole had already exerted a lot of precious energy explaining things to Dane when they were at home, but Dane didn't retain the information—ever. Luke and Thomas hung on their every word. She was certain the boys would like baseball just because Nicole did. They respected Nicole and valued her opinion enough to take her word on a sport being great. *God, that means more baseball games in my future.* She groaned mentally.

"Danny, not enjoying yourself?" Raymond teased, popping her in the shoulder and breaking her out of her thoughts. He was dressed casually, which she'd only seen a few times since she met him. He wore jeans and a shirt with the team logo.

"Don't get why you two like this. It's so boring," she replied bluntly.

"Your nephews like it." He nodded over at them, and as if on cue, the boys cheered.

The crack of a bat on a ball echoed through the stadium, and a ball sailed out of sight. Dane glanced down to see who rounded the bases and she chuckled. The rest of the stadium groaned.

"Yeah, they like it so much that they don't even know what team they're supposed to be cheering," she pointed out with a smile.

Raymond waved it off, while Nicole calmed the boys down. Dane laughed again. Two pairs of emerald eyes rolled, and Dane was left to be bored to tears for the time being. Her mind wandered over nothing in particular. *Has Haydn figured out how to unlock his new cage? He got the best of his last one pretty easily. But, the guys at the pet store were pretty certain he wouldn't break this one. Wonder what Crow's doing? Think she works today.*

Again, a hand on her shoulder interrupted Dane's pointless musings. Turning, she saw that hand belonged to Nicole, who offered her a sweet, if not apologetic smile.

"The boys are hungry for overpriced stadium dogs, and I thought you could go for some nachos if you're willing to wait in line with me."

Dane smiled. "You know I am. Nachos sound good."

The couple left Raymond with Luke and Thomas, who were talking Raymond's ear off. Dane couldn't help noticing how happy Raymond looked, as the boys pointed things out to him. *They're such little know-it-alls. Is that a trait from their dad?* She doubted she'd ever know. *Raymond seems like a good dad, though. I bet Nick had a blast growing up with him.*

"Baby, I'm sorry you're not enjoying yourself," Nicole said as they waited on the concessions line.

"It's fine, Chem. It's not that I'm not enjoying myself, but baseball just isn't my thing. I'm happy to be here with you and the boys and your father, but that's not going to make baseball unboring to me." Dane shrugged.

Nicole smiled and squeezed her hand. "That's sweet. So, you're okay?"

"I'm fine and I want to come to any future games with you."

Nicole's smile brightened. Dane meant her words, too. Baseball would never be her favorite sport, but Nicole and her nephews would always be some of her favorite people. She'd sit through a million games with them.

"Your dad's cool, too." Dane wasn't sure if she had ever told Nicole that.

Nicole nodded. "I'm glad you think so."

"The boys like him."

Nicole nodded. "You know my dad likes you, too."

Dane was silent for a bit. "Yeah, I know." She smiled and Nicole smiled back.

Snacks were retrieved, and the couple returned to their group with goodies for all. For a moment, the couple examined their charges and the food they bought for the children. It was doubtful they could make it through chilidogs without spilling something on their crisp, clean, brand new baseball jerseys. Nicole straightened the boys out with napkins in their laps as well as tucking napkins in the jerseys. The napkins on their shirts were held in place by hair clips that Nicole had in her purse.

Dane laughed. "You're the MacGyver for messy kids." She handed the boys their food.

Nicole chuckled. "The purpose of a purse is to be prepared for any number of situations."

"Hell, might need to start traveling with one of those if that's the case."

"Don't worry, baby. You know I got you."

Dane laughed. She noticed Raymond watching them, but he thankfully kept his opinions to himself. Dane tried not to think of what might be going through his mind, but she noted he was very interested in seeing them handle the kids. For some reason that she didn't want to contemplate, his scrutiny made her gulp. She got his attention away from them by handing him a cup of lemonade and a hotdog.

"Thanks," Raymond said, before taking a long drink.

"No problem," Dane sighed.

With the boys set up, Dane handed Nicole her lemonade. Nicole had a sweet tooth, but she couldn't bring herself to eat stadium food, especially chilidogs. She had no problem picking at Dane's nachos, which Dane didn't mind since she stole sips from Nicole's lemonade. The game pressed on.

"Is it over yet?" Thomas was done with his food, still perfectly clean, and sitting on Nicole's lap. He apparently didn't have the stamina for a full baseball game, eyes drooping from exhaustion. He curled into Nicole's chest, and she cuddled him close to her.

"Soon," Nicole whispered to him. There were a couple more innings to go.

Raymond's eyes drifted to Nicole while she comforted the little boy. Dane found herself breathing harder. *I'm sure it's nothing.*

"Whoa," Luke called out excitedly, as a loud *crack* echoed through stadium.

The ball screamed through air and actually came in their direction. Plenty of people in the area rose from their chairs, Raymond and Luke included. Dane glanced at Nicole, the only one amongst them that could probably catch the ball if it came their way.

"Baby, it's headed right for you! Give it a try," Nicole cheered, making sure to be careful of Thomas, who was now asleep in her lap.

Dane frowned, but she didn't really think about it as she got up. Truthfully, she couldn't catch for beans. She typically fumbled with stuff before dropping it. She didn't want to do that here and look like a chump in front of her girlfriend, her nephews, and her girlfriend's father. That was practically the whole world to her.

Dane just put her hand up and hoped for the best. She managed to keep from panicking and actually caught the homerun ball. The sting from the impact caused her to hiss. She held on tight, knowing if she dropped it, the people in front of them would scoop the ball up.

"Way to go," Raymond cheered, and he patted Dane on the shoulder roughly.

Dane laughed awkwardly to cover up a wince. She handed the ball over to her nephew, who looked like she had given him diamonds. She smiled at him and ruffled his hair. Luke wasted no time hugging her as tightly as he could for several long seconds. Nicole gifted her with a kiss on the cheek after she sat back down. That held Dane for the rest of the game.

"Oh, my God! Did you see the way Dane just caught that ball? It sounded like it hurt, but she got it anyway." Luke was talking Raymond's ear off again, as they walked out of the stadium. Clearly, there was another baseball fan amongst them. "And the way the catcher tagged that guy out to make sure we won the game, it was flipping awesome."

Raymond laughed. "Yes, it was."

Luke was still trying to talk to Raymond as he walked them to the car. Thomas was still asleep, carried in Nicole's arms. Dane strapped him in after Nicole placed him in the back seat. Raymond hugged Nicole farewell and shook hands with both Dane and Luke. He smirked at Dane...or she could've imagined it. She wasn't sure which, and she didn't know what to make of it if he had smirked at her.

"When do we get to go to another game?" Luke bounced in his seat.

"I'll try to set it up. We'll have to make sure your parents are okay with it, too," Nicole replied.

Luke pouted and settled in the back. "Mom might not let us."

"Why do you say that? She let you come this time," Dane said.

Luke scrunched his face up as he looked out the window. "Not really. She screamed at Dad and called you a lot of bad names. Called Nick some bad names, too. Dad took us out while she was still yelling. He went back in and didn't come back for a long time."

"Oh." Dane glanced at Nicole.

"Luke, you're old enough to know that sometimes people yell at each other when they're angry, but they're fine with each other later on," Nicole said.

"Mom's never fine with Dane," he muttered with a frown.

"That's okay because I don't hang out with your mom. I hang out with you and we like each other just fine, right?" Dane gave him a wide grin to lift his spirits.

Luke nodded. "I like hanging out with you and Nick. I don't wanna stop."

"We like hanging out, too, so we won't stop," Dane promised.

He smiled. Her word was enough for him. His level of trust amazed her, and she smiled over that. She reached over to Nicole and took her free hand. Nicole gripped her hand and smiled back.

***

Danny played with her nephews and Haydn, while Nicole fixed a light, healthy snack for them. She knew they were already wearing themselves out playing with the dog, which she was happy about. Luke seemed to have forgotten all about the trouble in the car, and Thomas was now wide awake.

"Apples and grapes," Nicole announced as she came out with three bowls of fruit. While the boys typically got along very well, they did not like sharing with each other, so they each had their own bowl. She'd share with Danny.

"Oh, food," Thomas cheered as if he had never had a meal before.

"Go wash your hands before you eat," Danny ordered the pair.

The boys ran off for the bathroom. Nicole smiled and eased down next to her lover. Danny reached for an apple slice, but Nicole popped her hand.

"Ow! What was that for?" Danny pouted.

"Did you wash your hands?" Nicole inquired with a playful smile.

"I'll have you know I never touched the dog." She laughed.

"I wish I could believe that. But, we both know you've never, never touched the dog.'"

Danny snorted. "You can't prove that."

Nicole smiled as they ate their snack. The brothers returned for their individual bowls. They ate quietly while watching a baseball game at the boys' request. It was a rebroadcast on an all-baseball channel, but it was all new to Luke and Thomas. All too soon, Adam was there for them.

"Dad! Dad! Dane caught me a ball!" Luke announced as soon as he saw his father. He waved the ball in his father's face.

"And Mr. Raymond taught us baseball stuff with Nick," Thomas added.

"Mr. Raymond?" Adam echoed with a craned eyebrow.

"My dad," Nicole replied.

"Your dad went to?" Adam asked.

"Yeah, he's the one who suggested the game in the first place. The boys really enjoyed themselves."

Adam smiled. "Thanks for that."

"No problem."

They got the boys ready to go and exchanged farewell hugs. They watched Adam put them in the car and drive away, returned to the sofa, and watched a movie until the movie was watching Danny. Nicole kissed her sleeping girlfriend's head.

"You're so great with kids. It'd be a shame for you not to be a mom. You'd show your parents how it's done," Nicole whispered.

Wet Sage

"YOU'RE GOING ON ANOTHER business trip? Can you smuggle me with you again?" Danny asked with a naughty grin from her place on the sofa. She rubbed her hands together at the thought of going on another trip with Nicole.

Nicole scoffed as she flopped down on the couch next to her partner. "I wasn't supposed to bring you on the last trip, and I honestly don't think it would be good for either of us for you to come on this trip."

Dane's mouth dropped open. "What? Why would you say that? We had a great time, and I was able to help you relax after that tense meeting. Why would this be different?"

"For one, it's not located in some boring town."

An interested ebony eyebrow arched. "Uh...where is this one?" She probably didn't mean to sound as intrigued as she did, but she was definitely eager to know.

Nicole sighed and glanced away. "Vegas."

And there Danny's mouth went again. "You're going to Vegas and you don't wanna take me? Why?" Her pout was enough to break Nicole's heart.

"Because it's a business trip. If you come with me to Vegas, my mind will be on everything but business!"

Danny laughed. "We can behave." That word and its volume caused Haydn to poke his head up from his chew toy. His large brown eyes said he was behaving, which earned him reassuring ear rub from Danny. He went back to his toy.

Nicole scoffed. "In Vegas?" She rolled her eyes, fairly certain that was impossible for a couple to do.

"We can behave to Vegas standards," Dane amended.

Nicole snorted now. "Vegas standards? Vegas has standards? Since when?" They'd be lucky to make it back by that logic.

Sighing, Danny threw her hands up a little. "Look, we can consider

217

it a victory if we don't get arrested or come back married with no memory of why we did it or when it happened."

That probably would be a victory, which is why I can't take her. "No, no, no. I have work to do while I'm there. I know if you come along work will be the last thing I think of."

"Come on, angel. I'll leave you be while you work. I can find something to do...unless that's what you're worried about. You think I'll go to Vegas and lose my mind?" Danny scrunched up her face.

"No! Baby, I know you have plenty of self-control. But, this is a business trip and I'm not going there for fun."

"And bringing me would mean you'd have fun? You're not going to be in business meetings the whole time. Have some fun, Chem. It'll be cool. We could catch a show, hit a few casinos, and do crazy things in a hotel room," Danny hit her with a huge grin.

"Baby, it is a business trip. By definition and name, a trip for business, not fun."

Grey eyes rolled and Danny scoffed. "Nick, did you handle the last business trip with the same level of professionalism that you always do, even though I tagged along?"

Nicole frowned. "Yes, but I don't want this to become a habit. If it does, I know, eventually, my professionalism will slip, and I'll just want to spend time with you. You'll end up being the only thing on my mind."

Danny nodded. "You're right. Okay, let's make this my last business trip for the next six months?"

Nicole sighed and gazed at the floor. She'd love for Danny to join her, but she needed to be able to focus on work. She definitely wouldn't be able to focus on work with Danny there, especially if they made plans. She'd just want to be with Danny like they were on vacation. But, Danny's presence helped relax her and that helped her stay focused during meetings.

"This can't become a habit."

Danny grinned and grabbed her into a tight embrace. "Don't worry, angel. It won't. I'll only come along when you invite me. I'll never request to go, unless you look particularly upset."

"Why are you so good to me? So good for me?" Nicole wondered aloud as she cuddled into her.

"Because, you're those things to and for me. I wanna take care of you in any way that I can."

"I feel the same. I love you so much."

"Love you, too."

***

Dane planned their downtime in Las Vegas. They were only going to be there for three days and two nights. On Friday and Saturday, Nicole would be booked from nine to three and she decided that, no matter what, she had to be in bed by one. Sunday was a free day. They had a late flight back home, and Raymond had actually volunteered to drive them to the airport and pick them up.

"Danny, I don't know how you talked Nikki into letting you go with her, but I'm glad you did." Raymond and Dane were loading the bags in the car trunk. Nicole was inside making sure she had everything for her meetings.

Dane blinked and regarded him as if he had grown a second head. "Really?"

"Yes, really. Honestly, sometimes, I do think she works too hard. Not in the sense that she has too much to do, but that she lets work become her whole life. Even her mother doesn't let the job totally consume her the way that Nikki does. Kate has fun, and I'm not going to bother you with the details, but she does, especially on business trips. Nikki should be able to relax after the meeting and if she has to bring you to do that, then so be it."

"Wow. Cool." One day it would seriously settle in her mind that Raymond liked her. Maybe today would be that day since that was practically approval of their relationship.

His eyes narrowed on her. "You'd better not come back married." His tone was deadly serious.

Dane gulped. "Uh...I'll make sure to avoid anyone who looks like Elvis."

Raymond laughed and patted her on the shoulder. She glanced at the hand, not sure what was going on. Dane was saved when Nicole joined them, and they set off for the airport. Raymond reminded them to call when they landed to let him know they made it all right. Dane wondered why, but Nicole just assured him they would do so.

***

They checked into their hotel room and had dinner in the restaurant downstairs. Dane was confused by the time change, mostly because the only clock she really ran by was her own internal one.

Sitting down to eat, they both scanned the casino just beyond the restaurant. It was busy with people and loud with slot machines and other things.

"This place looks like fun," Dane noted with a smile. There certainly were a lot of bright lights and exciting sounds.

"We will not find out tonight," Nicole said firmly.

Dane pouted. "Fine. But, we're going to play some casino games eventually. I am in charge of the free time, after all, and I'm taking that job very seriously." This was the truth. Nicole needed to relax.

Nicole only smiled. They finished their meal and returned to their room. They showered and fell into bed, going to sleep almost immediately. By the time Dane woke up, Nicole was gone. She remembered a fleeting kiss from her love and a mumbled "I-love-you." She ran her hand through her hair and frowned.

***

Nicole breathed a heavy sigh as she entered the hotel room, practically tearing her suit jacket off. She felt like she was drowning in her sweat. She did not expect it to be so hot just stepping outside from the air-conditioned building. It was not even spring yet.

"Hot enough out there for ya?" Danny smiled as she pressed a water bottle to the back of Nicole's neck as she tossed her jacket to the floor.

"All I did was get out of the cab and walk to the building." Nicole groaned, loving the press of the cold bottle. She moved her hand over Danny's hand.

"I've been out there all day."

"And you're not hot? What the hell, baby? Are you, like, immune to weather? You don't get cold, you don't feel heat, what's next?" Nicole teased with a gentle smile.

Danny laughed and flexed her bicep. "Strong like bull."

"That still doesn't explain you being weather resistant. I'm going to go shower and change, and we'll do whatever fun filled things you have planned for the day."

There was a nod and a smile from the younger woman. "I'll pack us some water."

"Thank you."

***

Nicole was a bit surprised that their first stop was the Shark Reef. The aquarium was a lot more involved than the last marine exhibit they went to, and they both had to consciously remember to act like adults. Just entering the place was breathtaking. Danny actually gasped.

"This is amazing," Nicole whispered. She clutched Danny's arm, as they strolled through the shark tunnel. She doubted her eyes could open any wider than they were, and she was still afraid she might miss something swimming by in the tank.

"Amazing doesn't begin to cover it," Danny replied. Nicole thought Danny's mouth might never close. "Oh, my God, they're huge!" Danny pointed to the green sea turtles, as they swam by.

Nicole nodded in agreement. They oh'ed and aw'ed like two little kids, which they acknowledged with shared smiles, blushes, and some giggling on Nicole's part. They even leaned against the glass a few times. Danny tapped on it a couple of times, trying to get the turtles attention. When they got to the touch pool, they touched everything and for a long time. They even passed each other creatures to touch. They circled the jellyfish display at least a half dozen times. Nicole had to be dragged away from the octopus exhibit.

"They're cute," she cooed.

"Not if you've seen some of the anime I have," Danny joked. Nicole was happy she didn't get that one and looked on for the next piece of amazing.

"Look at the crocodile." Nicole pointed at the creature in question, trying to pull her partner to that exhibit, but something else had Danny's attention.

"Look at the komodo dragon." Danny countered and plastered herself to that tank. She then went to look at the crocodile with Nicole. They eventually moved on from the reptiles.

"Wow, look at those fish," the redhead said, as they continued through the aquarium.

"Hey, those are the piranhas." Dane pointed into the tank.

Nicole's mouth hung open. "Have you ever seen them before?"

"Chem, you know I haven't seen half these things outside of when we went to the zoo and the aquarium back home. Sometimes, I do watch Animal Planet, though. I've seen some shows on them."

Nicole nodded; the channel had become a favorite of Danny's ever since they got their precious pup. They smiled and made their way to the gift shop. They slipped away from each other to get gifts. Danny ended up with a t-shirt and a turtle plushie. Nicole received a mug and a jellyfish plushie.

"Baby, this was wonderful." Nicole grinned and wrapped her arm around Danny's arm, pulling them closer together. She watched Danny visibly preen.

"Well, we're just getting started."

Nicole grinned even more. She couldn't wait to see what else her partner had planned. After dropping off their things, they went out for dinner at one of the other hotels. The musician had gone through a lot of trouble to pick out a place that served the exotic foods Nicole delighted in. Nicole spent the evening spoon-feeding Danny bites she thought her partner would enjoy.

"Big Dog, this is perfect." Nicole smiled as dessert was brought to the table. It was something else she'd have to let Danny taste.

"I'm glad you think so, but we still have more stuff to do."

***

"Why the hell are we so impressed by magic? We know it's an illusion, but we still acted like it was real," Nicole tittered. She clutched Dane's arm as they left the show, walking out into the cool desert night.

"How the hell did they do that thing with the bullets?" Dane almost screamed in disbelief, throwing her free hand up.

Nicole chuckled. "You are too cute, baby."

"Cute enough to have a nightcap?" Dane's grin was positively sinful.

A teasing glint sparked in emerald eyes. "You gonna wake up with me for breakfast in the morning?"

"Promise!" Dane held her hand up.

Nicole laughed. "Let's go back to the room and see what you've got."

Dane was ready to run to the room, but held back. There was something romantic about strolling down the strip with her girlfriend clutching her arm. It was a little slice of perfect, like many things with Nicole. She put her arm around Nicole's waist.

"You know what, let's walk for a while," Dane said in a low voice, leaning down to kiss her cheek.

Nicole smiled and patted Dane's arm. "Yeah, I'd like that."

They were silent through most of their walk, taking in the sights. There was some kind of quiet warmth between them that had nothing to do with the desert air, and Dane didn't want that to end.

"You feel it, right?" Dane hoped Nicole knew what she meant.

Nicole squeezed her arm and smiled. "Of course."

At the end of the night, they returned to their room and settled for some heavy petting. They showered together and fell into bed nude. They rolled around until Dane settled on top of Nicole. They exchanged heated kisses and caresses, but nothing more than that.

"You should go to sleep. You're the one that has meetings, after all." Dane wasn't sure where the willpower came from to keep her mouth from Nicole's breasts, to not bury her fingers to the hilt in her girlfriend; but it was late and Nicole had work in the morning. They had spent too much time wandering outside, but she didn't regret their time together.

Nicole groaned, but glancing at the clock, she conceded the matter. "It is bedtime. But, we are waking up early and continuing this." The yawn made her words seem doubtful.

***

Nicole was somewhat distracted from her meeting, silently lamenting the lack of playtime that morning and wondering how Danny was spending her time. After an hour, she gave in to her distractions, which bothered her somewhat. *This is why I didn't want Danny to come! I need to focus on business*. She stepped out of the meeting and called the hotel room, but there was no answer.

"I really need to get Danny a cell phone," Nicole sighed and returned to her meeting.

At lunch, her cell phone rang. She didn't recognize the number, but answered anyway. "Hello, Nicole Cardell."

"Hey, Nick, come downstairs," Danny said and then hung up.

Nicole's curiosity was piqued as she made her way downstairs. Danny was in the lobby. Nicole couldn't help the smile that conquered her face. Danny grinned in return. She was greeted with a warm embrace.

"Baby, what are you doing here?" Nicole inquired, still smiling.

"I dunno. Just thought you could use a friendly face and a break from the business end of this trip," Danny remarked with a dashing smile.

Nicole sighed. "Let's go get something to eat."

Danny's forehead wrinkled, but she followed Nicole to the small food court in the building. They quickly got their meals and sat down at an open table in the corner. Danny gave the place a quick once-over before focusing on Nicole.

"This place's pretty big."

"Uh-huh."

"You okay?" Danny reached across the table for her hand.

Nicole blinked. "Yeah, why do you ask?"

"Your face looks a little bothered. Did I do wrong by coming here?" Grey eyes were laced with worry, and the way her eyebrows curled up drew out a small smile from Nicole.

"No! I'm happy you showed up. I'm so happy you're here. I was thinking about you all day." She squeezed her girlfriend's hand.

Danny nodded. "That's the problem isn't it? You're supposed to be focused on your business meeting since this is a business trip, a trip for business, but you're thinking about what fun I might be having or what trouble I might be getting into."

Nicole looked down at the table. "How do you know me so well?"

A wide, amused grin settled onto Danny's face. "I read your diary late at night."

Nicole laughed. "I figured as much. So, what have you been up to?"

"Losing money in blackjack. Nothing big or elaborate for you to be concerning yourself over. I'm saving all of the fun stuff for when you're around. Because I'm trying to kill time, I just give back anything I happen to win."

"Where have you been playing?"

"All over. Wanna play with me later? We'll have time before I take you some place you'll love."

Nicole thought on it very briefly. "What the hell? We're in Vegas, after all!"

Danny's face lit up. "That's the spirit!"

Lunch was over sooner than Nicole liked, and she was back in her meetings. She was surprised to find she could now focus and was even reinvigorated for the rest the day. She actually left the day's meeting feeling good.

Danny waited for her in the lobby. They left hand in hand, returning to the hotel so that Nicole could shower and change. They hit the blackjack tables and Danny learned Nicole was much more prudent with her money. Her bets were small, and she pocketed all of her winnings, only using small amounts to add to wagers when she had a "good feeling."

"I think I should stop now and just hold chips for you." Danny laughed. She had lost a lot of her money, because she liked to play fast and loose.

"No, no. I like having you play next to me. Please stay, baby."

Danny smiled and continued playing. Nicole saw Danny check her watch, which she rarely wore. She wondered if her girlfriend's divided attention was the reason behind losing her money.

"Baby, if you tell me when we need to leave, I can set an alarm on my phone," Nicole offered. Of course, there was a chance they wouldn't hear it thanks to all of the casino noise, but it was worth a shot.

"No, no, no. I got this. You just worry about your cards. You support us, after all. Wouldn't do if you lost your money," Danny replied with a laugh.

Nicole laughed as well and continued playing until Danny pulled her from her seat. They cashed in their chips, and Danny looked ready to pass out when she saw Nicole had won almost seven hundred dollars.

"You must be lucky, baby." Nicole kissed Danny's cheek, which brought a smile to Danny's face.

"I think you're right because I know I hit the jackpot."

Nicole bumped her girlfriend with her hip. "Sweet talker."

"We should put the money in the room before we leave."

Nicole nodded in agreement. They wandered to their room and then were out and about. They ended up at a chocolate festival. Nicole's knees actually went weak; she clutched Danny's forearm to keep herself upright.

"Sweetheart," she whispered.

"We've got all night." Danny grinned as she watched Nicole become a kid in a candy store.

***

"Nick, how the hell are we going to eat all of this junk food?" Dane gawked at the bags in her hands, bags full of sweets. Packets of chocolates, cartons bearing cakes, boxes of pastries, and packages of candy. There was no way in hell they'd be able to eat everything and escape cavity or stomachache free.

"Not just us, Danny. Some for my parents. My sweet tooth was come by honestly and is genetic. Then there's Mina, Clara, and Crow. A few people I like at work and school." Nicole was holding bags of her own.

Dane couldn't help arching an eyebrow. "Crow?" She was shocked Nicole even thought about Crow, considering their still somewhat rocky relationship.

"Yes. She is your best friend, after all. We had to get something for her."

Dane shrugged. "Crow will appreciate it."

"I thought as much. After all, with the way she looks out for you, she deserves some kind of reward," Nicole teased.

Dane scoffed slightly. "She looks out for me? All of those chocolate fumes must've messed up your brain."

They laughed and teased all the way back to the hotel room. Dane planned for some sweets of her own, but Nicole showered by herself and fell into bed. She was sound asleep by the time Dane got out of the shower. Dane smiled softly.

"Well, I guess I won't get my sweet treat, but I'll settle for holding you in your sleep any time, angel." She put her hands around Nicole, who turned in her sleep and cuddled into Dane's body. Dane continued to smile. "God, I love you, woman. Even when you're too tired to sex me up." She laughed at her own joke before kissing her lover's cheek and falling asleep.

***

Dane awoke to the sensation of sweet lips floating across her own. She purred at the feeling and taste. It tasted like Nicole and chocolate. *Good combination.*

"You've been in the candy already," Dane accused, not bothering to open her eyes. She could feel Nicole's naughty smile against her mouth.

"You don't know that for sure."

"I can taste it on your lips."

"How about you try to taste it inside my mouth?"

She opened her eyes to see the devilish sparkle in Nicole's eyes. She wasted no time taking Nicole up on that offer. A moan echoed through the room, as Dane's tongue caressed and explored Nicole's delicious mouth. They broke for air, and Dane smacked her lips.

"That is definitely chocolate. How are you eating chocolate this early in the morning?" Dane asked, even though she had seen the redhead eat sweets before breakfast every now and then.

"Because it's unwrapped already," Nicole replied in a seductive tone, licking her girlfriend's neck. "And it tastes so good," she cooed.

Dane shivered and rolled over onto her back. Nicole followed her, settling on top of Dane. Her nerves danced as Nicole pressed against her. They kissed again, slowly and thoroughly. It was as if Dane was leisurely trying to get every drop of chocolate out of Nicole's mouth. Nicole returned the favor by trying to take back whatever Dane's tongue removed.

Dane's hands groped for soft skin, finding plenty of it and loving every second. She could not be more thankful that they had both forgone pajamas. She wanted to feel Nicole as close as possible, and she wanted to feel as much of Nicole as possible. Her hands roamed, grabbing, caressing, and kneading heated, heavenly flesh. Nicole trembled against her, which only made her want more.

She purred while Nicole moaned into her mouth. She swallowed each noise, feeling like they made her melt into the bed. Eventually, they had to break apart for air, but that didn't stop their hands.

"Wanted to do this all weekend," Dane breathed, one hand massaging Nicole's breast and the other on her hip posed to move her.

Nicole groaned and panted from the attention. She had trouble answering at first, pressing herself into Dane being a much higher priority than speaking. "I know. Sorry, I was too tired."

"I understand. Now, let's not waste any more time before we have to check out."

The redhead nodded and they went back to exploring each other's mouths and bodies. Dane pulled Nicole closer, wanting to feel her grinding against her thigh. Nicole obliged, drawing out a long, strained moan from Dane. Nicole purred as she moved against her.

"Goddamn, Chem, you feel so good against me. So hot, so molten. You make me melt," Dane growled, her hand pulling Nicole closer, harder, faster.

"You make me feel so good, baby. I wanna make you feel good, too," Nicole panted loudly. Leaning down, she peppered Dane's heaving chest with kisses. Her hands wandered down Dane's sides briefly before going to keep her breasts occupied. Nicole's hands adored Dane's breasts with caresses.

"Feels so good. You feel so good," Dane mewed. "Nothing better on Earth than you against me." She gently squeezed Nicole's heavy, heaving breasts.

Nicole's response was to flick Dane's nipple with her tongue. Dane inhaled sharply, and her mouth dropped open from the jolts of pleasure. Nicole obviously heard the noise and wrapped her lips around the area, sucking gently. Dane tried to return the favor, rubbing the pebbled apex at the center of Nicole's breast just the way the attorney liked it. Nicole cried out loudly and jerked against her girlfriend.

Dane pulled the redhead closer, needing to experience more of her. Her hand on Nicole's hip moved her faster. Throwing her head back briefly, Dane shivered as Nicole's passion spread all over her leg. She needed more. *Now.* The hand that had occupied a plump, jiggling breast moved in between Nicole's legs, as a shrill, high-pitched noise pierced the mood.

"What the fuck!" they both screamed, and Nicole flew off Dane, who frantically searched for the source of the accursed noise. Her heart felt like it was about to pound out her chest.

"It's my phone, baby." Nicole crawled over to the nightstand to the cell.

As Dane relaxed, she recognized the ring tone for Kathleen. Nicole answered and quickly began getting dressed. She had once expressed that she felt awkward being naked while on the phone with her mother. Kathleen had interrupted them many times. Even if Nicole ignored the call, Kathleen would just keep calling until she got an answer. *It's like she knows she's ruining our playtime.*

Dane heard Nicole start talking business and knew the moment was gone. She began getting dressed herself. She also made sure everything was packed away since she suspected Nicole would be on the phone until they had to check out. She was right.

"Baby, I'm so sorry. I didn't think she'd talk for damn near an hour," Nicole sighed, hanging her head in defeat.

"Of course, she would. She probably knew we were doing it and wanted to stop us." Dane laughed.

"God, I hope not. The last thing I want to think about when I'm about to have an orgasm is my mother knowing it's happening." Nicole shuddered.

Dane laughed even more. "Sorry, love. I have all day to make it up to you."

"I honestly feel like the chocolate festival was the best place you could ever physically take me. You're covered for the rest of your life as far as trips go."

"I figured as much, which is why today I thought we'd just wander the strip. Go in some stores, explore the casinos, maybe ride the roller coaster at New York, New York. I think there's an M&M store, which I'm sure you'd love, even though we just went to a chocolate festival."

Nicole smiled and they walked off, hand in hand, to enjoy their last few hours in Las Vegas. When they got on the plane, they had pictures and chocolate to occupy them. Raymond picked them up at the airport and was kind enough to give Nicole Monday off since it was so late and the business meetings went well.

"Thanks, Daddy. We got chocolate and cakes for you and Mommy. I'm leaving them on the backseat." Nicole walked around to the driver's side of the car and kissed him on the cheek.

"Thanks for that, Nikki. Danny." Raymond nodded to both ladies.

"No problem," Danny replied.

Once they were in the house, they tried to pick up where they left off in the hotel room. Kathleen called while Nicole was on her way in between Dane's legs. Kathleen claimed she was checking to make sure Nicole got in all right, but Dane was certain the woman's "Mommy senses" were tingling and she was purposely being, for lack of a better term, a cunt-blocker. Too bad it didn't work. Nicole feigned tiredness to get off the phone and went back to the task at hand. She turned the phone off; the voicemail could answer anything else for the rest of the night.

"Best business trip ever," Nicole whispered before her mouth was too busy to talk.

Honey

NICOLE DECIDED IT WAS her turn to plan a date. She had been slacking and letting Danny handle that aspect of their relationship for a while. She supposed it was because she was surprised when Danny wanted to go out. She was flattered whenever Danny planned an outing for them and she wanted to give Danny that feeling.

Checking the weather, she found a good day for a picnic. She doubted Danny had ever had a proper picnic. The first thing on the menu was her potato salad that Danny loved so much. She'd eaten the entire bowl on her own on more than one occasion.

Nicole spent her morning in the kitchen. She didn't tell Danny about the picnic, but had informed her they'd be going on a date later that day. Danny seemed agreeable to the idea.

"Hey, Chem, taking Haydn for a walk before it starts raining," Danny called from the den.

"Okay," Nicole replied, and then she realized what her girlfriend said. "Raining?"

She rushed to the window and frowned at the dark, grey clouds in the sky. Mentally, she let out every curse word that she knew. She had been too busy with their lunch and snacks to bother looking outside, instead trusting in a weather report that was days old.

"Stupid! I'd never do some dumb shit like this at work," she huffed.

She had to think of something quickly, while Danny was out, to salvage the rest of their date. *Okay, if this happened to Danny, what would she do?* As soon as that question left her brain, she knew what to do. She just needed to finish up before her lover returned.

"I hope this works just as well as it would in the park," Nicole prayed.

***

Thunder boomed through the air as Dane ran back inside with a whining Haydn. He was apparently more pissed off with being caught in the rain than she was. She took him straight to the downstairs bathroom and toweled him off, knowing he would shake the first chance he got and she didn't want him to make a mess. When she was done, he shook himself dry just because he was a dog and trotted off to play with his toys.

Dane grabbed another towel and dried herself off as best she could. She threw the towels in the basement, where the laundry awaited her. She realized how quiet the house was.

"Nick! You home? Hope she didn't try to go out in that monsoon," Dane muttered, as she scanned the first floor. Nicole was nowhere to be found. "Nick? Nick, you here?" There was always a chance there was some emergency at work, like someone couldn't find a paperclip and swore Nicole was the only person who could find it.

Dane made her way upstairs to be met by her partner coming out of their bedroom. They greeted each other with small pecks on the lips, but Dane kept Nicole at an arm's length to make sure she didn't dampen the redhead. Nicole gave her a little, amused smile.

"Go take a nice, hot shower. I have a surprise for you after," Nicole said in a gentle tone.

"Yeah, lemme do that." Dane moved to go into the bedroom to use that bathroom, as they generally did.

Nicole quickly stepped into her path. "Uh...baby, can you use the other bathroom, please?"

Dane's brow furrowed briefly, but she figured Nicole's surprise was probably in the bedroom. Nodding, she did a complete one eighty and marched off to the other bathroom. Taking a nice, long, hot shower, she felt better. She smiled when she exited the shower to see clothes waiting for her.

"My sweet, sweet seraph."

She dressed in her house clothes, a black camisole and cream sweat shorts. *Is she trying to tell me something with the clothes or is she just trying to get me to wear a camisole?* Instead of thinking on it, she went to go see the surprise Nicole had planned. She knocked on the bedroom door, which felt odd. Before she could contemplate the weird sensation, the door opened and revealed Nicole's beautiful smiling face.

"You look good in a camisole." Nicole blatantly looked Dane up and down.

"I feel ridiculous. Why didn't you just bring me a wife-beater?" Dane tugged at the top with two fingers.

"Because I wanted to see you in something different."

Dane leered, even though Nicole hid behind the door. "Are you in something different?" She purred at the thought.

"Sorry, baby, I am not." Nicole opened the door to show that she was wearing navy yoga pants and a matching t-shirt that used to belong to Dane.

Dane couldn't help her pout. Nicole laughed and removed the pout with a gentle kiss to Dane's lips, which instantly lifted the musician's spirits. The redhead took her by the hand and tugged her into the room. A surprise yelp escaped Dane, but they both pretended like it didn't happen.

"Welcome to our rainy-day picnic," Nicole grinned, motioning to the setup on the floor.

"Picnic?" Her eyes fell to the blanket on the floor and a nearby basket. There were candles lit and placed around the room. Nicole dimmed the lights in the room to let the candles do their work.

"Please, sit." Nicole tilted her hand toward the blanket.

Dane mutely nodded and followed instructions. Nicole sat down and opened the basket. She pulled out plates and silverware, setting some in front of her lover. The Tupperware containers of food came next.

"This is what you've been up to all morning." Dane smiled.

"Well, yes. I was hoping we'd get to have it in the park, so Haydn could enjoy it, too. I didn't know it was going to rain today, though. Sorry." Nicole began opening the containers.

"It's all right. This is amazing in its own right."

A light blush stained Nicole's cheeks and she smiled. "So, what do you want for lunch?"

Dane studied the layout. "Can I just eat the whole thing of potato salad?"

"What? No! You'll get some, but you have to eat more than that. Come on, I made fried chicken, rice and peas, salad, shrimp, meat balls, apple slices, and peaches."

"All this in one morning?" *I know I stayed out of her way, but how the hell did she make all of this and I didn't notice?*

A soft, amused smile graced Nicole's features. "Haydn distracts you very well and some of it I made last night while you were lost under your headphones. I fried the chicken when you took a nap, so you wouldn't smell it."

Dane could only laugh. While she no longer had a band, she found herself composing songs and writing lyrics as if she did. It didn't help that Nicole indulged her. First, Nicole had set her up a music room in the den. She also listened intently to Dane whenever she prattled about equipment, so Nicole knew what to furnish the room with. She often asked Dane to play things for her. Dane had never had someone in her life so interested in the process of creating her music and it was just one of the many things that made her love Nicole with all of her heart.

"Here, you'll have a little of everything, but the apple slices are all yours." Nicole handed over the large plate of food.

"Like I'm stupid enough to argue with that!" Dane laughed. Apple slices were one of her favorite snacks and everything else looked simply delicious.

Nicole smiled while making her own plate. She poured Dane some apple juice in a wine goblet. Dane couldn't help laughing again as they silently enjoyed each other's presence while the rain pounded against the house and the wind howled.

"Don't freak out over this, sweetheart, but I'd very much like to do this again," Nicole said.

"Me, too," Dane jumped in with a smile. This was really nice. It'd be great to relax on another rainy day with a picnic. Maybe she could arrange one. Or, they could do Nicole's idea of a picnic outside when the weather cleared.

Nicole smiled kindly. "With a child."

Dane's thoughts didn't slow down. "We could take Luke and Thomas."

Nicole's smile was now patient and she patted Dane's knee. "Our own child."

Dane's brain ground to a halt and she blinked so hard she thought she could hear it. After that, though, she couldn't blink again if she consciously tried. Dane was sure she looked like an owl, because her eyes wouldn't go back to normal. Okay, that certainly caught her off guard. She shoved some food in her mouth to have an excuse not to respond quickly and tried to sort her feelings out on the matter.

A child. Nicole mentioned it a couple of times, but I've never really put any thought into a kid. What the hell would I do with a kid? I am practically a kid myself. Stop thinking about it. She felt like she'd just freak out if she thought on it. *Wait, isn't that what she told me not to do? Well, how the hell do I not do that?*

Nicole laughed and patted Dane's knee a second time. "I told you not to freak out. I'm making a simple desire known. I told you, children aren't on my list until after marriage and since we're not about to be married, I know we're not about to have a child."

Dane could only nod for a moment before remembering she had the ability to speak. Of course, she wasn't totally sure she could trust her voice. "Should we talk about this a little? Whenever the subject comes up, we dismiss it almost as soon as it does. Never have a chance to think about it." *Okay, maybe I dismiss it because I don't want to think about it.*

Nicole nodded. "What do you want to talk about? Just the idea of having a child?"

"Yeah, I mean, even that's a lot. You trust me with a kid? I mean, I don't know a damn thing about being a parent."

The smile that graced Nicole's face was so sincere and lovely that Dane's heart thumped in her chest. "Of course, I trust you with a child. I trust you with my heart, so that means I trust you with all the hopes and dreams that come with it. Have you seriously never thought about a child of your own, like ever?"

Dane's eyes narrowed, fixed on her plate, as she thought on it. "In fleeting moments with the boys, I sometimes think I'd like to spend time like this with my own kid, but nothing beyond that. I mean, I don't know anything about taking care of a kid. I don't have anything to go on beyond fleeting moments with the boys."

"You've never thought about it in passing before them?"

"No, never." She'd probably given more thought to walking on the moon than having kids in her life.

Nicole's smile vanished and was replaced with a slight frown and big eyes as she rubbed Dane's knee again. "Baby, do you think you'd be like your parents and that's why you don't think about having a child?"

Dane's hand automatically went through her hair. "It's possible. I mean, I didn't have great parenting experiences. Will I hit our child the first time I have a bad day or the first time the kid makes a mistake? Will I try to push our kid on someone else because I don't want to deal with the kid? Will I resent the kid for taking up your time? Will I…hate our kid?" *After all, my own mother hated me, resented me because he hated me.*

Nicole moved closer, her hand on Dane's now. "Of course not, baby. You're not like that. Sometimes, things will be hard and you won't know what to do, but as long as you love this child, as long as you want this child, and claim this child, I know you'd never purposely hurt the child in a fit of anger or frustration. You'll do your best, like you do with the boys. You'll love the kid with your whole heart, just like you love the boys and just like you love me. There will be times when we won't know what to do, but we'll help each other through it, or we can ask my parents for help. Neither of us will be perfect. We're human and babies don't come with instructions."

"I know," Danny whispered. Her voice was hollow to her own ears and yet still full of despair. "It scares me," she admitted in a tone even lower than the whisper.

The very thought of a tiny life depending on her frightened Dane more than anything else, even more than the idea of never regaining the full use of her hand. So many things could go wrong and then she would have screwed up a human being. The responsibility of it all. Worse, she might see what others saw, she might come to understand why someone would abandon a child.

"What if..." Dane swallowed hard. "What if...what if I see it."

"See what?"

"What if I see in the kid what everyone else saw in me? What if I see a monster? A terror? A mistake?"

Nicole just stared at her with a stricken look in wide green eyes. She held Dane's hand tight. It was encouraging, but Dane still feared.

"Think about holding our baby, Danny. Our baby is beautiful. A full head of unruly black hair, sun kissed complexion, and smiling brightly at you, eyes full of wonder. The scent of the baby wrapping around you, blanketing you in the smell of something fresh, new, and innocent. The weight of the baby in your arms, leaning against you for warmth and security, trusting you completely, loving you completely," Nicole said in a low tone, as if frightened Dane would leave.

Dane swallowed hard again, but it did nothing for the tightness in her throat as the images flashed through her mind, drowning her thoughts in emotions she could hardly comprehend. Her heart beat heavier, and she was sure that the uncertain tattoo was louder than the rain patter outside. Her hand was now shaking as it traveled through her hair.

"I...I..." Dane was completely dumbfounded.

Nicole offered her a small, comforting smile. "Don't say anything, sweetheart. You don't have to decide if you want a baby right now. But, you should know you're very good with kids, and I suspect it's because you know what kids need by only having fleeting moments of it yourself. Just try to entertain the idea someday and when necessary we'll talk more about it."

Dane nodded, but her vocal cords still weren't working enough for her to respond. The topic was thankfully dismissed as Nicole began eating again. Dane wasn't so quick to go back to her meal, thoughts of babies flooding her mind.

Do I want a baby? What would I do with one? Would I be willing to share Chem with someone who'd definitely need her more than I do? Nick's obvious with her thought on this and she wants a kid. She'd be a great mom, but I'm a mess. Can I even stay with her if I don't know how I feel? What if I don't want a kid? Will I lose Chem? Would I deserve her? Would she resent me?

Dane had no answers for her questions and was far from brave enough to pose them to her girlfriend right now. She finally managed to start eating lunch, only to find that the discussion hadn't only robbed her tongue of the ability to talk, but also the talent to taste her favorite potato salad. She frowned as she tried her best to remember how delicious Nicole's cooking was.

"Sweetheart, please don't let it bother you. It's not the end of the world." Nicole reached over and patted Danny's thigh.

No, it's not the end of the world today, but damn, tomorrow looks like a decent candidate. Still, Dane tried to enjoy the food, which remained tasteless. The only silver lining she could imagine was that at least it didn't taste like bitter, defeated ashes. *That's gotta mean something...or I'm just a lovesick idiot, hoping against all hope.*

"Baby, tell me what I can do to make this better," Nicole implored with glistening eyes.

Dane could only imagine what she must look like if Nicole was begging to help her. She shook her head. "I'm okay. Just thinking about it for the first time, seriously thinking about it."

The redhead nodded and thankfully let the lie go. But, Dane knew she'd ruined the picnic, and she couldn't think of a single thing to make it better. Once they finished their meals, Nicole put everything back into the basket.

"Hold me for a while?" Nicole requested, as she settled down on the picnic blanket.

Dane did as asked, lying right next to her lover. The rain falling outside was the only noise in the room and it seemed to be a natural lullaby as Nicole was asleep within minutes. Dane was awake for a while longer, still plagued by thoughts brought on by their conversation.

***

Cries filled the blurry white room and Dane felt something small being eased into her arms. Curiosity got the best of her and she looked down to see what she was holding. Large, curious, green eyes in a chubby, peanut butter face were focused on her. "Who are you?" they seemed to ask.

"Who are you?" Dane countered.

No answer was forthcoming. Instead, a tiny hand slid across her index finger. Her brow wrinkled and studied the small, mysterious creature in her arms. Her heart beat suddenly picked up as she was flooded by a million and one emotions that she couldn't begin to comprehend. Overwhelmed didn't even begin to cover the sensation.

She managed a hint of pride in the simple fact that she hadn't dropped the little, green-eyed puzzle. She then found it more of an accomplishment that she was still on her feet as emotions swirled through her like a torrential hurricane, only to realize she was, in fact, sitting down. A good thing, too, because she felt a little dizzy.

"Maybe it's not too late to send you back," Dane considered as stomach acid decided to creep its way up her throat. *Why should I have to share the attention of the only person to love me for who I am?*

***

The park was green and vibrant without a cloud in the powder blue sky. The sound of a dog barking got Dane's attention and she found herself almost completely bowled over as Haydn barreled into her. She caught her balance on what she recognized as the picnic blanket she'd shared with Nicole. Glimpsing a basket across from her, she guessed she and Nicole were doing it again in the park. *Good, I can make up for screwing up the last one.*

Her thoughts on mending bridges were cut short by the familiar peals of Nicole's laughter. It brought a smile to her face until it was accompanied by similar, but very childish laughter. That wasn't familiar at all. Still, it settled something inside of her.

As she turned her head to find who the second voice belonged to, she was tackled for a second time. She went down this time and felt small arms wrap around her neck, hugging her. A familiar sense of being buried by a billion emotions narrowed her vision, and she had no clue how to fix that.

As she calmed down, she realized things weren't quite so horrible.

The emotions, while something akin to a tidal wave, didn't consume her. Instead, she felt warm, loved, and settled. It felt good to be embraced, good to be trusted, good to be loved. There was another giggle and it felt like home.

***

A thunderclap startled Dane out of sleep. She squeezed Nicole tightly, by accident, which woke her up, too. Dane blinked and looked around, wondering what happened to the park and her beatific hug. Rubbing her eyes, she finally realized what had happened.

"It was a dream," she mumbled.

"Hmm?" Nicole focused on Dane.

"Had a dream we got to do the picnic over in the park. It was really nice. The perfect day. Haydn was out with us. He was big. Adult dog size and there was…" Dane trailed off and motioned around her body. Her eyes softened. "Little hands hugged me…" Licking her lips, she whispered the last part. "Felt nice."

A soft smile conquered Nicole's features, and she leaned over to kiss Dane's cheek. "Glad you're not overwhelmed anymore."

"Oh, no, I am overwhelmed. Scared shitless really. But, there was something there beyond the panic and the fear. It gave me something else to think about. Something nice."

Nicole moved and hugged her. Dane smiled and wrapped her arms around the redhead. Nicole cuddled into her, and the feel of Nicole's steady breathing calmed her.

"Sweetheart, I don't want you to feel pressured about this baby business. If you want one, great. If you don't, then we'll work through it. It's not the end of the world."

"But, you want a kid." There really wasn't a compromise in between "you want a kid" and "I don't," not that she didn't. That dream certainly left her with something to think about.

"I've only entertained the idea and it was only a vague fantasy before you. You're the first partner I've considered kids with, but if you don't want them, that's fine. I want you to know that I'm comfortable enough with you, and trust you enough, and love you enough to want to bear your children. It's not an offer I make lightly."

Okay, wow. That's a lot, but really amazing. Dane smiled. "I'm touched by the gesture. Are you sure you'd be fine if I decided I didn't want kids?"

"Baby, I want you. I want you forever and always. If I have you, I'm fine. You're the person that brightens my day, makes my heart speed up just a little faster in a good way, and makes me feel warm inside. You're the person whose arms I feel safe in and who I can whisper all my secrets to. I refuse to compromise this for anything." Nicole's grip on her tightened a little.

Dane kissed Nicole's crown. "You're all of those things to me, too. I'd give you anything I could. I'd do anything for you."

"But, a baby's a big step, I know. You don't have to decide tomorrow. You don't even have to decide this year. Hell, you may never decide or you may decide you don't want any, but I'll always be here. I'm not going anywhere."

Dane smiled and her heartbeat finally went back to normal. "Thank you."

"No, thank you, for giving me all of that and more."

Dane wasn't sure what to say. Her eyes drifted to the window to see the rain was still coming down, but she felt like there was a ray of sunlight cutting through the storm clouds. "Can we try our picnic again?"

Nicole grinned. "Excellent idea!" She reached for their basket to set everything up again.

The second time was the charm. Nicole's laughter echoed through the room as they conversed. In the distance, just under the rain, Dane thought she could hear a childish giggle join in and she smiled.

Therapy

DANE YAWNED AS SHE awoke and found herself in bed alone. Frowning, she rubbed her eyes and sat up. *Where is she already?* She was about to get up and go search for her wandering partner, but footsteps in the hallway kept her in place. She smiled as Nicole nudged the bedroom door open and appeared with a tray of food in her hands. Emerald eyes lit up when they caught sight of Dane.

"Oh, yes, you're awake," Nicole happily chirped.

"Yeah, I was about to panic since you weren't here." Dane laughed.

Nicole's brow furrowed just a little bit. "Panic? You're not prone to panic when you wake up alone, are you?"

"Only when I expect you to still be in bed with me. Now, what's this for?" Dane asked, as Nicole put the tray down in front of her.

Dane looked down to see golden waffles with melting butter and syrup accompanied by a bowl of fruit and scrambled eggs. Her mouth began watering at the sight and smell of the food. *I must've done something real good in a past life to deserve Nick in my life now.*

"This is for our anniversary."

Dane's face scrunched up. "Our anniversary?" *Did I forget or sleep through a few months or something?* "Last time I checked our anniversary was not for another six months."

Nicole chuckled. "Not that anniversary."

"Then what—" Dane's question died on her tongue as she realized Nicole had on her skimpy robe, which tended to mean she had on hot lingerie underneath or nothing at all. The idea of either was enough to make Dane want to take her right now, forget everything else. "Chem, what are you wearing or not wearing under that?" She arched an eyebrow.

The redhead smiled coyly. "If you're a good girl, you'll find out what's going on under this robe."

Dane was sure she wore, at that moment, the most perverted smile that had ever graced her features. But, Nicole didn't seem to mind, so she just kept on smiling. She remembered she had questions about why she was getting served breakfast in bed.

"So, what anniversary is this?" Dane eyed the food.

"This, baby, is in honor of the first day we met."

Dane blinked. "What? Oh, yeah, you did this last year, too. I'm surprised you want to remember this day considering what happened before you met me. And considering what a pain I've been..." Her presence had certainly brought more drama and unwanted excitement into Nicole's life, she was sure of that, but Nicole didn't seem to hold it against her.

A soft smile remained on Nicole's face. "No more than I have. When you came into my life, everything changed for the better. Trust me on that. Yes, we've had problems, but that's life. Every couple has problems and arguments. We're both learning as we go here. I think we're doing excellent. Two years of friendship, a year and a half of dating, and we've stumbled a few times, but we always pick each other up. We'll always pick each other up, right?"

"Damn right!" Dane nodded.

"Then start eating and be sure to share."

Dane chuckled and decided to do just that. She cut into the waffles, dividing them as she liked them. Nicole made herself comfortable on the opposite side of the tray, hovering over Dane's legs, but not sitting on them. Dane took a bite of waffles, while Nicole made herself busy with the fruit.

While eating, Dane tried to guess what Nicole wore under her robe. Being able to see cleavage distracted her. Her mouth watered and it had nothing to do with the fine meal anymore. She stuffed more waffles in her mouth before she did something to ruin the special breakfast.

"Here, have some waffles, too." Dane picked up a bit on the fork and guided it to Nicole's mouth.

Nicole took the piece, dripping with syrup, into her mouth. Some of the syrup oozed out of her mouth as she savored the food. Dane felt herself throb at the sight. Nicole had the nerve to wipe the syrup away with her finger. It wouldn't have been a serious matter if Nicole didn't give her another coy, sweet look while slowly licking the syrup from her finger. Taking it even further, she proceeded to suck her finger for absolutely no reason at all. *Fuck breakfast!*

Dane grabbed the breakfast tray and dumped it on the nightstand, only slightly careful to not spill the half-eaten meal. Nicole's eyes went wide and her mouth dropped open a little, as if she didn't know what she'd done. Dane pinned her naughty, teasing girlfriend with a heated gaze. Nicole seemed frozen in place, hovering slightly above Dane's legs.

"You didn't finish eating," Nicole dared to say with that damned look of pure innocence.

"I haven't even started! Get up here." Dane growled.

For the first time that morning, Nicole looked confused. Her brow wrinkled as her eyebrows curled. "Up there?"

"On my face, right now!" Dane pointed to her mouth, just in case Nicole needed a visual cue. Dane slid down onto the pillow some and tugged Nicole by the hips to where she wanted her.

Nicole yelped as Dane made her straddle her face. Nicole seemed like she wanted to protest, undoubtedly uncomfortable with Dane demanding a position they hadn't used before in the middle of breakfast, but Dane really needed to just go right at Nicole's soul.

"Baby?" the lawyer whimpered.

"Just go with it. We try new things all the time now. I need to have you so badly," Dane growled.

Dane's hands groped Nicole's legs, loving how smooth and firm the limbs were. Wandering up to her ass, she discovered her sexy girlfriend wasn't wearing panties. She wasted no time pulling Nicole to her, lapping at Nicole like a hungry kitten. Nicole let loose a loud moan and her head fell back while her hands pulled Dane's head closer to her.

At this angle, Dane felt like she drowned in her angel, taste, smell, and feel. Nicole surrounded her, and she loved every second of it. Sweet honey danced on her tongue as she explored her love. She moaned wantonly, as Nicole rocked her hips, the motion begging for more of Dane's affectionate mouth.

"So fucking good," Nicole cried, as her grip tightened on Dane's head, and her hips moved with even more purpose. Dane's tongue and lips loved her with fervor.

Dane could only moan while making sure to please Nicole, drinking her in, living off of Nicole. Her hands enjoyed and delighted in every inch of soft, supple flesh that they caressed. Eventually, they settled on Nicole's ass, pulling her closer to Dane's devouring mouth.

She's so fucking sweet. Better than all of the chocolate that she eats. Better than the syrup on the waffles. Better than any fucking nectar of the gods. I want her only and always.

Nicole began loudly panting. Her breaths sounded like begging, pleading, longing, and singing heavenly music all at the same time. One of her hands left Dane's head and her cries became sharper. Dane could picture her lover fondling her own breast, which made her throb again. Her tongue and lips worked harder.

Suddenly, Nicole cried out what might have been Danny or just a nonsense word. Her hand fisted in Dane's hair, causing Dane to hiss in pain and pleasure. She liked the pull, though, just as much as she liked when Nicole dug her nails in or bit her. It all felt so good.

Nicole's hips slowed as she drenched Dane's face in her ambrosia. Dane moaned and made the attempt to clean her sweetheart off. Nicole shuddered and clutched Dane's hair again.

"Baby, don't. I'll climax again," Nicole whispered. She whimpered, as Dane made another sweep of her tongue.

"That's a bad thing?"

"We have all day and I don't want to fall asleep on you just yet. So, I'm going to get off."

"Okay then." Dane grinned and made another sweep of her tongue, which made Nicole whimper.

Nicole squealed. "Get off *you*! I'm going to get off of you!" She quickly swung her leg over Dane, falling to the empty side of the bed. "Now, let's finish breakfast and I'll let you see what you completely bypassed in your hunger."

Dane smiled and grabbed the tray again. She eased it in front of her and dug into the cold waffles and eggs. She fed some to Nicole, who fed Dane some fruit in exchange. Soon, breakfast was over and Dane continued to pulse. She was about to toss the tray aside, but Nicole moved swiftly and got to the tray first.

"I'll be right back."

"You'd better," Dane growled.

Nicole laughed. "I like you all feisty. It'll go along with what I have in mind next." Without a further clue, she rushed out of the room. Dane could only whimper in anticipation.

***

Nicole was surprised she was able to walk to the kitchen on her still-wobbly legs. She hadn't expected Danny to go at her so ravenously, even though she very much appreciated it. She had never considered sitting on Dane's face, but damn, it was wonderful. She shivered thinking about it. *I wonder if she'll want to do that again.* Knowing Danny, yeah, it was safe to assume she'd be able to do it again.

She went to check on Haydn to make sure he was fine with his toys. He was, thankfully, still gated off in the den rather than wandering the house. She was off for the next part of what was already shaping up to be a celebration of new things. In the bathroom, she slipped off her robe, revealing her naked and toned body. She had been surprised Danny didn't rip her robe off in her rush. As she put on her clothes, she tried—and failed miserably—to not think about riding Danny's face like a woman possessed.

She yelped and blushed from the memory. "Please, you can't blush from that considering what you're about to do," she scolded herself in the mirror.

Nodding, she knew that was the truth. She checked herself out in the mirror and felt her heart thump nervously. She immediately calmed down by telling herself how Danny would react when she laid those sexy, exquisite, grey eyes on her.

Returning to the bedroom, she found the bed empty and messy. Danny didn't believe in making a bed. She could hear the sink in their bathroom, so she suspected Danny was brushing her teeth. While Danny was occupied, Nicole started making the bed.

When she heard the water stop, she quickly made a pose out of fluffing a pillow. Danny strolled back into the room and gasped. Nicole smirked while Danny's mouth dropped open. *One day she's going to dislocate her jaw doing that.*

"I'm sorry. There was no 'do not disturb' sign up. Did you not want the room serviced?"

"Chem, you're...that's...you..." Danny's mind was officially blown. Now, just to have the rest of her join it.

"Yes, ma'am. Is there something you need? How can I be of service?" Nicole asked in a low voice as she stepped closer to her dumbfounded girlfriend. She was dressed in a sexy and very naughty French maid outfit. It had quite possibly made Danny swallow her tongue. *I hope not. I like that tongue a lot.*

"Uh..." Danny visibly took a deep breath. Her shoulders squared, so she'd clearly calmed down. "Yes, I do need your services. I've made a mess that needs to be cleaned up."

Nicole held back a squeal, delighted that her girlfriend would play along. She continued smiling and beckoned Danny to the bed with a single crocked finger. Danny was on the bed in an instant.

"So, please, madam, tell me where this mess is." Nicole leaned down, resting her hands on Danny's smooth thighs.

"In my shorts," Danny breathed.

"Let me take a look and then determine how to clean it." Nicole eased down the boxers. Danny sighed as the warm air hit her, while Nicole just marveled over the treasure waiting for her. "My, my. This is quite the mess. How did you make such a mess?"

Danny sighed and a smile invaded her face. "My girlfriend really made it. She's so hot and just fucking superb. The little minx licked syrup off her fingers, and I damn near exploded, right there. Help me, please."

Nicole couldn't help smiling. "My pleasure. I will clean this whole mess."

Nicole set about cleaning up "her mess." She lightly ran her fingertips down Danny's legs as she dropped to her knees, in between Danny's legs. She kissed caramel thighs and the kisses turned to long licks. When she got to the center of all that was Danny, she was touched to find a blazing river flowing from the guitarist.

"Danny, your reactions always make me feel so sexy, so desired," Nicole purred before taking Danny into her mouth and showing Danny all the love that she could.

Danny howled when Nicole's mouth covered her and her tongue tasted her. Danny's hands went to Nicole's hair. She caressed Nicole's hair as she did her own when nervous, but she was clearly far from anxious about what was going on. The gentle stokes set the tone for Nicole's mouth.

"Fuck, angel, you feel so good," Danny whispered, as if it were a secret.

Nicole devoured her love slowly, savoring her. Her tongue played with Danny until she felt Danny's hips moving. Nicole eagerly obliged, tilting her head for a different angle. She lapped, kissed, and feasted on Danny, who tightened her grip on Nicole's head.

"Fuck!" Danny's leg trembled uncontrollably. She held Nicole to her a moment and in that moment Nicole couldn't breathe. Somehow realizing her actions through her climax, or just needing to do something else with her hands, Danny released Nicole and seemed to float, tapping the mattress with her fingers. Maybe she was playing a song.

"All clean," Nicole remarked with a coquettish smile.

Danny blinked and focused down on Nicole. Her hand was still shaking as she caressed Nicole's wet face. She returned the smile with a lopsided grin.

"Get up here and gimme a kiss," Danny entreated, still trying to catch her breath.

Nicole couldn't resist the tussled look of her partner, so she merrily indulged both of them. Danny moved further back on the bed to accommodate her girlfriend. Nicole took her place on Danny's lap and wrapped her arms around Danny's neck.

"Look at the mess on your face," Danny teased. She ran a tender knuckle down Nicole's cheek.

"Can you do something about the start of a new mess?" Nicole asked with an exaggerated pout. The gentle stroke of Danny's finger sent shivers through her.

"I can try, but you're obviously the professional."

Nicole didn't get a chance to respond as Danny cupped her cheek and leaned in to kiss Nicole on her wet lips. The kiss was slow. Danny's hand continued caressing Nicole's face while her other hand was on the small of Nicole's back, bracing the redhead against her.

Danny's usual purrs echoed through the room, as their tongues and lips moved tenderly against each other. Each noise made Nicole whimper and burn. She pressed herself closer, needing more and more of Danny. The lace of her costume brushed against Danny's chest, earning a roaring hiss from the musician.

Danny's hand left her face and snaked down to her neck, leaving a trail of pure electricity that went straight down her body. Danny lovingly stroked her neck before continuing down until she was palming Nicole's left breast. Nicole moaned wantonly into Danny's mouth, as the musician massaged the globe. The moans grew longer and louder, as Danny's thumb lazily toyed with her pebbled nipple.

Nicole wasn't sure how long that lasted, but it eventually became maddening. She felt like she was melting while being set ablaze. She needed more than slow and gentle now. Nicole reluctantly pulled away from Danny's deliciously gifted mouth.

"Honey, I need more. I need you deep. I need you so deep," Nicole breathed.

Briefly, Danny's forehead wrinkled. "You want me to put *it* on?"

Nicole could only nod and make a rather pathetic noise in the back of her throat. Danny smiled and went to get their newest toy, which didn't require straps rubbing against her sweaty skin.

Nicole helped ease the toy securely into Danny, earning several wonderful noises from the musician. Danny looked down once the toy was in place, and Nicole noted her girlfriend looked proud, as if the toy was an extension of herself and not an item they both agreed to buy.

"Danny, what goes through your mind when you wear this?"

Danny, oddly enough, began sporting her goofy, lopsided grin. "You want to know the details?" The voice didn't match the expression since the voice was a sexy purr.

A shudder ran through Nicole. "Yes," she whispered.

"Lay down on the edge of the bed, let your legs hang, and I'll tell you."

Nicole wasted no time complying. Danny made herself comfortable in between Nicole's legs, but she didn't do anything beyond that. Nicole was so worked up that she was panting in anticipation.

"What goes through my mind when I don this particular piece or its friend? I imagine I can feel you. The fantasy, the mental space is amazing. The idea of feeling you beyond my fingertips..." Danny shuddered. "This one helps the fantasy more so than the other. I pretend I can feel you, feel your moist, warm, loving body accept me with fondness, eagerness, loving me as I love you. Feel how your whole body embraces me at a single point, feel how your grip pulses and pulls me, begs me, thanks me, takes care of me. And, of course, feel you explode in all of your glory and allure that puts all other members of this creation to shame. In my head, we're connected as one being, one mind, one soul," Danny whispered reverently, as she ran her calloused fingertips along Nicole's thigh.

Nicole was beyond panting now, beyond molten, beyond thought. All that was left was her need for Danny. Her lover didn't disappoint, running the now empowered toy along her to prepare them for the connection ahead. All Nicole could manage was a strangled, strange noise that basically equaled "Fuck me!"

Danny eased into Nicole, who hooked her legs around Danny's waist to pull her girlfriend to her with great haste. Danny slammed into her, causing them both to cry out. Danny growled at the move. "You don't follow instructions, dammit."

"You don't. Need more," Nicole managed to remind her.

Danny nodded, pulled back some before slamming back in. Nicole screamed and squealed, as Danny pounded into her. Danny cried out that time and kept on going. The sound of their bodies meeting and their ecstatic clamor almost shook the walls.

"Oh, God," Nicole shouted, getting just what she wanted. It made her body even hotter than before, her girlfriend building the blaze within her.

Danny used one hand to pull Nicole even closer, hitting everything just right to make lightning shoot through Nicole. The other hand yanked at the front of Nicole's costume, which was thankfully strapless, so bouncing breasts were easily freed. Danny's hand quickly occupied one of the wonders of the world.

"Love having my hands free to touch every part of you. You feel amazing, Chem. So fucking sweet."

The words curled into Nicole's stomach, knowing Danny was envisioning the feel of being inside of her and Danny was getting off on that. Nicole's mind swam with pleasure. Danny leaned down, kissing Nicole's neck as she slipped a hand away from Nicole's waist to a much more sensitive portion of Nicole's anatomy. A long whimper escaped Nicole as Danny's fingers stroked her, adding to her ecstasy.

"I'm gonna...I'm gonna..." Nicole howled and shot up off of the bed. She wrapped her arms around Danny as if to anchor her to the Earth. The world narrowed into nothing but pleasure and the love of her life giving it to her.

Danny wasn't done and continued moving as Nicole rode her wave of pure rapture. With Nicole closer, Danny ducked her head to suck on whatever bit of Nicole that fit into her mouth. The attention kept Nicole from coming completely down from her euphoria, which was fine by her. She continued pulling Danny to her and began nipping at her lover's neck.

Danny panted and made overwhelmingly adorable noises. Her body was slowing down and her hands wandered aimlessly. She was probably close and running out of energy considering how hard she was working. She reached in between them again, caressing Nicole's sweet spot and pushing her into sweet oblivion once again.

"Danny!" Nicole barely registering when Danny stopped moving.

"Damn," Danny breathed into Nicole's glistening, heaving chest. She kissed the tantalizing salt of Nicole's sweating flesh.

"Well, at least I know you're not dead," Nicole joked in a low tone. Her throat was slightly sore.

Danny smiled. "I think you only have the power to kill me when you're in control." She sounded a little hoarse as well.

Nicole tried to laugh, but she didn't have the energy to do so. She didn't have the energy to move. Of course, she didn't have much desire to move with Danny plastered against her. Hot sweaty skin pressed against her shouldn't feel sexy, but it damn sure did.

"Sweetheart, I wanna sleep," Nicole whined cutely.

"Me too," Danny yawned.

"I don't wanna move."

"Me too."

They were all too aware that they'd have to move if they wanted to sleep, but it took a while. First, Danny backed up to ease out. Nicole couldn't help whimpering and moaning at each tiny motion. Once Danny was gone, Nicole groaned in disappointment, feeling as if a piece of her had been taken away. She didn't have much time to lament, because she had to help Danny free herself of the toy, which she knew was Danny's least favorite thing about wearing this particular toy.

"Do it really quick, like a Band-Aid," Danny requested.

"I know how you like it." Nicole knew if she really did it the way Danny wanted, she'd hurt the musician. But, Danny always wanted the thing out immediately whenever they were done using it. *Hard to believe she likes this as much as I know she does.*

Nicole carefully removed the toy and dropped it to the floor, while Danny began pulling the covers back. They cuddled into each other. Danny pulled the covers over them.

"Baby, don't think the day's through yet," Nicole whispered.

Danny shivered. "I'm going to hold you to that. Don't feel right to have the whole morning in bed and only gave you three orgasms. Could do that on a regular night."

"Is that how you count success, by how many orgasms you give me?" Nicole teased.

"That is one of many factors."

"Are you being serious?"

"Very."

"So, what if we have a night where I just focus on you?" *I should do that more often.*

"Then success is measured by how many times you kill me. Of course, if you kill me once, that's success enough." Danny laughed.

"Oh, I only get once, but you set a high, three-orgasm-or-more limit for yourself? That's almost sexist."

Danny shook her head. "I don't think less of you, angel. It's actually me. You seem like you can take more than I can, so I want to give you more. I get wiped out, usually, after one, but especially after two. You're a sex goddess, you little vixen."

Nicole had to shift to look at Danny. *Is she just being cute or trying to sweet talk her way out of this?* "Are you serious?"

"Dead serious. For me...for me, you're the best I've ever been with. I know it's partially because I love you. Now, don't get me wrong, you're talented in bed. But, just seeing you breathe arouses me. You know how hot you get me from just regular clothes. You damn near blew my head off my shoulders with this little French maid number. You're just amazing."

"You made me this way. No way in hell would I wear this costume for anyone else. No way I'd do most of the things we do with anyone else. You make me adventurous." Nicole yawned. "You also make me sleepy."

"Then sleep," Dane mumbled, as they dropped off to sleep.

***

Dane put on a t-shirt before going downstairs. She put the toy in the dishwasher, as per Nicole's orders from when they first bought it. Something about the dishwasher would sterilize or something. She couldn't remember the whole reasoning. She just knew where to put it...*in more ways than one.* She smiled at the thought.

Of course, when she was first given that order, she tried to put it in the dishwasher with dishes in it. Nicole practically had kittens when she saw what Dane had planned. The only thing that kept Dane from sleeping on the couch was that she honestly didn't know Nicole would have a problem with the dishes sharing the dishwasher with a sex toy. To this day, she didn't see what the big deal was, but heaven help her if dishes and toys shared the same space.

She went to check on Haydn, letting him out of his crate for a while. He made a mad dash for the backdoor. She let him out. She barely had time to step away from the door, getting a blast of not-yet-Spring weather, before Haydn was back.

"I guess it's too cold for you, too."

Dane made tuna sandwiches for lunch, because she didn't want to have something that could get cold, and thus ruined, in case they got distracted. *I hope we get distracted.* She returned Haydn to his crate, much to his dismay. He whimpered and whined, so she had to pet and cuddle him a little before leaving him alone.

Going back upstairs, she put the lunch on the nightstand before shedding her shirt and easing back into bed. She stared at Nicole's sleeping form, debating if she needed more sleep or if she was ready for round two...or round four depending on how she looked at it. Her body ached a bit, but the temptation of Nicole in her disheveled maid's outfit proved to be too much.

Deciding to give Nicole a treat since she'd wanted things deep earlier, Dane slipped out of bed and slipped into her harness. It would do until she worked up a serious sweat and then she'd hate the feel of it moving against her. She couldn't remember being so particular in the past, but it was probably because she'd been too high or drunk—or both—to notice the harness giving her problems. *I should shop around for a new one sometime soon.*

She made sure to adjust the toy where it would press against her. She got back in the bed and wasted no time in showering Nicole with soft kisses. The redhead mewed and turned into the kisses without waking up. Dane laughed a little before going in for a passionate kiss that definitely woke Nicole and got her to return it.

"That's a nice way to wake up," Nicole sighed as the kiss broke.

"I have better things in mind if you still want me deep."

Nicole whimpered while nodding. Dane couldn't understand Nicole's pleasure here, but she certainly didn't mind giving it to her and smiled before going in for another kiss. The show of affection was slow, but quickly began to heat up as Nicole pulled Dane over her. She ran her hands up and down Dane's back tracing the muscles along her spine before moving to her breasts. Dane groaned as Nicole kneaded her breasts.

"You like that?" Nicole whispered.

"Of course," Dane replied with another groan. "Want that, too."

"Huh?"

Dane explained by diving mouth first into Nicole's breasts. The surprise attack caused Nicole to arch off of the bed. Dane purred and her mouth played with the gems at her disposal. Reaching down, she used one hand to caress Nicole to get her more worked up.

"God, yes, baby," Nicole moaned, clutching Dane tightly.

"Want me?"

"You know I do."

"Want me deep?" The response was a whimper. "Want me hard?" There was another, longer whimper. Dane moved back up to kiss Nicole. As their tongues danced, Dane continued stroking Nicole, building her up, earning more moans and whimpers. She was ready, so Dane got into position.

"Wait!"

Dane was fairly certain her heart stopped. "What? What did I do?" she begged in a panic.

"You didn't undress me and you know how I love to feel your skin against mine."

Dane chuckled to cover up a long sigh. "Oh, sorry. Don't scare me like that, though."

Nicole smiled. "Sorry, baby."

They both worked quickly to get Nicole naked, which caused Dane to purr at the sight. The redhead smiled and gave Dane a kiss on her partially gaping mouth. Dane grinned and once again got into position.

"Oh, God!" Nicole cried, as Dane joined them. Nicole wrapped her arms around Dane, digging into copper colored shoulders.

Dane's hips moved like powerful pistons, wanting to give Nicole exactly what she asked for. Nicole groaned and held onto Dane for dear life. Leaning down, Dane swallowed the noise with a sloppy kiss. Their bodies pressed together, touching breasts, which caused sparks to burn through both of them.

"So good," Dane breathed.

"Yes!" Nicole writhed against her lover as if she were a madwoman. She slammed her body against Dane's, meeting the powerful thrusts with her own movements.

Dane growled, feeling like she wasn't bestowing Nicole with all she desired. Moving, she dislodged herself briefly, earning a disappointed cry from her girlfriend. Taking hold of Nicole's leg, Dane placed it on her shoulder, and Nicole gracefully slid her other leg onto Dane's shoulder. Dane pushed herself up on her arms and then put her all into reducing Nicole into a puddle.

Nicole clawed around the bed, trying to find something to hold onto. In the end, she grabbed onto Dane's forearms. They locked eyes and connected, peering into each other's souls and seeing into their hearts. They were looking at the only person that existed in the universe for the moment, which was all Dane needed.

It took all of her willpower to not beak her stride as her world narrowed. Her focus centered on Nicole, who moved her hands to knead Dane's breast. For some reason, the wonderful attention made Dane move with even more purpose, giving Nicole all that she wanted and more. Dane wasn't even sure how her hand ended up between Nicole's legs, but there it was, her middle finger and ring finger stroked Nicole's clit as she moved the toy in and out of her love. Nicole screamed at the top of her lungs and bucked in a manner that would've put a mustang to shame. Dane wasn't sure what happened after that because everything went black.

When Dane came to, she felt gentle fingers stroking her back and soft kisses on her neck. She couldn't help smiling. She realized she was pressed against the warm, precious body of her love, which caused her to purr.

"You awake now?"

"Very much so. I'm not crushing you, am I?"

"No, I've been reveling in our closeness, my dear. Congratulations, too."

"On what?"

"You killed us both this time."

Dane laughed. "That explains a few things. God, that was freaking amazing. You're amazing, Chem." She blinked. "I'm still strapped in? I'm gonna move, okay?"

Nicole nodded and Dane kept her movement to a minimum. She eased out of her lover and dumped her attachment on the floor. Once she settled back down, Nicole climbed on top of her and used her as a mattress. They both smiled.

"You know, you might be onto something, celebrating this anniversary. It marks a new life for me, almost like a birthday. You made me come back to life, feel again, and feel new things. You brought music back to me. When I say you're an angel, I mean it." Nicole was like some mythic creature she couldn't even put into words. Angel was just the best word to sum it all up.

"I know. Just like when I introduce you as my soul mate, I mean that. I feel whole and complete with you. I've never felt like this for anybody and I don't intend to ever let you go. I'm spending the rest of my life with you, so you'd better get used to me," Nicole replied with a tired smile.

Dane smiled back. "I welcome you in my life because you gave it to me. Now, let's eat the lunch I made, take another short nap, and continue this wonderful day."

Nicole nodded. "Before we do that, I just want you to know that I love you, and I do want to spend the rest of my life with you. You are my soul mate." She placed the sweetest kiss on Dane's lips.

"Love you, too. I want the same, because you make me a better person, and I want to share everything with you. You made my life worth living, and I want to live it showing you how much you matter to me."

They exchanged one last kiss while gazing into each other's eyes. They saw the past, present, and future. Their past, present, and future. Their forever, together.

The End.

About S. L Kassidy

What is there to know about me? Not much. I was bred, born, and raised in New York and I have no desire to live anywhere else. One day, I would like to travel to a few places, but for now I am content where I am.

I started out writing poetry in junior high and continued to do so for ten years. I wrote short stories, usually fantasy and romance stories, for my own entertainment throughout high school and college. Back then, I wrote strictly for me and those stories remain locked in the back of my closet in little notebooks, written in my almost unreadable, tiny handwriting. In between writing those stories and poetry, I managed to get a college degree in history.

After graduating college, I had a semester off before graduate school and I didn't really have anything to do with my time. So, I took a chance and wrote a fanfic and dared to upload it to the Internet. I was surprised that other people enjoyed my work and I've been posting ever since. I had quite a bit of fun with fan fiction and eventually decided to try my hand in original fiction. I suppose it was sort of like coming back around to what I had been doing in high school and college, except this time the stories were for whoever wanted to read them. I uploaded my first original story a few years ago and haven't looked back. I plan to continue writing as long as I continue getting ideas for stories and it continues to be fun.

Contact Information
E-mail: slkassidy@gmail.com
Facebook: https://www.facebook.com/pages/SL-Kassidy
Desert Palm Press: www.desertpalmpress.com

Other Books by S. L. Kassidy

Please Baby
ISBN: 9781311485137

Jayce Newton's life is going downhill after she rescues her little niece from an awful situation. She plans to hold onto her niece and gain custody of her, but there are some factors against her. Her girlfriend doesn't want the baby around. Her mother wants to take the baby from her, and her brother has disappeared. Things only seem to get worse when Gus Tucker comes into her life.

Gus Tucker's life isn't going much better. She recently divorced her wife and moved into a new home. She's looking forward to a new start and spending time with her sister. Before she can do that, though, she ends up causing trouble for Jayce Newton, getting her fired from her job and kicked out of her home. She tries to make it up to Jayce by taking her in during her time of need. Now, it's just a struggle to see if they're able to coexist in the same house with a baby between them.

Desert Palm Press

Scarred Series

Scarred for Life
ISBN: 9781310171352

Dane Wolfe is a loner. Forsaken by her family and betrayed by people close to her, she has lost all faith in people and spends her days wandering the streets with no direction or meaning. She drifts through life, existing and nothing more. Nicole Cardell is a successful attorney. She has too much faith in people and is being taken advantage of by her boyfriend, Tyler, Dane's cousin. She's tired of his selfish ways and tosses him out. The bad relationship leaves her questioning her judgment. Circumstances bring Dane and Nicole together and a friendship brings them closer. They're able to heal each other and bring balance to each other's lives. Their peace is shattered when family causes trouble and tears them apart. Will they find their path back to each other and to the love that was slowly growing?

New Cuts, Old Wounds
ISBN: 9781310217289

In this sequel to *Scarred for Life*, Nicole Cardell and Dane Wolfe have been together for a year. They are doing their best to move forward with their relationship and open up to each other. It's time to meet family members. Dane's nervous about meeting Nicole's family, but she's even more nervous about Nicole meeting her family. Nicole is eager for both. Nicole thinks Dane should bond with her family while Dane thinks she needs to get as far away from them as possible. The Wolfe family seems to agree with Dane, but keep inviting her to things and Nicole keeps accepting the invites. Will family make or break Dane and Nicole?

Note to Readers:

We have made every effort to edit this book. However, typos do slip in. If you find an error in the text, please email lee@desertpalmpress.com so the issue can be corrected. We appreciate you as a reader and want to ensure you enjoy the reading process.

Bright blessing.

www.ingramcontent.com/pod-product-compliance
Lightning Source LLC
Chambersburg PA
CBHW070902180626
46817CB00003B/881